W9-AMT-254

THE TROUBLE WITH
MAGIC

*Also by Patricia Rice
in Large Print:*

Almost Perfect
Must Be Magic
Merely Magic
Nobody's Angel

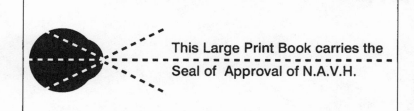

THE TROUBLE WITH MAGIC

PATRICIA RICE

WHEELER PUBLISHING

Published in 2004 by arrangement with NAL Signet, a member of Penguin Group (USA) Inc.

Wheeler Large Print Romance.

The text of this Large Print edition is unabridged. Other aspects of the book may vary from the original edition.

Set in 16 pt. Plantin.

Printed in the United States on permanent paper.

Library of Congress Cataloging-in-Publication Data

Rice, Patricia, 1949–
  The trouble with magic / Patricia Rice.
     p. cm.
   ISBN 1-58724-682-1 (lg. print : hc : alk. paper)
   1. Kent (England) — Fiction.   2. Psychics — Fiction.
3. Scotland — Fiction.   4. Large type books.   I. Title.
PS3568.I2925T76 2004
  813'.54—dc22   2004043044

To my wonderful readers,
who understand the magic of love

As the Founder/CEO of NAVH, the only national health agency solely devoted to those who, although not totally blind, have an eye disease which could lead to serious visual impairment, I am pleased to recognize Thorndike Press★ as one of the leading publishers in the large print field.

Founded in 1954 in San Francisco to prepare large print textbooks for partially seeing children, NAVH became the pioneer and standard setting agency in the preparation of large type.

Today, those publishers who meet our standards carry the prestigious "Seal of Approval" indicating high quality large print. We are delighted that Thorndike Press is one of the publishers whose titles meet these standards. We are also pleased to recognize the significant contribution Thorndike Press is making in this important and growing field.

Lorraine H. Marchi, L.H.D.
Founder/CEO
NAVH

★ Thorndike Press encompasses the following imprints: Thorndike, Wheeler, Walker and Large Print Press.

PROLOGUE

Kent, England, 1743

"The book, Mama, may I have it, please?" Six-year-old Lady Felicity Malcolm Childe stared longingly at the hand-painted folio of children's Bible verses lying open for patrons of the stationery shop to admire. It rested on a counter just out of reach of Lady Felicity's sticky fingers, but she reached for it anyway.

"Remember what I told you, dear." Hermione, Marchioness of Hampton, hurried to her daughter's side. Her hat ribbons blew in the breeze from the open door, and she caught the end of her scarf before it fluttered loose. "Do not touch until you've tested it."

"Yes, Mama." With her chubby bare fingers, Lady Felicity brushed the air above an open page depicting an angel with long golden hair hanging in silken ringlets that looked remarkably like hers. "Oh, it's filled with love, Mama. May I hold it, please?"

"Wouldn't the little girl prefer a candy instead?" The proprietor leaned over his counter with a tempting stick of horehound.

Before Hermione could intervene, Felicity accepted the offering with delight. "Thank you —" As her fingers wrapped around the treat she gasped, and with a flutter of dark gold eyelashes, collapsed in a puddle of silken skirts and petticoats upon the rough wooden floor.

Casting the startled proprietor an appalled glance, Hermione swept her daughter up in her arms and marched out of the shop, panniers swaying with indignation. Waving off footmen and nursemaids who rushed to her aid, she climbed into the waiting carriage, still cradling her frail daughter in her arms.

Within the private confines of the familiar coach, Felicity stirred and woke. With a sob, she clutched her mother and buried her face in the marchioness's ample bosom.

"Now, now, child, it's all right. You simply must learn to test before touching, as I've taught you."

"He's a *nasty* man," Felicity hiccupped. "He does *nasty* things to little girls and they cry. I don't want to go there anymore."

Her usually tender mouth firming into a tight line, the marchioness nodded her beribboned head vigorously. "I shall certainly see to that, dear. I will talk to your father, and Mr. Jones shall leave the village at once. You see, your gift is very useful. It will keep him from hurting any other little girls."

"I don't want to see bad things anymore," Felicity whispered. "I hate my gift. It hurts. Why can't I have another gift?"

Hermione sighed and rocked her daughter in her arms. "You are only given what you are capable of handling, my dear. I know you don't understand that yet, but your gift is precious and valuable. When you grow into it, you will learn to use it wisely."

"Christina's gift doesn't hurt," Felicity muttered with a rebellious pout. "She sees pretty things. Why can't I feel pretty things?"

"You felt love in the book," Hermione reminded her. "It's just that sometimes bad things feel stronger than gentle ones. It doesn't hurt when your family touches you, does it? Or Nanny?"

"Nanny has sad touches," Felicity murmured sleepily as her mother continued rocking her. "I don't want to touch any more bad things."

"Your family will always take care of you, dear. You'll be safe and happy around familiar vibrations until you're all grown up and know how to use your gift. Learning comes from experience, but we'll give you good ones."

"Can I stay in Papa's library? It's nice there."

Hermione laughed. "No, you cannot live in a library, dear, although your papa would let you try if you wanted."

"I want to. I don't want to see any more bad things." Setting her quivering lip in a firm manner reminiscent of her mother's, Felicity closed her eyes and slept.

ONE

Spring, 1754

"I *saw* him. Percy was there when his mother died, no matter what anyone claims," Felicity muttered fiercely, clinging to the rail of the family yacht as the ship lurched and slid into a trough between rough waves. Swaddled in a cloak, a scarf, and thick gloves, Lady Felicity stared into the April squall. She'd never seen the sea before. The salt spray stung her cheeks, and cautiously she licked her lips to taste the droplets gathering there. It even tasted of salt.

She ought to be afraid of the wild waves and the crack of lightning, but those were things she couldn't touch, so they had no power over her. Or she over them. At any other time she would have exulted in this new experience. Instead, dread of things she had set in motion churned her stomach. Beneath the dread shimmered a sliver of hope that her efforts would not be in vain.

The incident with Sir Percy had been her breaking point. Even her father had agreed that a relaxing journey to visit her sister in Northumberland might settle her nerves.

10

Leila and her husband were staying at his family's estate in Wystan. As much as Felicity wanted to see them and the new baby, it was the proximity to Scotland that drew her on. She prayed she could find some way to escape her family's solicitude to reach Edinburgh and the one frail hope of ever having a normal life.

She *must* reach Edinburgh. A lifetime of pain and loneliness, denied even the simplest of human pleasures, would be unbearable. *Was* unbearable. She had broken her papa's heart when she'd refused Sir Percy's proposal of marriage. And terrified herself.

"Quit saying that you saw Percy," Christina said. "If he really did murder his mother, he might murder you, too. How do you know he doesn't have spies following us?"

Exhausted by the constant tension and turmoil of touching strangers these past few days, Felicity still managed to cast her sister a look of incredulity. "Spies? Why in the name of the goddess would he do that? Nobody believes me. His servants swear his mother's death was an accident, that he wasn't at home the day she died. His steward swears they were together in London that day. I'm just an hysteric afraid of marriage."

"Well, you did become hysterical, and you *are* afraid of marriage," Christina said with equanimity. "That doesn't mean you aren't right, and if you are, you have made him very nervous."

"I have made *everyone* very nervous." Wrapping her mantle tighter, Felicity watched a seagull scream across the leaden sky.

"Come inside, Felicity," Christina urged. "The wind is increasing and will blow you off your feet."

Her sister was scarcely two years her elder, yet ages older in terms of experience and courage. Christina sheltered Felicity from life's buffets much as the rest of their family did, but Christina did it with impatience. With a shrug acknowledging her sister's concern, Felicity returned her spectacles to her nose and descended the companionway into the cabin below.

"The captain does not think we'll reach Northumberland today," Felicity said. Entering their private cubbyhole, she picked up her much-beloved and slightly bedraggled doll from the bunk, and gingerly occupied the bed's edge. Her doll exuded the joy of a long-ago Christmas and the memory of all the happy hours of play in the hands of her innocent sisters. It provided a balance against the cabin's dismal vibrations. "Leila and Dunstan will be worried if we're late."

"Perhaps Dunstan will tire of waiting for us in port and go home."

Christina said this with such glee that Felicity couldn't prevent a smile. "He's an Ives. He's more likely to set the Navy searching for us. I think Ives have gained the reputation of causing Malcolm disasters simply because they are such interfering creatures. They cannot leave well enough alone."

Christina laughed. "If *anyone* knew what we intend, they'd interfere." Sitting cross-legged on the bunk in an unladylike billow of skirts and panniers, she propped her shoulders against the wall. "This will be great fun, once we find some means of escaping interfering relations. I've never been to Edinburgh."

"I cannot see how we will go now," Felicity replied. Her dread roiled higher at the thought of such a reckless escapade. She was not an adventurer by nature. Only desperation drove her to this scheme.

"It will be marvelous fun," Christina reassured her. "We will see the sights and meet new people. It's a pity we cannot find you a husband while we're at it, one more to your liking than the stuffy ones Father prefers. Sir Percy would never have suited."

Felicity had thought bookish Sir Percy the ideal suitor — until she had seen murder in his touch. Half the reason for this journey was to hide her until her father could investigate her tale. She suspected the other half was his fear that this time her mind had taken leave of her senses, and a good long rest from the exigencies of London's social whirl was needed. Sir Percy was not at all the sort to make people think he could murder his mother.

"Well, Ewen Ives is still unmarried," Felicity said in wry jest, offering the worst possible example of a suitor she could summon, as far from wealthy, respectable Sir Percy as could be imagined.

Christina laughed at the notion of Felicity with one of the men in their brother-in-law's tumultuous family. "You'd spend the rest of your life chasing after the lot of them, attempting to prevent them from wreaking the havoc and ruin you'd discover on every object they touched."

"Well, it wouldn't be *boring*." But boring was what she wanted — needed. Safe and boring, no unpleasant surprises, no jolts of pain or anguish or visions of death and destruction.

"Besides, Ewen possesses nothing for which Father could trade your dowry, and Father lives for haggling with suitors." Christina giggled at the thought. "Although, you must admit, Ewen is the most handsome of the Ives. And charming, when he chooses to be. He would dangle you with all his other conquests like a watch fob on a chain."

Felicity sighed. One of her favorite objects was a mechanical bouquet of porcelain roses that twirled to tinkling music. Ewen Ives had given it to her for her come-out last year. It held only his fascination with the motor without any deep, dark secrets attached. But handsome, charming men were not for

14

dowdy, invisible girls like her. She had only briefly seen Ewen at a family gathering or two since then. Besides, her father would have a spasm of the heart if he knew she dreamed of an Ives. She loved her father and wished him to be happy with her choice.

The only way that would happen was if she found *A Malcolm Journal of Infusions*, which she needed to rid herself of this wretched gift — if it would do as promised.

First she must find the Lord Nesbitt in Edinburgh who had last owned the book — a century ago.

"More's the pity," Felicity said, "but it's best if we avoid interfering Ives if we can, although how we can avoid Dunstan when we are supposed to be staying with him and Leila is beyond my comprehension."

"We simply must convince Leila that we are grown-up enough to visit Edinburgh on our own," Christina declared.

Since Leila had married Dunstan Ives last year, she had become so engrossed in her studies of perfumes and scents that she'd scarcely traveled to London. Felicity couldn't predict how Leila would react to her younger sisters' dangerous mission.

"Perhaps she will be so busy dandling her new baby on her knee that she will not notice if we don't arrive at all," Christina suggested.

"She will more likely be pacing the dock with Dunstan. It's not as if I leave London with any frequency. Mama will have written her with lists and lists of instructions." Felicity clenched her fingers anxiously. "It's a wonder Mama did not lock me in my room for my own safety or that Father did not banish me to the Outer Hebrides after I swooned at Sir Percy's feet."

"*Percy,*" Christina muttered with disgust. "A milksop like that could not so much as murder a bank ledger. I think your gift has gone awry."

Felicity hunched over her doll, hugging its familiar vibrations of love for comfort. "If I cannot be rid of this wretched gift, I shall never marry. I will grow old living in Papa's library."

Christina bent forward to brush Felicity's hair out of her face in a gesture of sympathy. "I'm sorry. It's just so very hard to believe that a fop like Percy could be dangerous. But you're right. If you're forever seeing a suitor's mistress in his snuffbox or reading his lascivious ambitions in his touch, you'll never marry. Don't worry. We'll find your book."

That was the ray of hope to which Felicity clung. She'd received too many unanticipated shocks upon touching seemingly innocent objects to ever be as courageous and trusting as Christina, but she was willing to brave more than stormy seas if at the end of the journey she could find the journal.

She knew her mother would be horrified if

she was aware that Felicity was seeking the recipe that would rid her of her unwanted gift, but this latest incident had convinced her that she had no other choice if she wished to be normal and marry happily, as her family desired.

"I wish our great-grandfather had not been so spiteful as to sell off the Malcolm library," Felicity said, mourning the loss of so much knowledge. "There could be all manner of wisdom in those books, lost on people who understand nothing of their content."

"I cannot imagine why some Lord Nesbitt would buy a bunch of old journals." Standing, Christina stretched restlessly in the confines of the tiny cabin. "Perhaps he burned them. Scots have weird notions of witchcraft."

"It's not witchcraft," Felicity said crossly. "It is wisdom learned from experience. If I can find the recipe, I can be normal like everyone else. I can live a full life. I can dance and marry and have babies."

"If that isn't magic, what is?" Christina asked.

Buried beneath layers of protective clothing, untouched by any hand except her family's, Felicity peered upward at her sister with eyes glistening in wonder and anticipation. *Magic* was the world around her — the one she had never experienced.

The one she would never experience if she

didn't find the journal.

This wasn't the port where they were expected.

Felicity suppressed a shiver of fear as she stood at the rail, examining the huddle of unfamiliar stone dwellings built one on top of the other up the hillside.

Dunstan and Leila wouldn't be waiting for them here.

"There's an inn," Christina whispered excitedly. "Do you think we've landed north or south of our port?"

Tucking her gloved hands beneath her heavy mantle, Felicity glanced about for the captain. She wasn't inclined to speculate when she could ask. At her glance, the captain dismissed the sailor to whom he was speaking and strode briskly toward them.

He tugged respectfully on his cap. "Apologize, my ladies, but we must repair a loose spar before taking to sea again. The delay will be a short one."

"You handled the storm superbly." Christina rewarded the man with a dazzling smile.

"Could you tell us where we are?" Felicity inquired, gently slipping in their real concern while the man was distracted.

"Just north of our destination, not far from Edinburgh as the crow flies. We'll be repaired by nightfall, if all goes well, and be back to England tomorrow e'en."

Gadzooks, the opportunity she'd been praying for! No Dunstan, no Leila, and her destination almost within reach. Anxiety and anticipation mixed together until Felicity thought she might be sick of them, but she had to take this step, no matter how foolish it was.

"Might we go ashore while repairs are made?" she murmured, trepidation beating in her breast. Fate or fortune had brought them just short of her goal. Could they? *Dare* they?

Christina understood at once. With sparkling eyes she gazed adoringly at the gray-haired captain. "Oh, please, might we? I've never seen Scotland, and I need solid ground beneath my feet before we set forth on open water again."

Stoically, Felicity watched as her sister charmed the sensible captain into doing her bidding. Few men could resist her bewitching cornflower blue eyes, much less the provocative way Christina toyed with her silken tresses and offered just the right flash of pearly teeth and ruby lips.

Felicity tugged her hood closer around her own limp hair, hiding eyes she knew to be as gray-blue as the cold sea. She'd never had any desire to be charming and provocative.

"If we won't sail until dawn, might we take our bags and stay at that inn?" Felicity pointed at the ramshackle structure on the road leading into town.

More eyelash flapping and tearful pleas ensued. Felicity and Christina had partnered too often in these escapades to doubt their success now. Christina flirted and charmed while Felicity covertly solicited the information they wanted. Together they could spin their father and half-brothers in circles. The sea captain didn't have a chance against their wiles.

Within the hour they were aboard a rowboat bound for town. With no maid to accompany them and the promise of a single evening ashore, they could carry only what fit in one bag apiece. Felicity struggled with her doubt and fear as they approached the dock, but it was now or never. One took what opportunity presented itself or regretted it forevermore. She'd just never grabbed an opportunity so huge and frightening before.

"The captain said as to how I must stay with you, m'ladies," declared the lad who clambered with them to the dock and assisted them up. "I'll see if there's room at the inn, and ask for a maid for ye, if ye please."

The daughters of a wealthy marquess could demand anything they liked. The price they paid for that privilege was that they could never be left alone. Felicity had never argued with that fact of life, although Christina rebelled against it frequently. With their need to escape undetected to Edinburgh, Felicity could understand Christina's restless rebellion against the constant vigilance.

"How thoughtful of you," Christina chirruped to the cabin boy while tugging Felicity's elbow and surreptitiously pointing to a wagon hitched to two workhorses.

Felicity wrapped her fingers around the purse of coins in her pocket. *Now or never,* she repeated over and over as they walked toward the inn and freedom.

TWO

"Ach, and if it isn't Aidan, the Ives God of Trouble, himself! Has my brother Dunstan's son run away again? Or my sister-in-law Ninian stirred a cauldron she cannot control? A regular harbinger of doom you've become. Here, take a seat."

Sheltering from the storm in a port inn just inside of Scotland, where he expected to catch a ship to Edinburgh, Ewen Ives, fourth in succession to the title of Earl of Ives and Wystan, kicked a chair out from his table to allow his unexpected guest to sit. The tavern wench in Ewen's lap bussed his cheek and leapt to fetch a clean tankard for the newcomer.

Aidan Dougal looked more like an Ives than any Ives, although he claimed no branch of the family tree. Browner and brawnier than any of his tall, swarthy relations and bearing a more prominent proboscis, he carried the certain stamp of aristocracy despite his plebian appearance. He settled his lengthy frame onto the seat offered, crossed his boots at the ankle, and observed the twin serving girls filling pitchers and tankards at the behest of his laughing "cousin."

"I'm on my way south and sought to quench my thirst," Aidan said. "I thought the family had ordered you to stay put in Northumberland for a while, to oversee the mine and canal. Your boots must have wandering soles."

Ewen hooted with laughter, and the serving maids dimpled at the sight and sound of a handsome man enjoying himself.

Accepting a tankard of ale from one twin, Aidan ignored her inviting smile and threw back a hefty swallow. With a toss of her glossy curls, the maid turned back to Ewen, who rewarded her with a broad grin and a pat on the hip.

"He's an ogre who eats beauties like you. Fetch us a bite to eat, will you? Looks like the storm has blown away my ship, and we'll be lingering awhile." Ewen patted the second maid on her ample bottom so she wouldn't sulk, and sent both of them out of the private drawing room.

Sprawled in his chair like the lord of all he surveyed, Aidan quaffed his ale and regarded Ewen with a lifted eyebrow. "You have a way with the lasses."

"They have their way with me," Ewen returned. "All they ask is a little attention and a kind word. You should try it some time."

Aidan grunted, set down his mug, crossed his arms over his broad chest, and rocked back in his chair. "They cost too much for the likes of me. I've a mind to find one who will be a helpmate, not a drain on my pocket."

That subject veered too uncomfortably close to one Ewen was avoiding, so he sipped his ale in lieu of answer. As usual, his damnable interfering relation blithely disregarded his silence.

"I hear you promised to fund the rebuilding of the village that flooded when the canal lock gave way last winter."

Despite the fact that he had no discernible home or occupation, Aidan heard everything that had anything to do with the Ives family. Ewen wondered if there was some way of bottling Aidan's invisible method of communication. A man could make a fortune with a talent like that.

Aidan had heard correctly. Ewen had borrowed against everything he owned to restore the village, and still it hadn't been enough. And the first bank payment was fast coming due. He'd never been burdened with responsibility, and he didn't like it now, but he would do what had to be done. "It was my lock gear that gave way," Ewen said, shrugging.

"But the canal belongs to more than you." Aidan eyed him shrewdly. "I think all the investors should have pitched in for repairs. It's not as if you have funds to throw about."

"Not that it's any of your concern, but I have expectation of income," Ewen said carelessly, as if coins spilled from his pockets as he walked. People tended to accept his wilder statements at face value if he said them with bravado. "The other investors are family men and cannot spare the coin."

"The other investors hoard their cash and let you take the fall. Even if that mine turns a profit this year, it won't be enough to rebuild a village."

Ewen hid his pain with a broad smile. "Well, that's what banks are for, isn't it?" Of course, banks liked to have their money repaid within a reasonable amount of time, and his time was running out.

"There's some who say that is what marriage is for."

The conversation had taken a decidedly uncomfortable drift. "I never saw it that way," he answered stiffly.

One of the twins returned with a heaping platter of sliced bacon and eggs. Setting it on the table, she leaned her generous bosom against Ewen's shoulder. Absently, he rewarded her by circling her waist with his arm. She ran her fingers through his hair, loosing the ribbon of his queue. When she tried to sit on his lap again, Ewen handed her their empty pitcher. "Later," he murmured. Right now he had more important things on his mind — like avoiding the verbal web Aidan was spinning.

The maid pouted, trailed her fingers through his shirt lacing, and tickled his chest hair. Impatiently, Ewen brushed aside her marauding fingers. She'd already unfolded his jabot. Eventually he'd have to find a mirror and make himself presentable. He'd have to shave as well.

Fingering yesterday's whiskers, he reached for his coat where it lay across a chair. An idea for a razor that didn't require soap and water danced through his mind. He rummaged for a pencil lead and a wadded piece of paper in the pocket, and pulling them out, began to scribble a design instead of helping himself to the eggs steaming in front of him.

Aidan snorted as the maid sauntered away. "Marriage has its purposes," he said, continuing the conversation that Ewen had already forgotten. "Are you so comely you've never felt the itch without a woman about to scratch it?"

Truth to tell, Ewen had never had a problem *finding* women. Quite the contrary, he couldn't get rid of them. Women had been set on snaring him from an early age, although he could see no good reason why. He had no home, no fortune, and little interest in either. But he did enjoy women.

He frowned as he sketched, but the design didn't work as he planned. "It's not scratching the itch that's the problem," he admitted, "but avoiding a noose around the neck afterward." Giving up on the sketch and stuffing it back in his pocket, he reached for a plate. "I like each woman for a different reason and no one woman has it all. Marriage isn't natural for my sort."

"Then take your pick from wealthy ones, and your money problems are solved," Aidan said cheerfully.

Ewen spooned eggs onto his plate and shook his head. "I can't abide the clingy twits of society or demanding ladies who require constant attention. If I must marry, I prefer an experienced woman who will go her own way while I travel about on my own business." That's what he would prefer. He feared that wasn't what he would get.

"Sounds as if you have someone in mind," Aidan suggested, partaking heartily of his fare.

Dammit all, the man could pry words from the speechless. To avoid answering, Ewen glanced through the window at a yacht bobbing in the harbor. The ship he'd hoped to catch hadn't arrived yet. He wondered where that one was headed. He longed to be on any ship at all, heading for anywhere but where he must.

"There's a widow in Edinburgh, daughter of a wealthy Cit," he offered up to Aidan's insatiable curiosity. "We've dallied before, and she's made her interest clear. If I explain what I need, she'll be happy to exchange some of her wealth for my name and position, such as they are." And for a ball around his leg and a noose around his neck, as well.

Despite her clever mind, Ewen feared that Harriet Dinwiddie would not be the sort to understand his wandering ways. Like her merchant father, she held on to what was hers.

But it was that or debtors' prison in a month if he could not find the funds to make the bank payment. And there was the little matter of a promise to cough up more funds for expanding the mine or risk losing his investment. So far no one had lined his pockets with gold.

"You're daft, man." Aidan stood up and stepped in front of the window, blocking it with his broad frame. "A man needs a place he can call home and a woman who welcomes him there."

"And I see you're working hard to find one," Ewen scoffed, relieved to have found an opening to switch the topic from himself.

"Aye, I am. I've heard of a welcoming lass just south of here, and I'm setting out that way. A time comes when a man's bed grows cold and lonely."

Ewen didn't know what to say. He didn't know Aidan well. He'd appeared at his brother Drogo's wedding as an unknown relation and surfaced mysteriously every so often since then, like now. Ewen hadn't expected to find anyone he knew in this remote outpost.

Although the mines he supervised were close to the family estate in Wystan, he'd avoided the family's usual port in Northumberland. Having had word from his brother Dunstan that some of Leila's relations would be arriving shortly, Ewen had chosen to slip away to a more northerly port across the border in Scotland. He figured it simpler if he avoided his family until he was properly betrothed. "I don't suppose the object of your desire has a wealthy sister?"

"Won't know until I've met her," Aidan said with good cheer, turning to face the room. "Want to come with me?"

There was an offer he'd like to accept, but footloose and fancy-free would soon be a dream of the past. Shrugging, Ewen lifted his mug. "The bank is looking for its money. Unless you can promise gold at the end of your rainbow, I'll be traveling north."

"You could have done as your so-called friends and walked away from the village's woes," Aidan reminded him.

Ewen scowled. "What do you take me for? A scoundrel? I have a means to put roofs over their heads, and they don't. If a man must marry, it might as well be for a good cause."

Leaning a broad shoulder against the window frame, Aidan asked casually, "Are you certain it was your lock design at fault in the flooding?"

Excellent question, and one Ewen couldn't answer readily. "I can't see how it was, but the canal lock was swept away. I've nothing to show otherwise."

"What about your drawings? Wouldn't they show something?" Aidan suggested. "Instead of marrying, you could prove you were innocent of the damage."

Ewen sighed and took a healthy swallow. He'd been chastised often enough by his brothers for not keeping proper records; he didn't need Aidan doing the same. "I've no idea where the plans got to. I drew them a long time ago. And even if it wasn't my fault, the damage must be repaired, and there's no other to do it."

Folding his arms, the big man shook his head in disbelief. "Were you a woman, I'd call you a fibbertigibbet. You gave me the drawings, remember? I thought to use the canal design on a streambed. I've got them at home."

Ewen raised an eyebrow in disbelief. Aidan had a home? Most times Aidan barely had boots.

The musical tones of feminine voices penetrating the door of the parlor distracted Ewen from his companion's revelation.

In the past, he might have stepped to the door to investigate the rising argument in the hall. Women traveling alone were an oddity, and often appreciative of male assistance. But now he was practically a married man and didn't have the right to flirt.

Could he give up other women if he married? Harriet would expect it of him, he supposed. Could he expect it of himself after taking solemn vows?

His father hadn't abided by his marriage vows. Most of the men of society didn't. Yet his married brothers did. Besides, look what a mess his father had created with two households, one legitimate and the other illegitimate.

Confining his lust to a woman like Harriet wasn't very appealing. She had a man's grasp of money, and a fine, intelligent mind, but hardly a feminine wile to entice. In his experience, no woman could provide all the qualities he admired. He appreciated Harriet's cleverness, but it didn't seem fair to limit himself to a fine mind when there were so many other elements worth admiring elsewhere — like sweetness and full bosoms and laughter.

"Second thoughts?" Aidan taunted, returning to their original subject.

"I know my duty." Actually, he didn't. As a younger brother, Ewen didn't have many responsibilities, so he'd left the burden of family to his older brothers, Dunstan and Drogo. That didn't mean he couldn't shoulder his fair share when necessary.

"We'll pay well," rang clearly from the lobby beyond the door.

Even through the closed door, Ewen recognized something familiar in the distress underlying the woman's brash declaration. Ignoring the instinct to help, he reached for his fork. It was his damnable instinct to fix things that had him in this position in the first place.

A second female murmured something indistinguishable. Even Aidan watched the door with interest now.

"I ain't takin' two runaway females anywheres," a wrathful male replied.

"Do we look like runaways? How *dare* you, sir!"

"I'll lay odds they're runaways," Aidan murmured, slapping a coin on the table.

The amount wasn't enough to interest Ewen in the wager. "Let 'em run away. Didn't you ever run away as a lad?"

"This isn't a fancy lane between mansions in Surrey. That's a rough road out there. They'll be robbed the instant they set foot on it."

"Go save them, then. I haven't the time," Ewen said, digging into his cold eggs.

"If you won't rent them to us, we'll buy the cart and horses." A calm voice overruled the agitated shouts of the driver and the termagant. "How much are they worth?"

"Ten pounds!"

Ewen choked on his mouthful. If they were talking about the wagon outside the window, the woman would do better to make the cheat pay *her* for taking those broken-down, hay-burning nags off his hands.

"Two pounds, and you'll include the reins and harness," the soft-spoken woman offered.

The gentle timbre of her aristocratic accent struck Ewen's ear with odd familiarity, but he shook his head. Impossible.

"That's theft, it is! Nine pounds, and not a far-thing less."

"Felicity, take it," the louder of the two said frantically. "It's our only chance."

"Three pounds, and you'll include the feed," the soft voice demanded with authority, ignoring the frantic one.

"Who do you think you're dealing with, girl? Some high muckety-muck what can afford to throw away a man's wages? Eight pounds or I'm leaving without ye."

Ewen caught himself holding his breath, waiting for the soft-spoken woman to call the thief's bluff. He exchanged a glance with Aidan, who leaned nonchalantly against the wall, arms crossed, listening. The coin he'd wagered sparkled on the table.

They were runaways. Young and unprotected and obviously of good birth. And they were about to risk their few coins on a cart and horse that would no doubt leave them stranded in a robber's haven.

He must be daft to even consider intervening, yet he scraped back his chair with resignation and rose before the loud female could cinch the deal over the clever one's head. Had she called the clever one Felicity? How many

Felicitys could there be in this world?

Dunstan had been expecting visitors from his wife's Malcolm family. Dunstan lived a day's journey south of here.

With a sick feeling in the pit of his stomach, Ewen strode to the door beneath Aidan's knowing look.

"Then leave, sir, for I'll offer no more," the soft-voiced one declared.

"Felicity!" the loud one wailed. "We *need* that cart."

"I'll be off then," the cart owner said smugly.

With a sigh of inevitability, Ewen jerked open the door.

On the other side stood the two blue-eyed, golden-haired Malcolms his brother was expecting back in Northumberland.

His sisters by marriage.

Spoiled little witches who invaded Ives lives like pestilent locusts. It was always an ill omen when they appeared on a man's doorstep.

THREE

Felicity nearly leapt out of her skin as a door flew open, revealing a gentleman in an unfastened velvet vest and loosened jabot. In her cork-soled pattens, Felicity stood at eye level with the sprinkle of dark hair exposed by the gentleman's partially open shirt, and her heart gave a little extra thump at the muscled chest revealed.

Fascinated, she could scarcely tear her gaze away. Even her half-brothers never appeared in her presence in such dishabille. She supposed she should shriek and close her eyes, but intrigued by the appealing aroma of masculine musk and the breadth of velvet-clad shoulders, she forgot to say anything.

"You!" More forthright than Felicity, Christina confronted the intruder. "If Dunstan sent *you* to deliver us, he is sadly mistaken in his choice of escorts."

Dunstan? Oh, dear. At this mention of their conservative brother-in-law, Felicity tore her gaze from the fascinating chest and lifted it to a square chin with a hint of a cleft and covered in dark bristles. Above that she observed firm lips compressed with impatience and a nose —

Oh, my. This was definitely not Dunstan's

striking Ives beak, but a narrow Roman nose in perfect proportion with strong square cheekbones. Another tilt of her head and she was looking into the piercing intelligence of nearly black eyes beneath a sleek ridge of eyebrow raised in inquiry, except these eyes danced with curiosity and a hint of amusement rather than her brother-in-law's sternness. A curl escaped an otherwise straight queue of black hair.

Ewen Ives!

"I'd say my brother is sadly mistaken in his choice of guests," the mellow voice drawled in retaliation to Christina's insult. "Did your broomstick lose its course?"

Oh, dear, this was a dilemma indeed. Felicity chewed on the tip of her glove as her tall and comely sister stood toe-to-toe with the most handsome Ives in existence — Ewen, the youngest of the three legitimate brothers. She remembered siblinglike quarrels when these two had come together on previous occasions. This would never do.

A movement in the doorway drew her attention to the towering giant standing behind Ewen. Catching her gaze, the giant offered an informal tip of his finger to the place where his hat should be. Adonis. No, at her sister's wedding Dunstan had introduced him as Aidan Dougal. He only looked like an Adonis. Or Hercules, more like. He was undoubtedly an Ives, whatever his name.

Worse and worse. They'd be dragged back to Wystan, will-they, nill-they. Fuss and bother and gillywidgets.

Upon realizing the gentlemen knew the ladies, the cart owner backed away. Felicity simply couldn't let these wretched Ives men stop them now that they were so close to their goal. They'd sent the cabin boy on an errand while they dickered over the cart, but he would return any minute now.

As Christina and Ewen verbally tore each other into scraps, Felicity edged around them in the direction of the carter. "Sir, here are three pounds, and an extra shilling to wet your thirst. Do the horses have any quirks we should know about?"

The man shot the gentlemen a hasty glance, grabbed her coins, and shook his head. "None. Just lash them and they'll amble when they're ready." Tugging his forelock, he escaped through the tavern door.

"You didn't just pay that rapscallion, did you?"

Felicity jumped again at the smooth baritone speaking unexpectedly over her shoulder. This hallway was much too narrow. She could feel the lean length of Ewen Ives at her back, and shivered at his proximity. She didn't question how she knew it was Ewen and not the other one but drew a calming breath so her voice wouldn't tremble. "I did, not that it's any of your affair."

Turning, she couldn't believe she'd responded like that. Christina was the rebellious one. Ewen Ives merely thought her a child and exercised his gentlemanly instincts by seeing to her welfare. She shouldn't snap at him.

But his heat and solidity loomed much too close for comfort. Her fingers itched to touch — to push him away, surely. She never liked touching men.

"We must escape," Christina intervened in a breathless whisper. "There is a murderer after us."

Felicity clasped her hands and rolled her eyes, waiting for Mr. Ives' exasperated reply.

As expected, he snorted in disbelief. "And the sky is falling as well," he said in a scathing tone that caused Felicity to wince. "Providing you survived the packs of highwaymen on the road," he continued, "where did you plan to hide from this invisible murderer?"

Highwaymen? *Egad.* Inexperienced at escaping her family's security, Felicity hadn't considered the possibility that they would need an escort.

She clenched her gloved fingers beneath her mantle and gathered the courage to give the dashing gentleman the wide-eyed, innocent-child stare she'd perfected over years of Christina's company. "We'll be safe in Edinburgh," she said sweetly, not entirely feigning her terror. "Could you help us find our way there?"

Standing with arms crossed over his broad chest, Ewen Ives was devilishly pleasant to look upon, but exceedingly obnoxious in all other respects. She watched the black ribbon of his queue as he shook his head in stubborn denial, though laughter hid behind his attempt at sternness.

"You'll go back to Wystan, where I'm certain you belong. Is that your yacht out there?"

"They *abducted* us," Christina exclaimed, pursuing her tale with glee. "We're *escaping*. You must help us. Our father will reward you handsomely."

The mention of reward brought the first flicker of interest to their tormentor's eyes, Felicity noted. Ewen was the handsome inventor of the Ives family, the perpetually bankrupt womanizer. Did she dare encourage a known rake to spend time in the company of flighty Christina?

Glancing at Aidan, she wondered if he would not be the better choice — older, more striking than handsome, and far less apt to be swayed by a pretty face. He had rested his brawny, linen-clad shoulder against the doorjamb to observe the scene, as if it were a puppet show performed for his royal amusement. No help there, she ventured. They would have to play on Ewen's more chivalrous instincts. And his obvious need for cash.

"We can pay for your time," Felicity offered,

concealing her shrewd summary of the situation behind her demure demeanor. "It truly is a matter of life and death that we reach Edinburgh. If you will not help us, we must take our chances alone."

Tearing his exasperated gaze from the bold miss flaunting her best smile, Ewen examined the wisp of a child who was wrapped from head to toe in a gray mantle. He could detect the hint of a silver-gold ringlet beneath her hood, but even though she stared up at him with a child's clear gaze, long lashes and the hood partly concealed her expression.

He remembered this one as the Malcolm who had been presented just last spring. She'd been fascinated by the mechanical toy he'd given her. So she was old enough to travel with her sister. Yet experience made him wary of Malcolms. His brothers may have been foolish enough to fall into their snares, but he had far too many projects on his slate to join in any mischief this pair had planned.

"You would be far better off murdered in your sleep than taking that road alone," he admonished the younger one. "I'll escort you to Dunstan. He'll know how to deal with whatever pursues you."

"But then Leila and the baby will be in danger," Felicity answered, lifting her provocatively long eyelashes in an unblinking plea. "I suppose we could hire guards," she continued relentlessly. "Can you recommend any?"

"Excellent idea, Felicity!" Christina nearly danced with excitement. "We could buy muskets."

Ewen slapped the heel of his hand to his head to dislodge the insanity the women induced. Muskets and nubile females and fragile innocents were enough to twist any man's brain. "They don't sell muskets on street corners," he said. "And no man in his right mind would sell one to a woman."

He didn't believe their abduction story for a minute. Anyone mad enough to steal these two would have thrown them overboard long since.

"If we give you the coins, will you buy us a musket?" the young one asked. "We'd be much obliged." She held out a small coin purse.

With an impatient gesture, Ewen brushed the purse aside and turned to reprimand the elder sister.

Apparently startled by his abrupt motion, the child dropped the purse and coins spun across the worn floor. With a look of reproach, she crouched to gather them again.

Her uncomplaining acceptance of his bad behavior compelled Ewen to rectify his ill manners. Squatting down to help her, he scooped up the coins and held them out to her as a peace offering. "Many pardons, my lady."

To his surprise, she merely stared at his outstretched palm as if he offered her poison. Before he could urge them on her, the brasher sister stooped down and collected the coins and pouch.

"Felicity, the gentleman doesn't intend to help. We'll fare better on our own. Come along."

Returning to his feet, Ewen could only block their exit and stare at them in bemusement. What the deuce should he do now? Felicity regarded him with a wistfulness that would pierce his heart. The elder glared and waited for him to move.

Behind them, Aidan chuckled. "They're all yours. I've better things to do than grovel before pretty blue eyes. Why don't you take them to my home? It's on the way to Edinburgh anyway. They should be safe enough there until you can convince their family to reclaim them. While you're there, you can take a look at those drawings in my library and see if your canal design was at fault."

Ewen opened his mouth to protest. A staunch "no" was on the tip of his tongue, but two pairs of beseeching blue eyes assaulted him, awakening the germ of responsibility his mother had instilled in him. He glared at Aidan instead of the girls. "How far is your place?"

The bigger man shrugged. "You can be there in a day if you take that rotten wagon.

My home's a roof and walls and naught more," he warned. "They'll plead with you to leave as soon as they set eyes upon it."

"Is your home truly near Edinburgh?" Christina asked eagerly.

"With yon horse, it might take an hour downhill." He snorted in disdain. "My home's but a few miles from the city."

"Can't you take us, Mr. Dougal?" the little one asked with a hitch in her voice and a pleading gaze.

Ewen smirked. "Hear that? They prefer you. And it's your home. You can't deny your duty as host."

"I can and will," Aidan asserted without compunction, retreating to the window seat. "My direction is southward. I'll be happy to escort the ladies to Wystan, but not in the opposite direction."

"It cannot be so long a journey, can it?" Felicity asked, turning to Ewen. "And our father will reward you handsomely, I promise. We have no choice but to go, with or without you."

Ewen decided he was addled to even consider their plea, but what would it hurt to see them to safety? He'd leave them with Aidan's servants, thumb through the canal plans he'd drawn, and find a place to stay in the city where he could woo his lady after Dunstan arrived to claim the brats. It would delay his plans by only a day or two.

Besides, he was curious to see what kind of cabbage patch Aidan sprang from.

The light of hope flaring in the shy one's eyes cinched it. With a sigh Ewen returned to the parlor where he'd left his coat. "We need a map, Dougal. And an introduction, or your servants are like to turn us away. Don't see why you can't come with us. It's only a short delay."

Aidan's laugh shivered Ewen's timbers. "Right you are. And I'll miss the entertainment as well, but I'll overcome my grief. Come along, ladies. Take off your cloaks and warm yourselves by the fire."

With a regal gesture to one of the serving maids, Aidan requested pen and paper. Having achieved their wishes, the girls quickly made themselves at home, called for more coals, hot tea, and scones, and whispered between themselves.

Ewen supposed he shouldn't call the pair "girls." The elder had been presented to society several years ago and was betrothed to a duke's younger son, if he remembered rightly. The younger Malcolm must be of an age for marriage. Still, the way she huddled inside her enveloping cloak and looked at him as if he might eat her for breakfast spoke of youth and an annoying innocence. He'd rather argue with the loud one than coddle the helpless one.

He shrugged on his coat and tightened his

jabot. The slight Malcolm carefully averted her eyes while the taller one boldly watched. Hell.

A glossy-haired twin returned carrying a steaming tray of coffee, tea, and scones along with the supplies Aidan had requested. She shot the women at the fire a suspicious glare, then dimpled becomingly at Ewen. "Ale, sir?"

With a too-perceptive look, Aidan indicated the coffeepot. "I'd avoid ale until you're rid of those two. They're enough to muddle a man's mind as it is."

Strangling on his hastily tied collar, Ewen considered several rude remarks and congratulated himself on not speaking them. He'd chew his tongue off over these next days maintaining an even disposition. The burden of enormous debts and the penalty of marriage hanging over his head had tested his limits. Two flighty — and beautiful — Malcolms might be the death of him.

Tucking a coin into the maid's ample bosom and giving her a buss on the cheek to ease her temper, Ewen skirted the table and the Malcolms. He leaned his back against the wall next to his cousin and asked in an undertone, "Will you carry a letter to Dunstan?"

"Aye," Aidan murmured back, "and ye'd best think of something suitable to tell the cabin lad scouring the hall looking for the ladies. Methinks the captain of yon yacht will arrive shortly."

Shooting his companion a look of annoyance for lapsing into pirate dialect, Ewen shoved off the wall to grab one of Aidan's quills and carry it to the table. He hated writing. Ink splattered on the pristine vellum before he'd applied a single word.

"Perhaps I should write a note to my father," a polite voice said from the vicinity of his elbow. In the warmth of the fire, the young one had pushed back her hood to reveal tousled blond locks.

Her direct gaze held an innocence with which he had little experience. "Will you wreak your feminine wiles on him?" he asked teasingly, enjoying the slight blush coloring her cheeks.

Despite her blush, she answered with pragmatism. "He has something of a temper and will not be pleased that we've chosen to disobey his orders."

"Charming." Distracted from her innocence by an image of the powerful Marquess of Hampton bearing down on him, breathing flames through his nostrils, Ewen shuddered. "And I'm supposed to expect a reward for allowing you to do as you please?"

"I shall simply tell Father you are keeping us safe until he can send someone after us," she suggested.

"Oh, fine, and now I'm an accomplice to your escapades." But without words of his own to explain, Ewen pushed paper and pen toward her.

He watched as she retrieved her spectacles from her pocket and began writing to a man so powerful he could play heads of state like puppets on strings. Ewen had spent a lifetime staying out of sight of the powerful, aware they had more interest in the status quo than in his visions of the future. But a father had a right to know where his daughters were.

"I'll keep the cabin boy occupied until you're under way," Aidan drawled. "Leave a note for the captain while you're at it. The boy's like to fear for his head otherwise."

Felicity's blond head bobbed agreement, and Ewen noted the way fair wisps curled in artless abandon about her delicate nape. She was much too young to hold his interest, he decided, returning his gaze to the letter he should be writing to Dunstan.

Glaring at Christina smiling seductively at him over her teacup from the other end of the table, Ewen scratched a few curt words across the page. Beside him Felicity sat down to write a lengthy discourse to her father in a careful hand straight from a schoolbook.

"There's the directions." Aidan rose from the window seat to throw down the map he'd been working on. "The place is cold and drafty, but you'll be safe there."

Felicity looked up to give him a smile of unsurpassed sweetness. "You are very kind, Mr. Dougal. We owe you a great favor."

Even the intrepid Aidan looked flustered

beneath her shy regard. "Ninian would have my head if I did not offer my aid," he muttered.

At the mention of her married cousin, Felicity sighed and returned to writing. "She'll have my head should she discover what we're about, so please go nowhere near her until we're home again."

Ewen squeezed the bridge of his nose and sent up prayers at this revelation. Anything Ninian disapproved of her husband would disapprove of. And her husband happened to be Drogo, Earl of Ives and Wystan, Ewen's eldest brother and keeper of the family purse. "We'll have both my brothers and your entire family hounding us the instant your letter reaches London. Why don't I just drown myself in a loch and have done?"

Felicity offered another smile of pure faith. "Because you're too responsible a gentleman to cause us undue grief. It's good to know at least one Ives was brought up properly."

Startled, Ewen studied her virtuous expression for insult, but she merely returned to writing her lengthy tome as if she hadn't just shaken him to his toes.

Responsible? Him? "Rake," "rogue," "rapscallion," and "bankrupt scapegrace" were appellations that had been thrown at him frequently, but "responsible"? Not in his lifetime. He didn't have the time or patience to live up to society's impossible standards. She would be sadly disappointed if she thought him a *responsible* gentleman.

No, his sort only resorted to responsibility when they needed something. And he needed to get to Edinburgh to marry an heiress so he didn't end up in Newgate, begging for a living.

FOUR

"The innkeeper sold me the quilt you liked and I some warming bricks," Christina explained, hurrying through the muddy inn yard to arrange the articles in the back of their newly purchased cart.

"Bless you!" With relief, Felicity watched her sister tuck the inoffensive quilt over the highly offensive wagon bed. "I shall be perfectly content there."

"You always hated the pony cart after Rolly's spaniel died in it. We should have thought of that sooner." Christina leaned closer to whisper, "Isn't Ewen Ives the most handsome creature you've ever met? I vow, his aura is all lovely blues, with the occasional lustful purple. We could not have done better had we planned this encounter."

Since the subject in question was hastening toward them, Felicity refrained from replying. Inwardly, she groaned.

How would she ever explain to her father if she let Christina fall into the clutches of a penniless Ives when Christina was already promised to a duke's son? The marquess would have an apoplexy. Their father had only grudgingly accepted Leila's marriage to

Dunstan because she had been a wealthy widow and was free to choose as she pleased.

Felicity gazed out at the yacht bobbing in the harbor. They really should sail for Wystan and forget this mad errand. She was dragging Christina into something far beyond her ken.

But Felicity had only to touch the cart to receive the image of a child sobbing over something she couldn't see and was helpless to prevent since it may have happened decades ago. Why should she endure more of the chronic misery her gift caused when it made her family so unhappy as well? They were only a day's ride from freedom. How could she give up her quest now?

"Ladies, let us leave before the cabin boy lifts his head from the innkeeper's best ale." Ewen extended his hand to Felicity to assist her into the seat. "You first."

Earlier, when she'd refused to take the coins from his hand, he'd looked at her as if she were a peculiar strain of idiot. Still, Felicity couldn't accept his assistance. He didn't wear gloves, and she didn't trust the leather of her own to protect her against the impact of an Ives.

Disdaining his open palm, Felicity gathered her skirt and petticoats and with some difficulty clambered into the back of the cart to make a nest for herself in the quilt.

Watching her, Ewen ran his fingers over his

hair in confusion. "You can't ride back there. The road will jolt every tooth out of your head."

"Felicity suffers from motion sickness if she sees where we're going," Christina replied, arranging the warming bricks around her sister. "Help me up to the seat, and we'll be ready."

Without saying a word, the timid Malcolm pulled her hood around her face and huddled within the shelter of the quilt. Refusing to encourage the spoiled child's foolishness, not knowing what else to make of it, Ewen swung around to assist Christina. "Right. Let's be on with it then."

Settling on the cart bench, Ewen was more uncomfortably aware of the slight form wrapped in powdery scent behind him than he was of the curvaceous female ensconced at his elbow. As the horses swayed into motion, he winced at the hard jolt of the wagon wheels, but he refused to argue over the brat's choice of seating arrangements.

"I don't suppose either of you would be interested in entertaining me with the real reason for this journey, would you?" he inquired, by way of making conversation.

"London does not agree with us," Christina answered blithely.

Ewen frowned at the ridiculous reply. "*I* do not agree with you, but that doesn't stop you from blackmailing me into cooperation.

Should I be wary of outraged suitors leading small armies in your pursuit? Will your half-brothers come after me with brickbats, or worse yet, will your mother put a hex on me?"

"I think Aunt Stella has the hex manual," the petite one intervened before her sister could reply. "If you wrote to Dunstan, he's more likely than anyone to come after us."

Malcolms weren't really witches, Ewen knew. They just seemed to have extraordinary *instincts* that no one else possessed. His sister-in-law Ninian had empathic qualities that went beyond the normal. Dunstan's wife, Leila, apparently smelled character, which made no logical sense to anyone but her. They could do strange things, though hexing people didn't appear to be a habit they'd acquired. Still, he'd like to know how the innocent one had discerned he'd written to Dunstan.

Ewen rewarded her with a suspicious frown over his shoulder. In response, she batted her lashes and returned to watching the passing countryside. Had she been a full-grown woman, he would have distrusted her harmless pose, but a child had no reason to feign innocence.

His self-protective instincts chose that moment to remind him that she'd had her debut and was — officially at least — no longer a child.

"I can't protect you if I don't know what I'm protecting you from," he argued. "I'd suggest you tell the truth now, or we may all regret it later."

"We *told* the truth," Christina insisted. "One of Felicity's suitors is a murderer. No one believes us. It just didn't seem safe to stay in London with a killer haunting our doorstep."

"If Ninian didn't believe you, then you're lying," Ewen asserted. "She always knows when you speak the truth."

"Ninian's in the country. We didn't tell her," Felicity admitted.

Ewen shivered at her words. He didn't think the soft-spoken sister was quite as apt to make up tall tales as Christina. The possibility that they spoke some form of truth would complicate his life unbearably. He probed for more details. "All right, who is this murderer so I can watch out for him?"

"Sir Percy Larch," Christina answered. "He pushed his mother over the balcony rail to her death."

"Percy?" Ewen repeated. "The banker with no eyebrows? *That* Percy?" He definitely didn't believe them now.

"He has eyebrows," Felicity corrected. "They're just very light."

"Percy would not lift a hand to a quill if it spilled ink on him." Ewen vented his frustration that they thought him so gullible. "Now,

I could believe it of his cousin Robert. The man pinches pennies until they cry. Are you certain it's not Robert?"

"I don't know Robert. I saw Percy," the child insisted.

"You *saw* him? You saw Percy push his mother off the balcony?"

"I see things. Could we just leave it at that?"

"Not on your life," Ewen replied with deadly intensity. "I'm not a besotted fool like my brothers. Are you in the habit of 'seeing' murderers?"

"Of course not," Christina answered when Felicity retreated into her mantle and refused to explain further. "It's just that some memories and emotions are so strong, people and objects give off vibrations of them. Felicity is very sensitive to those vibrations."

Felicity waited with interest to see if Ewen laughed, threw them out of the cart, or took them apart to see what made them tick, like the machines he was so fond of fixing.

"Vibrations?" he scoffed. "You see auras and she feels vibrations? Useful tricks. What am I vibrating right now?"

"Disbelief," Felicity answered with a sigh. She shouldn't have expected more. He was an Ives, after all. He needed scientific, logical proof of things that had no scientific, logical basis.

"Excellent. You're better at guessing than

your sister, but you're way off the mark if you feel murder in Percy's vibrations."

"She doesn't —"

"Don't, Christina. Once we find the book, it won't matter. Let's concentrate on that." It was a pity such a handsome, intelligent gentleman couldn't believe in that which he could not see, but Felicity had long ago accepted that most men were like him.

"London is full of books," the far-too-intelligent Ives said, following another tactic. "Why go all the way to Edinburgh for one?"

"Why go all the way to Newcastle for coal?" Christina countered. "Because that's where it is."

"One could order it shipped."

Felicity admired his logic, but it would take a lifetime of explanation to dissuade him that logic did not apply in their situation. "Would you ship a one-of-a-kind book containing the result of all your experimentation?" she asked.

She caught her breath at the look Ewen Ives shot her over his shoulder. The flare of interest in his mysterious eyes beneath ebony eyebrows seared like a heated arrow. She pulled her mantle tighter and tried not to imagine what it would be like to have all that intense curiosity applied to her.

Something rebellious in her urged her to fling back the hood and face his curiosity fully, but she'd spent a lifetime living in caution and couldn't change readily now.

"No," he finally answered, "but then, I wouldn't see visions of murderers or run away from them either." He returned his attention to the horses and the path climbing into the hills, away from the village.

"Oh, so you would stay in London and let all society laugh at you while the murderer hunted you down and killed you?" Christina asked brightly.

Ewen grunted in exasperation. "Let's just accept that we have nothing in common to converse on and try silence for a while."

Felicity liked that idea, but Christina never held her tongue for more than a minute at a time unless she was asleep. And sometimes she talked in her sleep, too.

"Why don't you tell us what *you're* doing up here?" Christina asked him. "That should keep us occupied for hours and hours."

"I was hoping to catch a ship for Edinburgh," he said caustically. "And now I'm transporting two spoiled children for no good reason other than that you have a cart and the ship hasn't arrived. Has an hour passed yet?"

"Tell us about Mr. Dougal," Felicity interrupted in the interest of making peace. "Is he your cousin?"

"On the wrong side of the blanket, presumably. Ives family records aren't precisely complete."

"His aura contains a shade of rose I associate more with Malcolms than with Ives," Christina admitted. "But Malcolms keep good family records, and I know of no mention of him."

"Rose?" Ewen asked in disbelief. "You see *pink* in Aidan's aura?"

Giving up on keeping the combatants apart, Felicity let her attention wander to the rolling hills of the countryside. The brisk April air smelled pleasantly of what she assumed to be heather. Having lived most of her life in the smog of London, she enjoyed the refreshing scent. Even the air at their family estate in Kent did not seem so invigorating. Or was it her first brush with freedom that she tasted?

Facing backward, she frowned at a movement at the bottom of the hill they'd just traversed. She didn't wish to irritate the easily annoyed Ives any more than was necessary or to be the one who cried wolf, but it certainly appeared to her that a rider was following them at a dangerous pace.

Christina's tale of Sir Percy chasing after them was mostly for show, but what if the ship's captain had decided to take them back to where they belonged? Or if a highwayman had heard a marquess's daughters were out here?

"Do you think we might pull off the road for a bit?" she asked, trying not to sound unduly alarmed.

"And break an axle on a rock? Did you have some desire to spend the night under the stars?" Ewen asked without slowing down.

Christina glanced over her shoulder just as the rider broke through a band of trees at the base of the hill below them. Hoping her sister could see the man's aura and be able to judge him friend or foe, Felicity waited for her reaction.

Christina's eyes widened in alarm, and without warning, she leaned over and grabbed the reins from Ewen. She tugged hard to the right, and the horses obediently swayed toward the side of the road.

Cursing, Ewen jerked the reins from her hands and steered the horses back from the precarious edge of a ditch. "Must I tie you up for your own safety?"

"Highwaymen!" Christina cried, clutching his arm and glancing over her shoulder. "We must hide."

Felicity sighed at her sister's dramatics, but she had to admit, they often had the desired effect on gentlemen.

Staying firmly on the road, Ewen Ives ignored Christina's admonition. "It's broad daylight. No self-respecting —" He followed her glance to the road behind them.

Apparently unable to see the cart hidden by a curve of the road above him, the rider galloped over the path below, his cloak billowing in the wind as if he rode to escape the gates of hell. He didn't appear harmless.

"Plague take it!" Ewen expertly guided the lumbering wagon behind a large rock formation. "Out, both of you. Crouch down behind that stand of gorse. I'll lead him down the path a way until I know what danger he poses."

Felicity hated to part company with their only security, but she knew that as daughters of a rich man, they were obvious targets. If anyone on the yacht had mentioned who they were, it wouldn't take long for someone such as the cart's previous owner to figure out what road they had taken.

Unable to think of a better plan, Felicity slipped from the back of the cart. In a rustle of petticoats, Christina jumped down beside her, using the shrubs for concealment.

"Be careful," Felicity called as Ewen turned the horses toward the road.

His white teeth flashed in a devilish smile, and he saluted them with his pistol. "I don't fail damsels in distress. Hide!"

His Ives confidence warmed and encouraged her, but as soon as he drove away, Felicity had to fight her panic. "Could you see who it was?"

Christina shook her head. "I didn't recognize his aura, but I didn't like his pace. I thought it best to be wary."

Or elect the path that afforded the most

adventure. But Felicity didn't take her sister to task for that. "We can't stay here," she whispered. "What if something happens to Mr. Ives? Let's make our way along the side of the road where we can't be seen. Maybe we can help him."

Christina glanced dubiously over the bleak landscape of heather, gorse, and rocks, then down at her vivid blue gown. "I don't exactly blend in."

She might know little or nothing about the countryside, but Felicity knew how to play games. If she pretended this was just a game of hideaway, she could do it very well. "I blend in. Hide here in this hollow. Fill your pockets with stones you can use for warning or weapons."

Before Christina could argue, Felicity crouched behind a rock and knotted her gray mantle in place. She had never climbed hills before. Gingerly, she touched a gloved finger to a gray rock half buried in the ground. Although the April air was cool, she felt a slight warmth from the sun emanating from it. No dreadful vibrations hurt her here.

She heard the beat of hooves approaching at a gallop, and Ewen's merry whistle ahead as he urged their lazy horses into motion, leading danger away from them. She'd known Ives men could be stubborn and demanding. She'd not fully understood that those qualities could also be heroic.

He could be killed for their foolishness in taking this dangerous road instead of the safety of the ship.

Her gift might be singularly useless, but she had a clever mind. She would think of something to prevent him from coming to grief because of her.

Sliding into a narrow gully, she stirred a small avalanche of pebbles. Without thought, she grabbed a patch of gorse for balance and jerked her hand away. It was prickly and caused a purely physical pain. More determined now, she followed the gully down the hill.

Ewen was guiding the cart past the crest, toward the valley below, traveling no faster than Felicity could walk, so she stayed abreast. The highwayman would catch up to him quickly at this rate. The gully widened as it ran downhill, but the gorse became less dense.

She dropped deeper into the ditch as she heard the rider crest the hill.

"Ives!" the stranger shouted.

The highwayman knew him? Felicity peeked over the ditch edge. Ewen slowed, frowned in her direction as if he knew she was there, then halted the horses as if he hadn't a care in the world. "Who goes there?" he called jovially.

"It's me — Campbell. They told me at the mine that you were heading for the city. I just missed you at the inn."

Wishing she had Christina's ability to read auras, Felicity crouched in the gully and studied the newcomer. The stranger was wearing an old-fashioned ramillie wig and a coat decades out of date, and didn't appear dangerous. When Campbell scanned his surroundings, she ducked down again. He was old and stout. Surely Mr. Ives was safe with him.

"Is there something wrong at the mine?" she heard Ewen ask in alarm.

"No, not a thing. They were under the impression you were bound for Edinburgh, and I thought we could travel more safely together."

Ewen laughed. "Sorry, you'd best go on without me. I'm about to make one last visit before I'm imprisoned in the bonds of matrimony."

Felicity bit back a gasp. He was betrothed? No wonder he was irritated by the delay. But his reply led her to believe he wasn't happy with the prospect of marriage.

"Aye, Mick at the mine said as much. Can't imagine where you'll find a gal to dally with out here, but a handsome face attracts them, I wager. The innkeeper thought you'd gone off with a pair of them."

Fascinated despite herself, Felicity waited to hear how he'd charm the man out of believing that.

"I won't tell your secrets if you won't tell

mine," Ewen replied cheerfully. "Is there aught else I can do for you, Campbell? I hate to keep a lady waiting."

She sneaked another peek and saw Campbell fish an oilcloth-wrapped packet from his coat.

"I'm delivering this to Robert Larch, or that young cousin of his who's handling the London financing for us. He's expected in Edinburgh this week. I dislike carrying cash through this robber's paradise, but if you're not free to watch my back, I'll chance it alone."

"Sir Percy is Robert's cousin, isn't he?" Ewen idly inquired.

"That's the one. I hear Percy has a fancy for the London ladies. A Scots lass isn't good enough for him."

"They're all bonny in my eyes," Ewen said easily. "Next we meet, then?"

"Aye. I'll buy you a round to celebrate your impending nuptials." With a tip of his hat, Campbell dug in his heels and galloped off.

Now that the moment of danger had passed, Felicity froze. Should she race back up the hill to Christina and pretend she hadn't disobeyed orders or boldly step forward and take her punishment? She disliked it when people were angry with her, and she had a real aversion to this man's ire. She'd much prefer he not think her a ninnyhammer.

Before she could decide, a mellow baritone rang over her head. "Do you want to guess what I'm vibrating now?"

Cringing, Felicity tilted her head back to meet the black gaze of Ewen Ives as he towered over her. Bare fists pulled back his unfastened coat and vest to reveal narrow hips encased in supple doeskin. He radiated masculinity and — could it be curiosity?

FIVE

A hail of pebbles forced Ewen to duck, drawing his attention away from the slight figure cowering in the ditch. He had no notion what she intended by following him, but his curiosity was diverted by a more urgent need to avoid being crowned by a rock.

"What the devil are you doing?" he shouted at Christina, who was pelting him with pebbles from above. He dipped behind rocks and gorse to avoid the deadly accuracy of her ammunition.

"Christina, for the love of the goddess, leave poor Mr. Ives alone."

Poor Mr. Ives? *Poor?* Taking a seat upon a bed of heather out of firing range and leaning back against a bare rock, Ewen basked in the sun's warmth and attempted to rearrange his view of the world. *Poor?* What did he look like to them, a muddling milquetoast like Percy? A trapped rabbit? Women *fawned* on him. Threw themselves at his feet. Men respected him. He'd dammed an entire river and made it navigable, harnessed lightning, built a steam engine, and saved a mine.

And this timid mouse thought him so

pitiful he needed her protection from a rock-throwing vixen? Disgruntled, he remained hidden where he was, rethinking his desire to protect this pair of idiots.

"He was shouting at you," Christina called to Felicity.

"I did not mean to shout." In disgust, Ewen rose to his full height.

Christina nearly fell off her perch in surprise. Reacting swiftly, he caught her and hauled her down to the ground. "I don't yell at ladies."

"You yell at me!" she shouted.

"Precisely my point."

The younger sister leapt to her feet but wisely held her tongue as Ewen caught the termagant's elbow and escorted her toward the cart. He was beginning to rethink his position regarding helplessness. The coddled one behaved with considerably more sense than the independent one.

"If you don't trust me to get you safely to Edinburgh, why did you ask for my company?" he demanded of them.

"Because we knew that as a gentleman, you would never let us leave on our own," Felicity said simply.

He scowled as Christina scrambled into the cart with a careless exhibition of stockings and petticoats. He turned his back on the display, not wanting to wallow in feminine pulchritude while fate meant to chain him to only one woman, and a sharp-tongued, narrow-hipped one at that.

"I can drive the cart," Christina insisted as she caught up the reins. "You ought to stand as guard, prepared to fight off attackers."

Before climbing into his seat, Ewen turned to the sensible sister. "She reads novels, doesn't she? Do you think you can convince her she's not Gulliver or Moll Flanders or whoever she thinks she is today, and that I'm perfectly capable of escorting you to Aidan's home?"

A smile flickered across Felicity's deliciously bowed lips, and Ewen forced himself to tamp down his lascivious response. She was little more than a *child*. He had no right to contemplate how her lips would taste against his. The threat of marriage must be stirring him to madness.

"Unlike you, we have little opportunity for adventure in our lives," she replied. "Christina does what she can to make her own."

"Not while she's with me." He glared at the female next to him. "You will pretend to be a docile, pleasant-tempered lady on a family visit until I'm a day's ride away from you, or I'll leave you here to find your own way. Understood?"

"Does this mean you will pretend to be a gentleman until then?" Christina asked with a haughty lift of her eyebrow.

"I'd like to eat sometime before nightfall,"

Felicity intervened. "Didn't the innkeeper mention a place a little farther on?"

That took the dash out of both of them.

"Will you let me assist you into the cart?" Ewen asked in the same courteous tones as she had just employed.

Felicity eyed his ungloved hand and shook her head. "I mean no disrespect, but I'd rather not. I suspect it would be very much like shaking hands with lightning."

Through dark eyes, he studied her before dropping his gaze to his callused brown hand and shoving it into his capacious coat pocket. Felicity could see the curiosity and intelligence burning behind Ewen's thick lashes as he worked through that puzzle. It was a trifle unsettling to be studied by a dashing gentleman, but Felicity figured she would be immune to his charms as long as she couldn't touch him. With as much modesty as she could summon, she edged into the cart on her own.

"I haven't murdered anyone," he said quietly as she settled in.

The knot of anxiety in her insides unraveled at this sign that he was trying to understand. So many people did not try. "But I suspect you may have done many things with those hands that you wouldn't like me to see, haven't you?"

A wry smile transformed his manly visage into one of boyish appeal. "If you can see all a man has done with his hands, then you had best retire to a nunnery."

Felicity held his gaze. "Exactly."

Seeing his shock, she pulled her hood close and settled back in the cart. If she could rid herself of her cursed "gift," she could open up to the pleasure of seeking charming, handsome men like Ewen Ives. Until then there was no point in making herself miserable dwelling on what she could not have.

She could see what a man had done with his hands?

Ewen tried to work his mind around the concept and failed. No maiden should have any inkling of some of the things men did with their hands. Did she see *all* things, or just some? Or did she simply have a screw loose in her head?

Did he really want to know the answers?

As the mild spring day slipped toward chilly evening without any sign of Aidan's home, Ewen debated his wisdom in pressing on past the village they'd stopped in earlier. They'd dined well, but the inn offered only a single open sleeping room for travelers. At the time, continuing on had made sense.

But being stuck on a freezing hilltop for the night in the company of two unpredictable unmarried females didn't make any sense at all.

"Mr. Dougal's map shows a stone fence, an

oak, and a barn after the village," Christina said, peering closely at the sketch in the fading light. "We've followed a fence all the way up here. That half-dead tree might be an oak. And I suppose that could be a barn."

Ewen slowed the horses while they studied the scattered stones of a tumbled-down edifice.

"I thought Mr. Dougal said he lived but a few miles from Edinburgh," Felicity said in bewilderment. "There is naught but sheep and stones out here."

"Perhaps we have missed the road." Christina attempted to sound confident that they would find it again.

Ewen had had all day to become accustomed to being on the outside of these sisterly discussions. The pair was up to something, no doubt, but it was none of his concern. They had their schemes; he had his. He'd leave them in the hands of a competent housekeeper, get a good night's sleep, find his papers, and set out for the city at dawn.

If he didn't think too hard about the leg shackle awaiting him, he could do what must be done.

"That's an odd-looking pile of rocks on that next hill," he commented.

He could feel Felicity shifting position so she could see the road over his shoulder. She wore some subtle scent that reminded him of apple blossoms. In the cool night air she radiated a comforting feminine warmth. Had she been any other female, he would be dreaming of spending a hot evening in her beguiling arms.

He needed a *woman* wrapped around him, not a helpless maiden like this one. Harriet had offered him a warm bed and welcoming arms in the past. Better that he should think of a widow of her maturity and independence.

"Let me have the map, Christina." Felicity held her gloved hand over his shoulder, interrupting his morose thoughts.

"Are you sure?"

"I'll try it with gloves first. We can't wander aimlessly around the countryside all night. We need to know if we should turn back."

Ewen watched in fascination as the younger sister caught the corner of the map with two gloved fingers. He stopped the horses so he could watch her weigh the paper in her palm. Apparently deciding that Aidan's sketch wouldn't hurt, she pulled off her glove, curled the map in her fingers, and concentrated.

In the interest of science, he studied Felicity's features in the twilight. With the hood flung back, he could better see the shadows beneath her eyes and the hollows of her pale cheeks. She truly did not look well. Guilt crept over him as he realized she shouldn't be out here on a cold Scots night. He should have stopped at the village and commandeered the entire inn for them.

He didn't have that kind of money.

In total honesty, Ewen knew he wouldn't have thought of it even if he'd been a wealthy king. He'd never learned to look after anyone but himself. He didn't know how he'd ended up taking care of this pair.

"Oh, dear." Felicity opened her eyes and stared into the fading gloom of the hill ahead.

"What?" Ewen demanded.

"Your cousin is somewhat of a jester, is he not?" Felicity returned the map to Christina and began tugging her long glove on again.

"I don't know him well enough to even call him cousin. Is there a house up ahead or should I turn back?" He couldn't believe he'd just asked that. How the hell could she tell by squeezing a piece of paper?

"A castle," Felicity replied. "If we go on a little farther, we should see it."

Ewen felt both sisters waiting expectantly. Feeling that he was the butt of some joke, he shook the reins and set the horses in motion again. *A castle*, he scoffed. Aidan hadn't owned a decent pair of boots until Dunstan bought him some. He was unlikely to own a sheep, much less a castle.

"That isn't a pile of rocks." Christina leaned forward to see more clearly. "Look, you can see a tower beyond that first section. The rocks must be the outer defense walls."

Narrowing his eyes, Ewen studied the

73

oddity they approached. He'd picked through an old castle or two on occasion. Most of them were piles of stone these days. It was growing too dark to see clearly, but he didn't think nature could duplicate that sharp jut of broken crenellation outlined against the last remaining ribbon of light. A man could almost imagine a flag flying and archers at the ready along the parapet.

"Gadzooks," Felicity murmured in fascination. "It's a castle just like in the storybooks."

"That's a generous description," Ewen muttered as the details became clearer. Most of the outer defense walls had been carried off. What had once been a guard tower on one corner had tumbled down the hillside. Three more towers stalwartly guarded the remaining corners of the square, three-story keep. The stones glowed rosily in the sunset, and light sparkled like diamonds in the stained glass of the solar, but Ewen wasn't fooled by the beauty.

Judging from the beams jutting from the roof, the residence hall had holes in its ceiling. He wondered if he should turn the horses around and head back. For all he knew, the walls were held together by the ivy covering them.

"I don't see any lights," Christina said. "I don't think anyone's home."

"Of course no one's home. Would you be

home if you lived there?" Ewen made a mental note to pound Aidan into the ground next time he saw him. *Bats* wouldn't live in a cave like that.

"Perhaps the lower floors are safe and snug, and he leaves the upper story like that to deter thieves," Felicity said with optimism.

"No one could live there," Christina declared. "There must be another house somewhere about."

Ewen didn't think so, and Felicity's silence warned that she didn't believe it either, but he urged the horses onward. Dreams of warm fires and soft beds popped like bubbles one by one as they drew near.

"Who will let us in?" Felicity whispered.

With no lane to follow, Ewen guided the horses across the overgrown yard and halted the cart at a crumbling stairway. Not a single light flickered behind the windows. At least they appeared to contain some form of glass, so perhaps the place wasn't entirely abandoned.

"Wait here. Let me check the door. We can always go back to the village if no one is home."

He took the stone steps two at a time and pounded a heavy iron knocker against the massive oak. Nothing. It would take a giant to persuade enough noise out of the knocker to be heard past the threshold. Glancing around, Ewen discovered a rope hidden between two squared outcroppings of stone arching upward into a pointed roof. Praying he wasn't lowering the portcullis on his head, he tugged the rope and heard the distant echo of a bell.

"I daresay we could just open the door and let ourselves in."

Had he not recognized her voice, Ewen might have jumped six feet off the ground at the unexpected advice at his elbow. Glancing down, he found Felicity wrapped in her quilt and studying the door with interest.

He had the inexplicable urge to wrap her in his arms and carry her to a warm fire and safety. The very notion of being provoked into such an action shook him back to reality. She'd think he meant something by it.

The echo of footsteps on the other side of the door was a relief.

Christina joined them as someone threw a squeaking iron bolt. So much for telling the women to stay in the cart. Ewen debated throwing himself in front of both of them should a carnivorous dog or an ax-wielding madman appear on the threshold. With a return of his usual wry humor, he was half inclined to let the dog and madman have at them.

One massive door creaked slowly open, revealing a flickering candle flame. With a sigh of exasperation at himself, Ewen grasped Felicity's quilt-wrapped shoulders and shoved her behind him. She jerked out of his hands before he realized his faux pas in touching her, but she obediently stayed where he placed her.

"Ah, there you are, lovies. Do come in. We've been waiting for you."

Holding up a candle, a tiny old woman materialized in the gap between the doors. Wearing brocaded skirts from a century ago, she beamed at them through a face more wrinkled than crumpled parchment. Ewen clung to the word "we" as he observed the cane supporting her. He couldn't leave two sheltered women in the shaky hands of this housekeeper, but there must be more servants within.

"We're Miss Felicity Childe and Miss Christina Childe, and this is Mr. Ewen Ives. We're sorry to intrude at this hour," Felicity said, "but Mr. Dougal said we might stop here for the evening. If we'll be an intrusion, we can return to the village."

The woman beamed with approval. "Oh, no, dearies, here you'll stay. I'll hear no more of it. Come in. I'm Margaret, though there are some as calls me Meg."

She looked Ewen up and down as if he were a horse she might buy. "My, you're a fine one. You've the mark of the old man about you, of a certainty. Bring in the bags, would you? I've a fire started in the ladies' chamber."

"Is there a groom to handle the horses?" Ewen inquired, too overwhelmed by the various responsibilities facing him to choose one over the other, much less try to interpret the old woman's strange observations.

Their hostess chuckled. "Not unless they're ghosties. There's none here but myself. Bring the bags, and I'll see to the ladies while you look after the creatures. There'll be hay and water in the stable."

None here but herself. Then who was the "we" who had been waiting for them? A pall of gloom dropped over him as Ewen returned to the cart. He'd hoped to leave the women in the hands of a staff more reliable and responsible than he.

As it was, he couldn't go courting in the morning unless he took both women with him.

On the other hand, he thought, spirits lifting, that meant he could explore this fascinating pile and put off negotiating a marriage arrangement with a woman who could squeeze shillings out of stone.

SIX

Ewen had *touched* her. And it hadn't hurt!

Felicity contemplated the wonder of that as she gazed around at the impressive hall they entered. She'd actually enjoyed Ewen's protective instinct to shelter her as the door opened — once she'd recovered from the shock of his brief touch. The quilt and her clothing had apparently buffered her, and for a brief moment she'd felt like a normal, cherished woman.

She longed to feel that way again.

She bit her lip anxiously as Ewen turned away to collect their bags from the cart. She disliked exploring the unknown castle without the security of his presence.

But he was betrothed to another and eager to be rid of them, so there was no point in pretending he would accompany them on their adventure. She must learn to face the world on her own.

Gathering up her quilt and skirts, she followed the housekeeper and Christina through the cavernous hall. With trepidation she studied the moth-eaten tapestries between leaded glass windows, a cobweb-covered iron chandelier overhead, and bulky furniture covered in yellowing linen. Aidan lived here? It didn't look as if the hall had been used since the last knight rode away.

The air echoed of ghosts, but no doubt that was her imagination. She wasn't touching anything but her skirts, and she held them high off the cold slate floor, so there was little chance that she was sensing vibrations.

"Is there anyone else living here?" Christina asked, striding through the towering room and casting fascinated glances into the dancing shadows of the medieval living quarters.

"The master comes and goes, and the wee ghosties appear from time to time, but I'm all that's left of the staff that was. Grand, we used to be, with cooks in the kitchen and grooms in the stable, but all that's gone now."

A mystery. Christina liked nothing better than a mystery. Felicity could think of nothing worse. Nervously checking over her shoulder, she forced the others to walk slower. She didn't want to leave Mr. Ives too far behind.

She sighed in relief as he swung through the door, hauling one portmanteau beneath his arm and the others in his hands. She breathed easier at the ringing of his masculine boots against the slate.

"Here's another candle, dearie, if you'll carry it, please." The old woman handed a candlestick to Christina. "There's a nice snug chamber above for the ladies, and the gentleman may use the master's chamber below."

Felicity felt Ewen's reassuring solidity behind her and didn't startle when he dipped his head to whisper near her ear, "Will you feel safe alone? I can sleep outside your door, if that would help."

The intimacy of his breath against her skin, as much as his gallant offer, shivered down Felicity's spine. She liked that he requested her opinion rather than treating her as if she hadn't a brain of her own, even if he had every right to think of her as a squeamish miss. "The castle seems safe enough. And I felt no harm in Mr. Dougal."

"Laird Dougal, if this pile of stones is his." Ewen fell into step beside her, taking in the solid wood stairway, the headless suit of armor at its foot, and the collection of broadswords decorating the timbered mantel. "Dunstan or Drogo should have looked into his background."

Not heeding them, Christina hurried after Margaret, eager to explore their new surroundings.

"Well, this is your opportunity." Felicity reminded herself that Ewen Ives was a busy gentleman, but she hoped he would linger a day or two with them here. She had no idea how she and Christina could get into Lord Nesbitt's library to find the book she needed.

Ewen Ives would have far more experience and knowledge for such adventures. "Drogo and Dunstan are busy with family, and you're not."

"And don't want to be," Ewen retorted. He dropped his battered bag at the foot of the stairs as the sprightly old lady led them up.

"Families may be annoying," Felicity observed, "but they're the ones who must take us in and care about us when times are difficult. You should treat yours with respect."

"I regard them with such respect that I keep my distance lest they discover what a ne'er-do-well I am," he said with good cheer. "The illusion of success is much easier to achieve from a distance."

"I am certain you're too modest to admit that you have many fine qualities that they admire," Felicity replied, shocked by his perception of himself. "Christina and I will be forever grateful to you for the speed with which you came to our rescue. I hope we have not caused you too great a delay."

"As Aidan said, this is on my way." He stopped politely in the entrance of the bedchamber where Christina and Margaret were already in earnest conversation about linens.

In no hurry to encounter whatever ghosts resided within, Felicity lingered in the security of Ewen's presence. "It seems a pleasant enough room," she said, trying to reassure herself. "I wonder why she has a fire already laid? Surely we traveled faster than any message Mr. Dougal may have sent."

"Someone in the village warned her, no doubt. Don't go seeing more than there is," he said, waiting for her to precede him.

She flashed him a skeptical glance and, gathering her limited courage, entered the room behind her sister.

"I dinnae have time to bring in help this evening, my ladies." The old woman's smile wreathed her lined face as she used their titles, even though they hadn't mentioned them. "But there will be hot water and fresh scones in the morning. If you can make yourselves comfortable here without me, I'll lead the gentleman to his room."

"If you don't mind, I can make myself comfortable on a floor in an adjoining chamber," Ewen insisted. "The young ladies aren't accustomed to being on their own."

Felicity nearly fell to her knees in gratitude at his offer. She wasn't prone to seeing ghosts, but the castle was old and bound to contain the remnants of far more human misery than she was equipped to deal with in her current state of exhaustion. Ewen's knowledge and cheerfulness offset her lack of courage and bolstered her spirits.

Margaret studied him shrewdly but nodded. "If the ladies dinnae mind and ye're comfortable with the floor, it can be arranged. There's a sound roof in the next room. I cannae say that the chimney's clean enough for a fire."

"I've slept beneath the stars. A fire isn't necessary." Ewen accepted a lit candle from the housekeeper and raised it to study Felicity's face. "You should be safe enough. I'll unharness the horses and bed them down. If you need anything in the night, you need only call out."

Grateful for his assistance, Felicity offered the only valuable in her possession. "Would you like my quilt to sleep on? It is nice and thick."

Ewen accepted the threadbare cover Christina removed from the bed rather than the quilt Felicity had used as buffer against him. "This will do. You need something familiar with you."

With that considerate statement, he strode off. The old woman cackled in appreciation. "Aye, and there's a gentleman. One of you better catch him before he gets away." Laughing softly, she hurried out in his wake.

Christina looked thoughtful as the housekeeper disappeared into the gloom. Afraid to know what her perceptive sister had seen, Felicity drifted toward the crackling fire. The low-ceilinged room still hid in shadows, but she sensed no ominous vibrations waiting to leap out at her.

"He's an Ives, and we're both in his proximity," Christina warned, setting her candle down on the bedside table. "That can't be good." She didn't look particularly worried.

"I heard him say he's betrothed." Felicity held her hands out to the fire. "We really don't know that Ives are worse than any other men. Ninian and Leila seem happy enough with their Ives husbands. They are quite capable of precipitating catastrophes without any help from anyone. Ewen will be on his way shortly, so we have only ourselves to blame if disaster strikes."

"He's an Ives. And we're Malcolms. That's like placing nails to lodestone. He'll stay." Christina took the quilt Felicity handed her and flung it over their new bed.

Felicity shivered, and not from loss of the quilt.

A chunk of plaster bounced off his nose, waking Ewen the next morning. He rubbed the bruised extremity in the groggy hope that it wasn't broken. Wrapped in an ancient bed cover with his portmanteau for a pillow, he gazed upward at the bare lath where the chunk of plaster had been. A leak somewhere overhead, he surmised.

A ray of sunlight speared the broken glass in the narrow window of the tower in which he slept. A wooden window frame leaned against the wall, as if someone had attempted to figure out how to widen the archer's slit to a more modern size. It would take a stonemason to widen that opening.

Except for the frame and a pair of wooden benches, the room was empty. A blackened fireplace had probably warmed the castle's guards on a chilly night. Ewen suspected the glass came much later, so someone must have lived here in the centuries since.

Another chunk of plaster fell, and a female scream jarred him from his contemplation bringing him to his feet.

His abrupt movement released a cascade of plaster and a maelstrom of dust from the crumbling ceiling.

Coughing, groping for the door or his boots, whichever came first, Ewen stumbled into the bench where he'd left his coat and stubbed his toe. Hopping about, grasping his injured foot, he cursed in startlement as the door swung open.

"Oh," a surprised feminine voice said from the opening. "I meant to knock."

"That would have been simpler than screaming," he answered, still nursing his toe and trying not to curse too loudly.

"That's what I came to tell you — do not mind Christina. She was a little startled but not harmed."

Resigned to having a conversation with a maiden while he was half dressed, Ewen gingerly returned his throbbing foot to the floor. He beat the dust out of his shirt as he crossed the cold wood in his stockinged feet.

Swinging the door fully open, he let in the sunlight beaming over Felicity's shoulder from a hole in the corridor ceiling. Nearly blinded by the sudden light, he saw only a vision wearing silvered robes and a halo of white gold.

For a moment he thought he'd glimpsed heaven. Struck dumb, and shaking his head to dislodge the plaster dust, he studied her slight figure.

Felicity wore her fair hair pulled back in a queue much like a man's, but the effect was strickingly feminine. She carried a book in her hand, and sunlight sparkled off her spectacles. When she smiled, it was like watching a new day rise.

"What the devil is your sister about at this hour?" he finally blurted, awaiting her sensible explanation.

"Christina has always wondered if ghosts have auras, so she went exploring."

All right, he told himself, so "sensible" meant one thing to her and another to him. Cocking his shoulder on the door frame, Ewen glowered just to see if that would cloud her rosy good cheer. Mayhap his black whiskers would terrify her into leaving him alone. "I don't suppose a ghost carried her off and that is why I woke covered in plaster."

Felicity gazed with interest at his unfastened shirt, and he regretted his taunt at once. He had to remember she wasn't an experienced flirt. A maiden such as she needed a husband to teach her about masculine bad habits. He didn't qualify. He straightened and prepared to close the door.

"Apparently your room is part of a tower."

"*Was* part of a tower," he corrected, diverted from the proprieties by his curiosity.

"I will not argue technicalities. There is a staircase leading up and Christina followed it. The flooring is not sound, I fear."

"Is the brat safe? Must I come to her rescue?"

"No, as I said, you needn't disturb yourself. I knew your gentlemanly instincts would cause you to run to her aid, which is why I knocked. Christina rescues herself quite well."

"My instinct is to wring her spoiled neck," he warned. "Now, if you'll excuse me, I had best get dressed before the remaining tower tumbles down on me."

"It is a very interesting tower," she murmured shyly, removing her spectacles and stashing them in her pocket. "I believe Margaret has hot tea and scones prepared. She's found a servant from the village to help out."

She turned away, and Ewen couldn't resist watching her walk through the bars of sunlight beaming through the broken roof. Felicity had spent the better part of yesterday wrapped in a shapeless quilt, but today he

88

could admire the slender waist above the sway of her bell-shaped skirts. She carried her slightness with grace. No one could mistake her for less than the daughter of a marquess, despite her youth and timidity.

Felicity had come to his rescue — not precisely the act of a timid child.

Disgruntled at not being able to easily dismiss the younger Malcolm as either a child or timid, Ewen slammed the door, precipitating another shower of plaster.

Felicity clasped and unclasped her hands as she hesitated at the top of the stairs, glancing over her shoulder toward the door that had just slammed shut. Oh, my, there must be something dreadfully wrong with her. Even though she knew Ewen Ives no longer stood there, she could still see him in all his rumpled maleness — unshaven jaw black with bristles, half-open shirt, silky black hair falling into intriguing dark eyes. He looked a ruffian, and every inch of her that was a woman had wanted to touch him.

She *never* wanted to touch men, and certainly not worldly rakes. The very idea terrified her. My heavens, touching Ewen Ives would be akin to sticking her hand in the fire. But twice now she'd longed to reach for him.

Perhaps she simply needed breakfast.

Just in case he might open the door and bellow something after her, Felicity glanced over her shoulder again. She had never noticed how closely men's breeches conformed . . . No wonder men always covered themselves with long coats and vests.

With heat rising in her cheeks, she hurried down the stairs. Male anatomy could be of no interest to someone with her affliction.

She really must go to Edinburgh and find that book, or she would never learn how it felt to touch a man.

"There ye are, my lady! I've sent hot water up to your sister, and I have hot porridge for ye. Is the lad awake?"

Felicity breathed a sigh of relief at Margaret's pragmatic intrusion. "He'll need warm water as well. Christina showered him in plaster dust."

"And he did not tear her limb from limb? 'Tis the mark of a true gentleman, it is. There are Ives, and then there are Ives, if you ask me. This one could be worth keeping."

Felicity ignored Margaret's sly glance as the housekeeper led her toward the kitchen. "He's betrothed and will be on his way now that he's delivered us safely here. How far is it to Edinburgh?"

"Well now, that depends on how you go, doesn't it?" Clapping her hands as they entered the kitchen, Margaret caught the attention of a plump young maid sweeping the floor. "Take the young master a pitcher of hot water, Dora, and don't be lingering with your flirting ways. He's already spoken for."

That didn't appear to deter the new maid, who eagerly filled a pitcher from the tank beside the chimney and departed with a saucy grin.

"Thinks too highly of herself, does that one," Margaret muttered, slapping bowls on the wooden trestle table.

"Edinburgh?" Felicity gently insisted, trying to divert her thoughts from the saucy maid and the halfdressed man above and what they might do together. "We have a cart."

"Aye, and it's not a far walk. Just beyond the next hill or two."

"And Lord Nesbitt? Do you know aught of him?"

Margaret sent her a sharp look. "And what would I be knowin' of gentry? There's them that have, and them that have not and glad of it, if ye ask me. Enjoy the earth the good Lord gave ye and let them be as would dance to the devil's tune."

Oh, my, that did not sound promising at all.

While anxiously awaiting the arrival of her braver sister and Mr. Ives, Felicity pondered how to borrow a book from the library of a man who might dance to a devil's tune.

SEVEN

"We cannot simply roll into the city, ask for Lord Nesbitt's residence, and peruse his library as if it were open to one and all," Christina announced over the remains of breakfast.

Felicity sat beside Christina at the wooden trestle table in the castle kitchen. A fire crackled merrily on the enormous hearth where a kettle boiled, though no servant lingered to tend it. Margaret and Dora had disappeared into the nether regions.

"You should have thought of that before you started out on this harebrained adventure," Ewen pointed out from his position halfway up the towering fireplace, where he'd climbed to examine a set of bells that had apparently been designed to be rung from the castle door.

He'd recovered valiantly from his earlier disarray, Felicity noted with admiration. He'd washed the plaster out of his hair until it gleamed with blue-black highlights, shaved his stubble-roughened cheeks, and donned a coat that emphasized his manly shoulders. He'd scarcely touched his oatmeal after he'd seen the bells, though. Their operation apparently fascinated him.

"Do we know anyone in Edinburgh who might introduce us to Lord Nesbitt?" she asked.

"Sir Percy Larch." Christina crumbled the last of her scone into a pool of clotted cream and idly stirred it with her spoon. "His family comes from there."

"Now there's a thought." Ewen jumped down from his perch and regarded them with disbelief. "Call on the murderer. If that's your only suggestion, perhaps I'd better send you back to London."

"You mustn't do that!" Alarmed, Felicity almost reached out to grab his arm. At the last minute she refrained, astonished that she'd even lifted her hand in his direction.

He turned to her anyway. "Why is this book so important?" he asked, then looked as if he would bite back the words if he could.

Oh, dear. Felicity clasped her gloved fingers and sought words that wouldn't make him laugh at her. Despite his cheerfully eccentric propensities, Ewen Ives looked even more authoritative and impatient than her father. If she didn't say the right thing, he might leave them to fend for themselves. And for some reason she didn't care to examine, she didn't wish to risk that.

"According to my grandmother's diaries," she said carefully, "the Nesbitts acquired the Malcolm library over a century ago, during Cromwell's reign. I'm certain it is a very long and involved story, but the crux of the matter is that the Nesbitts now own a great deal of Malcolm history. I do not know how much it would cost to buy back the library, so I thought to just ask if I might borrow a particular volume."

"Which begs the question — why must you have *that* book?"

Felicity glanced at her sister, but Christina said nothing, leaving the success of their venture in Felicity's hands. With a gesture of helplessness, she attempted the impossible. "I cannot live with my peculiarity any longer. That book might tell me how to become a normal person."

She thought it best not to mention that her mother would lock her in a tower and throw away the key should she discover what they were about. She was still amazed that they'd escaped without one of their elders somehow sensing their intention and flying after them. Aunt Stella had a peculiar ability for that.

Ewen studied her with an intelligence that had Felicity believing he could see right into her head. He might appear the handsome, carefree rake, but behind the façade lurked a man of formidable accomplishment. Ninian had related his exploits with great pride. Felicity knew he'd blown up a mountain to save the village of Wystan from a flood, conquered rocky soils to build canals, and had the temerity to play with lightning.

In medieval times he might have been called a powerful sorcerer and been feared and revered. The part of her that was very much Malcolm felt the pull of his spell.

"You might learn to handle your 'peculiarity' with a little more finesse rather than give up on it," he suggested.

Frustrated by her inability to explain how terrifying, demeaning, and destructive her visions could be, Felicity shoved back her chair and rose from the table. "I do not expect you to understand. Go to your betrothed. We can proceed without you."

It was the very last thing she wished to say, but she couldn't take the words back now. Frozen in horror by what she had done, she dug her fingers into her palms and waited for him to walk away.

"Felicity, we really —" Christina began.

"No, you can't." Towering over her, Ewen spoke over Christina's objection. "The two of you will blunder about causing scenes until someone becomes irritated enough to call you witches. For all I know, they hang witches in Scotland."

"We're not witches," Felicity murmured, but, in fact, he'd called up one of her ancient fears.

"I know that," he answered impatiently. "You're simply interfering women who can't leave well enough alone. By my definition, that's witch enough, and I'm a generous man. Others may not be so kind."

Christina looked prepared to swat him with a broom, but unlike other men, Ewen ignored her beautiful older sister to hold Felicity's gaze, so she felt compelled to respond.

"I'm painfully aware that all people aren't kind," she told him. "But it is difficult not to react when one sees visions of abuse. Or even beautiful visions of fireworks or fields of flowers. I startle easily. Men hate it when I faint." The touch of bitterness in her voice surprised her, but her tongue had come unstuck, and she couldn't halt it. "I'm not at all certain that being thought a nervous twit is better than being called a witch."

"How often do you have these visions?" Instead of derision, Ewen's voice brimmed with fascination, and his piercing eyes pinned Felicity like an insect under glass.

She tried not to squirm. "I'll not satisfy your idle curiosity, sir. Mine is a singularly useless and potentially dangerous gift, and I want no part of it. If you will not help us, we shall go on without you."

Instead of rising to the challenge, the man turned his capricious curiosity on Christina. "Can you turn your gift off and on?"

"Of course not." Christina drained her teacup and rose from the table. "Auras may change from one minute to the next, but my ability to see them does not."

"But you can ignore these colorful halos

floating around everyone's heads?" he demanded, not letting the subject drop.

"Not just heads," she corrected. "And it's no different than seeing the nose on your face. They're simply there. If you frown, I notice. If your aura changes color, I notice. It's not startling like Felicity's gift is."

"What kind of hocus-pocus is required to be rid of something that seems as much a part of you as breathing?"

Felicity almost smiled at that. Other men scoffed at any hint of Malcolm abilities. Even Christina's betrothed called her an "imaginative little creature." But Ewen Ives wanted to understand how they worked.

"If we knew what to do, we wouldn't need the book," Felicity said. "This is getting us nowhere. We must go to Edinburgh and find Lord Nesbitt. You needn't accompany us."

Felicity turned to leave the kitchen, and almost tripped over the huge timber separating the servants' quarters from the main hall. She would like to explore this fascinating structure, but not while she was still terrified of touching anything. When Ewen offered his arm to steady her, she hastily drew her hand away.

"You won't know if you have anything to fear from me unless you try," he suggested, obviously irritated by her refusal to touch him.

"And I'd like to leave it that way," she

retorted. She would become as snippy as Christina if he kept tormenting her.

She couldn't bear it if Ewen vibrated of something disastrous, and with his background, she couldn't imagine anything less. She preferred the security of his presence without knowing that he'd seduced virgins or beat horses.

"You can't take that cart into the city and ask directions like country bumpkins," he warned. Like the gentleman he was, Ewen waited until Christina had joined Felicity, then followed the rustle of their gathered skirts up the stairs. "I think I should go into the city and make some inquiries first."

"So you can take the cart to Edinburgh and leave us stranded here?" Christina demanded.

"For the last time, I will not abandon you to your own devices," he said with exaggerated patience. "My brothers would lop off my head before your father could. I'm stuck with the pair of you until someone comes along to collect you. I know people in Edinburgh. We can start there."

Ewen derided himself for admitting so much, but Felicity's beaming smile of gratitude puffed up his pride too much to allow retreat. He would start riding a white steed and carrying a lance if she smiled like that more often.

"And you say you're not a gentleman," she said.

"He's not," Christina protested. "He's calling us nuisances."

"He's offering his aid, and we should be grateful. Thank you very much, Mr. Ives. We will accompany you into Edinburgh. Give us a few moments."

"No hurry." Hoist with his own petard, almost relieved at the excuse to take the women with him and thus delay his courting, Ewen halted to examine the crudely installed lamp on the staircase wall. "And could you call me Ewen?" he said. "There are too many of us to use the surname."

Christina ignored his request and continued upward, but he caught a glimpse of Felicity's pleased expression as she halted to look back at him.

"We will return promptly," she called, before hastening up the stairs.

Ewen waited for his pulse to slow after they were gone. He knew better than to play with Malcolms. He really did. Any other time he could have locked the tall one in a closet and walked away, whistling. But the young one . . .

It would be like kicking a kitten.

Plague take it, falling short of her expectations would be like telling a child there was no Father Christmas.

Well, she'd learn differently soon enough. For now there was no harm in taking the pair into the city if it was but a few miles away. He'd inquire about Lord Nesbitt, then come back to locate the papers Aidan said he kept. By the time Dunstan or the marquess arrived, he'd know where his plans for the lock gear had failed, and he could begin courting Harriet.

Maybe he could take a look at that bell rope while he was waiting. He glanced up to follow the ancient soot-blackened rope across the enormous beams supporting the medieval hall. Clever of someone to install that. It had possibilities. If he attached different ropes and ran them upstairs, could they ring for the maid from there?

Taking the stairs down to the hall two at a time, Ewen thought he would investigate while the women prepared for their outing.

Wrapped warmly in a fur-lined mantle, hood, and muff, Felicity clattered halfway down the stairs, halting on the open landing at the sight before her.

Legs akimbo, Ewen Ives stood braced on the massive iron wheel of the chandelier suspended from the vaulted ceiling of the great hall high above her. He'd discarded his outer garments and was back to shirtsleeves again — filthy with the soot and cobwebs of the ancient hall. Wrapping his muscled arm around the enormous chain bolted to the ceiling, he reached for a high rope. Felicity caught her breath as the chandelier tilted precariously.

The motion didn't daunt him. Dangling from the ceiling, he grabbed the heavy rope over his head, knotted it to a smaller one, and let the free end of the light rope fall to the floor.

Biting her lip, thinking she ought to slink back into the shadows, Felicity watched in awe as the inventive Ives grasped the lighter rope and used it to descend hand over hand toward the slate floor. In the distance, she could hear a noisy clamor of bells, but it was Ewen Ives who held her attention.

Muscles bulged across his back as he twisted in circles with the rope, then leapt to the ground as gracefully as any cat. She thought she might expire on the spot when he glanced up, caught sight of her, and flashed her a brilliant smile that reminded her of a mischievous boy.

"If Margaret's in the kitchen, we'll hear her tearing into us shortly," he called up.

Sure enough, Margaret and Dora both came running, wiping their hands on their aprons and looking amazed. "Is it the roaring kelpies risen out of the loch?" Dora cried as she raced ahead.

"Is it a fire?" Margaret called from behind her. "Have the redcoats come thievin'?"

"It's only Mr. Ives," Felicity reported. "He's been climbing the bell rope."

"Lord have mercy!" Margaret leaned against the newel post to catch her breath.

"Don't ever do that to me again, young man! You've taken the air out of me. I never heard such a clangor."

"It's an excellent fire alarm," Ewen mused, circling the rope and gazing upward, preoccupied with his thoughts rather than with the chaos he'd caused. "We could attach it to a bell outside and awake the town, if need be."

"Back in '46 that might have done, but no longer." Growing irate now that she had her breath back, Margaret placed both hands on her skinny hips and glowered. "Be off with ye now, and leave the bells be."

Felicity hurried down the last few steps to prevent the housekeeper from beheading the oblivious Ives. "He's trying to help, Margaret. I'll make him warn you before he does that again."

Unrepentant now that Felicity had distracted his attention from the problem at hand, Ewen grinned at the irate housekeeper. "This isn't the Highlands, and it's a decade too late for the Butcher to come after you. From what I can tell, it's old age and lack of maintenance that's bringing this place down, not cannon."

"Well, and what if it is? Be along with ye, now. I've better to do than waste my breath on another heathen. You made me drop my dough. It's your own fault if your bannocks have feathers in them." She stalked back to the kitchen.

The plump maid lingered, gifting Ewen with a seductive smile. Felicity bit back a scowl as he chucked Dora under the chin and returned her smile with one that could make grown women swoon. But his attention swiftly returned to the overhead ropes, and Dora flounced off, throwing one last lingering look in hopes of some sign of his admiration.

Ewen merely followed the path of the rope across the ceiling. "I could run the rope upstairs, and you could ring for help if ghosts vibrated the walls," he suggested.

Oh, he was doing this for her. She wasn't accustomed to men noticing her or caring about her needs. Wide-eyed, Felicity approached the rope. "Will I be able to pull it hard enough?"

"If not, you can always wrap it around your sister's neck and give her a push," he said cheerfully.

Unsure what to make of that, Felicity nodded dubiously at the contraption, and gravitated away from him toward the door. *Concentrate on retrieving the book,* she told herself. She couldn't afford to let the meaningless smiles of a rake like Ewen Ives distract her from her purpose.

Overhead, Christina's shriek of surprise, followed by a cry of pain, jarred Felicity out of her worries and into a run.

Ewen was already halfway up the stairs before she reached the first tread.

EIGHT

"Where the devil are you?" Ewen shouted, following what sounded like a moan. Fear coiled and spat in a corner of his brain. The marquess would hang him from the ramparts if anything happened to one of his daughters.

"The tower," Felicity called from behind him. "She said she saw an aura there, and I told her we didn't have time —"

Ewen didn't wait to hear the rest. The tower's stone stairs were worn but sturdy. He couldn't say the same of the beams holding the wooden floors between landings.

"Christina, answer me! Where are you?" He raced up the enclosed staircase he'd located after this morning's incident of tumbling ceiling plaster.

A stream of unladylike invectives issued from higher above him, and Ewen breathed easier. She'd live — until he strangled her. "Stay put, we're coming up."

That was easier said than accomplished. The first set of tower stairs led to a room that might have once stored weaponry for medieval guards. In the years since, it had collected broken remnants of chairs, enormous picture frames, and giant bedsteads.

To reach the outer stairs, he had to scramble over, under, and between the hodgepodge of furniture. He cursed for not thinking to bring a candle. The gray day outside did not allow much light through the narrow windows.

At a soft "ouch" from behind him, Ewen was reminded of the other female he was supposed to be protecting, and doing a damned poor job of it. Biting off a curse, he swung around. "You needn't kill yourself for Christina's sake. You said she rescues herself. I'll just see that she does so safely."

The tenacious child glared at him, untangled her mantle from a protruding nail in a picture frame, and flung the garment onto a table. "If she's hurt, you'll be useless. Go on. I'll be right behind you."

She wore a delicate gown with billowing silk sleeves and a petticoat with lace frothing about her feet. She'd snag every nail in Aidan's attic. "You'll do no such thing," Ewen exclaimed. "Stay right there. Let me see where she's got to."

Fair eyebrows rose and long lashes swept upward to reveal the disapproval in her crystal eyes. "By all means," she answered in a frostier tone than usual.

Satisfied she'd listened even if she disapproved, Ewen climbed over a moth-eaten stuffed wolf, dodged around the rusted remains of several suits of armor, and reached the open staircase door. "Are you safe?" he called up the poorly lit stairway. "Or should we send for a regiment of soldiers?"

"I'm fine," Christina called back in disgust. "I just can't pull my foot free."

Edging around a fallen lintel that did not bode well for the arch above him, eyeing an overhead beam to see if it supported the load of the doorway, Ewen examined the stairwell circling the outside of the tower. At least the stones appeared to be free of dead birds and vermin, but dislodged mortar, rocks, and a storehouse of old timber made traversing the stairs a lesson in perseverance. "How the devil did you get up there?" he called from the doorway.

"By ladder," Christina called down. "It's in the privy."

A soft imprecation behind him distracted Ewen. A rattle and bang followed by a frightening cascade of metal objects jerked him around in time to catch the appalling sight of the younger Malcolm tripping over her skirts and falling into an armory of shields and lances.

A sharp battle-ax fell from the wall, missing Felicity's head by inches, and Ewen's gut twisted as the remainder of the armory began to tumble in domino fashion. Shoving aside a three-legged table blocking his path, he winced as she lurched forward and landed hands down amid shards of metal.

Ewen lunged past falling lances to haul her to safety, shielding her from the brunt of the collapse with his back. She shrieked in surprise at his touch, but he had no intention of letting two Malcolms come to disaster under his care. He'd prefer that her magic fingers uncover all the black marks on his soul before he'd watch her break her neck.

"Let me down!" she squealed in panic, writhing as he caught her waist and swung her into his arms. "You arrogant ape, set me down!"

Ignoring her flailing feet, Ewen carried Felicity over the debris and up the outer stairs in accompaniment to her litany of imaginative insults and her sister screaming at him from above. Briefly, he contemplated the power of flight. If he had wings, he could carry both of them off the tower and drop them in the nearest loch.

His captive fought not to use her hands on him, but ultimately she had to grab his shoulders or she would end up being dumped unceremoniously on her rear.

She grew dangerously quiet as they reached the floor above. Surprisingly for one who looked so fragile, she had a satisfying heft to her. Under different circumstances, he might have appreciated the nicely padded curves cuddled against his chest and her subtle scent of apple blossoms.

He didn't often have the opportunity to

protect or to cherish, and he rather enjoyed this feeling of omnipotence.

Christina's shouts of fury and Felicity's ominous silence warned him he didn't have the right or the leisure to hold her at all.

Warily studying her frozen expression, Ewen lowered his curvaceous burden to the floor. He wanted to know what visions or vibrations he'd emitted that had silenced her so effectively. Or maybe he'd rather not know, given the hedonism he'd enjoyed in his lifetime.

Sternly, he pointed at the floor where they stood. "It's wood. It could be rotten. Do not step anywhere I do not, and stay several paces behind me."

"Felicity! What's wrong? Where are you?" Christina's frantic cries emanated from a doorway on the opposite side of the tower.

Grim-lipped, Ewen tested the worn floor, pounding with his boot and looking for soft spots. "She's fine," he called back. "We're almost there."

Far too aware of the silent female trailing behind him, Ewen strode as swiftly as he dared to the privy chamber. If the fool woman had climbed the garderobe and got stuck, he had half a mind to leave her there.

He eased the heavy panel open and dared to breathe again at the sight within. Wrapped in a velvet mantle, Christina sat upon the dusty floor of the empty room, her face set with a look of disgust. A ladder with broken rungs led up to the roof. Ewen judged that her abrupt fall from the ladder had punched a hole in a rotting floorboard. Like a cat, she'd landed feet down, but her foot appeared to be caught in a maze of splintered wood.

"What have you done with Felicity?" Christina demanded before he could say a word.

It occurred to him that, generally, Felicity took far better care of herself than her older sister did, and that it was rather incongruous for the one who had caused this trouble to be worrying about her. He didn't have time to mention that observation before the subject in question arrived.

"I'm here." Quietly, Felicity slipped past Ewen. Before he could stop her, she gently tapped the boards in front of her as she'd seen him doing. Assured that they would hold her, she made her way to her sister.

Testing the floor for his heavier weight, Ewen reached the rotten board and crouched to examine it. "You'll have to hold back your skirt so I can work the broken bits away from your ankle."

Blessedly silent for a change, Christina lifted acres of skirt, petticoat, and panniers to reveal a badly torn stocking and the hole trapping her. "It hurts when I move it," she whispered.

Kneeling, Felicity clasped Christina's chilly

109

fingers and watched anxiously as Ewen snapped the broken board with his bare hands — strong hands that had held her against his hard chest and rapidly beating heart. She could scarcely breathe when she thought of it, so she tried not to. She'd have to consider all the implications of Ewen's embrace later. For now, her concern must be for Christina.

"You screamed," Christina murmured, searching her face. "What did he do to you?"

"Nothing, nothing at all." She dared not meet her sister's eyes. Christina could see enough in her aura without reading her expression as well. "Does your foot hurt?"

"My ankle hurts. And I've scraped my leg trying to free it. I'll be fine," Christina said loudly enough for Ewen to hear.

He didn't look at them but broke off another splinter of old wood.

"He must have done something. You're looking at him as if he were a god and a devil rolled into one," Christina whispered.

Felicity was spared from answering when the final splinter broke free, and Ewen tugged Christina's ankle through the hole. Her cry of pain distracted them from all other concerns.

"She may have twisted it." Ewen examined Christina's torn stocking and bleeding ankle with dismay. "I'll have to carry her down."

A spear of jealousy struck Felicity at the thought of Ewen's magical arms holding

Christina as he'd held her. His touch had inspired sensations she had yet to sort out except to know she wanted to feel them again, and she didn't want to share the experience with her sister.

She quelled that inanity and shifted to examine the injured limb. "We'll need to soak and wrap it. I don't think you should stand, Christina."

Christina moved her foot, winced, and looked resigned. "I suppose this is what happens when one follows ghosts. Apparently, they dislike being chased. I wonder if it would help if I apologize."

Ewen snorted and Felicity fought a smile. "I don't think ghosts can heal you. Mr. Ives — Ewen — would it be better if she just held on to our shoulders and we helped her down?"

"I can carry her," he said. "But you'll have to keep her injured foot from bumping into things."

Christina glanced from one of them to the other, then donned a stubborn expression. "I don't want to be carried. Help me up."

"Don't be foolish. You will be in bed much sooner if Ewen carries you." Felicity would give anything in the world to experience his arms around her again. Generously, she offered the opportunity to her injured sister.

Christina didn't appreciate her magnanimity. Gathering her skirts in one hand, she imperiously held out her other to Ewen. "Help me up. I'm certain I can do this."

Instead of taking her hand, Ewen grabbed her waist and hauled her upright. Felicity watched Christina's face grow pale, then regain color and a determined expression. She was certain that the relief she felt was because Christina was well enough to stand. She could not possibly begrudge her sister the strength of Ewen's aid.

Which was a good thing, because Ewen ignored all protest to wrap his arm around Christina's waist and help her across the floor. Felicity fought a stirring of jealousy as the tall couple walked ahead of her. She could take care of herself and didn't require anyone's attention, she told herself. Thank goodness for that, since she was always invisible in the shadow of Christina's loveliness.

With a look of concern, Ewen glanced over his shoulder. "Would you go ahead of us and clear the way? I'd feel better if I could keep you in sight."

Startled, but inexplicably pleased, Felicity hurried to clear a path.

"It's not broken," Christina insisted for the thousandth time. "You must go on to the city without me. I'll just lay about and rest it for a while."

Ewen had quit pacing and disappeared once Margaret announced the ankle was merely sprained. Felicity didn't want to imagine him hanging from a chandelier as they bandaged Christina, but she kept listening for the distant sound of bells. "I cannot possibly go to Edinburgh without you," she protested, hiding her dire disappointment. The book was so tantalizingly close . . .

"Father will be here soon," Christina warned. "We can't ask Ewen to dally much longer. This is your one chance. You must take it."

Felicity fought a flutter of alarm. She had never gone anywhere on her own. Her family always hovered around her, shielding her from the shock of strange places. Her duty was to look after Christina, not go charging off on an adventure into a strange city with a man who —

She stopped that thought in its tracks, but some flicker of it must have shown in her aura, for her sister looked at her with curiosity. "Something happened between the two of you, didn't it? Did he touch you?"

Nervously, Felicity clasped her hands and gazed out the mullioned window to the barren hill beyond. "I was too worried about you to notice." That had to be the explanation. Or perhaps her clothes had protected her. She wore gloves and had touched only his coat, and he'd held her through layers of bodice, corset, and underclothes. She hadn't touched his bare hand, after all.

Maybe she should.

"He touched you and you didn't notice?" Christina asked incredulously.

He'd *carried* her, and she'd felt sheltered. It didn't seem possible. She must have been hysterical. "I was terrified."

Christina accepted this comment with suspicion. "Don't let him use my accident as an excuse not to take you with him. Go find Lord Nesbitt, I'll be fine. I promise not to chase any more ghosts."

"You couldn't talk to them if you caught them." Glad to steer the conversation away from herself, Felicity faced the room again. "Just admire their pretty colors and leave them alone."

"Bring me a book from the library, and I'll be quite content."

Christina never read books. Felicity frowned, but she didn't have any gift for reading people's minds. "Keep your foot up, and I'll be right back."

Feeling oddly unnerved as she traipsed off in search of a book, Felicity gazed down the long hallway outside their bedchamber, wondering where libraries might be found in castles. Perhaps this one didn't have a library? After all, books had been scarce at the time of the original keep's construction.

But she could tell that the old keep had been updated in some prior decade. Fascinated, she wandered the upper hall, wondering what manner of people had lived here. She ought to feel afraid to be wandering alone for the first time in her life, but she felt strangely bold.

The familiar arrangement of evenly spaced windows, ornate plasterwork, and decorative mantels welcomed her in the rear of the house where the roof was still intact. Plaster had fallen, wallpaper had peeled, and mold had set in, but the floors were sound and spring sunlight peeked through the clouds to illuminate the glassed windows. Not a stick of furniture begged her to linger, though. She was beginning to think the only reason she and Christina had a bed was because the ancient tester was too massive to carry through doorways.

Giving up on what she assumed was the family floor, she reluctantly took the stairs down to what ought to be the public rooms, as she should have done in the first place. She wasn't avoiding Ewen, was she? He had been all that was considerate and thoughtful, despite Christina's ability to cause mayhem.

Or had he given up on her and left for Edinburgh without her?

It might help if he were as thoughtless and irritating as she expected all men to be. Then she wouldn't have to consider why his touch had generated a seductive sensation of pleasure instead of horrifying images of his worst memories. Or did Ewen's memories only include seduction?

She must stop thinking like that if she meant to steel her resolve and go into the city with him.

She would have to ride beside him without Christina to shield her. On that dreadful little cart.

Find a book for Christina and don't think about it, she told herself. Studying the great hall and seeing no sign of Ewen, she held up her candle to explore the dark outer edges of the room. The massive entry doors filled one end. The doors to the corridor leading to the kitchen broke the opposite end. Several narrow windows allowed gray light in along the two longest walls. One of these walls contained a fireplace large enough to roast a team of oxen. A rotting tapestry of unicorns and medieval ladies swayed lightly in a draft beside it.

The far wall seemed most likely, then. Crossing the stone floor that once would have held tables and benches for a garrison of knights, Felicity examined the tattered tapestries at the end of a row of narrow windows. She simply needed to be brave and move the cloth, which was no doubt permeated with centuries of memories. She would be less likely to faint if she was prepared for the assault on her senses.

Gritting her teeth, Felicity touched a corner of the first tapestry. A blur of sounds and smells and movement washed over her, but she held fast, willing the sensation away. The vibrations were as old and faded as the cloth, and they dissipated without causing harm. Peering beneath the cloth, she discovered a partially opened door and gently shoved it with her booted toe.

A maze of pipes, tools, and odd metal connectors littered a long library table and frayed carpet within. Illuminated by a crackling fire, ancient volumes covered the library shelves in disorderly stacks coated in cobwebs.

Metal pipe in hand, Ewen glanced up from his seat at a table strewn with papers and documents. He'd washed the soot from his hands and face and changed into a clean shirt and stock, but he still looked rumpled and dusty. The afternoon shadow of his beard would have added a disreputable aspect had it not been for his air of distraction.

"I think Aidan's been trying to use my drawings to piece together his plumbing," he announced without preamble. "Is the hoyden tied to the bed and unlikely to cause more trouble today?"

Oh, gadzooks! Felicity couldn't tear her gaze from the smudge of dirt on Ewen's perfect nose or the interest lighting his eyes as she entered.

Her heart fluttered as she realized she would have to touch him again, just to see if her earlier reaction to him would be repeated.

NINE

Garbed in a tidy blue gown adorned with sparkling white lace, the petite Malcolm drifted into the room as if Ewen were the spider and she were the wary fly.

Occupied with matching an elbow fitting to a ball valve from the pump mechanism of Aidan's fascinating sink, Ewen attempted not to notice her hesitation. After this morning's incident, he had a thousand questions he'd like to ask her, but he refrained. He wasn't certain if he did so out of fear of frightening her with his curiosity or frightening himself with her answers.

"Christina's resting. I . . . I came to find a book for her."

He glanced around at the poorly lit shelves of moldering tomes. "There might be a medieval manuscript or two, but I doubt anything relevant to your sister's romantic tastes."

She ignored his dry tone and fastened her attention on the first wall of shelves. "I shall endeavor not to disturb you."

She might as well try to stop the world from spinning. Distracted, he'd forgotten to stand when she entered the room, but she didn't seem to expect it.

Sitting back in the torn leather chair, Ewen made a pretense of cleaning off the valve as Lady Felicity discreetly ran her gloved fingers over the fading volumes on the shelves within her reach. Apparently satisfied that the books contained no violent vibrations, she cautiously removed her glove and ran her bare fingers over their spines. Finding a volume that caught her interest, she donned her spectacles to read the faded lettering.

She wasn't *reading* the titles first. She was *feeling* them.

Impossible. Grimacing at his fantasies, Ewen dipped a cog in the bowl of ammonia beside him, and scrubbed the aging iron with a brush he'd found in the kitchen. He ought to be searching through the stacks of papers for the ones on the lock design, but he couldn't tear his fascinated gaze from the lady. Besides, looking at faded ink was tedious.

"They're all very old."

He scrubbed harder at the rust and grime, trying not to hear the disappointment in her voice. "Books are frivolous wastes of time," he said. "They either tell lies or repeat what we already know." From his limited experience, anyway. Fiction bored him, and the few scientific treatises he'd perused had been wrong. He'd long ago decided he could figure things out more accurately on his own.

Ewen watched her test the library ladder for

sturdiness. She was more petite than fragile, but she'd scared the hell out of him when she'd nearly been beheaded by the falling ax. He'd prefer not to repeat the experience.

Of course, after he'd recovered from the horror of watching medieval lances bounce off her, he'd rather enjoyed carrying a squirming bundle of silk and curves.

He had to quit thinking like a rake and start thinking like a married man, he told himself. He returned his attention to the work at hand. Damn, but this marriage business wouldn't be easy. How the devil did his brothers do it?

"It's a very odd collection."

Her voice came from just in front of him. Ewen finished scrubbing the cog and dared a glance up to see that her fingers were rapidly scanning the volumes on a nearby shelf. "These are religious tracts mixed with treatises on magic. The ones above are historical accounts of druids and books of legends. Quite odd."

"They should suit your sister, then." Ewen dried the cog on a wool rag, then wiped the metal with an oily rag. In front of him lay news sheets covered with similarly cleaned metal parts.

"Christina doesn't like books any more than you do." She pulled down a volume so old, pages fluttered to the floor when she opened it. "She'd rather hunt ghosts. I apologize for the trouble she has caused."

Ewen deliberately averted his gaze from the sway of Felicity's skirts and slender waist as she bent to retrieve the pages. He had a weakness for women as some men had a weakness for gin. He liked sampling them all, but he shouldn't indulge in lustful thoughts about a female ten years his junior who didn't seem aware that she shouldn't be alone with a disreputable bachelor.

"I would think if ghosts existed, they must give off vibrations of what killed them, at the very least," he said offhandedly, trying to stay with the conversation. "You could probably find ghosts easier than she can."

"Ugh. Which is why Christina hunts them and I do not." She carefully tucked the pages back where they belonged and returned the volume to the shelf.

"Coward." He reached for the next gear.

"Sensible," she retorted.

Before the argument could escalate, buxom Dora appeared in the doorway, tray in hand. "Tea?"

Ewen heard the flirtatiousness in the maid's voice and appreciated the provocative wink she sent him as she entered. He liked even better the way she leaned over the table so he could enjoy the view of her abundant curves beneath the modesty piece covering her bodice.

"And thee," he responded easily, knowing this game well.

Dora giggled and brushed his arm with her breasts as she set out his cup and saucer. "That could be arranged," she said saucily.

"He's promised to another." Felicity's matter-of-fact comment abruptly ended the game. She drifted over to the table and added sugar to Ewen's cup, pouring his tea, then her own.

Ewen curled his eyebrows in surprise when Felicity added just the right amount of cream. She didn't even seem aware she was doing it. Instead, she was studying Dora, who had not bowed respectfully and departed, as a well-trained servant should.

"He's a free man until then," Dora said with outrageous good cheer. "It's not in a man's nature to be faithful."

"Please, you'll note I'm still in the room," Ewen said, but he might as well have been talking to the wall. Being ignored by two attractive women was an entirely new experience for him, even if the argument was over him.

"That's not entirely true," Felicity answered thoughtfully, sipping from her cup. "I have observed that Ives men are faithful once their interest is caught. Admittedly, my observations are limited."

"To two," Ewen murmured, but the women weren't listening.

"Pleasure's where you find it," Dora said without rancor. "If you can't hold him,

122

someone else will."

Ewen watched with interest as pink flushed across Felicity's cheek to her delectable ears. Then, recovering his senses, he rose from his seat. "That's enough, Dora. I'm sure Lady Christina would like her tea as well."

Dora flounced off. Silence descended. Another woman would have laughed off the foolish exchange, but Felicity was much too innocent to understand half of it. Ewen felt responsible for letting it go so far.

"Dora needs to be trained in propriety," he offered in apology.

"You don't suppose she's Mr. Dougal's mistress, do you?" she asked.

She tilted her head to look at him, caught his astonishment, colored, and took her teacup back to the shelves to examine them.

"Devil take it, Felicity! I'm not your father or your brother. You're not supposed to say things like that to me."

"You're my brother-in-law. I fail to see the difference."

She failed in no such thing. He could see it in the stiffness of her spine. She had stepped over the edge of propriety and knew it. But then, when had that ever stopped a Malcolm?

With a sigh of acceptance, Ewen returned to his seat. He'd be damned if he'd continue standing until she decided to settle somewhere.

"Come and eat these tea cakes. You'll not

find anything in those musty old tomes, and I'll not get the plumbing repaired until you sit down."

She glanced doubtfully at the metal-strewn table. "You're repairing the plumbing? What plumbing?"

"It looks to me as if someone with mechanical ability and a good grasp of Roman bathing facilities added running water in that elaborate garderobe system your sister was exploring. But the pipes are plugged and rusting. It appears Aidan thought he might save a few pieces and fix the lower floor, but he doesn't know what he is doing."

Seemingly fascinated, she studied the metal he'd strewn around him. "Water runs through these pipes into the castle?"

He shrugged. "Most castles have wells in the cellar. This is a pretty simple system that might fill wash basins. If the tank on the roof were repaired, it could be used to flush the garderobe." He winced as he realized what he'd just said. Another reason why he shouldn't be left in polite company for any length of time. His fascination with mechanical things overcame propriety.

Oddly, she didn't seem to mind. She sipped from her teacup, her brow wrinkled in thought as she studied the pipes. Sunshine broke through the clouds outside the window and a ray caught a nearly silver tress resting on her shoulder. He liked that she didn't wear her hair in unnatural curls pinned to her head or covered in powder and grease. She could be a forest sprite, an unaffected creature of the woods.

"I thought you needed to go into Edinburgh," she finally said.

"And leave the two of you here alone? That would be the same as asking for lightning to strike." He thought she smiled at that, but he couldn't read her eyes.

"It could be days before Christina can stand on her own. I don't think we have days to spare."

Ah, now he saw the direction of her thoughts. Scrubbing rust from another fitting, Ewen surreptitiously studied her. He'd more than touched her today, and she hadn't fainted. So what had she seen that made her so wary of him? Or was all that business just an elaborate ruse of some kind? "I sent a note off earlier to Lord Edgemont, one of my fellow investors in the canal."

"Lord Edgemont?" she inquired, watching him with the wide-eyed look that so fascinated him.

"We share a financial interest in a mine and canal in Northumberland," he answered, "as do several other gentlemen here, including your suitor, Sir Percy, and his cousin, Robert Larch."

"Oh." She considered that information. "And the gentleman on the road, too? Mr. Campbell?"

"He owns much of the land back in England where the mines are located, so he's part of the consortium as well." Like Ewen, the other investors weren't wealthy men, but those hoping to earn wealth through scientific advances. He tried not to begrudge their refusal to help the village that had flooded. After all, he'd been the one who had convinced them that the canal lock would work.

"I see. So you were headed for Edinburgh on business?"

That was one way to state his intention of marrying Harriet to pay off his debts. "And entertainment," he added with good cheer, just so she didn't have any wrong impressions of him. "Edgemont returned my inquiry with an invitation to visit."

She looked both interested and doubtful. "Do you think he would know Lord Nesbitt?"

"Edgemont is well connected. I should think he'd know most of Edinburgh society, unless Nesbitt is a recluse. Do you know for a fact that Nesbitt has the book?"

He was starting to enjoy watching rose color her cheeks.

"I only know that a hundred years ago the Nesbitts bought our library."

He generously refrained from scoffing aloud, but had to point out the obvious. "That's a wild risk. Nesbitts could have died out, and the books could be in possession of a MacDuff or a collection of people. The books could have been burned or sold. They might be moldering in an attic, just as that armor is rusting here. You have very little chance of ever finding one book after a hundred years."

"I know. And I know that the information it contains might not help me." She sighed, lowered her cup to the table, and gravitated toward the shelves again. "But I cannot give up the chance of a normal life without trying everything." She said that matter-of-factly, as if she'd just announced she would have to give up sweets.

Ewen frowned as she returned to waving her fingers over the spines of old books. "What does that mean, precisely?" he demanded. "What do you give up if you don't have that book?"

She threw him a surprised glance over her shoulder. "Touching. I thought you understood that."

"That's ridiculous. At this very moment you're touching those nasty old books filled with heaven knows what atrocities." Ewen didn't understand his anger but simply reacted to the idea of her never touching anything again. He'd touched her, and she hadn't died of it.

She smiled and gestured at the books. "Books are my friends. They can't think or feel, and seldom hold memories. If they're truly awful books, I can sometimes feel the horror readers have experienced while reading them, and I know to avoid those. But mostly, people read for enjoyment, and I pick up vibrations of laughter or interest — positive emotions. These books are so old and haven't been read in so long that they seem to hold no vibrations at all."

"So you're not searching for titles, but for books that held someone's interest?" He couldn't believe he was asking this. Her so-called gift seemed preposterous to him. He was dying to test it but reluctant to become too involved when he had matters of more importance to attend to.

Felicity smiled in such approval that Ewen felt as if he'd given her the ideal gift, although he had no clue what he'd said right.

She returned to examining the shelves. "I was hoping to find a book that evokes a woman's happiness or romantic feelings, but I'm thinking this is a fairly ancient and learned library. Christina won't be pleased."

"Give her the book on druids. If we're lucky, she'll change into a tree."

Felicity's laughter floated through the murky library like a fresh spring breeze. Already half aroused by her sweet scent and close proximity, Ewen almost groaned aloud.

"Christina would like nothing better than to become part of the forest," Felicity admitted. "She wasn't meant for civilization. I, on the other hand, would be content to spend my life inside a library."

There — that proved she wasn't meant for the likes of him. He'd sooner cut his throat than spend time in a library. "Fine," he said in a disgruntled tone that surprised even him. "While you're at it, spend some time in here looking through these stacks of trash Aidan collects and see if you can locate my drawings for lock gears."

To his amazement, she obediently crossed to the table to examine the papers buried beneath his mess.

"I'm not at all certain I will recognize a lock gear, but if I can find the drawings under all this, I might be able to put together ones that look alike or feel alike. Then you could look through them more quickly."

He didn't want to know what she meant about "feeling" alike. All paper felt alike. But if she could find what he needed in the stacks, he could do something more constructive, like putting these pipes back together.

He saw her hesitation as her hand hovered over the pipes, and he grasped her dilemma instantly. Standing, he filled his arms with cogs and fittings and dropped them to the carpet and out of her way. "This was the only spare room with a working fireplace. Sorry."

She gifted him with a look of surprise and pleasure that nearly robbed him of breath.

Damn, but it had been a long time since a woman had admired him as a responsible gentleman instead of a charming rake good for toying with but for little else. He'd accepted his role as charming ne'er-do-well for so long, he'd grown into it.

"I'll ask Margaret which rooms Mr. Dougal prefers." Unaware of his reaction to her, she passed her gloved hand over the stacks of drawings and notes, lingering over some. "Perhaps we could fix up his rooms a little, and keep warm at the same time."

Ewen couldn't tear his gaze away. In fascination he watched her touch a roll of drawings, then a sketch of a latrine that had caught his eye. Aidan must have been working from that sketch. What the devil had possessed the man to accumulate all this wastepaper?

Once satisfied that the sketches contained nothing harmful, Felicity began sorting through the stacks as if she knew precisely what she was doing. Under her nimble fingers drawings of canals and locks fell unerringly into one stack. Scribbled notes of uncertain origin and odd sketches landed in another. Papers that didn't look familiar and probably belonged to Aidan moved to the end of the table. What had seemed like a torturous task to Ewen became a few minutes' play to her.

"You're amazing," Ewen said in genuine awe as she began sorting the stack of lock drawings into some order he couldn't discern.

She blinked and lifted her gaze as if he'd just drawn her back from another world. "You leave a very strong pattern of your thoughts on these. I cannot understand them well since I know nothing of what they are." She gestured over the papers. "But I can see what you're seeing."

"And you want to be rid of this marvelous gift? I don't suppose you could transfer it to me? It would have taken me all day to make sense of those."

Startled, she glanced over the stacks she'd gathered. "It's very simple, really. I don't need my gift to do this. It's just faster this way." She sent him a curious look. "And your thoughts don't hurt me."

Ewen opened his mouth to say something witty, then shut it again as he realized the importance of what she'd said. "I didn't hurt you when I carried you earlier?" He'd been dying to know but had feared to ask. Something in her gaze told him it was safe now.

"No," she whispered, flushing. "But it's not quite the same as . . ." She gestured vaguely at his hands. "I was very agitated. It means nothing."

It meant *something*, but he wouldn't press her on it. That was a lot to ask of a man who liked nothing more than to explore the mysteries of the world. He shuffled through the stack of canal papers until he found the one on the gear that had malfunctioned.

Handing it to her, he watched warily as she accepted it. "Was I out of my mind when I designed this?"

Her eyes widened as she glanced from the paper to him. She crumpled it a little in her bare fingers, concentrated, and looked perplexed. "Why is this paper so important to you?" she asked.

"Because that design failed. The gears cracked from the pressure of the water in the lock, the lock broke open, and the river flooded part of a village, wiping out houses and livestock. It was a miracle it did not take lives."

She looked appalled, then fascinated, as she studied the drawing. "You copied this from a previously successful design. The images look almost identical to me, although I can see some differences that at the time you seemed to think were improvements."

"Obviously, I was wrong," he said dryly. "I owe a great sum of money for rebuilding that village."

Taking a deep breath, she met his eyes. "Is there any possibility that the materials used to create this design were at fault?"

He wanted to fall at her feet and kiss her slippers. Grabbing the drawing, he hastily scanned it. He knew the gear would work. There was no reason under the sun why it shouldn't.

Maybe it *wasn't* his fault that the village had flooded.

Merely easing the burden of guilt opened his eyes. If it wasn't his fault, then whose? And how? And why?

TEN

"How long do you think it will take for my father to arrive?" Twisting a button of her glove, Felicity nervously watched as the cart navigated a perilous curve on the road to Edinburgh the morning after Christina's accident.

Both Christina and Ewen had spent the previous evening assuring Felicity that this trip was perfectly proper, and even Margaret had agreed that Scots society didn't abide by the same formalities as that of London. Other than her own foolishness, Felicity had no reason not to accompany Ewen into the city.

She was desperately trying to keep in mind that it was dangerous to touch an Ives, and that finding the book was more important than her interest in the gentleman sitting next to her, who guided the horses with such expertise.

If she could quit fretting, she might even enjoy the journey. She'd shed her mother's protective guardianship, the shelter of an army of servants, and now she'd even left Christina behind. She was free to act as she pleased but wasn't certain what to do with her first opportunity.

She took in a deep breath and admired the scenery. The rugged Scots countryside was only just shedding the drab browns of winter. On a sunny hill, the first yellow of gorse blossomed. A butterfly alighted on her glove and, enchanted, she watched blue and black wings flutter as the creature found its balance and tested its surroundings with twitching antennae.

Butterflies and countryside conveyed no destructive vibrations. She let that notion soothe her rattled nerves.

"How long did it take your yacht to reach Scotland?" Ewen asked, interrupting her reverie. "We sent the letter back in the captain's hands."

"Almost three days," she responded. She'd forgotten her nervous calculation of how soon they could expect to be dragged back into the family fold. "But we were caught in a storm. If Father sails right after receiving the letter, he could be here in less than a week. How can I find the book in less than a week?"

"Dunstan and Leila live closer and will no doubt show up before your father does. Perhaps they can persuade him to let you stay."

Felicity clasped her hands and considered the possibility. Beside her Ewen nearly vibrated with a passion she'd never experienced and didn't understand. She cast a sideways glance at his fine dark brows drawn in concentration, watched an errant strand of his hair lick at his sharp cheekbone, and knew the answer to Ewen's suggestion. Her father would never leave her in the company of a penniless — and attractive — Ives.

"I could persuade Father only if he thought he would make more money or gain more power by doing so," she said with a sigh. "He really is a good man, but he's achieved his position through stubborn single-mindedness. It's a little late to ask him to change now."

"He thought marrying you off to Percy would gain him an advantage?"

"Percy has a substantial shipping venture that my father was interested in controlling. He was deeply disappointed by my rejection of his suit." Felicity didn't hold her father's obsession with making money against him. The marquess would never force her to marry where she didn't wish. She simply hated disappointing him.

"I must marry or serve no purpose to him or anyone else. The book is my only hope, but I'll never persuade him of that," she continued. Or persuade her mother, but Ives men tended to hold her mother and aunt in some awe, so she thought it best not to mention all the family objections to her pursuit. If Ewen knew her formidable Malcolm relations would fly here on the wings of fury did they know what she was about, he'd have her on the next ship out.

"I think you could learn to control your gift a little better, put it to good use, and you might be far happier than ridding yourself of it," Ewen argued.

Felicity turned a resentful look on him. He didn't understand what he was suggesting. Perhaps it was time to show him. Preparing herself mentally for the shock, Felicity clenched her teeth, removed her furred muff, and rubbed her hand over the cart's rough footboard.

She winced as a vision leapt clearly in front of her. She bit back a cry of anguish at the sight, and tried not to fall headfirst into the vivid scene.

Ewen's reassuring presence seemed to balance her between the real world and the one in her head. Steadying her whirling reaction, Felicity described what she saw. "A woman sat here. She's crying and feeling so hopeless she wants to die. Her son is in the back of the cart. He's holding the head of a calf that is moaning in pain. The boy is as ill-nourished and sickly as the animal. The woman knows both the calf and the boy are dying."

Felicity took a deep breath, knowing that if she let the vision open wider she would encounter a terrifying violence. Reminding herself that Ewen was beside her and the vision was of the past, she opened her mind to the man sitting beside the woman, driving the cart. "The woman is afraid to whimper,

137

afraid to say a word, and she's biting her tongue very hard for fear that if she makes a sound, the brute beside her will strike her. She already bears the bruises of his fist."

"Bloody hell."

Grabbing her arm, Ewen jerked her hand away from the board.

Startled by the abrupt departure from the world in her mind, Felicity fell back against him. She was shivering, and wasn't really aware when Ewen wrapped his arm around her and drew her against his comforting shoulder. She didn't want to weep. The vision was weak, so she knew the woman and boy were long dead. They were beyond her help. She knew that intellectually. But it was difficult to prevent her heart from breaking at their plight. Tears spilled and shudders racked her as she fought to shut out the woman's fear and despair.

The cart had halted, and through her tears Felicity gradually became aware of a consoling hand caressing her hair and a muscular arm pressing her into a warmth that smelled of leather and smoke and something masculine she could not name but inhaled with pleasure. The visions drained her, so she didn't think, just relaxed, and let the anguish seep away.

"You didn't need to prove it to me in such a painfully graphic manner," Ewen's angry voice exclaimed above her head now that she'd stopped shuddering.

Much to her amazement, now that the vision had faded, laughter crossed her lips. Felicity looked up, and only then did she fully comprehend that Ewen Ives was holding her as if she were a cherished possession, looking as if he'd like to wring the neck of anyone who harmed her — which he thought he'd done. Since he couldn't strangle himself, he was taking his fury out in words.

"You live very much in the moment, don't you?" she asked with startling comprehension.

Ewen filled his hand with her hair and tilted her head back so he could scan her face for signs of injury. She liked the security of his big hand cradling her head and his arm sheltering her. Pain and regret had furrowed his forehead, but the fascination in his dark eyes thrilled her. She really needed to pull away, yet she understood so much more when he held her like this.

"Don't ever do that again," he growled.

Chuckling, Felicity sat up, away from the dangerous pull of his warm arms. "Yes, sir," she murmured with false meekness.

She could tell he knew she was teasing, and a smile flickered on her lips as he gave her a disgruntled look and took up the reins again. Men never treated her like a fascinating phenomenon or even a real woman. She thought she could learn to like it very much.

Except it appeared that only Ewen Ives could touch her without causing harm — and Ewen Ives was betrothed to another.

Ewen boldly rapped the door knocker to Lord Edgemont's Edinburgh town house. The narrow, winding street of the old city would possess some charm were it not for the chill wind reddening his companion's cheeks. He chafed again, knowing he was ill suited to look after a gentle lady, but she seemed determined to pursue this search.

She stiffened as a servant answered the door and ushered them in, and he wondered how she was reacting to the thick woven rug under their feet and the dark paneling of the entryway. He offered his arm, but she ignored it, preferring to keep her hands shielded in her muff.

Before Ewen could wonder more, Edgemont appeared in the back hallway and hurried forward.

"Ives! Good to see you. Percy and Robert are here. We've been discussing financing."

Ewen mentally cursed as Felicity disappeared behind him, as if she were a ghost who could blend in with the woodwork. He hadn't realized Percy had returned to Edinburgh, although if Felicity had rejected his suit, he should have considered the possibility.

Too late now. Reaching behind him, Ewen tugged her mantle, forcing her forward. With

140

a proprietary hand at her back, he presented her to the Scots laird. "Lady Felicity, this is Lord Edgemont, one of the investors in the canal. Edgemont, Lady Felicity Malcolm Childe, my sister-in-law. She's a bibliophile."

The laird seemed somewhat taken aback by her presence, but adjusted rapidly. "My pleasure, my lady. You are interested in the libraries of Scotland?"

"The private ones," Ewen spoke for her. "We're on a mission in search of old books. One can never have enough of them."

Knowing Ewen's aversion to reading material Edgemont snorted, but spoke respectfully to Felicity. "Perhaps my wife can help, my lady. She's in her sitting room. You might share a cup of tea and discuss Edinburgh's shops."

Ewen recognized Felicity's reticence, but he told himself she needed to learn how to go about in the world on her own. He wouldn't be around to look after her for long. Besides, she wouldn't wish to encounter Sir Percy.

He watched as she followed a maid up the stairs and out of sight. Ewen felt rotten about letting her go, but he'd prefer to argue with the gentlemen without her presence.

"When Campbell said you were courting, he didn't mention you were pursuing an innocent," Edgemont said, leading Ewen down the dark corridor. "I trust her income will be adequate."

Ewen contemplated spinning the older man

around and plowing his fist into Edgemont's weak chin for the implied insult to Felicity, but he'd learned a modicum of restraint over the years. He'd put himself in the position of explaining Felicity's presence. As one of his investors, Edgemont was more concerned about Ewen's ability to repay his loans than with social niceties. How would he explain about Harriet?

And how the devil could he visit Harriet while in the company of a female who might faint from merely touching his intended's hand? He was just discovering the full difficulty of insulating Felicity from physical objects. How could he protect her from the far more volatile presence of people?

"It's no concern of yours who I court," he said curtly, stalking into the library to greet the gathering of some of the mine's most influential investors. "Gentlemen." He nodded at the men seated around the long mahogany table.

Squire Campbell, in his rough country woolens, his round face chapped from the wind, his fading brown hair worn clubbed and unpowdered, appeared surprised by but not unhappy about Ewen's arrival.

Sir Percy Larch, wearing a powdered wig that added pomposity, not age, to his youthful, unlined features, merely looked morose as he sipped from his cup. The blue silk of his coat and the extensive use of lace on his sleeves bespoke London's finest tailors and a large pocketbook. At a young age Percy had inherited a trustee position in the London bank that had loaned Ewen funds to repair the flooded village.

Robert Larch, Campbell's peer in age and roughness, scowled, crossed his arms, and sat back in his chair. He wore neither powder nor wig, but he'd attempted more finesse than the squire in his choice of full-bottomed coat and clean jabot. His blacksmith's shoulders strained at the silk, revealing him for the tradesman he was.

"Thought you were courting," Campbell said with bluff good cheer.

"My sisters-in-law insisted on seeing the city, so here I am, waiting for my brother to retrieve them." Wondering why his investors had thought to meet without him, Ewen awaited an explanation.

Sir Percy widened his pale blue eyes. "Sisters-in-law? Your brothers married Malcolms, did they not?"

Ewen stifled an inward grimace, pulled out a chair without invitation, and assumed a negligent pose in the seat. Resisting the crystal whisky decanter on the sideboard, he poured a tepid cup of coffee from the silver pot on the table. "They did." And there must be a hundred and one Malcolms, so Percy could keep guessing. "Now, gentlemen, what is this meeting about?"

He didn't think the diversion would prevent Percy from trying to determine the identity of Ewen's in-laws, but he could try.

"We need funds for more equipment for the mine. Will you and your brother be good for them?" Robert Larch demanded.

Ewen needed to take money *out* of the mines, not put more money in. And if Drogo had money to invest, Ewen would rather his brother repay the bank loan. These men knew that.

Still, rather than let them get under his skin, he shrugged. "I'll ask."

Ewen studied Percy as he sipped his coffee, and listened with only half an ear to the rest of their report on finances.

All the men present had invested different amounts in the canal and mine. Percy, the banker, liked investing his funds in promising ventures that could produce more return than simple interest. He and his cousin, Robert, owned a shipping enterprise contracted to carry the coal produced by the mine, which was located on land owned by both Ian Campbell and Ewen's brother Drogo.

The canal lowered the cost of transporting coal to the port where Larch's ships waited, so they'd developed an interest in Ewen's plans for it. Besides the shipping venture, Robert Larch also owned an iron foundry here in the city. Ewen had met him when

144

Robert helped produce the mechanical contraptions for stabilizing the Northumberland mine.

Lord Edgemont owned much of the land through which the canal ran. So did Drogo, but he had parliamentary duties in London and generally left Ewen to attend investors' meetings.

Since Ewen had neither land nor wealth to invest, his shares in the mine and canal had been earned from his investment in time and expertise. Now that the canal was almost operational and the mine ready to produce a profit, he stood to earn a comfortable income, depending on the choices these men made. They'd already refused to advance him the wherewithal to repay his personal bank loan, insisting the cash was needed to satisfy debts that they'd taken to build the canal. Now they were considering purchasing more equipment rather than distributing some of the profit.

From the discussion at the table, it could be years before Ewen saw any real money, and from their talk of expansion, they'd soon be asking him how quickly he could marry so he could invest his wife's dowry. Grimacing at the thought, Ewen returned his gaze to Felicity's young suitor.

Percy's interest seemed to be as distracted as Ewen's. He kept glancing at the exit and tapping the papers before him. Ewen calculated that Felicity's ex-suitor would make his excuses as soon as he gave his report. Ewen damned well wouldn't let the mother-murdering macaroni near Felicity if there was any way he could prevent it.

Did he actually believe the lace-dripping dandy would murder his own mother? Or had Felicity simply made up the tale to avoid marrying a milksop?

Don't be an idiot, Ewen. Felicity was an innocent who loved books and would adore being waited on hand and foot by this harmless twit. And nothing short of murder — literally — was likely to deter her from her duty to her father.

He was the kind of impetuous, inconsiderate man she would avoid.

Disgruntled by that observation, Ewen added a dollop of whisky to his cold coffee and tried to focus on Percy's rambling report, but he had no interest in pounds and shillings he'd never see. He owed a king's ransom and must court a sharp-tongued merchant's daughter to obtain it.

That was unfair to Harriet. She was a fierce bedmate and a woman who knew how to bargain, fair and square. Harriet could deal with these investors, freeing him to invent and wander.

Smiling at the thought of Harriet sitting across the table negotiating with the Larches, Ewen almost missed Percy's exit line.

"Gentlemen, I've other engagements this

morning. Unless you have further questions —"

Ewen also rose. "And I promised the lady an outing. Since I cannot make heads or tails of your numbers, I'll leave wiser minds than mine to it."

Loud objections followed, but Ewen had no desire to be raked over the coals again for the lock disaster or interrogated about his finances or lack thereof. Mostly, he didn't intend to let Percy near Felicity.

"I'll walk you out, Larch." Pounding the slighter man on his silk-clad back, Ewen all but shoved the baronet from the library.

"I must make my farewells to the ladies," Percy grumbled, righting himself. "You needn't leave on my account."

"The ladies are discussing shops and spending money and won't appreciate the intrusion." Realizing that in his haste to escape he hadn't questioned Edgemont about a Lord Nesbitt or his library, Ewen used the topic to divert Percy. "You know more of the city than I do. Is there a Lord Nesbitt in residence who possesses a rather eccentric library?"

Startled by the change of subject, the banker allowed himself to be led down the corridor toward the street door as he contemplated the question. "The place reeks of Nesbitts. Have you no more to go on than that?"

"Nesbitts who have held titles for over a century?" Ewen assumed they had titles, since Felicity had referred to the purchaser as a lord.

"You don't know what title?"

Ewen sighed. "If Nesbitt is the family name, doesn't that indicate a lesser title? If he were a duke, wouldn't he be duke of something or other?"

"That still leaves a lot of leeway," Percy said dryly as they reached the door and a footman returned Percy's hat and gloves.

"Well, in my experience, not many nobles have extensive libraries. It's the books I'm after."

Percy tapped his tricorne against his palm, glanced anxiously up the stairs toward the lady's quarters, and then, giving up, shrugged. "The Earl of Middlesea is a Nesbitt, but it's an English title and he doesn't live here. His ancestors are from Edinburgh, though. Come to think of it, he's some relation to Baron Nesbitt, I believe." Percy made a moue of distaste. "Although I don't believe you would wish to become acquainted with a man of his ilk."

Ewen was in no position to quibble over a man's reputation. "That's a start. If you think of anyone else, pass it on to Edgemont, would you?" He all but shoved the baronet out the door and waited until the footman locked it before spinning on his heel and running up the stairs.

He disliked deception and wasn't fond of

dancing to a lady's tune, but the sooner he solved Felicity's problem, the sooner he could return her to the safety of her family. So he'd do what he had to do to keep her away from Percy while seeking her damned book.

Or so he told himself as he followed a maid's direction to the elegant sitting room where the ladies chattered.

Felicity leapt to her feet the instant he entered. He liked that she didn't play coy or gush or show him off like a prize she'd won at the fair, as some women did. Instead, she retreated to him as if he were the man she wished to see above all others.

He made a gallant bow to the ladies. "A sight such as this is a treat more rare than a spring bouquet on a raw winter's day."

Several of the ladies giggled. Fans flapped and rouged cheeks reddened. Ewen normally delighted in these feminine reactions, but today his only concern was for the maiden at his side waiting for rescue.

Lady Edgemont, her hair powdered, curled, and capped in a useless frill of lace and streamers, eagerly appealed to him. "I do hope you will persuade Lady Felicity to attend the Nesbitts' ball tomorrow. I can assure you she will meet all the best people there. Lady Nesbitt is a particular friend of mine and will be delighted to introduce my guests."

So much for stodgy Percy's opinion of the baron. Clearly the man was accepted by the finest society. With an inquiring lift of his eyebrows, Ewen waited for Felicity to respond. He didn't know how her gift affected her in a room full of people, although he knew she'd attended society's functions in the past. He wouldn't commit the error of assuming he knew what was best for her.

"That is very generous, Lady Edgemont. Thank you," Felicity replied, modestly clasping her gloved fingers and looking enchantingly young.

Ewen had come to realize that look was deceptive, but he admired it anyway. Felicity had a backbone beneath that quiet demeanor.

Several of the other ladies raised their voices in excitement at her agreement. Any newcomer made welcome entertainment in this narrow society. Before Ewen could pry Felicity away, a nasal voice sounded in the hallway below, and he froze.

Oh, gad, no! Not here. Not now. Harriet was a proud, uncompromising woman. She'd never accept his explanations about Felicity. Visions of debtors' prison danced in his head as Ewen hastily calculated how he could escape before Harriet could catch him here.

He contemplated the windows — no balcony. He glanced down the far hall — only closed doors. By the time he started searching for furniture large enough to hide behind and thinking of excuses for doing so, the newcomer was behind them, waiting for them to move out of the doorway.

With a mental sigh, Ewen plastered a smile of genial welcome across his features and steered Felicity away from the door.

Tall and thin — Ewen knew full well she wore plumpers to fill out her fashionable gown — Harriet Dinwiddie swept into the room, glanced in startlement at him, and then at Felicity on his arm. She wore her golden hair unpowdered and swept into a smooth coiffure beneath a cap adorned with an amount of lace that exhibited her wealth if not her good taste. Narrowing her eyes, she swung her expensively beaded purse and waited for introductions.

Taking the offensive before Harriet's sharp tongue could wound, Ewen bowed effusively over her hand. "Mrs. Dinwiddie, such a surprise! I had not hoped to have the pleasure of your company so soon."

"So I see," she said acidly, unmoved by his charm.

"Harriet!" Lady Edgemont patted the seat on the sofa beside her. "Come in. Lady Felicity, might I introduce Harriet Dinwiddie? Her family has been a part of Edinburgh society for eons. Harriet, Lady Felicity is a bibliophile who has come all the way from London to visit our libraries."

"With Mr. Ives as her guide," Harriet said, studying Felicity from beneath disdainful brows. "I cannot see how you've ended up here, my lady. Edgemont hasn't a book to his name, which is why he and Mr. Ives get on so famously. I also fail to see why you would choose an illiterate for your escort to *libraries.*"

"Lady Felicity is my sister-in-law, and I'm merely being helpful," Ewen answered cheerfully, immune to her slights.

Felicity set her gloved finger beside her lips and regarded Harriet with peculiar interest. "Surely you are aware that knowing people is the best way to accomplish anything, Mrs. Dinwiddie. I am a stranger here and could not have entrance to the best libraries without the aid of Mr. Ives, who knows all the right people."

Caught off balance by her perception, Ewen recovered swiftly. "You are most kind, my lady." He didn't waste effort on interpreting the glance Felicity bestowed upon him, but bent over Harriet's hand, heart pounding in fear that he'd lose this one opportunity to avert disaster. "My dear Harriet, if you would be so kind as to give me leave to call on you once my family duty has been fulfilled, I would be the happiest man in the world."

He hoped there was a slight softening in Harriet's attitude as she withdrew her hand and murmured acceptance.

He offered Felicity his elbow, relieved that she accepted it so they might make their escape.

Leading her down the stairs and out of the house, Ewen heard her expel a sigh of what he assumed was pent-up anxiety.

"I did not expect such company," he said apologetically. "It was a mistake bringing you here."

"No, not at all. It has been most enlightening." Her tone sounded more thoughtful than worried. "You are much too nice to people. They take you for granted. I had not realized it was possible for people to ignore the substance behind a person's surface charm."

Again, she had caught him unaware. Ewen glanced down at her demure expression but saw nothing except her wonder at learning something new. If he attempted to explore why she thought he had any substance for people to take for granted, he might be disappointed in the result. He preferred to continue thinking she admired him. She was young. It was excusable.

"Are you certain I shouldn't send you back to Dunstan?" he asked as they strolled toward the stable where they'd left their unfashionable means of transportation. "Percy is certain to be present at the soiree. This is a very small society here."

Her gloved fingers pressed into his arm, but she did not falter.

"I shall do whatever it takes to find that book. Percy cannot accost me in a room full of people. Once we have permission to view the library, we can leave." She threw him an

153

anxious glance. "Oh, I'm sorry. I didn't think . . . Will you mind escorting me? Your fiancée —"

"We're not betrothed. I have yet to ask her."

"Oh." She sent him a thoughtful look. "Then perhaps you should make certain she is not the sort to take your good nature for granted, as Mrs. Dinwiddie does. You deserve better than that."

Stunned for the third time in less than half an hour, Ewen could not summon a single affable word with which to brush off her observation.

Maybe he should look in his mirror to see if he was still the ne'er-do-well he'd always been. It was hard to imagine anyone who deserved to be saddled with a bankrupt scapegrace. Harder still to imagine that he deserved better.

"Harriet is the woman I've chosen," Ewen admitted with great reluctance. "She is an extremely intelligent, capable woman."

Felicity's crystal eyes seemed to look into his soul before she abruptly turned her head away. Was it tears he'd briefly seen in them? Or disbelief?

ELEVEN

"What the devil are you doing up here?" Ewen demanded from where he lay on the tower roof the morning after their visit to the city. Leaning over the well shaft, he lifted his head to investigate the shadow falling over him. He still hadn't come to terms with his reactions to Felicity. But that wasn't the reason for his anger now. The sight of her petite form silhouetted against the cloudy sky, winds whipping her skirt, gave him shivers of fear that she would simply blow off the roof like a kite. He wasn't accustomed to being afraid for anyone, and it shook him mightily.

Crows screeched outrage at this invasion of their territory but had the sense to keep their distance.

"I could ask the same of you," she said mildly. "What does that contraption do?"

"It should carry water to all floors, but the rope and the wood have rotted. The cistern works for the garderobe, but the winch for the well is useless." Ewen sat up and leaned back on his palms to gaze up at her. "The ramparts are dangerous. I trust you're here for some urgent reason?"

He knew better, of course. He simply had the idle hope she might listen to his warnings if he couched them in less threatening terms.

"Christina is grousing about being confined, and Margaret is threatening to seal her into the oubliette. Would this place even have a dungeon, much less a torture chamber?"

"It might benefit us all to find out." Leaning back on his elbows, Ewen gazed over the rolling countryside, drinking in the fresh wind. He loved days like this, when he was free to explore the world around him without a care.

Aware that Felicity awaited an explanation for his foolish remark, he flashed her a grin. "If your fear for Christina is your only reason for being out here, then you may go back now. I have no desire to be sealed in an oubliette, which is what will happen if your father discovers I've let you blow off the roof."

Had she been any other woman, he would have caught her skirt and pulled her down to him. He was grateful when she shattered that improper thought.

"A messenger has arrived." She held out a package she'd hidden behind her. "I thought it might be important."

Oh, hell. Papers. Just what he needed. More rubbish to clutter up his life and pin him down. With resignation Ewen clambered to his feet, took the packet, and shoved it into his pocket.

At least in this position he could look down on Felicity's fair head, catch her arm, and steer her toward the tower stairs. She hesitated, but it seemed she was becoming accustomed to his touch — at least through layers of clothes. He'd not think about her naked skin. Or try not to.

"Is the messenger waiting?" he asked, opening the heavy door for her and all but pushing her out of the wind.

"No. He was on his way to the mine and simply delivered that. Said he'd come from the city."

Ewen growled under his breath, and Felicity shot him a look of curiosity. He shook his head and took the narrow stairs first so that if she tripped, he'd break her fall. "Business, that's all. Shouldn't you be preparing for this evening?"

"I left Christina and Margaret arguing over which lace to use. Since we only brought one bag apiece, they've little enough in the way of suitable attire to work with. They've been rummaging through wardrobes, stealing fripperies."

She followed close on his heels, and Ewen gave up any attempt to chase her away. He could hear her sister's voice carrying up the stairwell and sympathized heartily with Felicity's plight.

"I don't think Aidan will mind if they raid the wardrobes. A bit of lace here and there can't hurt. You could hide in the library and read."

"I was, until the messenger arrived. I feared it might be bad news."

Papers generally were. Shoving his wind-blown hair behind his ears as they emerged on the floor where feminine voices discussed some vital point of attire, Ewen strode briskly toward the main stairs. "I'm sure they're of no importance," he said. "You can go back to your books."

"You don't mean to read the papers, do you?"

There wasn't an ounce of accusation in her voice, but Ewen whipped around to glare at her. Blue eyes brimming with questions stared back at him. "Does your gift include mind reading?" he demanded.

"Certainly not." Felicity pulled back from Ewen's harsh tone. On the roof he had held her arm, and she had felt safe instead of threatened. Now that he had focused his formidable attention on her, she might have the vapors simply to avert his intensity.

He caught her arm again and steered her onward. "Why don't you scream in horror when I touch you?"

She didn't want to discuss that either. He was deliberately diverting the conversation from himself, and doing an excellent job of it. He was forever steering her about. She couldn't understand why he could when no one else dared.

He headed for the towering front doors.

"Where are we going?" She shook his hand loose to catch up her skirt. She really ought to return to Christina and her dressmaking, but Ewen didn't seem to mind if she followed him.

"Outside."

He held the door open for her, and pleased that he did not order her away, she hastened out before he could change his mind. The day was breezy and slightly overcast, but more like May than April. She had donned her gloves when she'd gone up to the roof, but she thought she might not need her mantle now. "Does the well shaft extend down here?"

"No, it extends into the dungeon."

She cast him a glance to see if he jested, but he was striding blithely over the rocky terrain away from the castle. Another gentleman might have offered his arm to help her, but Ewen had a habit of forgetting all else when his mind was focused on one of his projects.

"Do you not even have any curiosity about your message?" she inquired, catching up with him.

"Not particularly. Messages seldom contain good news." He halted on a hillside behind the castle and looked down upon the damaged tower and the wall of solar windows. "Aidan seems to have had some very forward-thinking ancestors. They modernized this heap of stones far beyond what some houses have today."

"Until they ran out of money," Felicity added dryly.

"Well, if he's an Ives, that's the common result." With a wicked grin, he sat down on a boulder and pulled up a blade of grass to chew on, basking in a ray of sun escaping the intermittent clouds.

Felicity sought a similar stone so she might sit, too. Deciding the one near his feet would suit, she gingerly arranged her skirt, petticoat, and mantle and lowered herself. She could not remember having sat on the ground in a long, long time. She had forgotten how harmless the earth could be, how comforting. Exploring, she ran her gloved hand over the stone and the nearby soil, feeling nothing but the air and the activity of insects. Daringly, she poked a beetle lumbering over a pebble. It tickled.

The presence of Ewen's long, masculine legs inches from her stirred less innocent vibrations, though, ones she wasn't certain how to respond to.

As if sensing her sudden nervousness, Ewen abruptly leapt up and put some distance between them. He pulled the packet of papers and a stubby charcoal pencil from the capacious pocket of his long coat, then hastily sketched an angle of the keep on the outer sheet. Removing an odd tool from still another pocket, he appeared to measure the sky.

Fascinated, Felicity remained where she was and watched. He seemed to reap much enjoyment from whatever discovery he was making. She loved the way he threw himself into his ideas.

When he had the measurements down to his satisfaction, he returned his perceptive gaze to his surroundings. With a grin at her wide-eyed expression, he scoured the broken bailey and plucked a handful of wildflowers from a sheltered alcove to present to her. "For your patience, my lady."

"It was not patience but fascination. What did you just do?" She accepted the bouquet. Through her gloves she could feel the warmth of his regard on them.

"Not much." He shrugged. "I think it would not be difficult to rebuild the foundation of that tower using a system of levers and pulleys. I was taking some simple measurements."

"You measured the sky?" That seemed almost as awesome as the wildflowers she held in her hands. She sniffed their delicate fragrance and admired the variety of shapes and colors. As she touched a ferny leaf she could feel Ewen's joy in it, although she could not quite differentiate among his joy in the day, his project, and her.

He enjoyed *her*. The wonder of that swelled up inside her.

He laughed, and she admired the way he threw himself into laughter as easily as he threw himself into thoughts. Shoulders back, face to the sky, he gestured with his hand and a cloud parted, as if on command. A sunbeam illuminated his brown features when he returned his gaze to her.

"I used a theodolite, a crude but effective tool when combined with a little basic geometry. I wanted to calculate the height of the tower." He dismissed the math lesson with another wave of his hand. "You are not afraid of flowers?" He observed the way she traced her finger over the petals.

"Flowers don't have thoughts," she said without thinking.

"So you *can* read thoughts!"

"I cannot," she argued, wondering how they had arrived at this subject again. "If I could, I'd know where you were going with this conversation."

"But you read the woman's thoughts in the cart." In pursuit of the answer to the puzzle, Ewen wouldn't give up. Instead, he took the seat beside her and began to braid the cowslips blooming alongside the rock. Finding a particularly delightful one, he tucked it into her hair without a moment's apprehension of her reaction.

The petals brushed her cheek and felt wonderful. "Wood tends to absorb more vibrations than other materials." She attempted to continue with the conversation while he teased her with a primrose. "The poor woman's thoughts were so powerful, they left a presence on the wood."

"You can read *powerful* thoughts, then. If you touch me and I'm concentrating intensely, you can feel what I'm thinking." He caught a pretty caterpillar crawling across his boot and held it out on his palm for her inspection.

"That would be frightening," Felicity blurted without intending to.

"I don't think scary thoughts," he assured her. "I think your gift frightens you as much as people do."

Timidly, she stroked the wiggling, furry worm. Again, all she could sense was Ewen's delight in showing her these things. And perhaps a little of his curiosity about the world around them. "You would be frightened if you saw the things I did."

"You said yourself that your visions are of things that are long gone and that you cannot control. Try thinking of them as scenes in a book. Examine the details and not the emotions." He continued to hold his bare hand extended to her even as the caterpillar crawled to the end of his finger and fell off.

Eyeing Ewen's outstretched palm, Felicity fought the urge to caress it. It would be so much easier if she could frame her visions in neat little pictures like her cousin Lucinda's paintings. The paintings occasionally revealed frightening things, but they were simply oil and canvas.

But the things she felt often vibrated with pain.

"How can one concentrate on facts when one is feeling anguish?"

"It would take practice," he admitted, retrieving his hand when she would not accept it. Without rancor, he continued braiding the flowers. "You could start with easy things. Touch familiar objects and study those with which you feel comfortable, perhaps."

Comfortable. Out of the corner of her eye, Felicity studied the long fingers of Ewen's brown hand. He had strong, callused fingers, with clean, neatly clipped nails. He'd held her with those hands more than once. He'd wrapped his arms around her, and she'd felt safe. But now she felt far from safe. She felt nervous and excited.

She wanted to hold his hand. She longed for his reassuring grip so much that she nearly whimpered with the strength of her need.

As if sensing the direction of her thoughts, Ewen held out his hand again, this time including the temptation of a bracelet of flowers. "Trust me?" he inquired softly.

She wanted the flowers. She also wanted those capable fingers on hers. *Touch familiar things and study those with which you feel comfortable,* he'd said. And then maybe she could learn to control her response to her visions?

Gathering up her courage, Felicity glanced

down at her gloves. Did she dare? Deciding it would be easier if she did not think too hard on it, she bit her lower lip and offered her hand. Carefully, Ewen unfastened the tiny buttons. She held her breath as he drew off the glove, looped the flower bracelet over her wrist, and brushed his fingers against her uncovered palm. When she didn't flinch, he left his palm upraised so she could press hers to it.

She did.

He watched her and waited.

And inside her head she saw him, watching and waiting and battling excitement. She didn't understand his excitement. It possessed undercurrents of some powerful emotion she couldn't quite grasp. Mostly, she felt safe.

No man's hand had ever made her feel safe. In wonder, she curled her fingers around his. Imitating her action, Ewen closed his hand carefully around hers. His skin was warm and rough, and his strength held her steady as her nerves jumped at this unaccustomed intimacy.

She could feel the solid beat of his pulse. Heat flowed through their joined hands. It was odd seeing and hearing these things through him, wondering if his thoughts were hers as she tested the boundaries of her vision, if vision it was. She sensed satisfaction, but was it hers or his?

How did he do it? How did he push out

the past and concentrate only on the moment? For that's what he was doing. He didn't have a thought in his head beyond her hand and her presence and the flowers between them.

Reluctantly lifting her bare fingers from his, Felicity pulled back from her vision to study the depths of her companion's wise eyes. The interest flaring in his gaze scorched hot enough; she didn't need to see more.

She'd learned that Ewen Ives desired her. That she could touch him and it didn't hurt.

What would happen if he kissed her? Could he concentrate on the moment then?

"I do hope these are the proper Nesbitts," Christina fretted, sitting up in bed to adjust the pink bow at the back of Felicity's gown.

"Well, I should think they would at least *know* of the right ones and could introduce me." Felicity frowned down at the plain gray taffeta gown she wore. It was newly adorned with a pink stomacher and bows, with lace at the hem so it might fit over Christina's frilliest petticoat and panniers. Margaret and Dora had helped by adding the pink roses taken from an old gown they'd found in the attic, but the taffeta would never be more than adequate. And on a night when Felicity wished to look her very best.

She didn't know why she cared. She merely wished to meet the Nesbitts and find her book. No one ever noticed what she wore anyway.

"You should wear pink more often."

Felicity nearly dropped her gloves at the sound of Ewen's voice behind her. She hadn't seen him since he'd returned her to the castle that morning.

Before she could recover, he crossed the room, picked up a cloth rose lying on the table, and tucked it into the ribbon holding her heavy hair on top of her head.

In his blue evening coat, silver-embroidered blue vest, and gray silk breeches, Ewen was no longer the heedless, windblown inventor, but an elegant gentleman accustomed to the companionship of sophisticated company. Had it not been for the moment on the hillside, Felicity would have believed it was simply a part of the charm he bestowed on all women that he bothered to look at her at all.

Perhaps it was merely that *all* women fascinated him. Still, she couldn't forget his joy and satisfaction as he had held her hand. He'd enjoyed *her,* an insignificant infant in the eyes of most men of his stature.

Felicity's corset tightened and her breasts pressed tighter against the confining bodice. She could scarcely breathe as Ewen stood close to arrange the flower to his satisfaction. She could smell his sandalwood soap. He'd just recently shaved his heavy whiskers, and she longed to rub her fingers over his smooth jaw.

"I look like a little girl in pink," she protested

when he stepped away.

"You look like a spring rose in pink," he corrected. "But you're right. The color is much too young for a lady of your advanced years."

Christina flung a hairbrush at him, but Ewen gazed only at Felicity. He handed her a second rose from the collection on the table. Felicity didn't like the shrewd look in her sister's eye as she observed his actions.

Briefly, she wondered if Christina wasn't faking her sprain for reasons of her own. Dismissing the notion, Felicity made the mistake of taking a deep breath to clear her head. Instantly, she felt her handsome escort's interest swerve to the embarrassing amount of bosom revealed by her neckline.

"I think I need the modesty piece," she whispered, turning to search the bits and pieces of clothing strewn across the bed.

"One doesn't wear neckerchiefs in the evening," Christina scolded, slapping her hand. "Go on. You'll be late. Take my mantle. It will be warmer."

Maybe she could wear the mantle all evening. Or locate the library while Ewen cut a swath through the ladies.

Finding the blue velvet, fur-lined wrap Christina indicated, Ewen dropped it over Felicity's shoulders. "Come along. I need you to keep Edgemont and his cronies from chewing my ear off about percentages and pounds per ton and things no man should need to know."

"You'll never make your fortune that way." Distracted, Felicity allowed Ewen to take her arm and place it in the crook of his elbow. Not until she tightened her fingers against the satin of his blue evening coat did she realize that she was boldly touching him with a bare hand.

Ewen hurried onward, not giving her time to think. "I'm not in search of fortunes," he said as he propelled her past Margaret and Dora and toward the stairs.

Margaret looked quite pleased with their handiwork, and even Dora sighed in pleasure as Ewen gallantly bowed and swept Felicity away.

To hasten their progress down the stairs, he grabbed her ungloved hand in his. Felicity instantly received a sudden vision of — herself?

With her hair tumbling to her naked shoulders.

Pulling her hand free, she furtively tested the pins holding her curls. Nothing tumbled loose. The vision disappeared with her action, and she sent Ewen a suspicious look.

He didn't appear to notice. Clattering down the stairs ahead of her, he simply seemed eager to depart.

Had she just seen what he was thinking?

It gave her heart palpitations to think of it. Was that how he saw her? If it hadn't been for the pink rose tumbling from her hair, she would scarcely have recognized herself in the vision she had seen. Her eyes had been shiny and wide and excited. Her hair had looked like spun gold. She'd never given her shoulders much consideration, but she'd been seeing them through a man's eyes, feeling a man's lust, and —

No, no, she mustn't think like that. It was much too odd.

"Put your gloves on. It's cold outside." He took the gray kidskin from her limp fingers and held one out so she could insert her hand.

She wriggled her fingers into the tight leather. She could feel his breath upon her bare wrist as he fastened the tiny buttons, and excitement coiled tight inside her.

"Thank you," she murmured.

Ewen's too observant gaze searched her face. Fastening the last button, he offered his arm again, and looked satisfied when she took it. "You no longer fear touching me."

"I do," she replied stoutly. "I never know what you'll be thinking."

He escorted her outside, and his dark eyebrows rose in the light from the hall before he closed the front doors. "So you *can* read my thoughts?"

"Not exactly." Although it certainly seemed as if she had. Embarrassed, she started down the stone stairs, then stopped at the sight of the carriage at the bottom. "Where did that come from?"

"A far less interesting question than the one you're avoiding," Ewen said dryly, leading her toward the dilapidated vehicle. "I found it over in the village. The wheel casing needed repair, and I had to be creative with the shaft, but it should get us there in warmth." He stopped to verify the safety of the harness and patted the horse's rump.

"The lamps are unusual." She studied the gleaming brass of the oil lamp illuminating the door. "We could see without moonlight."

"I've been meaning to try them on Drogo's chariot but never had time. You don't think they look odd?"

"New things always look odd until one adjusts to them." Felicity watched as he consulted with the driver, and wondered how he'd paid for a carriage and a driver if he were as penniless as everyone claimed.

Returning to her side, Ewen indicated the stout man holding the reins. "Tell Mort that. He thinks the lamps are an embarrassment. But he leapt at the opportunity to have the carriage working again, so he's willing to put up with my fancies."

"Mort owns the carriage?"

"Actually, I think Aidan does, but it's been moldering in a barn for years. Mort used to drive it when it was new, so he thinks of it as his."

"Oh." Felicity pondered these fascinating facts. She didn't know Aidan and didn't care that he owned a disintegrating castle and carriage. But she wanted to know more about the man beside her who could invent lock gears and fix plumbing and magically produce carriages.

A man who could touch her bare hand and bring her pleasure.

She thought it might be time to explore her gift just a little bit more before she gave it up.

TWELVE

A breath of Felicity's perfume tortured Ewen as he helped her into the carriage and signaled Mort to drive on. She hadn't powdered her hair, so the scent must come from the cloth roses she'd twisted into her coiffure. The women had pulled silver-gold ringlets into some kind of puff at the back of her head and adorned it with lace and roses to match the gown. The high-heeled shoes and up-swept hair fooled his eye into believing she was sophisticated enough to be gallivanting about the countryside with a worthless rogue like him.

In the light of the swinging lamp, he could see the high swells of Felicity's bosom beneath a tantalizing band of silver lace. A slight tug of her bodice would reveal pink crests that would match her gown more effectively than roses. He wanted to do far more than simply tug on her bodice.

A child did not display cleavage of such generous proportions as Felicity's. She was a woman, all right. She simply didn't know it yet.

Biting back a groan as his manly parts fought the constriction of his silk breeches,

Ewen shifted in his seat.

"I would like to learn to explore my gift," Felicity's soft voice whispered unexpectedly through the darkness.

Imagining all the ways he could teach her to touch, Ewen debated pounding his head against the door to alleviate his instant arousal but decided that would only alarm her. He pinched the bridge of his nose and tried to remember she spoke on intellectual, theoretical levels and was innocent of the abyss of lust into which his mind had just plummeted.

"You must learn to observe instead of responding emotionally," he replied.

"Then I cannot explore with you," she said. "You're a cauldron of bubbling passion."

"All men lust," he told her.

"Perhaps I should learn that for myself," Felicity said primly, folding her hands in the billows of her skirt.

May the stars in heaven fall! Ewen braced a hand against the ceiling to be certain he didn't bounce off it in panic. Beside him, the clever little witch sat demurely, as if she'd said nothing of moment. "Leave other men be!" He tried not to shout too loudly. "Experiment on some doddering old lady who will not murder you should she realize you know her darkest secrets."

Ewen thought Felicity's lips curved upward, but the shadows were too deep to be certain.

Dammit, he was the more experienced of them. She shouldn't have the power to toy with him. He took a deep breath to regain his equanimity.

"I've been thinking," she said after a moment's hesitation.

Ewen loved the way she ducked her head when she was embarrassed. A tendril of pale hair curled loosely along her cheek, and he fought the urge to wrap it around his finger, draw her close, and kiss her until both their heads spun. "Sometimes there are better things to do than think," he teased, since he didn't have the right to kiss her.

"You said I should learn to observe," she reminded him, disregarding his banter. "Shouldn't I learn on someone I trust?"

Damn. He should have been prepared for this suggestion. He wasn't a man with a great deal of restraint; he tended to accept what was offered and worry about consequences later. Allowing her to touch more than his hand would be a path to certain disaster. "What about Christina? Surely you must be able to touch her."

"I've learned to shield myself from people I grew up with. It's the rest of the world that poses a problem."

Yes, he supposed it would. He didn't have to be a mind reader to know what she wanted. For whatever reason, women were drawn to him. He never took advantage of that attraction with maidens, though. The world was full of experienced women who were willing to share their warmth and laughter.

He would be married shortly, barred from ever sharing another woman's kisses, and frustration grated. "And your idea is?" he asked, forcing her to state it.

"To practice touching babies," she said crossly, folding her arms and glaring at him with a righteousness that enchanted him. To Ewen's delight, she even tapped her adorable little foot. "Shall I tell you *exactly* what I see when you touch me?" she asked.

"Plumbing," he asserted, tamping down his curiosity.

"And very interesting plumbing it is." Her voice held laughter, as if she really did connect his declaration to the very human plumbing on his mind.

Trapped, Ewen sought a way out. She couldn't really have read his mind. That was impossible. But she might have read his intentions. It was difficult for a man to disguise those, and Felicity was much too perceptive. He tried not to adjust his uncomfortable breeches too obviously.

"It was your suggestion," she reminded him. "If you do not wish me to practice on you, simply say so. I shall go back to hoping I find the book."

"And hope that the book contains the answer

you seek and that it's not only a sensible answer, but also one that works." He knew he sounded scornful, but her gift had immense potential, and he hated to see her waste it.

And the dangerous part of his soul, the sensual part that adored women, hated to pass up the opportunity to show a fascinating woman like Felicity the wonders to be had in the physical world she'd yet to explore.

"Well, I can always find a book on midwifery and retire to Wystan," she acknowledged with a sad sigh.

Unable to resist her vulnerable acceptance of his rejection, Ewen laid a finger under her chin and tilted her face up. "Don't claim later that I didn't warn you."

Before she could reply, he bent his head and captured her delectable lips beneath his.

Heat lightning, Felicity decided, gripping her fingers into her palms and closing her eyes to better absorb the sensation of Ewen's warm breath as he lowered his mouth to hers. The brush of their lips excited nervous vibrations that demanded further exploration.

His lips softened before pressing more urgently, and the northern lights exploded across her brain. The taste of ale and the scent of maleness seeped gradually into her senses, combining with the intoxicating friction of his demanding lips against her vulnerable ones, nearly spinning her off the seat.

He didn't touch her elsewhere, but she could feel his burgeoning desire to do so. Her breasts tingled, and places lower awakened and stirred. She parted her lips as he did, felt his urge to grab and hold her closer, and desired the proximity as much as he. Unconsciously, she slid closer.

She could feel their mutual resistance as well as their longing for more, but she couldn't bear to stop. Instinctively, she understood that he could teach her so much —

Ewen's tongue tasted her parted lips and electricity sizzled. She wanted to reach, to grab, to feel him against her —

She wanted to curl up in his arms and shake with fear at the power of this attraction.

Releasing her mouth with a gasp of desperation, Ewen hugged her close and buried his face against her hair. "You set me on fire, Felicity," he murmured. "You have no notion of what you do to me."

"Why can't I do this with anyone else?" she wailed into his shoulder, finally daring to dig her fingers into the soft linen over his chest.

"Because you haven't trusted anyone else?"

Maybe. Or she hadn't trusted herself. It was much too confusing. And disconcerting.

She pulled back, breaking his hold. "Do you love Harriet?" Her bare hands gripped Ewen's shirt, resting lightly against his chest. She could feel his reluctance to answer.

"It's time I married, and Harriet will suit," he said curtly, disengaging her sensitive fingers. "She won't mind my tendency to roam the countryside."

"Well, at least you know better than to lie." She released him, but she still shivered from being wrapped inside and out in his intoxicating hold.

He'd kissed her as no man had ever done, and she had nearly expired of pleasure. She might never have the opportunity again — unless she found the book or another man like Ewen Ives. She may as well wish for the moon.

"I'm not young and romantic. Harriet and I are practical people," he said.

"And she's wealthy and you need her funds. I think you would do better to discover why the lock gear failed than accept that you're the one who must pay for it."

She could see his startlement that she understood his dilemma. He shouldn't be so surprised. He was an honorable man without a romantic notion in his head. She doubted marriage had ever crossed his mind until someone had forced him to consider it.

"Discovering why the lock failed is about as practical as searching for your book," he said dryly.

"I can help. I can try touching others who worked with you, if you would point them out to me. I feel safe enough in your company. I think I draw something from you that gives me balance." She ought to be stunned to realize this, but from the very first she had sensed that Ewen was different. Special. She had been taught from birth to rely on her instinct, and she had.

The light of interest illumined Ewen's dark features, and not because of her offer to help, she knew. Her admission had given him a new mystery to explore. She loved that he was willing to accept her gift. Now, if he would only accept what she told him instead of pushing her to learn more —

"Perhaps it's like having a positive charge to counteract the negative one. We should test how that works," he said with barely disguised fascination.

She wanted to laugh at this evidence of how his mind worked. Instead, she thrilled beneath his perceptive gaze. She had to remember she was just a scientific experiment to him. Their kiss meant nothing. Less than nothing. Men had desires, that was all. She was flattered to be the object of his passing fancy — rather like his experiment in electricity — but they were both much too sensible to act on it.

Rebelliousness welled inside her, but she pummeled it down. She was the sensible Malcolm. She had to be. She didn't overset gentlemen with her beauty like her sister Leila, or with her liveliness, like Christina. She must use her wits, and her wits said that a wandering rake like Ewen Ives was the last man on earth for someone who must be insulated by the familiar.

"I wish I could imagine how anyone else could be at fault," he said. "I've thought and thought about it, but it does not make logical sense for the materials to be faulty. I designed the locks. The others invested time, money, and materials to build them. We all oversaw the construction. It had to have been a freak accident."

"If nothing else, perhaps we can learn more about your investors," Felicity answered. "I cannot think them all upright and moral if they are thick with Percy."

"Percy isn't a murderer," Ewen scoffed. "There must be more to what you saw than you realized at the time."

She didn't see how, but if Ewen was right —

If Percy hadn't murdered his mother, there would be no impediment to her marrying him.

The thought was far more depressing than it ought to be.

By the time they arrived in Edinburgh, Ewen understood the source of the fairy tales of witches and enchantments and spells. After that mind-spinning kiss, Felicity's presence had wrapped him in a fog. He would try to think of plumbing, and the scent of roses would waft over him, distracting him. He'd look ahead to see how close they were to the city, and she'd shift in a rustle of silk and taffeta, and he would strain for a glimpse of a stocking beneath her skirts. He'd listen for the sound of cobblestones beneath the wheels, and she'd sigh and his gaze would drop to watch the rise and fall of her bosom. It was enough to drive a man mad.

He ought to be interested only in her gift and its uses, but he couldn't get past the fascination of Felicity herself.

Ewen cursed inwardly as the carriage halted in front of a stone mansion, with candlelight streaming from all the windows. Their arrival jarred him from the sensual world in which Felicity had wrapped him.

Sedan chairs and their bearers jockeyed for position near the mansion's steps. Down the narrow cobble-stoned hill, a line of carriages waited to release their occupants. Footmen guarded the stairs from the mob of pedestrians straining to glimpse the grandly dressed ladies and gentlemen.

Instead of wanting to dash into the fashionable crowd inside the mansion as he was wont to do, Ewen wanted to linger in the cozy darkness of the carriage with this woman who was more intriguing to him than any puzzle he'd attempted to solve. A woman more seductive in her innocence than any experienced female of his acquaintance.

Had he not been committed in his mind to marrying a woman who would save him from debtors' prison, he would have succumbed again to the temptation of Felicity's moist mouth. But marriageable maidens expected far more in return for kisses than he was prepared to give.

Climbing down as a footman opened the carriage door, Ewen held up his hand for Felicity to take. She did so without hesitation, and he took pride in that. She possessed a quiet beauty that enchanted him. He waited for her lips to curve in one of her rare smiles, and anticipated the play of wonder and intelligence in her eyes when she encountered a new idea or experience. He found himself eager to hear her opinions of the gathering tonight.

Unlike his country bumpkin brother, Dunstan, Ewen enjoyed rubbing shoulders with the wealthy. On the whole, the lower level of nobility tended to be more aware of the new industries cropping up on their doorsteps. He could usually find someone of foresight with whom to converse.

He needed to tear his mind away from Felicity's temptations and back to the packet of letters he'd received earlier. The bank had sent a warning that he'd missed his first due date. That notice had been forwarded with one from Edgemont stating the company's decision to purchase the new mine equipment immediately. They wanted to know how soon they could expect his contribution.

He felt the noose tightening around his throat at the thought of Harriet waiting inside. She would know of his predicament by now and would be expecting his offer. He had only to announce their betrothal, and money would pour into his pockets.

But he couldn't tear his gaze away from Felicity as they were swept into the social whirl. Telling himself his first responsibility was to protect her, he set aside his worries and focused on escorting her safely about the crowded room.

It amused him when she offered merely the tip of a gloved finger to those of social stations beneath her. As the daughter of a marquess, she held a position higher than the better part of the crowd. In another woman, the gesture would have been considered haughty. In Felicity's case, her silver-pale beauty distracted, and if anyone noticed her reticence, they forgave it as timidity.

After watching her wince when she suffered the full clasp of an elderly earl's hand, Ewen learned to put himself between her and anyone of rank, intercepting any further eager grasps.

He ground his teeth as he caught sight of Harriet entering on the arm of Robert Larch. Far from feeling jealousy at his intended's escort, Ewen suffered an urge to shield Felicity from Harriet's sharp tongue. Harriet could keep her jealous pride to herself until he was officially hers.

"Would you care to dance?" he whispered into Felicity's ear. His breath shivered the dangling pearl of her earring, and a flush pinkened her cheeks.

"The minuet is safe enough," she murmured, nibbling adorably at her bottom lip as she watched the other dancers. "But the country dances involve too much touching."

"Unless it is one where you stay with your partner throughout," he pointed out as the musicians began the next set. He loved the way her startled gaze turned thoughtful and drifted to the dancers forming a circle. He'd wager she'd never had a partner with whom she could dance anything but the minuet until now.

"We could try," she whispered, excitement further pinkening her cheeks.

The earth would have had to swallow him whole to stop him after that.

Standing side by side with the other ladies in the circle on the ballroom floor, Felicity could scarcely keep her heart from pounding. Ewen Ives was the most handsome man in the room, and while every lady around her flirted provocatively with him, his attention was entirely on her, the little mouse who had been overlooked at her own come-out.

She tried to tell herself he merely regarded her as a fascinating enigma, but as he wrapped his arm around her in the allemande, she could sense his hunger for closeness. A thrill of a kind she'd never known warmed her when he bent his dark head to listen to her and his gloved fingers traced a design on her corseted waist. The strength of his arm as he swung her back into the circle nearly robbed her of breath.

Heady excitement ensnared her senses as she swayed to the rhythm of the music, drawing Ewen's admiring gaze to her bare shoulders. When she lifted her skirt and panniers to reveal her slippers and stockinged ankles, his gaze fell downward, and she felt as if he had wrapped his hand around her foot. She almost tripped and fell at the sensation, but the steps of the dance carried him to her side, and he caught her elbow to swing her about again.

His strong fingers wrapping around the thin silk covering her elbow was almost as explosive as his kiss. She could see herself as he saw her, feel his fierce desire, and her body responded in kind. She would have turned and run had they not been caught up in the steps of the dance.

It was as if no one existed but the two of them. The music thrummed, perfume filled the air, and the heat of a thousand candles caressed her skin. And Ewen's gaze burned straight through her layers of lace and silk.

He thought her beautiful. And desirable. Ewen Ives desired her as a man desires a woman.

She couldn't think clearly. Her head was too filled with sensation and wonder. She met his eyes and nearly fell into their dark depths. The music ended, and had he not steered her toward a table in a side room, she might still be standing in the middle of the dance floor, frozen in awe.

"We had better start searching for that library," he murmured, pouring her a cup of punch.

She thought that was the very last thing they ought to be doing, but she kept her opinion to herself. She swallowed the sweet liquid thirstily before realizing its potency. She choked and dabbed her mouth with the linen he hastily handed her.

"I'm sorry. I should have tasted it first." Ewen took the linen from her shaking hand and caught a droplet on the corner of her mouth. "You have me so distracted that I cannot think straight."

"I do?" She was relieved to know it wasn't just her, but if she couldn't rely on his good sense, they were in deep trouble. The charmingly wry twist of his lips at her reply enthralled her.

"You haven't learned the power of your charms yet. Leave off your cloaks and scarves more often, and men will flock about you."

She didn't want other men flocking about her. Other men terrified her. This one attracted her so strongly that she could scarcely prevent her hand from tracing the embroidery of his vest just so she could feel the heat and strength of him again. She stared at his lacy jabot, only jerking back to the moment when she realized she wondered what his chest looked like beneath it.

He muttered a curse, and caught her elbow as if to lead her away. She was quite ready to go anywhere he wished to take her, but as she looked up she saw the reason for his dismay.

Lady Nesbitt bore down on them, clutching Harriet's arm. Both women seemed intent on something and Felicity shivered in trepidation. In Felicity's over active imagination the two women seemed to be Destiny, about to separate her and Ewen forever.

Their hostess released Harriet and reached for Felicity. Ewen sought to prevent that by taking the lady's hand and bowing over it. "My lady, have I told you that you are all that is beautiful this evening?"

The rouged and wrinkled baroness tapped him flirtatiously with her carved ivory fan. "Of course you have. You tell all the ladies that, you rogue. Talk to Harriet. I must introduce Lady Felicity to some friends of mine."

As he straightened, Lady Nesbitt whisked Felicity into the crowd, leaving Ewen to face his future.

THIRTEEN

Felicity caught one last glimpse of Ewen over her shoulder before her determined hostess steered her to her private circle of friends. In his elegant London clothes, Ewen appeared impressively authoritative, standing with one hand in his pocket, his dark head bent to listen to Harriet. The pair of them were worldly creatures, and it was obvious that there was more between them than a few gallant promises.

Disgruntled, Felicity sighed and offered pleasantries as Lady Nesbitt paraded her about. She clasped her fan between both gloved hands to prevent anyone from reaching for her, but it was impossible to avoid brushing up against billowing skirts and flowing lace. Without the security of her cloak and scarves, she felt exposed, defenseless. Traces of thoughts and emotions assaulted her as surely as did the heavy perfumes and powders. Every inch of her skin crawled until she thought she must leap out of it if she did not soon escape this overheated room with its noisy throng.

She couldn't bear watching to see if Ewen escorted Harriet outside. Was he this minute offering the words that would bind him to her forever? Dread tormented her as she considered all the implications of Ewen bound forever to that wicked blond witch, escorting her to family functions, having babies with her. The notion couldn't be borne. She didn't try to question why this was so. She simply knew he deserved better than a woman who had called him illiterate.

Desperately, she kept her eyes open for a hallway that might lead to the library. She'd not had a chance to inquire about its whereabouts, and she didn't wish to reveal her escape plan to her hostess. If Ewen was cementing his future, she really must see to hers.

Surmising that the closed doorway beyond the buffet table might lead to the rest of the house, Felicity gathered her flagging courage and abruptly disengaged herself from the gossiping matrons.

A drunken gentleman nearly stumbled into her before she took two steps. She dodged so that he no more than grazed her shoulder, but the brief contact, vibrating with lechery, shook her. She had to escape this crowd before she became completely rattled and caused a scene.

Nearly weeping, she hastened her pace, but before she could work her way past the crowd at the punch bowl, a hand clasped her elbow, and she staggered.

The wavy vision of Percy's mother falling

to her death mixed with the memory of fainting the last time Percy had touched her. Desperately grasping for the objective viewpoint Ewen had advocated, Felicity steadied herself and attempted to block out her hysterical need to scream. Percy's shame at her earlier rejection overpowered the fleeting image of his mother.

"Lady Felicity! I have wanted to speak with you." Anxiously, he steadied her with a firm grip on her arm.

"Then you must release me if you wish a sensible reply." Giddiness left her spinning, but to her amazement, she was still standing.

"My apologies." Looking embarrassed, Percy hastily withdrew his hold. "I have been concerned since you disappeared from London so soon after we last met. I had hoped to find that you were not ill."

She must remember that no one but her thought Percy capable of murder. Even Ewen assumed he was an upright gentleman who buried himself in books and numbers. She had not seen the vision clearly this time. She could not say for certain that he was responsible for that deadly fall. Stay calm, she advised herself. Amazingly, the admonition almost worked.

"I'm very seldom ill," she replied. "I'm simply afflicted with the usual Malcolm eccentricities." There, that should discourage him. "I apologize if I behaved rudely the last time we met. If you'll forgive me, I must find my escort."

He reached to grab her again, and this time Felicity did cringe. Percy hastily dropped his hand. "I cannot seem to approach you rightly. I had hoped I might still find your favor. Perhaps if we could learn to know each other better?"

The idea appalled her, but she had no rational basis for that reaction. Sir Percy was a fine-looking gentleman. Not so large or as dangerously appealing as Ewen Ives, perhaps, but Percy possessed wide, expressive eyes, and a gentle demeanor that should have attracted her. He was fastidious about his clothing, without Ewen's arrogant disregard for the conventions. Percy spoke to her as if she were a precious object that might shatter if treated harshly, whereas Ewen tended to argue and mock.

To Felicity's dismay, she discovered that she preferred being argued with. Her family had always treated her with the same insulating caution as Sir Percy, and she resented it. She wasn't a fool or an idiot; she just had an affliction she needed to manage.

"Sir Percy, I don't think you would like the person I am," she said with as much confidence as she could muster. "You see only the daughter of a marquess, but in reality I am my mother's daughter," she said bluntly.

His eyes widened with comprehension. Lady Hampton was known far and wide for her oddities. London accepted her mother's eccentricities because Hermione was charming and the wife of a powerful man. Felicity watched as Percy calculated the prestige of marrying a Hampton against the embarrassment of marrying a woman who was capable of doing or saying anything.

To his credit, he did not bow and make his excuses.

"Your father explained, to some degree. I fear I did not quite believe him," Percy admitted. "You have always appeared to be all that is admirable in a woman. You would do me a favor if you would remain my friend."

"Why would you wish to be so? I cannot help you in any way." Nerves shattered, she clasped her hands and fought the urge to flee. She simply wanted to be alone, to find shelter within herself as she had always done.

Percy gestured in supplication. "I am not a man who attracts ladies. I don't possess a great title or fortune, don't have the kind of dramatic reputation the ladies sigh over." He glanced over Felicity's shoulder, and resentment colored his next words. "I am not handsome and charming like your brother-in-law. He is heavily in debt, you realize, and must marry for wealth."

Felicity followed Percy's gaze, and her heart fell to her stomach. Ewen stood in one of the emptier corners of the parlor, holding Harriet's hand. Mrs. Dinwiddie wore the ruffles of the

193

latest Paris fashion, and her fair coloring contrasted nicely with Ewen's dark handsomeness. They appeared to be in earnest conversation as Harriet's head fell to rest against Ewen's shoulder. Ewen's sober mien as he wrapped his arm around her waist said all Felicity needed to know. Surely even now he was asking for her hand in marriage.

Spirits plummeting, Felicity turned back to Percy. "Ives men always manage to prevail. I don't think we need concern ourselves for him," she finished wryly, understanding that Percy didn't have Ewen's best interest in mind by bringing him to her attention.

She must think of her own interests. She was just having some difficulty accepting it. That she was actually thinking of Ewen in anything remotely resembling romantic terms shook her.

"Then you will consent to see me?" Percy asked eagerly. "Where are you staying? With the Edgemonts?"

Thoroughly distraught by now, desperate to escape the crowd and recover her senses, Felicity said the first thing that came to mind. "Percy, I know you were there when your mother died. I cannot trust a man who lies."

Without waiting for his response, she veered past his frozen stance and headed for the corridor she prayed led to the library.

She'd done it again, reacted without

thought. If Percy were truly a murderer, he'd come after her now. She hated herself for her sudden panic. She hated Ewen for making her think she could be logical and scientific like him. She wasn't. She never would be.

She all but shoved people aside in her haste to escape Percy, to escape herself, to escape the explosion of colors and scents. She tried to make herself small as she slipped between chattering groups. If people turned to stare, she didn't notice or care. She simply wanted to disappear in a puff of smoke.

Felicity plunged headlong down the darkened corridor leading deeper into the house. Surely the library would be this way. She didn't hear voices here. She would be safe. She could look for the book. If only she could find the book . . .

A small fire crackled invitingly in a room to her left. Felicity glanced past the heavy paneled door and nearly wept with relief at the sight of row upon row of floor-to-ceiling books. Far from the frightening crowd, she could seek shelter here.

She slipped inside, ascertaining that she was alone, and wrapped her arms around herself. She took a deep breath. She could do this. She had to do this. She had to learn to navigate the chaos of her senses or live forever as a helpless invalid.

Determined to think pleasant thoughts, she

admired the promise of towering shelves of books. She would need to climb the ladder to examine the top shelves, but she could start with the lower ones and work her way around the room.

Now that she could see the enormity of the task ahead of her, her mind reeled as fear again took root. But she understood books, at least. There might be thousands of them and it might take a very long time, but she could handle the written word far better than she could handle people.

Refusing to think of Percy, shoving Ewen and Harriet to the deepest, darkest recesses of her mind, Felicity began methodically scanning the books on the bottom shelf, discovering tomes on the ancient Romans. Checking the next few shelves and finding the same, she gained confidence. If the library was catalogued appropriately, it should take no time to discover the shelves dedicated to journals of natural science and the mysteries of life.

She glanced up at the shelves above her head. Given most filing systems, she suspected such books were banished to the darkest reaches of the room. She really ought to begin there.

Locating the library ladder, testing its movability along the rail, Felicity rolled it to the first column of shelves. She almost wished for Christina's breeches instead of billowing panniers, but she would manage.

Unfortunately, she could not manage without a candle to light the way.

No matter. Setting one slippered foot on the first rung, she waited for her skirts to settle, crushed them against the ladder, and took the next step.

She was halfway up the ladder and had her fingers around a promising tome when the library door slammed open. Startled, she swayed, her fingers clasping the book more firmly.

Before she could steady herself, Ewen's strong hands grasped her waist, and she was propelled back to the library floor. The book flew from her hand, landing with an echoing crash as she gazed directly into his flashing dark eyes.

"Dammit, Felicity, do you wish to give me failure of the heart?"

Pulse beating unevenly, the noise of the falling book still ringing in her ears, she studied his face rather than wrench from his hold. Her gentlemanly champion did appear a trifle pale beneath his dark Ives coloring. Perhaps it was the grim line around his normally smiling mouth that unsettled her already rattled nerves. But that didn't explain the heated rush flowing through her lower parts. Perhaps her corset was too tight.

"I saw you with Percy, and then you disappeared," Ewen said in low, forceful tones.

"I've been searching the house with visions of finding your murdered remains in the ash heap."

He wasn't angry, he was *terrified* — for her. A smile curved Felicity's lips at the idea of the insouciant Ewen Ives afraid for her. She enjoyed a little thrill at possessing the power to raise his concern. "Percy wishes to court me," she said with a hint of mischief.

"I saw him touch you." His panic hadn't completely lessened, but he modified his voice slightly before asking, "What did you see?"

"The vision was muddier this time." Felicity retreated from his grasp as she realized Ewen's gaze dipped to her bosom every time she breathed. Her gown was definitely too low. Even a lace modesty piece wouldn't disguise the fullness of her breasts, not from the vantage point of Ewen's greater height.

"You didn't faint." Now that she was out of his hands, he flexed his fingers and glanced around, deliberately avoiding looking at her.

She understood his reaction. Given their inexplicable effect on each other, it was dangerous to be in the same room together. She glanced longingly at the ladder but picked up the book she had dropped to examine it. It wasn't the one she sought.

"I tried to concentrate, as you said," she answered with the logic he had demanded, "but watching a woman fall to her death isn't easy to see objectively. And Percy had this image of me fainting, which was far more recent, so I really saw nothing new."

Ewen crossed to the library entrance, checked the hall, then closed the door. "Then I assume he doesn't know what you've seen and you're probably safe."

She winced. "Umm, well, I wanted to discourage him." She returned to running her fingers over the shelf — government treatises, political histories — without looking at him.

Ewen spoke from directly behind her, making her jump.

"You *told* him. Are you insane, woman?"

"Everyone keeps telling me how he could not have done what I saw him do. How else am I to find out if he did?" She looked up at him.

Ewen's lips tightened in exasperation.

In sympathy, she patted the snowy cravat adorning his broad chest. "I just frightened him a little, is all. People never believe me when I tell them things that I can't possibly know."

He shook his head in disbelief and twitched his broad shoulders inside his coat as if to throw off his fears, then scanned the shelves. "Let's see if your book is here and leave."

"There isn't enough light at the top, where I suspect the baron would hide the books I need. If you will guide the ladder, I could —"

Ewen's glare halted that suggestion. Ever obedient, Felicity folded her hands and waited for a better one.

"You will break your neck climbing that ladder in those skirts," he declared — nonsensically, in her opinion. "That would certainly solve your problem, but I'd rather not be hanged for your murder." He grabbed an oil lamp from the library table, lit it with a burning stick from the fireplace, then searched the pockets of his coat.

Felicity watched in amazement as he produced a mangled bit of wire. What else did he keep in his pockets? Then again, perhaps she was better off not knowing.

Climbing the ladder with lamp in hand, Ewen found a step that apparently satisfied him. Setting the lamp in place, he wrapped the wire around the ladder rail and through the lamp handle to prevent it from falling.

"Did you and Harriet have a pleasant conversation?" Felicity asked, turning back to the shelves and pretending disinterest.

"That could be said," he said, turning to examine the topmost shelves.

"I trust she accepted your explanations about me."

"She does not believe them, but she'll come around."

Despite his attempt at cheerfulness, he sounded the smallest bit peeved, and Felicity's wayward heart pattered faster. Ewen Ives was not the kind of man who liked being pinned down or manipulated. Even married, he would resist being held back from his explorations. He was a rover and always would be. He had that sort of mind, and it would be a crime to change him.

Shaking off the panic that thought instilled in her, she tried to concentrate on the shelf before her. Medieval English history, Roman history . . .

"Religious tomes," he said with disgust from the top of the ladder, pulling it along the rail to the next section. His shoulder muscles strained against the tight fit of his coat as he rolled the ladder, and the lamp cast shadows along the interesting planes beneath his angular cheekbones.

Felicity did her best not to swoon from just looking at him. From her position beneath him, she could see the shape of his muscled calves. Ewen Ives didn't need padding beneath his stockings.

She had to look away. "Some people call witchcraft a religion. You may be close."

She wanted to be up there exploring with him, but Ewen was stronger and could pull the ladder better than she could. As much as he seemed to detest books and paperwork, he appeared to be working through the shelves almost as fast as she was.

"Drogo has been reading up on druids. He

thinks your Malcolm traditions have a strong relation to that ancient religion. Naturalism, not magic." He pulled out a volume, glanced at the opening page, and shoved it back on the shelf.

"Ninian gave him that notion, I daresay. She is the herbalist among us, and I believe druids were very effective with herbs." Sensing a strong vibration of excitement from a nearby shelf, Felicity circled her gloved hand over the book spines there. Caught by surprise at the image that arose, she threw a surreptitious glance at Ewen, and assured he was otherwise occupied, pulled the volume from the shelf. Gingerly, she turned the first page.

"Druids were also the storytellers, the carriers of history and legend," Ewen went on. "Your Malcolm journals and legends could be a product of that belief."

Silence.

Returning a moldering book to the shelf, Ewen glanced downward. The fire cast light and shadow over Felicity's angelic ringlets as she bent over a book that had caught her interest. The pink and silver of her gown seemed to blend naturally into the shadow and firelight, highlighting the paleness of her throat and bosom.

How could he ever have found Harriet's angular cheekbones and sallow complexion attractive? After Felicity's pink-and-white perfection, he would never be able to look at another woman again. He knew women well, had studied them as he had studied the other mysteries of life. Felicity's fair skin would stay as firm and unwrinkled as her mother's. Her youthful slimness would mature into a welcoming roundness meant to comfort and hold young children — and to tempt a man's soul.

Physical perfection wasn't all that a man required, he reminded himself, returning to his search of the shelves. Harriet had a perfectly adequate mind.

And a sharp tongue. Having just borne the brunt of it, he could vouch for that. But he traveled. He would not have to listen to her often.

Felicity had a fascinatingly clever mind, and a much more pleasant demeanor.

Damn. Ewen scanned the next row of books, attempting to divert his thoughts. "More religious tomes," he called down. "No druids."

More silence.

What the devil was she reading? He glanced down again, and she didn't seem to have moved except to don her spectacles. Uneasiness stirred, and he started down the ladder. "Have you found something?" He wasn't at all certain he wanted her to find the confounded book she sought.

The rattle of the ladder jarred her back to

the moment, and blushing, Felicity hastily shut the book and returned it to the shelf. "Not what we were looking for." She slipped her spectacles into some hidden recess of her skirt.

Curious, Ewen dropped down beside her and examined the shelf she'd been perusing. Recognizing the foreign lettering, he wagered the first title he read was the *Kama Sutra*. His eyebrows shot up as he examined the others. He'd heard rumors of Nesbitt's hedonism but hadn't realized his hobby was collecting books of erotica. With a chortle, he pulled out the book that had fascinated his modest companion.

FOURTEEN

"I didn't know such things existed." Felicity drifted away from the shelf, but not so far that she couldn't follow Ewen's reaction.

He seemed to be enjoying himself hugely. He flipped pages, studied them, and grinned. Felicity thought she might disappear through the floor. Malcolm women liberally discussed the natural human mating process among themselves, but no one in her family had ever explained the specific details. And she could not imagine even passionate Leila experimenting with the acts. . . .

Ewen held the volume open and chuckled. "This book shows how to seduce by touch. Aren't you interested?"

She was enthralled. Nervously, she bit her lip and studied his expression, but Ewen had returned to flipping through the bookplates, not at all concerned about propriety. Of course, the book was merely an object of curiosity to him.

She slipped her spectacles from her pocket, donned them, and peered around his shoulder, keeping him between her and the book. She tried not to gasp at the page he studied. "They look like preening peacocks."

Nude peacocks, but she did not think that necessary to note. Thank goodness it was a book. Books were safe — she thought. Staring at the naked couple made her tingle but it didn't hurt.

He laughed. "Men and women are not so far from animals that we do not strut and show our best features."

"That shows *her* best features, not his," she protested. She was eager to see the front side of the muscular man depicted, but the book was more intent on showing women.

"It's showing where a woman likes to be touched." He could not hide the laughter in his voice as he flipped the page. "Sensual massage," he read from the caption, proving that he wasn't illiterate.

Forgetting caution, Felicity moved closer, letting her skirts and panniers spill around Ewen's legs. The image he studied seemed innocent. The woman was on her stomach at least. "Why is he rubbing her back?"

"It feels good. With aromatic oils, it smells good, too."

She inhaled abruptly at the image of Ewen rubbing *her* bare back and hastily removed her hand from his arm. Ewen Ives was far too experienced in carnality. Her spine tingled from just thinking about it. "Rose oil," she murmured. "So that's what Leila does with it."

He laughed aloud. "I shall have to sniff

Dunstan next we meet."

Blushing at the image of burly Dunstan and her sensual sister rubbing each other with oil, she hastily flipped the page to the next plate, and instantly regretted it. She tried to slap the book closed, but Ewen held his palm over it.

"Progressive massage," he murmured in a thoughtful tone that still managed to sound seductive. "I hadn't thought of that."

She didn't want him to think of it at all. Wide-eyed, she stared at what the man was doing to the woman's — oh dear, she couldn't even *think* it. Her breasts tingled from just looking. Did men actually — oh, gosh and gadzooks. "It is an extremely well done sketch," she said stiffly, to hide the odd sensation of fluidity she was experiencing in her lower parts.

"That it is. Nesbitt is an excellent judge of material." As if sensing her agitation, he flipped to an earlier page. "This might be applicable to your problem. . . ." His voice trailed off as he examined the series of etchings.

Seeing feet and arms and other less embarrassing parts, Felicity leaned closer. Ewen absentmindedly caught her waist and shifted her to a more comfortable position beside him for reading. Overwhelmed by the sensation of his hand taking casual possession of her person, Felicity did not immediately understand his absorption with the pictures.

"I like this feather device," he said, obviously caught up in the excitement of a new idea.

Feeling brave and worldly, Felicity leaned forward to follow the path of his gaze. She shot back up at once and tried to put some distance between herself and the book. "That is . . ." she sputtered, not knowing how to speak her dismay. "People do not . . ." She removed her spectacles to polish them.

"Of course they do." He flipped the page, oblivious to her amazement.

Of course they do? Felicity tried to imagine feathers applied to such places, then imagined *Ewen* applying feathers to those places, and her face flooded with such heat that she covered her cheeks with her hands.

Finally acknowledging her embarrassment, Ewen chuckled and hugged her. "Just think, goose. Birds don't have painful memories that could hurt you. Perhaps if you had a suitor who touched you with feathers, you wouldn't be so averse to his fondling."

"If someone touched me in those places, I'd have to cut off his hands," she answered tartly, attempting to recover her better senses. Both appalled and intrigued, she couldn't seem to find it in herself to end this diversion.

And Ewen Ives wasn't inclined to adhere to propriety when his inventiveness was aroused. He'd discovered a new path to explore, a lusty one that suited him, and his agile mind galloped along it. "What would happen if I touched you with a feather?" he asked with seemingly scientific detachment.

Felicity knew better than to be deceived by the mask he donned as he turned his regard from the book to her. She could feel the desire carousing through him, see it burning in his dark gaze. He really wanted to know the answer to his question, but he knew as well as she that it wasn't experimenting with her gift that most intrigued either of them.

"If the feather was plucked painfully from the bird, I don't want to know how it would feel if it touched me." Removing her spectacles, she backed away as his gaze dropped to her exposed bosom. She felt as if her breasts might swell to twice their size and pop right out of her corset.

Ignoring her irony, Ewen carried the book to the library table, found a quill, and eyed her with growing mischief. "Chicken," he taunted, spinning the feather in his fingers.

"Goose," she retorted in kind, but she couldn't tear her gaze away from the quill twirling between his masculine fingers — fingers that had no doubt rubbed rose oil into a woman's bare back. And other places.

One etching had shown a man using a feather to tickle a woman's . . . No, she could not even name it to herself, but that part tingled now.

"Birds probably have no memory. Unless the quill contains the memory of someone holding it, it should have no effect at all." Felicity tried to sound discouraging, but the words hung in the air as a challenge.

Ewen approached her slowly, still twirling the quill in his fingers. "Perhaps we could rid you of your fear of touching by employing pleasure."

His voice was low and seductive and held Felicity captive. She watched his sturdy hands and not the feather. A frill of white lace at his wrists emphasized the weathered brown of his hands. The book had showed her the places men liked to stroke with their hands — the places where she ached to be caressed.

"You avoid touching, don't you?" Ewen said thoughtfully.

She was barely conscious of his words as the feather lowered to the only bare flesh exposed by her clothing: her face and breasts. Her spectacles fell from her hand as the feather brushed her cheek.

"I don't avoid you," she managed to murmur as he traced the quill along her chin. She barely felt it. No pain, no distress — nothing. She hadn't expected any. Instead she watched Ewen's dark fingers and satin-clad arm, and absorbed the intimacy of knowing he was touching her without actually touching.

"I'm far from harmless," he reminded her, drawing the feather in circles on her throat.

He didn't have to tell her that. His closeness fluttered her nerves, but she couldn't tear away from the intimate brush of the feather, or prevent herself from wondering what his hand would feel like in place of the feather.

"We ought to be looking for the book," she faintly reminded him.

"Not if books on touching fascinate you. Perhaps instinct is telling you something."

Ewen gave off more heat than a blazing fire. Wrapped in his warmth, Felicity tilted her chin up to give him better access.

She met his eyes with a courage she hadn't known she possessed. The intensity of his desire pulled the muscles taut over his sharp cheekbones, devastating her defenses, and she offered no protest as the feather lightly descended along her throat. In response, the tips of her breasts tingled and pressed demandingly against the silk of her gown.

As if he knew, he lowered his gaze to follow the path of the feather. "Perhaps you simply need to be touched all over."

Yes, *yes!* That was it exactly. She needed to be touched. She wanted his fingers on her, not the feather. Please, let him touch —

The feather drifted to the narrow cleft between her breasts, and Felicity sucked in her breath at the shiver shooting downward to places she pretended didn't exist. She didn't know what to do next. Should she fling aside the feather? Stand on her toes and kiss him? How could she persuade him to touch her as she desired?

How could she persuade him to touch her as the book depicted?

Ewen swirled the feather along the upper curve of her breast, then drew it with excruciating slowness toward the aching tip. "Should we try other objects?" he asked thoughtfully.

Your hand, she wanted to shout, but she hadn't the temerity to say it.

"Or other places?" Without warning, he pulled the feather away, caught her waist, and lifted her to the table.

Startled, Felicity did not protest as Ewen knelt on the carpet beneath her dangling feet. "What are you doing?" she whispered as he tugged off her slipper and a shudder of expectation coursed up her leg.

"Has anyone ever touched your toes?"

The book had listed erotic sensation points, and the bottoms of the feet had been one of them. And behind the knees. Felicity nearly levitated from the table as Ewen ran his hand beneath her skirt and touched both places at once to release her garter. Her stocking slid downward, leaving the awareness of Ewen's desire shivering across her skin.

"Ewen, we can't —" she murmured, but her stocking fluttered to the floor to join her shoe, the quill caressed her bare toes, and words failed her.

"You have adorable feet, you know." He said it as casually as if he were admiring a particularly fine painting. "It's a shame to keep them hidden."

Oh, dear. Her head spun, her breasts ached, and her toes tingled. She clung to the desk's edge for fear of floating off it. And then Ewen caressed the back of her knee with the quill and touched her toe with his tongue at the same time.

Felicity slid straight off the table and into his lap.

Without an instant's hesitation, Ewen wrapped her in his embrace and lowered his mouth to hers.

The room whirled as his lips molded to hers so expertly that she parted her lips without thinking. She thought he moaned against her mouth. His tongue slid inside, and Felicity tasted wine and felt the blood thundering through both of them and knew exactly where this led. And craved it.

She ran her hands beneath Ewen's coat and vest, found the fine linen of his shirt, and reveled in the ripple of muscle beneath her touch. His mouth licked flames across her skin as he tried to resist by ending their kiss, but it was far too late for that. She tilted her head to find his mouth again, and their lips met more surely than if drawn by magnets.

This time he drew his hands upward, finding the curve of her bodice, tracing his fingers where the feather had tormented her earlier, then dipping where the feather hadn't gone. Before Felicity could react to the vision forming in both their heads, Ewen tugged her bodice down, and her breasts emerged from the frill of lace.

Cool air blew across the puckered tips, arousing her more. When he didn't immediately touch her where she needed it, where she could tell he wanted to, she opened her eyes to study him.

A lock of raven hair fell across his forehead. His bronzed visage had grown taut with desire. Black eyes studied what he'd uncovered with such longing that she was pulled more strongly than by his physical touch, yet his hands stubbornly gripped her gown instead of reaching for the swelling curves exposed to his gaze.

She saw what he saw, the creaminess of her skin, the fullness of her breasts, the way the tips grew tight and eager for plucking — and she felt his restraint warring with his longing. His need to protect her from himself decimated any caution she may have felt.

Felicity knew better than to take this one step farther. He offered the opportunity to stop. She wanted to stop.

But not just yet. She had to know what his hands on her breasts would feel like. It seemed more important than anything else she'd ever wanted.

Capturing his gaze, she wrapped her fingers around his hands and drew them upward, away from the silk of her bodice to bare flesh.

FIFTEEN

Ewen almost groaned in gratitude and joy at Felicity's sensual gesture. Following the guidance of her slender hands, he reverently cupped the generous curves of her breasts. Delaying their pleasure, he gloried in the firm mounds filling his palms, watching the rosebud tips pout for his attention, but not putting his mouth to them. Not yet.

The library door slammed open.

The lamp on the ladder flickered out, and the fire in the hearth leapt with the rush of air.

Muffled exclamations of surprise and disapproval shattered their lingering fantasy.

Ewen bit back a curse at Felicity's wide-eyed shock. Filled with regret at this humiliating conclusion to what should have been a pleasurable experience, he drew her bodice back in place, sheltering her from prying eyes with his back. He didn't know how much the new arrivals could see, but any way they looked at it, the scene was compromising. Felicity's abrupt drop to the floor had thrown her skirts above her knees, and he knelt between them. Her stocking and garter lay somewhere amid the froth of lace, and he could not cover her exposed limbs quickly enough to prevent detection.

The sharp wrench of pain in his gut advised him of the immensity of his folly — too late to do him a bit of good.

Even if shadows concealed her kiss-swollen lips and the arousal pressing against his breeches, no observer in his right mind would mistake this scene for anything but what it was. They were doomed.

His fertile mind raced over possible explanations, but he knew when to admit defeat. No matter who stood in the doorway behind him, he'd bungled everything. At some better time, he'd have to examine why.

After adjusting her skirts as much as he could, and buttoning his hip-length vest to better cover himself, Ewen took Felicity's trembling hand and helped her to stand. Her small gasp as she recognized their audience told him he didn't want to turn around. A pity he'd never been a coward.

Keeping a protective arm around her waist, noting she didn't flinch from his touch, Ewen surveyed their unwelcome visitors, and his stomach dropped. "Harriet." He nodded at the only female in the group. The image of a great bundle of money flying out the window popped into his head, right before the one of iron-barred doors slamming in his face.

"Baron Nesbitt." He acknowledged his host's rank before continuing to the third interloper. "Sir Percy, what a surprise."

Felicity's shoulders jerked at this comment. The normally placid banker had fire in his eyes, and Ewen figured she could forget him as a suitor. The prim and proper types seldom possessed a compassionate streak.

His gaze drifted to Harriet, and any hope of applying his persuasive tongue in that direction died a brutal death. She'd been angry with him earlier for his neglect. This time her pride had been mortally wounded. *Hell hath no fury like a woman scorned* screamed through his mind.

What the devil would he do now? What he should say and what he wanted to say tied his usually facile tongue in knots.

"I thought it was my library my wife said you wished to explore," the baron said dryly, breaking the embarrassed silence.

"Forgive us." Ewen considered stepping in front of Felicity to shelter her from the condemning glances and harsh words, but he didn't want to release her. She was shaking, and he knew he was responsible for ripping open her sheltered world and exposing her to vicious gossip. Even pretending a betrothal wouldn't relieve her embarrassment. In the eyes of society, there was only one thing he could do to save her reputation. He had to offer her the full protection she deserved.

"We are newly wed and temptation overcame good sense," he drawled with the casual arrogance of one who does not regret his deception.

The baron's eyebrows shot upward as his face registered shock, then beamed pleasure. He nodded his bewigged head in acceptance of this excuse. A man of notoriously hedonistic reputation, he seemed more interested in the tableau than the consequences. His eyes glittered with appreciation.

Harriet and Sir Percy glared in appalled shock. Ewen cared little for what they thought. The stiffening of Felicity's shoulders warned he'd overstepped in her opinion, but he'd been out in the world far longer than she and knew the consequences of what he'd done. He would protect her with his dying breath.

"Congratulations! My, I must say I'm not surprised." The baron stepped forward and offered his hand. "Ives and Malcolms do seem to attract, don't they? Excellent connections for both of you." He glanced back at Percy. "You sly dog, you must have known. Is it a secret, then? Keeping the lass's meddling father out of your financial affairs, are you?"

Ewen's mouth dried as he waited for the banker's reply. Percy and his comrades were anticipating Ewen's marriage to an heiress so that he might invest in their machinery. Would they suspect that Felicity's father would see him rot in prison for molesting his delicate daughter before he'd hand over a dowry?

To Ewen's relief, Percy gave a curt nod. "Cat's out of the bag now." Swinging on his heel, he marched from the room.

"Humph, sore loser that," the baron mused. He glanced back at Harriet. "And you, madam? Do you not offer your best wishes?"

"Of course, Baron. As you said, the match was inevitable." Harriet's cool gray eyes assessed the situation, and counting her losses, she smiled chillingly at Felicity. "I wish you well of him, my dear. He's not a man who settles easily, is he? As I understand it, Ewen is the Ives who most takes after his philandering father."

Ewen could almost feel Felicity's Malcolm ire on his behalf. He squeezed her shoulders, attempting to prevent words she might regret later, but he knew better than to stand in the way of a woman's fury.

"The sins of the father are not necessarily passed on to the offspring," Felicity declared with deceptive calmness, "and historically, once an Ives chooses his mate, he is more loyal and faithful than most of man-kind. Ewen's father did not choose his wife, but he did choose the woman who followed her and with whom he remained until his death. That is not the act of a philanderer."

That wasn't a view of his father that Ewen had ever contemplated, but now that she mentioned it, he supposed she might be right. Now wasn't the time to meditate on his late father's perfidies and promises, though. Her father would not accept that rationale. Ewen's reputation preceded him too well.

"Then I wish you every happiness," Harriet replied sweetly. "Did you marry here in Scotland?"

"We did," Felicity responded.

Ewen tried not to cringe at the boldness of her lie.

The baron clapped Ewen on the back. "Good man. Why should a young couple wait for licenses and banns, church circuses, or old age before swearing their vows? If a man makes a promise to a woman, it's a promise, no matter what the circumstances. A lot of bloody lawyers drumming up business is what I call that pernicious Marriage Act your English parliament forces upon one and all south of the border."

The baron jovially pounded Ewen's back. "Taking advantage of our freedom up here was an excellent idea. A pity we cannot put asunder what we so rashly declare upon occasion, but I'm certain the two of you won't have that problem, not from what we've seen."

His laughter rose the hackles on Ewen's neck. A vague memory of a discussion on marriage laws buzzed at the back of his mind. He'd never had reason to pay heed to laws concerning matrimony — until now.

From the malicious look on Harriet's face, she knew something he didn't. Obviously, she wasn't heartbroken. If such was her character, he was relieved that he hadn't succumbed to her snares.

"Well, if you hadn't already wed, you'd be well and truly joined now," she said with a smile dripping scorn. "In Scotland, contract marriages are still valid without need of church or state. Declaring yourselves married before witnesses seals your fate. Come, Baron, we should leave the newlyweds to their privacy."

With a bark of laughter, their distinguished host followed Harriet from the room.

Deafening silence descended after their departure.

Married? By simply declaring themselves so?

Shock began shutting down Ewen's mental processes. He dropped to the floor to locate Felicity's stocking and slipper. *Married?* Never. Not possible. He would be a disastrous husband to someone as sweet and unassuming as Felicity. Harriet might have learned to deal with his irresponsible habits, but Felicity — No, he couldn't hurt her like that. Harriet was simply being spiteful.

The heiress he'd hoped to wed to pay his debts had just walked out the door. Panic punctured his normally cheerful outlook. What the devil would he do now? He'd have to find another rich woman, and quickly, before the wolves gnawed down the door.

Felicity couldn't really expect him to marry her, could she? She was intelligent enough to know what a disaster that would be. He didn't want to hurt her by explaining — or by marrying her.

He almost fell over in relief when he located the missing stocking under the desk. "Sit down so I can put this on you," he bid her, although the garment was too tangled for him to find its opening.

Felicity sat on the floor and rescued the stocking from Ewen's grip. Finding her spectacles on the carpet, she donned them before attempting to unknot the silk.

Not daring to study the gallant gentleman who had just saved her reputation at the cost of his hopes, she slowly worked out the tangles with shaking hands. Perhaps there was something to be said for hysteria and vapors. Either would be much simpler than his humiliating silence. If what the baron said was true, Ewen must surely despise her.

"Harriet was hurt and struck out blindly," he finally said. "I'm sure there is more to a Scots marriage than that."

"The baron agreed with her." Quietly, she attempted to don her stocking without raising her skirt, although why she bothered to hide what she'd already revealed she couldn't explain even to herself.

When Ewen didn't respond immediately, she understood their predicament was dire indeed. Of course, since both Percy and Harriet had just dismissed them as suitable prospects, neither of them had any likelihood of marrying soon. Ewen would have difficulty finding an heiress in time to repay his debt, and she would never find a suitor she and her father could agree on.

It was a pity she had no wealth of her own. Her father would deny her dowry to an unsuitable husband, and in her father's eyes, a man couldn't be more unsuitable than Ewen.

The Malcolm side of her family had wealth, but her entire family would be appalled by her wish to be rid of her gift. They'd blame Ewen for aiding in her search, so she could not expect help from that quarter. They might take her in, but not a bankrupt Ives who in their eyes had provoked this disaster. Malcolms were only just beginning to trust the turbulent Ives men. This incident could set back their familial relationship by centuries.

Ewen crouched down beside her, his blue coat and vest filling her field of vision. Felicity gulped as she remembered boldly running her hands over his wide chest, wrapping her fingers around those broad shoulders. Whatever had possessed her?

Without asking permission, he pushed back her skirt and expertly tied her garter in place as if he did it every day of the week.

As he might, she assumed, with any other woman but her.

When he held her ankle with firm fingers as he slid her slipper onto her foot, she stifled a cry of protest. Now wasn't the time for maidenly vapors.

"I don't think apologies will help, but I'll offer them anyway. I'm sorry," he said.

Panic lessened the impact of his touch, but Felicity sensed his sincere regret. Somehow that calmed her a little. They had a problem. He admitted it. Together they would solve it. He truly did provide the steadiness she lacked.

"It's not your fault. I cooperated fully. I've cost you an heiress," she whispered in apology.

"And I've not only cost you a suitor, but no doubt ruined your reputation. I cannot believe we fooled anyone with our declaration of marriage." He studied her reaction with concerned eyes.

Her reputation did not worry her overmuch. She just didn't want him to hate her. "I can't believe a little white lie can have permanent consequences."

"It wasn't a *little* lie. I was afraid Percy would run directly to your father, and I preferred to divert him with mistaken news of marriage and not gossip that would ruin you. I'd hoped we would have time to come up with a reasonable explanation."

"I'm sure you're normally much more adept at escaping these dilemmas," she said soothingly, then stared at him in sudden horror. "You have not declared yourself married to anyone else, have you?"

Laughter wrinkled the corners of Ewen's eyes at her look of panic.

"I have never so much as mentioned the word 'marriage' within a mile of any marriageable female," he assured her. "Until you," he corrected.

The handsome gentleman she so admired appeared uneasy at his admission. Amazed that someone as insignificant as she had brought this brilliant man to a state of uncertainty, Felicity tried to gather her scattered wits. "My father will kill us both." She winced as Ewen frowned. That wasn't exactly the effect she wanted. "Surely we cannot be legally bound. Should we consult someone about the legalities?"

Dark eyes studied her, then seemed to soften as he realized she wouldn't come after him with a butcher blade. He obviously had not kept company with many reasonable women in the past.

Ewen tucked a fallen silk rose into her tumbling tresses and offered his arm. "First thing in the morning. Come along, Mrs. Ives. We had best depart before they break out the champagne in our honor and decide to put us to bed together."

Mrs. Ives. Oh, dear. Could she really be his wife? Casting an uncertain glance at Ewen's taut jaw, she could tell he believed they might be.

Married. To Ewen Ives. Christina would laugh herself silly.

Perhaps champagne and being carried to bed together would be the best solution. She couldn't envision consummating their marriage any other way.

Accepting Ewen's skillful guidance as he steered her down dark corridors and out the back way, Felicity finally grasped that they had ended up in this situation because she *wanted* to go to bed with Ewen Ives.

May the goddess help her.

The carriage hit a rut in the road, propelling Felicity against Ewen. Reflexively, he caught and held her. She stiffened, but now that they weren't sitting like two icebergs a mile apart, he refused to let her go.

"I'll not make a biddable husband." He had no idea why that popped out of his mouth. Perhaps Harriet's angry accusations earlier had driven home the difficulty of adjusting his bachelor life to a woman's expectations.

"What woman wants a biddable husband?" Felicity asked with scorn, surprising him. "Men have their purposes, but being biddable isn't one of them."

Ewen grinned against her ringlets as she pushed upright, but he didn't free her from his hold. In his panic, he'd forgotten he was talking to a Malcolm. Their minds operated on planes of existence unknown to most of womankind. Or so it seemed. "I think I'll not ask what purposes you think I have. It might embarrass both of us."

"We've already embarrassed both of us," she said dryly. "And I'll thank you to wipe the memory of this evening from your thoughts."

Amused, he glanced down, regretting that her velvet cloak concealed the lovely swell of her breasts. She elbowed him, and he chuckled. "You're seeing my memories, are you?"

"Only because they apply directly to what you're trying to see now. All women have breasts. Why on earth are men so fascinated by them?"

"Because we don't have them?" Ewen asked. So much for maidenly modesty. Behind Felicity's quiet demeanor lurked a mind like a steel trap. She'd snap what little sense he still possessed in two if he didn't stay one step ahead of her. Intrigued by the possibility of a woman who might stay abreast of him instead of clinging to and holding him back, Ewen snuggled her closer. "Because men know that touching a woman's breast arouses her, and we can't resist temptation? Have I

227

succeeded in embarrassing you yet?"

"Of course not."

But her words were muffled against his coat, where she'd buried her face, and he laughed. "Be honest. Were we anyone else but who we are, we'd be exploring the freedom marriage offers right now."

This time she shoved away, removing every point of contact between them, probably to avoid seeing the image dancing through his head — the one of a woman who knew what he wanted, when he wanted it. His arousal reached nearly painful proportions at just the prospect.

"You want a far more experienced lover than I am," she asserted. "You think I'm a useless bit of fluff. I want a husband who respects me."

"You want a husband who can touch you and teach you to touch him," he replied. "With your gift, you'll know what I want even without experience. Lovemaking is not our problem. Your father and my debts are our problem."

Ewen astounded himself with that admission, but as he examined what he'd said, he knew he was right. He didn't know if he could be faithful, but despite his panic, his aversion to maidens had died the instant she'd fallen into his arms. He felt as if she belonged to him. It had felt natural and right and . . .

Damn, it was impossible, given their differing positions and outlooks. He had to be sensible and remember that reality and wishful thinking weren't the same thing at all.

"Perhaps . . . if we could prove your lock gear didn't fail . . . we could find some other means of settling your debt?" she suggested.

"Oh, yes, certainly," Ewen agreed dryly, "and we'll accomplish that before your father arrives and cuts off my most treasured possession. I think we're better off hiding until this blows over." He was not usually one to run away, but disappearing with Felicity had a certain appeal.

"Mr. and Mrs. Ives: wandering tinkers," she mused aloud. "Do you think Mort would drive or would you prefer the cart?"

Ewen laughed and hugged her to him again. "A wife with a sense of humor. Come along, lass, our castle looms. Let's explain this one to your sister and see if she takes up the blade in our defense."

Felicity shuddered. "We'll do no such thing. Christina would have us legally tied, bound, and locked behind closed doors before Dunstan and Leila arrived to do the same."

Having been reminded of his older brother's imminent arrival, Ewen felt far less jolly. Dunstan's overdeveloped sense of responsibility would include his wife's sister, and there would be hell to pay.

"A solicitor, first thing in the morning," he

agreed as the carriage jolted to a halt in front of the castle.

The front door opened before they stepped from the carriage, and a light from the hall illuminated a towering, broad-shouldered giant who threw more terror into Ewen's heart than Dunstan did.

Aidan Dougal had returned.

SIXTEEN

"Aye, and it's about time the both of ye came home," Aidan roared as Ewen and Felicity hurried through the nipping spring wind into the castle's less drafty hall. "The she-devil is poking holes through my ceilings with her dratted cane, raising ghosts long dead."

Felicity bit back an hysterical laugh at this greeting. So much for thinking themselves the center of the universe.

"Stow the blather, Aidan. You can speak the king's English as well as I can." Ewen appropriated a lamp from the hall table, and with a hand at Felicity's back shoved her gently toward the stairway. "Why didn't you just take the cane away from the termagant?"

"And come within speaking distance of that Malcolm? Are you mad, lad? I'd like to live to a ripe old age with my mind intact, thank you. You're the caper-wit who prefers to live dangerously."

Aidan bowed at Felicity. "My apologies, lass, but your sister has roiled my temper."

Felicity resisted Ewen's push and stopped before the giant to study Aidan's fascinating countenance. He might be called Dougal, but there was no doubt that beak of a nose and those glittering dark eyes belonged to an Ives. But there was something else there, something familiar she could not put a name to. She considered touching him so she might discover it.

Ewen had made her reckless. Drawing back her gloved hand, Felicity simply nodded. "Christina has that effect on most men. Only her betrothed, Lord Harry, seems oblivious of her temperament."

"Then this Lord Harry is a sot," Aidan stated.

"My opinion exactly." Ewen pushed Felicity past their host. "I thought you had business in the south, cousin. What brings you back here?"

Felicity balked at being led away from this interesting creature, and dug in her heels until Ewen tucked a falling rose back into her curls. A rush of emotion swept through her with the brush of Ewen's hand at her nape, giving her an image of how he saw her and Aidan just then.

She cast her "husband" a speculative glance. Did he actually shield her from his cousin because he was jealous? Of her? Perhaps her own feelings of jealousy over Harriet were mixing with Ewen's somehow.

"My business did not turn out as I hoped," Aidan replied, "and Dunstan grows more respectable with each passing day. He insisted it was my place to return and chaperone the lot of you until he can get here."

"Chaperone?" Felicity and Ewen repeated in astonishment. They glanced at each other, and her heart warmed at the laughter sparkling in Ewen's eyes. They were beginning to think alike.

Aidan eyed them suspiciously. "You think this amusing?"

"How are Leila and the baby?" Felicity asked, abruptly changing the subject. Gathering up her skirts, she obediently followed Ewen's silent instruction to start for the stairs. "Did you find them well?"

"The baby eats and wets and wails, just as she should," Aidan said grumpily, following in their path. "Leila sprayed me with some abominable perfume and went into a trance, so I didn't stay long. You won't be spraying me with scents, will you?"

Felicity decided she'd write Leila instantly to discover what her sister had found out about this elusive stranger, but she thought it best not to mention her intention to either Ives. Ewen might be marvelously understanding, but Leila's ability to detect character from perfume and her unsettling habit of seeing visions generally rattled the most staid of men. Aidan was already wary enough of her family.

"I can barely tell a rose from a violet," she admitted. "Books are my preference, not perfume."

"Good. A sensible Malcolm at last," he said gruffly, stamping up the stairs after them. "Your sister Christina will break her fool neck in those attics. What the devil is she after?"

"Ghosts," Ewen replied for her. "She's already sprained an ankle in her search. Perhaps breaking her neck would finally slow her down."

Felicity giggled, knowing he merely indulged in sarcasm while worrying that Christina would truly hurt herself. She did adore knowing how a man's mind worked. It was quite enlightening and allayed many of her fears, allowing her to relax in Ewen's company. A pity she had not been able to achieve this insight with another man. "I should have known a turned ankle wouldn't be enough to stop her," Felicity said. "I apologize, Mr. Dougal. I'm sure Christina did not realize she was disturbing your peace."

The rattle of a cane on the floor overhead and the thump of a loose board falling almost drowned out Felicity's apology.

"Aye, and Malcolms seldom do. A more selfish lot never existed, unless it's an Ives. Tottering damned idiots, the lot of ye. She'll have the walls crumbling in on us if she does not watch out." Shoving past them, Aidan took the stairs two at a time, bellowing at the top of his lungs. "If I have to come up there after you, I'll tie you to a rafter and hang you from the parapet!"

"Not a good approach with Christina," Felicity murmured with a sigh, hurrying after him.

Ewen caught her waist and prevented her from racing for the tower. "Let them fight it out. They're both adults. Tell me how you want me to handle our situation. Shall I ask for Aidan's aid in investigating the legality of our marriage?"

Breathless from being hauled so unexpectedly against his masculine chest, Felicity soon calmed in Ewen's welcoming embrace. She wanted to lean against him and accept his familiarity, but that seemed foolhardy to an extreme. Instead she disentangled herself to give his question some thought.

"If you ask him for the name of a solicitor, will he provide it without question?"

Ewen released her. "I don't think I know him well enough to answer that. Dunstan calls Aidan an interfering nuisance, but he respects him."

A bellow, a scream, and a loud clatter resounded overhead. Felicity winced but did her best to ignore the interruption. "Do you know a solicitor we could trust?"

Ewen shrugged. "The only solicitors I know are the ones the investors use. I can't say for certain that they would hold their tongues."

As the reality of their situation finally

seeped in, Felicity bit her lip and fought panic. They couldn't really be married, could they? She didn't like to cry, but it seemed the only response available.

Before tears could fall, Ewen caught her chin with his finger and lifted her face. "Don't fret, please. I'll take care of everything, if you'll let me." He rubbed his thumb beneath her damp eye. "I'll talk to Aidan. I know he hoards secrets as if they were gold."

Relieved, Felicity nodded. "I'm not strong like Leila or independent like Ninian. I fear I am of very little use in a crisis."

Ewen brushed a kiss across her lips, and though Felicity hungered for more, he stepped back.

"You have an excellent head in a crisis. You do what must be done, and when you don't know what must be done, you're willing to admit it and let someone else step in. That's a far more admirable trait than forging ahead without heed of danger."

Watching his eyes, sensing his sincerity, Felicity longed to believe that she was as strong and as smart and as brave as he thought her. She knew she wasn't, but she pinched back the protest. Let him believe in her. She liked that someone did. Someday she would be the person he thought she was now.

"Thank you," she whispered. "I will do whatever you think I must to help you out of this situation."

"Would you tie Christina to the bed?" he asked hopefully as her sister's screams echoed down the stairs.

She smiled, and the knot inside her relaxed. "Even tie Christina to the bed." Although this time she was the one who had caused the catastrophe, and not her reckless sister.

Ewen bent and kissed her again, and the tantalizing excitement was worth whatever difficulties lay ahead.

"She's an heiress," Aidan reminded Ewen as he paced the library before a roaring fire. "You could go to her father and tell him that if he wants a roof over his daughter's head, he should deliver the funds."

Ewen was aghast at the idea of blackmailing the powerful marquess into providing Felicity's dowry. But the possibility that there might be some means of keeping Felicity for a wife raised a wild hope in him.

Which he should damned well squash right now.

How could a rambler like him even think about taking as a wife a sensitive woman who needed the shelter of familiar surroundings to survive? He seldom stayed in one place longer than a week or two, yet she couldn't sit on a bloody strange cart without wrapping herself in blankets. He would make her miserable.

Even should he gain her dowry, how could

he pay his debts and still have enough to support her? His future income relied on the mine and canal, and to hold those he needed even more money.

He might desire Felicity in his bed, but there was nothing new about that. He liked women in his bed. That didn't mean he should ruin the life of an innocent.

"Malcolms take care of their own," Ewen finally answered. "The marquess knows that even if he doesn't provide a farthing, Felicity could live with family. I'm the one who is homeless. I don't want to expose her to the humiliation of a husband who can't support her, or one who would never be around when she needed him. She deserves better. Just tell me how to undo this thing."

Aidan crossed his massive arms and looked Ewen up and down. "You know you're spitting into the wind. The two of you are destined for each other, no matter how you twist and fight it."

Ewen took a deep swallow of the fine Scotch malt in the glass he held. It burned all the way down his gullet, giving him something to think about besides Aidan's prediction.

"If we're legally bound and there is no way out of it, then I'll do what I must to see her settled safely, but it's no life for her." He was spinning backward faster than logic could follow, but mindless panic had that effect. "She needs the opportunity to choose her own life, not be forced into mine."

Rocking back on his heels, Aidan nodded and seemed to accept that. "I can give you the name of a solicitor in Edinburgh, or you could write Drogo, but I suspect they'll both tell you the same. The English Marriage Act is too new for anyone to understand all the nuances. It probably makes your marriage questionable under English law since it requires Felicity to be twenty-one or have her parents' permission. But you are legally bound in Scotland. To do the right thing, you'll either have to file for a Scots divorce or marry her legally in England. Or you could return to England and never come back here, and hope the subject is never raised again."

Ewen didn't like any of these alternatives. They all felt shabby. He'd wanted to hear that Harriet had lied and the marriage wasn't valid.

He was married. Ewen dug his fingers into his hair and tried not to pull too hard. Practicality and logic would have to prevail — if he could just silence the banshees shrieking inside his mind.

He didn't want to taint Felicity with the scandal of divorce or the shadow of bigamy should she choose to marry in England.

Beggars couldn't be choosers. He'd have to present the options to Felicity and see her reaction. He'd have to present them in such a way that she would make the right choice and cut him free.

"It's an inane law," he muttered. "Why in the name of all that is holy would anyone abide by it?"

"Tradition." Aidan shrugged. "In rural areas we have no churches or preachers to hear our vows. So if a man stands before witnesses and says he's married, even if it is just to seduce the lass, the law holds him responsible for his actions."

That made a warped sort of sense, Ewen thought begrudgingly. A man who made such promises ought to be held responsible. A chill of the inevitable shivered down his spine.

"I thank you for your advice. I'll mull it over." Ewen emptied his glass and poured another. He didn't feel inclined to go to bed now that Aidan had come home. He would have to return to the floor of the drafty upstairs chamber — a chamber a wall away from where Felicity lay sleeping.

"And have the ladies been plagued by foul murderers as they claimed?" Aidan asked, refilling his own glass and changing the subject.

"Not unless you call Percy such. They are merely after a book, but Felicity and I were interrupted in our search this evening. I'll have to go back and ask Nesbitt if he has a catalogue of his library, but I doubt Nesbitt is interested in old journals."

Reclining in an oversized chair beside the fire, Aidan stretched his long legs and crossed his boots at the ankle, looking for all the world like a prince on his throne. "Old journals?" he inquired idly. Flames cast his face in light and shadow as he regarded Ewen through knowing eyes.

"She's taken one of her Malcolm notions that she can rid herself of her gift if she can only find one of her ancestor's journals." Why did he have the feeling that Aidan's interest was anything more than idle? Pacing the library, Ewen tried to study his enigmatic cousin but could see nothing in his cousin's lazy sprawl to give credit to that notion.

"You are wasting your time with the baron, then," Aidan replied with a yawn. "He'll have sold off anything he inherited on the subject."

"I cannot deny her the chance to look," Ewen insisted.

"Aye, I can see that's your only concern," Aidan said dryly. "Far be it for me to interfere in young love."

Taking a chair near the decanter, Ewen tried to calm his racing thoughts and ignore Aidan's wry jest. "How about you? I thought you were in search of a wife? What did you discover?"

"That all women are not created equal," Aidan answered. "I'm a fool to think any would come to this decrepit old place and make it into a home. Although your bell rope should improve the service should I ever have servants." Glancing around at the cobweb-enshrouded shelves, he snorted and took another swallow of whisky.

While wincing at his companion's sarcasm, Ewen gazed at the enormous fireplace. What if he added a reflective surface to convey heat into the room? If he combined it with Ben Franklin's vent and added a good flue damper for draft control, more heat would stay inside instead of going up the chimney.

He put his feet on the table and drew plans in his head. Life would be much simpler if men didn't need women.

"So, when is Dunstan coming to take the pair home?" Ewen asked idly, warmed by the whisky and trying not to think too hard.

"His Malcolm wife persuaded him to wait a little longer. She is not overly concerned that her sisters will come to trouble."

All he had to do in a few short days was find a book that had been missing for a century, get a divorce, and figure out how to pay back his debts. He had a creative mind. Surely he could think of something.

But all he could think of was the golden-haired nymph lying in the room next to where he'd be sleeping tonight.

His wife.

SEVENTEEN

"You know, if you would write down your ideas instead of simply creating them and walking away, you would do the world and yourself a great favor." Sitting on the library table, biding time while they waited for their appointment with the solicitor, Felicity shuffled through Ewen's drawings. She could tell he had just created this stack last night. She could feel the fervency still on them. She lifted one sketch to the light and wrinkled her nose as she attempted to discern what it meant.

"You sound like Drogo." Lying on his back on the cold hearth, Ewen finished banging the breastplate from an old suit of armor to fit the chimney and adjust its angle.

Soot covered him from head to toe, yet Felicity couldn't help but admire the flat abdomen and long legs protruding from the depths of the fireplace. Stockings and tight breeches clung to muscled calves and narrow hips, and it was all she could do to breathe while just looking at them.

She'd not thought of physical things like men's hips until she'd seen the naked pictures in that book last night. She'd not imagined how Ewen's legs might feel against hers until she'd studied the drawings. Now she couldn't stop thinking of them. She'd spent her life avoiding touching people, but now she craved the opportunity to touch this man all over.

He was making it rather clear that he didn't share her desire. Or perhaps, like her, he was unnerved by what they'd done and needed time to ponder all the aspects of their predicament. Pounding on metal seemed an unlikely but particularly male means of thinking.

"I've always thought your brother a very smart man," she declared, returning the drawings to the table.

"Bookish," Ewen retorted, his voice muffled with his head up the chimney. "And you're avoiding the question at hand."

So she was. She shuffled the papers some more, but no clue to Ewen's thoughts was on them. "I fail to see how we could keep something like a divorce quiet. Would it cost a lot of money? How does one go about it?"

"I'll have to ask the solicitor." Ewen popped out from the chimney. "Or would you prefer to tell your father and let him handle the matter?"

"By lopping off both our heads? He sent me away to protect me. He won't thank either of us for undermining his efforts," she said wryly. "I'd rather resist until there is no other choice. May I go into the city with you? I'd like to see more of Lord Nesbitt's library."

"You don't think we've found enough trouble in there?" Sitting up, he brushed futilely at the soot covering his shirt and breeches. "I'll ask him if he has catalogued the volumes. Let's see if he has Malcolm journals first."

"I'd still like to go with you," she said stubbornly. "I want to know more about the other investors in your canal. I cannot believe you're responsible for the failure of that lock."

Ewen scowled, but she could not fear a man with soot on his nose. She handed him her handkerchief, and when he didn't take it, she leaned over and scrubbed his nose for him. She wore a modest neckerchief this morning, but she could tell her breasts still distracted him, and the knowledge made her giddy. She'd always considered them embarrassingly large for her size.

"How the devil do you plan to do that?" he demanded, grabbing the linen and scrubbing his own nose.

"I don't know," she said. "My gift is quite useless in most ways, but it cannot hurt to try. Perhaps we could take Christina with us, if you fear being alone with me."

"I don't fear being alone with you. We're alone now." Standing and dripping soot, Ewen grabbed the stack of drawings she'd sorted. "And Aidan has taken your sister into the village to hunt for ghosts at the inn. He says the flooring is safer there."

Felicity chuckled. "I think those two are too much alike and will no doubt kill each other if we stay here. We must hurry not only to find my book and talk to your solicitor, but also to keep Christina from being murdered."

"I'm not certain murdering Christina is such a bad idea," Ewen grumbled, scanning his drawings. "She is bound to cause more trouble than she is worth."

Felicity couldn't prevent a thrill of selfish pleasure that a man as worldly as Ewen Ives preferred her company to that of her more attractive sister.

"What are these notes scribbled over here?" He pointed at the corner of the top sketch.

"You can't read my writing?" she asked, picking up one of the drawings he had discarded. "I merely jotted down what you were doing. I don't know the formal name for that thing you just installed in the chimney, but I described it with the words you were using earlier."

Felicity didn't know whether it was astonishment or anger in his face as Ewen set down the paper.

"You wrote down what I said?"

She lifted one shoulder casually, hiding that she quaked inside. "Is there something wrong with that?"

"Why would you do that?"

He seemed genuinely puzzled. Felicity clasped her hands in her skirt to steady herself. "Because it made sense to me to keep a record of what you do. You have so many projects that surely you must forget things from time to time. I sought to keep note of them."

"I'll hire a secretary if it comes to that." He threw the sketch and her handkerchief back on the table. "I'll wash and meet you down here in an hour, although what you might do in the city is beyond my comprehension."

He stalked off, leaving Felicity deflated. For a moment, she'd had a wonderful daydream of following Ewen about the country, keeping track of his drawings, making notes, and writing articles for the journals so everyone could benefit from his genius. Obviously, a secretary would know far more about these things than she. How stupid of her to think otherwise.

But she wasn't stupid. Leaping down from the table, Felicity set her jaw and began examining Aidan's cobwebbed shelves again. Just because the stubborn man didn't want her help didn't mean she was stupid. In fact, maybe he wasn't the genius she'd thought. Maybe he was just a stubborn Ives who needed her help and wouldn't admit it.

Miffed, she began dusting off a volume at a time. These books were certainly far more interesting than anything in the baron's library. Except for the baron's picture book, anyway.

Trying not to think of inked sketches of manly body parts, Felicity pulled down a tome of sermons and prepared to edify her mind.

"Ho, Ives! I'm amazed to see you again so soon. Thought you and the lass might be enjoying your wedding sojourn." Baron Nesbitt rose from his desk chair to welcome Ewen and Felicity as his servant ushered them in.

The visit to the solicitor had verified Ewen's fears, but he'd set the man to examining all angles of the law. The lawyer had agreed there might be argument to nullify the contract. The sum he'd quoted for research had nearly emptied Ewen's pockets, but he would beg on the streets if necessary to protect Felicity from his irresponsibility.

"I promised her a book as a wedding gift," he explained to the baron, "and we have not yet found the one she wants." Uncomfortable with the lie but beginning to relish the role of husband just a little, Ewen stroked Felicity's shoulder to make her look at him. He no doubt imagined the admiration he saw in her gaze, but he liked to believe she at least continued to think of him as a gentleman.

"We did not have a chance to inquire last night — has anyone catalogued your library?" she asked timidly.

In a moment of insight, Ewen recognized her uncharacteristically halting tone. She'd used it when paired with Christina. Christina blatantly flaunted her plumage to hold a man's attention, and Felicity slipped beneath his regard with a pretense of timidity. She was using *him* in the same way she used Christina. Damn, but she was clever. With books of erotica on his shelf, the baron might never agree to give out his catalogue.

"Had the whole lot catalogued after my father died," the baron admitted. "The place was a disaster, books and papers all about. Hired a professor to come in and straighten it out. He threw out or sold the duplicates and the worthless ones and tidied the place considerably. Blunt well spent, I say." Crossing the study, the baron removed several huge tomes from the top of a secretary. "Keep the catalogue in here so people don't poke about in it."

Ewen stifled the urge to grimace at the spidery writing on the pages Felicity flipped. It would take a hundred years to read through all that. "It's more than kind of you to allow us the opportunity," he acknowledged.

"If you gentlemen would prefer to talk privately while I peruse these, I can go elsewhere," Felicity suggested hopefully.

Ewen knew she'd rather be left alone, but he hated letting her wander off. Still, she couldn't come to harm in Nesbitt's library in broad daylight.

"I'll have the footman carry those for you," the baron offered. "I suppose I needn't worry about a married lady seeing the wrong sorts of things." He chuckled as if he'd said something clever.

Felicity smiled, and without even looking at Ewen obediently followed the footman and the catalogue from the study to the library. Only he knew that her obedience held an air of triumph.

After impatiently waiting for the servant to lay the books on the table, Felicity opened the first one the instant he departed. Line after line of titles and authors and subjects appeared beneath her fingertips.

Another time she might have lingered over the fascinating contents of this enormous library, but she didn't have moments to waste. Fingers flying, she turned pages, gathered some sense of the order listed, and began searching for subject matters related to ancient mysteries.

So engrossed was she in her search that she failed to hear the library door open. She didn't sense another presence until Sir Percy greeted her. She nearly jumped out of her skin.

He caught her elbow. "I'm sorry. I always seem to startle you."

She didn't hear his apology. The vision of a woman falling over a balcony rose before her eyes.

Felicity took a deep breath and attempted to wipe the image away, dreading the deadly crunch of a skull meeting unforgiving marble tile. Only this time she felt the horror of the man who'd caused the fall. The horror was almost worse than the fall. With tears filling her eyes, she began to shake.

Forcibly, Felicity tugged her arm free. Dropping into the nearest chair, she buried her face in her hands. She wouldn't faint, she vowed. She wouldn't, wouldn't, wouldn't. She didn't want to know how Percy felt or how his mother had died. Damn Percy for interrupting her search.

He crouched before her and tried to take her hands, but Felicity jerked them away. "Don't." She tried not to shout but, from the look on Percy's face, hadn't entirely succeeded. "Do not touch me. Every time you do, I see your mother die. I cannot bear it. I do not know how you live with it." If she were thinking clearly, she wouldn't know how he'd let *her* live with the knowledge, but the words spilled out before she could halt them.

As the vision faded, Felicity took deep breaths to control her rattled nerves. There — she hadn't fainted. She hadn't seen anything new or understood anything better or prevented a horrible death, but she hadn't fainted.

Still crouched at her feet, Percy rubbed the heel of his hands over his eyes. "What you

251

say is impossible. You cannot see such things. No one can."

Recovering, she almost felt sympathy for the man speaking with such terrible agony. It didn't seem likely that a murderer would experience regret.

"She was wearing a silver-embroidered scarlet robe à la française," she murmured, "and powdered curls. She must have been dressed for the evening."

Pulling his hands from his face, Percy stared up at her. "How can you know these things?"

Felicity didn't know if she was being very brave or very foolish. Malcolms had good reason for not proclaiming their gifts to the world at large. Only fifty years ago, witches were burned at the stake. She wasn't a witch. She was simply afflicted, but how did one explain the difference?

"I'm a Malcolm," she answered warily. "We have odd gifts. I thought you said my father explained."

"He said you could tell me things that other people didn't know and that if I listened carefully, you could be useful to me in my business. He did not mention that you see impossible things." Agitated, Percy stood up and looked as if he would flee.

"I don't see impossible things. I see memories of the past."

"If you saw my mother die, then it's no

252

wonder you fainted. I nearly did so at the time." With that admission, Percy moved to the farthest end of the library, twisting his tricorne between his fingers.

Knowing she trod perilous ground, Felicity fumbled for words. "I do not always see clearly or understand well. Shock tends to blur the image."

"I should think so." He shot her a sharp look and began to pace. "Your new husband does not mind that you see what he would prefer you did not?"

Oh, she'd forgotten that Percy thought her married. She'd never been very good at lying. Although she supposed if she and Ewen were legally bound, then she wasn't lying. "Ewen didn't murder his mother," she answered a trifle more caustically than she should. "He does not provoke unhappy visions."

"I didn't murder her." Hands behind his back, Percy stalked up and down with increasing agitation.

"You swore you weren't there, but I know you were. Why should I believe you now when you lied then?"

With shoulders slumping, Percy faced her from across the room. "You shouldn't, I suppose. You were right to refuse me. I'm a coward and a liar, but I'm not a murderer."

She truly didn't want to hear this confession. It ought to be none of her concern. But Percy looked haggard, as if he hadn't slept all night, and she simply couldn't let anyone suffer, even a murderer. "Would you like to tell me about it?" she asked cautiously, half praying he wouldn't.

His sigh could be heard across the room. Falling into a chair beside the fireplace, he glared into the fire rather than face her. "I was there."

She waited. Now that he'd confessed this much, she had to listen.

"I had just come in from London. I was little more than a boy, and I'd been exploring the city's vices too freely."

"You were sotted," she clarified.

He snorted. "That's a polite way of putting it. I was so sotted I can remember little of that evening. I learned later that I'd gambled my quarter's allowance away, so I probably rode home to ask for money."

"Your mother refused and you became angry?" She didn't hide her own horror well.

Percy ran his fingers up under his wig and shook his head. "I don't know. I can't remember what I was thinking. At that age, you think all the world is against you, that parents are deliberately holding you back and keeping what is rightfully yours. My father was dead, but I argued continuously with my mother. I thought I ought to have control of my estate before my majority."

"The servants would have reported that to the magistrate, would they not?"

"Yes," he said curtly. "I don't know that it occurred to me that night, but when I woke back in town the next morning to the news of my mother's horrible death, I knew I would be under suspicion. I didn't have any memory of the evening, didn't even remember returning to town, but I remembered her fall as if it were a drunkard's dream. So I said I'd been in town all week. I had plenty of witnesses willing to testify, should matters come to that."

"No one knew you rode home and back in the middle of the night? No one saw you come in?"

He shook his head. "It must have been late. She'd probably just returned from some party and was on her way to bed."

"And you argued and pushed her over the railing."

"No!" he shouted, leaping from the chair. "I wouldn't do that. I know I wouldn't do that. I loved her. I'm not a violent person."

Felicity certainly hoped not since she was trapped here alone with him. She glanced over her shoulder to see how quickly she could escape.

Percy noticed her glance. "I won't hurt you, I promise. You may call the baron and have me arrested if you wish, but I could not harm you."

She wanted to believe him. She wanted to believe he was suffering. Just imagining herself in his place gave her cold tremors. She didn't know how to relieve her doubts or his pain, unless —

Closing her eyes against the stupidity of what she was about to say, she offered, "Would you like me to see the scene again?"

He froze. She could sense his hesitation and fear. She'd be terrified if she were him. She was terrified of herself.

But Ewen had said she must learn to look objectively, without fear or judgment or hysteria. What was done was done, and could not be undone. She knew what to expect this time. There shouldn't be any shock in it.

"What if I did it?" he whispered. "I cannot remember anything but the horror of seeing her fall."

"Well, at least you'd know." That sounded cruel, but she didn't know what else to say. "It would be up to you to decide what to do about it. It's not as if a court of law would listen to me."

He thought that over for a minute, then hesitantly approached her. "What would I have to do?"

"Not catch me by surprise, for one thing." Clenching her teeth, twisting her hands in her lap, Felicity watched him kneel before her. She didn't want to do this. She was insane to do it.

Percy lifted tortured eyes to hers. "Please, I have to know. I cannot go on living like this any longer."

Wishing she could bind his arms, wishing Ewen were here, Felicity nodded. "Give me your bare hand." Stripping off her own glove, she held out her palm.

Percy ripped off his riding glove and flung it aside. "Shall I call for someone first?"

"And have everyone think I'm an hysteric if I faint?" Without waiting to think about it, she wrapped her fingers around his outstretched palm.

A vision of the woman in powdered curls rose before her. Ire flashed across her painted face. *"How dare you come to me stinking of gin!" she shouted, raising her hand. "I'll not have you grow up to be the sot your father was!"*

Felicity winced from the pain of the blow, as if she received it. She staggered and held her hand to her aching cheek . . . and watched in shock as the lady caught her heel in a carpet wrinkle, twisted her ankle, and fell backward against the balustrade.

Felicity bit back a scream as the ancient railing pulled loose from its mooring and the lady sailed into the emptiness below.

EIGHTEEN

"Excuse me, sir, my lord, but the lady has urgent need of your presence."

The warning in the footman's brief message shaved ten years off Ewen's life. In the time it took to race down the corridor to the library, he died a hundred deaths. How could he have been so careless as to leave her alone? She was so fragile, so helpless. . . . How could he bear it if she came to harm? How could he face a world bereft of Felicity's trusting eyes and clever mind?

Propelled by fear, Ewen crashed through the library door with the baron at his heels. He stumbled to a halt at the sight of Sir Percy weeping with his head in Felicity's lap.

Ewen had to stop and let his heart return to his chest before he could speak. Her dazed smile of welcome smote him so thoroughly he thought he might fall to his knees beside Percy.

He longed to go to her, to reassure himself that she was all right, but he didn't know what to do with a weeping banker. Puzzled, he searched her face, reading serenity there rather than alarm.

Later, her eyes promised.

Daunted by the confident look of a woman instead of the delicate child he wanted to think she was, Ewen nodded as if he understood and approached with caution. "Can we be of assistance?" he asked quietly.

"It's all right. Sir Percy and I have reached an understanding, and he'll be fine now. Perhaps we could call for some brandy? It's a trifle chilly in here."

Percy rose clumsily to his feet, wiping his eyes while pretending to turn up the feathered brim of his hat. Ewen couldn't comment in front of the baron, but he wondered how Felicity had managed to touch Percy for an extended period of time. Now that he was close enough to see her clearly, he read exhaustion in her eyes.

"Didn't know you were such a sentimental man, Percy. Let the best girl get away, did you?" Without an ounce of sensitivity, the baron bellowed for a servant and ordered his brandy brought in.

"Percy is a man of exceeding compassion," Felicity said with a benign smile as Ewen took her hand in his, offering her what comfort he could. "You are fortunate to have such a man interested in your ventures."

Ewen swallowed her nonsense like a lump of coal. His glare must have been evident. Felicity squeezed his hand, and Percy sensibly backed away.

"Lady . . . Mrs. Ives is all that is kind. She

has made things clear to me that I did not understand. I must make haste, if you will excuse me —"

Pulling his hat over his wig, Percy stumbled past Ewen and the baron, nearly knocking over the footman bearing the tray of decanter and glasses.

"Shall I ask for an explanation?" Ewen asked, ignoring the proffered tray to concentrate on the woman still clinging to his hand as if he were her connection to reality.

She gave a slight shake of her head and turned to her host. "Baron, I have not had time to read through your catalogue. Would you mind terribly if I linger a little longer?"

Ewen considered strangling her for her reticence but thought better of it when she sent him a look brimming with laughter, as if she saw his frustration. The little witch was seeing too much again. Dropping her hand, he handed her one of the tomes and took one for himself. It would give him the devil of a headache, but he'd read through the damned thing if he must. "She's looking for old journals, Nesbitt, specifically a book titled *A Malcolm Journal of Infusions*. Her family collects such things."

"I told the professor I had no interest in the gibberish my ancestors collected," the baron admitted, pouring a brandy and offering it to Felicity.

Much to Ewen's surprise, she accepted it.

"He sold off a lot of musty old volumes, along with a few medieval manuscripts that paid his expenses several times over. Good fellow that. I'd recommend him to you if he had not died last winter falling off a ladder in someone else's library."

Ewen could hear Felicity's dismay as if she'd expressed it aloud. Glancing down, he could see her tracing a line in a long listing marked "sold." He looked closer at the spidery writing, saw that many of the items contained "Malcolm" or "mysteries" or "herbs" in their titles, and knew what she'd found.

He squeezed her shoulder reassuringly. "I suppose you kept some record of who bought the materials?" he asked, trying to ignore the grinding in his midsection caused by Felicity's unhappiness.

The baron shrugged and sipped his drink. "Professor might have, but he merely submitted that listing of books sold and the amount paid. Have no idea who was foolish enough to buy the things."

"Booksellers, probably." Ewen probed deeper, although he held little hope of receiving an answer. He desperately wanted to give Felicity what she wanted. At the same time, he was almost glad that she wouldn't be able to relinquish the fascinating gift she'd been given.

"No doubt. City crawls with them. Sorry I

couldn't help you with your wedding gift. You may use my name if it will help in your search. Perhaps some fellow will remember the collection."

"That is very generous of you, Baron. Thank you." Felicity spoke softly as she set her glass aside and rose. "You have a marvelous library. I hope I'll be able to explore it more thoroughly someday."

The baron brightened. "I know how to compensate for the missing book! Newlyweds and all, I have the perfect thing."

Ewen hid a grimace of chagrin as he recognized the shelf the baron perused. "Here you go! Ideal for newlyweds. It will keep you warm on a snowy evening." Beaming broadly, the baron handed the volume to Ewen.

Feeling as if he were accepting an explosive device, Ewen expressed his gratitude, took Felicity's hand, and all but dragged her out of the library into the cold damp of a Scots spring.

"You don't have to look at me as if I'll burst into flames at any minute," Felicity muttered as they hurried down the narrow hill to their waiting carriage.

He should have hired a sedan chair. The damned alleys they called streets in this town were too narrow and steep for decent transportation.

Except that he didn't think he'd be any safer in a sedan chair while holding a volume of erotica in one hand and this woman in the other. He didn't know if he ought to fling away the book or let go of Felicity's hand.

She started to giggle and hastily covered her mouth with her glove. "I'm sorry. It's a charming wedding present, don't you agree?"

"It's an obscene wedding present." Reaching the carriage, Ewen threw the book on the floor, and helped Felicity climb inside.

"Bit of weather on the way," Mort called from the driver's seat. "Head home now?"

Despite her seeming acceptance of the baron's disastrous news, Ewen understood the depths of Felicity's dismay. He'd ruined her reputation and caught her in a trap they might not escape. Edgemont and his own business could wait another day. He had to help her find the prize that could offer her some glimmer of promise for the future. "Do you have a booksellers' row around here?" he called up to their driver.

At Felicity's smile of relief, Ewen felt as if he added another yard to his six-foot height. Even Mort's surly objections couldn't dissuade him after that.

"Thank you," she murmured as he settled into the seat beside her. "It may be looking for a needle in a haystack, but I can't help hoping we'll find it. How many books on Malcolms can there be?"

"I would have said none, but I fear that's being overly optimistic." Grimly, Ewen placed his boots on the volume of erotica on the floor.

"Oh, certainly. Ninian has my grandmother's collection, and Mother has an entire shelf of candle recipes alone. Our ancestors kept copious notes. You would do well to learn from them."

"Learn from Malcolms?" he asked incredulously. "Not likely."

"That's where your ancestors went wrong," she said in all earnestness. "They listened only to themselves and not to others. That's always a mistake. I'm sure they were good men at one time, but look what they've done to your fortunes and prospects."

Since the Ives fortunes and prospects had diminished in direct proportion to the Malcolms rise in the world, Ewen had no desire to debate that. Crossing his arms, he glared out the window at the first falling snowflakes. "Ives arrogance is our downfall. I doubt that listening to others could have changed that."

"Maybe, maybe not. Perhaps it was arrogance that prevented them from listening. But you're different. You hear and see everything around you and put your observations to good use. If your mother had anything to do with that, then you owe her much."

"Having no father fifty weeks out of the year probably had more to do with it." Knowing she thought him different from his worthless ancestors returned him to better humor, though. Most people thought his observations a foolish waste of time. Harnessing lightning might be foolish to some, but he could think of endless possibilities should he have time and the wherewithal to experiment. "I'm sorry about your book. I'd hoped finding it would be easier."

"I have to try. And keep trying."

Her words were soft and faraway, and Ewen left her to think her own thoughts. He had no right to express his opinion on the subject.

The volume of erotica burned a hole in his boot soles as the carriage rolled into the marketplace.

Felicity stepped out of the bookstall, and a cascade of snow slithered down her back before she yanked her hood into place. Glaring at the awning sagging over her head, she hastily stepped out of the path of the snow sliding toward the edge. It was bad enough that they hadn't found the confounded book. Having snow dumped on her head was the outside of enough. She wanted to stamp her feet and throw a tantrum.

Following her out, Ewen slapped his tricorne on his head just in time to catch the avalanche in his hat brim. Dodging the rest of the snowfall, he stepped into the street, cursing and beating his hat against his boot to shake the wet stuff loose.

"I think I lingered too long in there." Felicity

gazed in dismay at the unexpected blizzard covering all sign of the cobblestones beneath their feet. Shop stalls they'd visited not an hour ago were now boarded up and empty.

"He had the best display of old journals we've found today. It's a pity he didn't keep better records." Ewen looked up and down the street for some sign of their carriage and grumbling driver.

Distracted from her tantrum by his comment, Felicity glanced at him in amusement, but Ewen didn't seem to comprehend the import of what he'd said. "Do you ever listen to yourself?" she asked.

Studying her face, he apparently attempted to find an answer in her expression. Succeeding, he laughed and returned to looking for their carriage through the blizzard. "Record keeping and books make my head hurt. I'd rather remember things without them."

"Your head is hurting now?" Horrified that she hadn't sensed his pain, Felicity wished she had Ninian's talent for healing. She would be much more useful if she could touch him and cure his aches.

"It's nothing. It will go away now that I'm not looking at scratchy scrawls and fading ink." He caught her elbow and held her closely as he guided her down the street toward the intersection where Mort had let them out.

"Have you tried spectacles?" Felicity tucked hers into her pocket so she wouldn't lose them.

"Yes, but that's not it. I can see fine when I'm working on something. Sitting still to read books hurts." He sounded brusque, as if hating to admit a weakness.

"My grandmother called headaches like that the megrims."

"Megrims?"

She shrugged. "Ninian would better explain it." She touched his forehead in concern. "Is it pounding now? I am so sorry I dragged you into this. If you had only told me —"

"Which is why I don't tell people. I don't know why I did now." When she slipped and almost fell on an icy patch, he caught her and held her steady.

She liked the intimacy of sharing confidences, but she wanted to fuss just a little. It would make her feel better than pondering her abyss of a future without the journal.

The wet cold began to seep into her slippers, and she shivered. "I see a gray shape ahead. Is that him?'

"Come along, let's see."

She gasped as Ewen swept her up in his arms and carried her to the corner as if she were no more than a stack of books. His headache obviously did not diminish his strength. Wrapped in the fur-lined mantle, held effortlessly against his chest, she felt as snug as if she sat before a roaring fire. She laughed with glee as he deliberately skated through an icy patch and the wind whistled around them. She caught a snowflake with her tongue and basked in Ewen's broad grin.

"We'll not make it back to the castle this e'en!" Mort shouted down from the driver's seat as Ewen reached the carriage. "I took the liberty of booking a room down at the inn. It be the last room they had. All sensible people are already off the roads."

Felicity felt Ewen stiffen at this news. They'd have to spend the night here? Alarm began to beat in her chest. She disliked strange inns and alien beds. And they would truly be married if anyone learned they'd stayed out all night together.

No doubt Ewen saw the peril as well, but he merely deposited her in the carriage and gave Mort the signal to drive on. As he slid onto the seat beside her, shaking his hat out, she withdrew into the farthest corner. She didn't dare touch him now. She could almost hear the mighty wheels of his brain churning.

"I'm not used to doing the responsible thing," he muttered, still tapping his hat on his knee even though the snow had fallen off. "How the hell am I supposed to determine the responsible thing in a situation like this?"

She didn't have an easy answer for him. "I suppose it is more important to see that the animals and Mort are safe," she said cautiously. "And if Mort says the snow is too fierce to go home, we must believe him."

"I can't leave you alone in an inn crammed with strangers!"

Inns terrified her, but she didn't think now was the time to tell him that. She needed Christina with her before she even dared touch an unfamiliar bed. "Well, it can't be much worse than declaring ourselves married in front of witnesses," she said with far more cheer than she felt.

Through the gloom, Felicity couldn't verify that the look Ewen threw her was one of disbelief, but his lapse into silence said quite enough. Her father would slay them both if he learned they'd spent a night together.

NINETEEN

"We saved the room with the fireplace for the lady, sir." The innkeeper bowed and touched his forelock as he backed out of the chamber he'd opened for them. "The house is full of travelers, but gentlemen can be accommodated in the common room," he responded in answer to Ewen's inquiry about separate rooms.

Standing by the fire, warming her hands and still wearing her mantle, Felicity watched as Ewen slipped the man a coin. When the door closed, leaving them alone, she shivered and tried not to be afraid. The room was large by inn standards, yet Ewen filled it with his masculine presence. She sensed his closeness as if he stood beside her. The book of erotica they'd dared not leave in the carriage lay on the table between them.

"Since we are staying with Aidan, Christina and I do not need our coins." Nervously, she tugged her purse from her pocket and laid it on a table. "I cannot ask you to pay, considering it was my foolishness that brought us here."

After flinging his hat on a bed that filled one wall, Ewen ran his hand through his hair and didn't look at the purse. Or at her.

"Allow me some pride. I do not need a lady to pay my way."

"Ives arrogance again," she murmured, leaving the coins where they were. "Is Harriet not a lady? Would she not have paid your way?"

"No, Harriet isn't a lady," he replied in a tone that for Ewen was unusually testy. "Nor is she a dewy-eyed innocent. She wanted to buy my name and position in society. You have no need of either. And the cost of an inn room isn't quite the same as paying a debt larger than my income for the last ten years. I can afford the room."

"I apologize if I offended you." Stiffly, she pulled her mantle close, although she no longer needed the warmth. She needed a shield from all the vibrations he exuded as he paced up and down the worn floor.

"You never explained what happened with Percy. How could you let him touch you like that?"

That was a subject she could take some pride in, and she preferred it to wondering how they would share this room all night without one of them losing their self-control. Even as ignorant as she was of what happened between a man and a wife, she recognized that the awareness building between them was climbing to volatile proportions. "I did as you said and concentrated on observing instead of feeling. It was easier when I was in command of the situation instead of being shocked into it."

Felicity sensed that she held Ewen's interest, but she didn't dare watch the light of excitement or admiration in his eyes. It would be too much for her raw nerves right now.

"What did you see?" he demanded. "Presumably he didn't murder his mother if you let him get away."

As if she could have stopped Percy had he murdered ten women, but she liked that he thought her so powerful. It made her feel important, as if she were an adult whose opinion he respected rather than the child everyone else thought her. "He was drunk and could not remember what happened. But I saw it all, saw her raise her hand to him, saw her trip and fall. The railing broke from her weight. It was a dreadful accident, but Percy did not touch her. You were right, he could not have done so."

At Ewen's lack of reply, she glanced up. With his coat pulled back from his narrow hips and muscled thighs, he stood tall and strong and so masculine and capable that she could easily throw herself at his feet in desire. And he was looking at her as if she had grown wings and a halo. She didn't want to know the thought behind that look, so she returned to warming her hands, although Ewen's admiration had already toasted her through and through.

Abruptly, he stalked toward the door. "I'll have a maid bring a meal up here for you. I'd best find a bed in the common room."

"I'd rather not stay here alone." The words were out of her mouth before she thought about them, but it was true. What Ewen did to her with just a glance might shake her, but staying here alone was impossible. She willed him to understand, even if it sorely tried his gentlemanly instincts.

He hesitated. "Your cloak will not protect you?"

She breathed relief that he'd understood at once. "I don't know. I don't want to find out." He had trusted her enough to tell her his weakness. She took a deep breath and blurted out hers. "I don't always faint because of shock. Sometimes the visions drain me. And if I touch something else shocking . . . It's better if I have time to rest, and I do not dare rest on that bed unless I know it's safe."

"I don't think I will make it safe for you," he said dryly, forsaking the door to come up behind her and remove her mantle.

His masculine height and breadth at her back provided the shelter she craved. "You will," she assured him somewhat breathlessly. "You steady me. And you're a gentleman. I know I can trust you."

"That's more than I know." Draping the wrap over his arm, Ewen massaged her tense shoulders with strong, reassuring fingers.

"Men are men, no matter what clothes and manners we put on."

Under his gentle kneading, Felicity relaxed. Ewen looked to the future instead of the past so that his touch never poisoned her with regrets. "You would never do anything I did not wish," she said confidently.

His hands stilled, except for the rotating pressure of his thumbs. "You're right," he said with some degree of wonder. "Although I suppose, given our behavior, I should worry about what it is you wish."

She tried to elbow him for that improper thought, but he only dodged and chuckled.

"I'll hide the book, I promise!" he said, laughing as she spun around to glare at him. He held up his hands in surrender. "You'll have me fretting as much as you do. I'll go fetch some supper, shall I?"

"If you're concerned about your reputation, then I retract my offer," she replied tartly. "We needn't share a room or supper or anything else."

Instead of arguing, Ewen tilted her chin up and brushed his lips so softly against hers that she could scarcely catch her breath even after he lifted his head. The understanding burning in his gaze nearly melted her.

"You're an innocent, my sweet," he murmured. "I have no fear for my wicked reputation. Give me credit for trying to do what's best for you."

She gulped, but when he withdrew his hand, she stood as straight and tall as she was able. "Then give me credit for knowing what is best for *me*."

She could read the concern in his eyes, knew the experience from which he drew, and sighed in relief when he nodded.

"Bolt the door and do not open it until you hear my voice."

The instant he departed, Felicity drifted to the table and the baron's book. An experienced man like Ewen knew far more than she about what was happening between them. She needed to understand these odd sensations before she did anything more foolish than she already had.

She flipped the book open to see where the pages fell.

An etching of a male in a full state of arousal leapt out at her.

Hastily, she slapped the book closed again and rubbed her hands over her burning cheeks. She had wished to know what a man looked like, and now she knew. She would never be able to look Ewen in the face after this.

But she couldn't keep her imagination from leaping from the figure on the page to Ewen and juxtaposing the two. Her cheeks flamed hotter.

She was pacing the room by the time Ewen returned with a maid and their meal. With gloved hands she slipped open the bolt and tried to act naturally as the food was laid out. She wasn't the least bit hungry.

"You are regretting your decision already, aren't you?" Ewen asked after the maid had departed. He covered a chair with her cloak and held it out from the table for her.

"I regret many things." She took the seat offered and tried not to notice that his hips were of a height with her shoulders from this position. And she now had some knowledge of the fascinating equipment his breeches hid. "I regret looking at that stupid book, and I regret letting you test my limits."

Ewen pulled a chair close to hers and spooned food onto her plate. "You can't change what's done. You can only look forward and choose the best course with the information you possess right now."

"How can I?" she wailed, then bit her tongue. She didn't want to sound like a child. "You never have qualms or misgivings?"

"Don't have time for them," he admitted. "I know it's a failing of mine, but I seldom worry about what I'm doing while I'm doing it. Life is too short, and the future beckons. I could wish I had prepared better for a time when I might have a wife or family to support, but I never honestly thought it a possibility."

"And it shan't be. Your solicitor will challenge the law. I meant to retire to Wystan if I did not find the book, so you need not worry about my reputation. But I've cost you Harriet's dowry, and I cannot see how we will free you from debt."

She was fretting again. She could see his urge to laugh at her for doing what he'd just told her not to — worry over what couldn't be changed.

"Let us take one thing at a time," he said with remarkable restraint for a man whose lips were twitching. He polished the handle of her fork with his bare fingers before handing it to her. "First, we must make it through the night. Now stop fretting; I'm really not worth it."

"I cannot be like you and think of nothing but the moment!" Felicity slammed the fork down and tried not to wail in frustration.

She wrinkled the napkin in her lap so she needn't think too hard on Ewen's laughter and masculine proximity and how much she enjoyed both. His booted legs brushed much too close to her skirts, and her mind kept traveling to the book on the table and the picture she'd seen and the things he had done to her the night before.

Ewen forked a succulent bite of beef and held it to her lips. "You must worry about eating your meal without dripping gravy on your pretty dress, since we have no change of clothes."

Felicity glared at him with such hostility that Ewen had to chuckle again. Placing the food between her lips, he leaned over and kissed her pert nose while her mouth was too full to protest.

"You really cannot change the world or me, my sweet. Accept that, and life will be much simpler."

Her shoulders sagged, and he wanted nothing more than the right to take her in his arms and make her fears go away. But he wasn't completely irresponsible. He wouldn't take away the few choices remaining to her. He might wish to make love to her all night long, but he had no desire for her to end up wed to a man destined for debtors' prison.

Felicity snatched the fork from his hand and began to feed herself, although she toyed with the food more than she ate it.

Ewen knew he ought to feel guilty, but it wasn't an emotion he was well acquainted with. He finished his meal and rose from the table. "I'll go down and ask for an extra blanket to give you time to wash and prepare for bed."

She paled at his plain speaking, but he saw no reason to beautify the matter. She'd asked him to stay. He would be certain she meant it.

"Please don't leave. This is a new gown," she whispered. "I cannot . . ." She gestured at the bodice. "Christina helped me . . ."

And a maid would overset her already rattled nerves, he understood at once. He liked feeling worthy enough to buffer her from life's little bumps and stumbles. And he really didn't wish to leave her alone.

With expertise he flicked open the hook at the neck of her bodice, and, for good measure, released the lacing of the attached corset. Beneath the bodice a ruffled chemise caressed the hollow of her slender shoulder blades. She clutched the front of the gown to keep it from falling, but Ewen leaned over to kiss her cheek and catch a better view of plump young —

"Ewen!" she protested, struggling to pull up the loosened bodice.

Color tinted her cheeks. Laughing, Ewen brushed his finger over the pink, marveling at the silkiness of her skin. "If I were a rich man, I'd hunt down your father and tell him we're wed and that there isn't anything he can do about it. But since I'm not, I'll try not to tease."

Her eyes widened at this declaration, but he had teased her so often that she apparently did not take him too seriously.

Acknowledging that she truly feared being alone more than being with him, he exercised a restraint he hadn't practiced in years. Setting up the dressing screen in front of the fire, he politely turned his back so Felicity could scurry behind it. When she stepped out from behind it wearing her frilly chemise, he held out her cloak and did his utmost to keep his gaze on her face until she was safely wrapped in its folds. He rewarded his restraint with just a quick peek at her rounded shoulder as he pulled the wrap closed.

She studied him worriedly, forcing him to think of her comfort rather than his own. It reassured him that he wasn't totally beyond the ability to think of others, and he rather enjoyed the feeling of protectiveness. "I'll stay up until you are asleep to make certain nothing disturbs you."

Even cloaked in velvet, Felicity was a goddess of sensuality. Her full pink lips were moist and begged to be tasted. She had done nothing to her hair, and silken ringlets fell temptingly from their knot against her slender throat. And her eyes — if he thought of those beckoning pools, he'd never sleep again.

With a nod she held the cloak around her and escaped between the covers. Ewen arranged the folds of the heavy wrap more securely over her shoulders, checked that the sheets didn't touch her, and settled into a chair beside the fire so she could call to him if she needed.

"Thank you," she murmured so softly he almost did not hear her.

For those words he suffered the torments of the damned, listening while she tossed and turned and finally lay still, breathing evenly.

He wanted to lie beside her, to hold her in his arms so nothing could ever harm her again.

He wanted a hell of a lot more than that.

Before he did anything irrevocably reckless, he called down for a bottle of whisky and did his best to pretend that damned book didn't lay there, teasing him with new pleasures he could apply to Felicity's virginal defenses.

He timed with care both his drinking and the quantity consumed. His headache had slipped away while he'd massaged Felicity's shoulders. For that he was grateful. He needed his wits about him tonight. Now he must drink enough to send him off to sleep and not enough to give him mistaken assumptions about the woman whose bed he could be sharing if he was evil enough to seduce her.

Once satisfied he'd reached the right stage of intoxication for sleep, Ewen rewarded himself with a glance toward the bed. No man could drink enough to blind him to the beauty of Felicity's fair hair shimmering against her fur mantle in the glow of the fire. Long lashes curved against her pale cheeks, and her pink lips had parted in slumber. The mantle had fallen from her shoulders, and the frill of her chemise didn't entirely conceal her bare skin. He had to pry his gaze away while he threw off his coat and vest and hung them on a chair.

Stripped to shirtsleeves and breeches, he refrained from torturing himself by watching the last light of the fire die down.

How could he bring her here to a bed where strangers had done who knew what? Before he could recognize the first stirrings of guilt, he heard a soft whisper behind him.

"Ewen?"

Her voice tugged dangerously on his heart-strings. It was the only invitation he needed to cross the room and gaze down upon the woman in the bed — his wife, if he wanted to believe solicitors. When her gaze fastened on his open shirt, he became aware of his dishabille. "I thought you were asleep. Does the mantle not shield you?"

"The mattress seems fairly new, with lots of feathers," she said teasingly, her blue eyes peering up at him from beneath a tangle of silver hair. "I do not want you to sleep in a chair. I trust you."

Ewen lifted a wary eyebrow. "That's more than I do."

Felicity smiled sleepily and snuggled her cheek into the fur-covered pillow. "You cannot be a worse bed partner than Christina. She wants her half of the bed in the middle."

Devil take it, Ewen fumed, unable to tear his gaze from the full curve of her hip beneath mantle and bedcovers. He pictured how his hand would fit there, and almost groaned with the surge of blood to his already aroused loins. She had no idea what she asked for, if she thought him as tame as her blasted sister. "I've just enough drink in me to accept that offer if you make it again."

"The bed is strange," she murmured, "and the mantle does not comfort me as you do."

No man in his right mind could refuse that plea.

TWENTY

"I've never crawled into bed with a woman who isn't opening her arms to me in welcome. I'm not certain I know how to do it." Seductive amusement tinted Ewen's voice as he circled to the far side of the bed.

Digging her fingers into the fur lining of her mantle, Felicity kept her back to him. She'd seen enough in the firelight to know he'd undressed down to his breeches and shirt. Perhaps she had just imagined the curl of hair above his untied shirt laces, and surely she could not have seen the way his breeches molded to his muscled thighs — and manly parts.

Ewen placed one knee upon the mattress, and she could not deny the weight and scent of him as the bed sagged and shifted, bringing him closer.

"How can I sleep without a kiss good night?" he murmured, propping himself on one elbow to lean over her.

His breath tickled her ear, and Felicity could smell the whisky on it, but what she noticed most was the masculine aroma that was all Ewen's own. She longed to be sheltered in his embrace, to taste his kiss again, but she had learned where kisses led: to those titillating positions in the book.

Although her curiosity about the images didn't cause her fear, she knew that if she and Ewen did more than share a mattress, he would feel responsible and would do whatever it took to make her his wife.

A free-spirited man like Ewen would only be hampered by an anxious spouse who could not endure strange places. She couldn't bear to cripple him like that, even though he hovered over her, offering sin and temptation and the answer to all her questions. All she had to do was reach out . . .

As if sensing her weakening, wicked man that he was, Ewen leaned closer to brush a kiss across her cheek. "Just one kiss, my sweet, to tide me over till dawn."

She shouldn't. She'd just listed every reason why she shouldn't.

She didn't say no.

Like butterfly wings, his lips caressed hers, warming her with the heat of the sun and arousing her as no other element of nature could. He didn't use his hands, merely tasted, urging a response she gladly offered.

Her toes tingled when his mouth pressed hotter. Her belly writhed in excitement as his tongue swept the seam of her lips, teasing her into wanting more. Felicity dug her fingers into the fur mantle, trying to resist touching, but liquid heat flowed through her from where Ewen's tongue entwined with hers, and she had no will of her own.

His passion whipped through her. His need and hunger and loneliness mixed with a confusion of other vibrations — admiration, desire — as his hand slid slowly and seductively to cup and fondle her breast.

With bliss Felicity closed her eyes and surrendered to the sensations evoked by Ewen's talented hand. No feather between them this time, just his hand on her bodice, teasing her nipple to a taut, aching pucker that tightened her womb and liquefied her resolve. She wanted to part her legs, but his knee blocked her with the solidity of a tree trunk.

She reached for his shoulders to pull him closer, but Ewen caught her wrist, halting the wonderful caress. Her eyes flew open to discover his handsome features contorted with the strain of resisting her. She could *feel* the desire raging through him, and she ached with it.

"I will not be the man who causes you regret, Felicity," he murmured. Perhaps their kiss had seared the alcohol fumes from his senses, and he realized he'd gone too far. "I will apply my experience to better purpose than I've used it in the past." He rolled onto his back, crossed his arms under his head, and even though he still breathed heavily, he closed his eyes.

Felicity wanted to scream her frustration,

but she could not. Ewen had been accused of irresponsibility all his life, but he was far more trustworthy than she. She could not hurt his opinion of himself by tempting him to go beyond the bounds he had set between them. She should be ashamed of herself for teasing him like a common flirt.

When he made no further move toward her, she tried to breathe shallowly and pretend she slept. She heard his breathing gradually calm, although she sensed his uncomfortable stiffness beside her.

She would have to make up her bad behavior to him. Perhaps she could begin investigating Lord Edgemont and the Larches on the morrow. She didn't know if Mr. Campbell would still be in the city. Until now Ewen had applied himself to her problems, and she had done nothing for his. That really should stop. His situation was far more dire.

She must have dozed, for the mantle slipped from her shoulders. With Ewen's heat to warm her she didn't miss the fur. In fact, she slept more heavily once she turned to snuggle closer and wrap her fingers in the shirt he'd loosened from his breeches.

It wasn't until she was fully relaxed and only the thin layer of her chemise separated her from the sheet that the memories hidden in the bed crept up on her.

Heat. Excitement. The brush of a rough hand opening her shift, lifting her breasts free. A heavy

pressure between her legs, one she accepted will-
ingly, spreading her knees to accommodate it.
She ached. She wanted her breasts sucked. She
wanted more than that. She let him pull the
linen over her head and reached to tug him
closer, ready and eager for what he could show
her.

"Felicity?" Waking to heavy breathing and delicate hands clutching his shirt, Ewen rolled over on his side and cradled her against him, uncertain whether she woke or dreamed. She curled eagerly into his embrace, and his whole body caught fire at her sensuous caress.

He shook her gently until her eyes popped open. Her fingers continued to wrap in the hairs of his chest, her breasts heaved, her lips parted invitingly, and if he hadn't been so terrified of what she was seeing, he would have ravished her right there and then.

Slowly, she recovered herself. Taking deep gulping breaths, she clung to his shirt and buried her face against his shoulder.

Assured that she was awake and not hysterical, Ewen returned to his pillow and cuddled her against his chest. The pins had fallen from her hair, which spilled over him in a cloud of apple blossom scent. He could feel the prick of her aroused breasts against his side and recognized her sensual shiver as he ran his hand down her spine, but he wasn't a beast in rut. He could hold her like this. For a while. "Was it a dream?"

"I don't know," she murmured in confusion. "Oh!" She buried her face against his shoulder again with something akin to desperation. "The bed."

He glanced at her half of the bed and saw that her mantle had fallen to one side. The sheet appeared wrinkled where she'd snuggled against him. "You touched the bed," he affirmed. He should never have brought her here. If he ever gave half a thought to consequences, she would now be safely home and not quivering like a frightened bird. "I'm afraid to imagine what you saw."

"Newlyweds." She tried to giggle, but it sounded more like a sob.

Newlyweds. Rolling his eyes, Ewen brushed a tendril from her forehead. "That isn't the way I'd choose for you to learn about men."

She probably didn't even know what she was feeling right now, but he was familiar with the signs of sexual excitement. He could help her ease the frustration. All he had to do was move his hand higher to cup her breast, and within minutes she would do anything he asked of her. He could satisfy her arousal and take nothing for himself — but would she let him?

He didn't dare risk it. Her trust that he was a gentleman sat on his shoulders like a yoke. "Shall I send down for some warm milk?"

She shook her head and sought the safety of his shoulder again. He couldn't deny her the comfort. He retrieved her mantle and pulled it back around her. She weighed next to nothing, but the heaviness of her breasts against his side shot dangerous impulses straight to his groin.

"I'm sorry," she whispered into his shirt. "I hate being like this."

"I'm not doing a good job of taking care of you. I'll deliver you to the safety of your family, and you'll be fine." Ewen stroked her hair, willing his words to come true, wanting to do the right thing for her.

"It's not your job to take care of me," she hiccuped. "You cannot fix everything that is broken."

He wanted to, though. It was his way of dealing with his fractured world. She knew him too well already. "You're not broken. You simply have more to deal with than most."

"The book is lost, isn't it?" she whispered, revealing the fear she'd bravely hidden all day.

"I'll hire someone to keep looking. They can buy all the Malcolm journals in the city, if you'd like."

He might be able to afford it. He was certain the chimney reflector he worked on in Aidan's castle would keep rooms warmer. He simply needed to talk to Robert about the metal he required, and then sell the idea to a few investors.

The bank would have to find him before they could throw him into debtors' prison, he supposed. How much time did he have before then?

"Sometimes you're much too honorable a man, Ewen Ives," she whispered into his shoulder.

He didn't know what she meant by that, but her admiration soothed his disgust with his current situation. He'd spent a lifetime believing he didn't matter much to anyone but himself. Maybe this business of looking after someone wasn't quite the burden he'd thought it would be.

Ewen could feel her relaxing beneath his caresses, and his lips curved. She was so easy to please. He could imagine making love to her for a thousand nights and never growing bored. She would tease and scold and laugh and cry, and then she would rest in his arms just like this, and they would come together as easily and perfectly as sipping cold water on a hot summer's day.

She was his wife.

Ewen let that knowledge seep into him as she slipped into slumber.

She wouldn't need the missing book if she had him for a husband. She'd said he balanced her visions. He could calm her fears.

Lady Felicity — bookish child, clever witch,

serene woman, and beautiful temptress — was his to explore and claim at will.

He ought to be frightened. Maybe he was. The sheer enormity of the future she represented would overwhelm any sane man.

But the reward, should he succeed in persuading all the parties involved, would be more than he'd ever dare dream. Glimpsing the wonders of a future with Felicity in it was akin to dreaming of the possibility of flight.

He had no idea how to dig his way out of debt or how to persuade her formidable father that a roaming inventor could provide for her.

He would also have to persuade Felicity, and that could be a task in itself. Or not. Feeling her breath against his throat, Ewen fell asleep dreaming of scenarios in which he would seduce her. It would be so easy —

"Mort says the city streets should be passable. And if the sun continues to shine, we should make it home tonight," Ewen announced, breezing into their chamber just as Felicity finished fastening a ribbon in her hair.

He'd assisted her in dressing this morning rather than call for a maid, and carried up her breakfast tray so she need not encounter more strange vibrations than was absolutely necessary.

Had she really sensed his thoughts last

night? Did he really want her for a wife? Or was that just her wishful thinking?

She would never be able to look at Ewen's chest again without hearing his heart beat against her ear and feeling his desire.

Nervously, she tried not to look at him as he paced the room, filling it with raw energy. "Do you think we could find more booksellers?" she asked.

"No. I think the one we saw yesterday was our best hope." With impatience he added, "I wish he'd kept better records —"

Felicity smiled at his abrupt silence and dared to glance in his direction.

He made a wry face as he noted her laughter and raked a black lock off his forehead. "My sketches and notes are meaningless when I'm working out an idea," he protested. "It's not the same as record keeping."

"Writing out what you did after you've succeeded is the same," she pointed out.

"All right. So when I'm rich, I'll hire a secretary." To escape the subject of his careless disregard of his inventions, he grabbed the blue mantle and threw it over her shoulders. "Right now I must speak with Larch at his foundry. I've an idea that will make some money. And while I'm there I can try questioning him about the materials for the canal lock."

She loved the excitement chasing through

him and didn't protest his haste. She was beginning to understand that he didn't value his genius as he should, that he merely enjoyed the challenge of conquering a problem. Someone really needed to show him that his inventions were important enough to be recorded. If only he would let her into his life —

She stopped to grab the book he had left on the bedside table. She shouldn't. She really shouldn't. After her dream or vision or whatever last night, she knew better than to look at any more pictures. But the excitement had been so delicious, and she'd learned so much more about how Ewen felt . . .

"I'm tempted to burn that thing," he grumbled as he tucked the book under his arm. "It will teach you just enough to make you dangerous."

"I love the idea of being dangerous," she said demurely as they hurried down the stairs.

"That's what frightens me." Without further explanation, he delivered her to the waiting carriage.

The soot from thousands of smoking chimneys already dirtied the snow, and Felicity turned her attention to the much more interesting sight beside her. Ewen Ives was practically bursting with energy. She didn't know what his idea was, but she loved watching his expressions as he worked out the details and explanations in his mind.

"If I had some paper, I could jot down notes of what you're thinking. It's all in your head, isn't it?" she said as the carriage rattled over the cobblestones.

He glanced at her in surprise, as if he'd forgotten she was there. Instead of being insulted, Felicity was elated. He didn't feel the need to entertain, charm, or otherwise garner her favor. Ewen Ives treated her as an independent equal. She could learn to like that very much. If he would let her. If she could persuade him that they could make their marriage work.

"You would have to write fast," he replied. "I think of new ideas as I work over the old ones, and sometimes my thinking gets ahead of my tongue and you'd be lost."

She nodded in understanding. "It wouldn't be easy, especially in a carriage. I'd have ink all over if I tried to do anything proper. But some bound blank pages and a pencil would suffice for notes. I would simply have to force you to go over them later so I could write them correctly."

He smiled at her with such approval that she felt warm the rest of the way to the foundry.

There they ran into an impromptu meeting of Robert Larch, Lord Edgemont, and Ian Campbell, and she felt Ewen's excitement escalate. Now he could investigate all three men at once.

Robert was a barrel-chested man of middle age, Felicity noted as he shook Ewen's hand with vigor. She dodged any such touch by keeping her hands inside her muff. Lord Edgemont bowed to her, and Ian Campbell grinned hugely, making a gesture as if to doff his hat, except he wasn't wearing one. Of the three, only Robert Larch scorned a wig, wearing his fading hair pulled back in a leather string as if he were the village blacksmith.

The men cheered Ewen's arrival and variously looked knowingly or speculatively at Felicity. Shrugging off their curiosity, she let them wander into the shop to discuss whatever men discussed. She could not inquire of lock materials as Ewen could. Instead, she roamed Larch's office. A small grate heated the cluttered room, and she warmed her toes near it while noting the papers on Robert's desk.

Recalling last night's decision to help, she glanced over her shoulder to see where the men had gone. She couldn't see them through the half-open door.

She wasn't a brave person. She'd seldom done anything daring in her life unless she was pushed into it — usually by Christina. But since meeting Ewen Ives she'd learned that touching didn't always hurt and might even be helpful on occasion — as it had been for Percy. Didn't she owe Ewen the same opportunity she'd given Percy?

What if she could find some hint, some evidence that Ewen wasn't to blame for the canal accident? Might he take that information and use it to force the other investors to help him pay for the repair of the village?

It was a remote possibility, perhaps, but surely worth trying.

Keeping an eye on the doorway, Felicity swept her gloved hand back and forth in the air over the desk, searching for anything shocking that might hurt her. Finding nothing, she slipped off her glove and touched a finger to a ledger that was giving off a strong vibration.

Riches. The cash in the secret bank account was growing steadily. His pen wrote quickly over a column of figures. He reached for a second book and wrote a sum of half the amount of the original. What they didn't know wouldn't hurt them. They all had money enough and wouldn't miss this.

Slowly drawing her finger back, blinking away the memory of a man consumed by greed, Felicity fought a churning in her stomach. Weakness engulfed her, but she held steady, refusing to give in to it. Greed was a disgusting sensation, but not harmful or shocking. Mostly, she wanted to scrub her hand to rid it of the imprint of avarice.

Listening for the footsteps of the men returning, she glanced around the room, searching for other objects of interest. She assumed the ledger must be Robert Larch's, but one could not indict a man for greed. She could not even say whom he cheated or if this book belonged to the investment company. It certainly didn't free Ewen from guilt for the canal lock's failure.

Lord Edgemont's walking stick rested against a cabinet spilling over with invoices. Checking the doorway again, reassured no one approached, she tested the cane for violence and finding none touched it.

And jerked her hand away as if burned.

Not violence but fury. And guilt. And worry. A flash of anger at a man standing nearby. She thought it might have been Larch, but she didn't have the strength left to touch the stick again and verify the image.

Lord Edgemont had not been a happy man when he'd held this stick at some time in the past. It could have been an hour ago, or a month, but the anger was strong enough to leave a lasting impression. She had no way of knowing why he'd wanted to pound the heavy knob over some man's head, but that had been the strongest memory imprinted on it.

Trembling, wishing only to sit down and curl up in some safe place until the shivers stopped, Felicity bit her lip and forced herself to keep looking. Ian Campbell was a rough countryman. That had to be his wool cap upon the shelf. No gentleman would wear such an outlandish thing.

This might be the only chance she had. Resigning herself to the inevitability of it, she touched the cap without thinking.

In her mind the cap slapped against a wooden floor and boots stomped upon it in a fit of fury.

Dizzily, Felicity collapsed into a nearby chair and sank her whirling head into her hands.

TWENTY-ONE

Reaching the foundry office, laughing over Campbell's ribald tales, Ewen shoved open the door, eager to return to Felicity. He'd hated leaving her alone, but she would come to less harm here than at the inn.

The sight of her slender figure slumped and swaying on a hard wooden chair sent Ewen into a panic. Shouting in alarm, he elbowed past the men in his way.

"Felicity," he murmured, trying not to terrify her as he scooped her into his arms. "What happened, my sweet?" He collapsed in the chair with her across his knees. She was as pale as death, and her teeth chattered as he wrapped her in his arms.

"I'll call for a physician." Hastily taking in the situation, Campbell backed from the room. The other two gentlemen merely stared with unease.

"No, don't." Rocking Felicity against his chest, Ewen could feel her shudders calm and realized what had happened. She had said the visions weakened her. She'd had a vision.

He should never have brought her here. He was a dolt. "She's subject to the megrims if she becomes too cold," he told the others. "I'll take her back to the inn." If a megrim in any way resembled a headache, it sufficed as an excuse.

Accepting that explanation, the men hurried to heat bricks and find blankets while Ewen carried Felicity outside. She started to protest, but he ignored her remonstrations. She was too weak to even rip into him for leaving her alone in a strange place.

As he lifted her into the carriage, accepted the bricks and blankets, and tucked them around her, Ewen gave Mort directions, said his farewells, and climbed in. He could question Larch later. Taking Felicity to safety was more important than chimney reflectors or lock failures.

"I'm sorry, I should never have left you alone," he said as she stirred beside him. Without asking permission, he lifted her onto his lap again as the carriage rolled precariously down a steep hill. "What the devil could you have run into in that haystack Larch calls an office?"

He could have bitten his tongue after the words escaped. He had no right to shout at her. He knew full well she couldn't help herself. That's why she wanted the damned book. He would scour every store in Christendom to find the thing if he had to. He couldn't bear seeing her suffer. And he'd thought he had some right to ask her to leave her safe world for him? He was a horse's ass.

Weakly, Felicity giggled against his shoulder. "I don't know why you're thinking of horses, but please don't. It feels terrible. Think of your chimney thing. It's much more relaxing."

"You're reading my mind again," he accused her.

"No, really, I'm not. You're just so . . . evocative. I have this strong impression of a horse, and that you're upset, but that's something anyone could see."

Thank God. Leaning his head back against the faded velvet squabs, Ewen relaxed his grip and let her settle more comfortably against him. "No wonder your family cosseted you for so long. You're enough to unhinge a person."

"It's no worse than a headache," she protested. "I overdid it a little today. I'm sure if I practiced enough, I could learn to be stronger."

"Practiced what?" Alarmed, Ewen fought a surge of fury that she should risk herself so.

"Touching, like you said. If I can concentrate on observing and not on feeling, I might put this accursed affliction to some use." She sleepily rubbed her eyes. "It is so demeaning to collapse like that. I didn't mean to alarm you. I need to find some way of remaining strong."

He wanted to shake her until her teeth

rattled for listening to him. One more sign of his incompetence as a caretaker. Instead of shaking her he cradled her closer, until he could feel the beating of her heart and knew she wouldn't fade away before his eyes. "Nothing is worth making you suffer. Don't ever listen to me again."

She slapped his chest with dainty fingers. "And so I won't listen to you now. I'm perfectly fine. And I've learned something." She hesitated. "I think."

Ewen scowled at her. Color was gradually returning to her cheeks, and her eyes sparkled again, but she made no move to leave his arms. That proved she hadn't regained her strength. She needed him. Triumphantly, he adjusted his legs and continued holding her. "You're perfectly fine only because I'm holding you. Don't ever do anything so nonsensical again unless I'm around."

She snickered, and he thought maybe he hadn't phrased that quite right, but she didn't give him an opportunity to reword.

"Robert Larch is keeping two sets of books. I don't know whose books they are, and I know nothing about bookkeeping. I simply know he has a secret bank account in which he's accumulating money that rightfully belongs to someone else, someone he thinks is rich. Maybe several someones."

Ewen didn't really want to hear this. Robert and his cousin, Percy, handled the investment company's finances. They were canny businessmen who had accumulated wealth without any help from family. He admired their acumen. He didn't want to believe them thieves.

But if they were thieves, his own future was at stake. If his investments weren't paying out because Larch had stolen the profits, he'd heave Larch into his own damned furnace. But how could he know for certain that what Felicity had seen had anything at all to do with him?

"What did you actually see?" he asked. "Perhaps you misunderstood."

After she described what she'd seen and felt, Ewen could only trust her interpretation. He still didn't know whose books Larch diddled with, but just knowing he was dishonest was enough to twist his gut with fear.

Plague take it, he couldn't do anything until he had proof. He'd have to bring Drogo up here and have him apply his mathematical brain. Frantically, he calculated how long that would take. Parliament was just coming into session. Drogo wouldn't want to leave London until it was dismissed — too late to save him from bankruptcy. He couldn't afford to hire a bookkeeper. He couldn't afford not to.

"And Lord Edgemont is guilty of something," Felicity said, interrupting his racing thoughts. "I just couldn't quite grasp what.

He wanted to break his walking stick over someone's head, but that wasn't the cause of his guilt. I think . . ." She paused to sort out her impressions. "I think someone told him something, or he found out something, and he was furious and arguing with him. But all along he knew he wouldn't do what he should, so he felt guilt."

"That sounds like Edgemont, all right," Ewen growled, trying to fit this bit of information into the other and not succeeding. "He's crafty as a fox. He might find some way of getting even with whoever angered him, but he'd never let anyone know he was anything but blameless. He has a position to uphold and is very careful of it." Could Edgemont be involved in embezzlement? He couldn't believe it of him. Had he misjudged *all* his investors?

With effort, he returned his attention to what Felicity was telling him. "And Campbell?" he asked, hating to believe the bluff countryman was involved in some conspiracy, too.

"I don't know. He's a very blunt man. He threw his cap down and stomped all over it, but I sensed no guilt, only anger. I told you, my gift is singularly useless."

"Not at all. You've given me insights I'd never have had without your help. I can go from there. I don't want you touching anything else for my sake, understood?"

"No," she said decisively. "I shall do as I

wish, and you have no say in it."

He raised his brows in shock. He'd created a monster.

And a beautiful monster she was, Ewen decided, gazing down at Felicity's pink cheeks and parted lips when she fell asleep in his arms on the ride back to Aidan's castle. Her hair spilled in a golden drift over his coat sleeve, and he spared a few minutes imagining this rare gem was his to have and to hold.

But he wasn't meant to own gems. Dashing all his foolish dreams, Ewen reluctantly accepted that the responsible action would be to deliver her to her rightful caretaker. He would find some way of obtaining a quiet annulment. Money could buy anything. He hated asking his brother for money or explaining why he needed it, but he couldn't allow his chronic lack of funds to tie Felicity to him any longer. He owed so much money that nothing could save him, but at least he could save her.

They arrived at Aidan's crumbling castle far too soon.

Felicity woke with the halt of the carriage. Reluctantly loosening his embrace, Ewen waited for her to wake enough to climb out the door Mort had opened for them.

"It's been a grand adventure," she said sadly, looking at the castle through the open door but not stirring from his lap.

"And now it's time that you return home.

Your family can take care of you far better than I. They need never know what we have done. Drogo can use his influence to have our vows annulled once the solicitor discovers a way."

She paled and her big blue eyes grew wide with shock and what appeared very much like pain. What fantasy had she been creating in her head to make her look at him so? She didn't give him a chance to ask.

With a tearful cry she leapt from his lap into the trampled snow and raced for the castle.

Dashing after her, Ewen growled as the massive front doors opened before he could reach them. Without hesitation Felicity fled through them, as if a pack of wolves were on her heels. By the time Ewen stepped across the threshold, she was racing up the stairs, weeping.

Arms crossed over his massive chest, Aidan blocked Ewen's progress with the look of a gladiator about to pound his opponent into the floor.

"I didn't do anything! I've been a damned saint." Frustration exploding through every inch of his skin, Ewen flung down his hat, stomped his boots to remove the snow, and stalked toward the library. He'd done the right thing, by Jupiter. No one could tell him otherwise.

"You've been gone all bloody night," Aidan

shouted back. "You left me here with that heathen witch, fretting myself to the soul over whether to fetch your frozen bodies from the snow." He followed hard on Ewen's heels.

"We're not fools. We took shelter at an inn." Although Mort had been responsible for that. Ewen wasn't in a humor to be reasonable. He was tired of being treated like an incompetent, selfish child just because he was younger than his blasted noble brothers. And cousin. "Surely you can deal with one lame witch for a few hours. Where have you stashed her?"

"In the cellars," Aidan said with satisfaction, slamming the library door after they entered. "The floors there are made of stone so she cannot poke holes in them."

In another time or place, Ewen might have laughed. As it was, he grabbed the notes Felicity had jotted about convection heat, scanned them quickly, and picking up a hammer, slammed it into the piece of armor that hadn't cooperated the last time he'd worked on the thing. "It's a wonder she hasn't brought the whole damned place down on your head."

"She tried that before I locked her away. She's safer down there. What the devil are you doing?"

The library door opened again, and Margaret appeared with a tea tray in hand. "What did you do to the lass?" she asked threateningly. "She's weeping her wee eyes out, she is."

"I told her she's going home." That seemed safe enough. Grabbing the piece of metal, Ewen shoved past the housekeeper.

Through the open door Christina's angry voice echoed, overriding the quiet sounds of Felicity's crying. She'd obviously escaped the cellar and joined her sister.

Shame and guilt and emotions he couldn't name scalded Ewen's insides, but he continued across the hall to the room Aidan claimed as his own. The sooner he figured out how to make the reflector work, the sooner he could start selling it.

Though the sobs were faint, they were heartwrenching. Aidan's glare pierced Ewen like a knife. Margaret merely gave him a dirty look and hastened up the stairs with her tea tray.

"The lass isn't a weeper," Aidan protested as Ewen flung the metal to the stone floor with a clash and clangor to match that of the bells ringing in the kitchen. "You must have done something to upset her."

"I married her. Isn't that enough? And now I've got to unmarry her." Grabbing the largest piece of armor, Ewen climbed into the cold fireplace and began pounding it into place.

"Devil take it, quit making that racket! You can't walk in here out of the cold —"

From close range, a shrieking feminine voice nearly drowned out Aidan's loud complaint.

"Ewen Ives, I'll cut out your filthy heart and shove it down your throat until you gag!"

Ewen didn't bother climbing out of the chimney to investigate the wielder of that threat. Christina's shrill anger was unmistakable. "I thought you said you'd locked her in the cellar," he snarled at Aidan.

"Aye, but the ghosts keep letting her out," Aidan admitted dryly.

A broom swatted Ewen's boots with all the effectiveness of a gnat buzzing in his ear. "Get out of there this instant, you reprehensible oaf!"

Ewen contemplated remaining in the chimney for the rest of his life. He gazed longingly into the dark tower above his head. He could reach the roof, climb out, and escape over the hills, never to be seen again.

What the devil is going on here? a familiar male voice roared over Christina's shouts, Aidan's grumbles, and Felicity's sobs. Felicity's weeping rang loudest in Ewen's ears, even though the chimney protected him from actually hearing her, and his brother's thundering bellows obliterated all else. Just what he needed right now — Dunstan.

"Oh, dear," a new feminine voice exclaimed. "I think Ewen has finally found what he sought. I had better go to Felicity."

Leila. Dunstan had brought his unnaturally perceptive witch of a wife. There'd be hell to pay now, Ewen fumed, leaning his shoulders against the chimney's interior and continuing to gaze longingly upward.

Found what he sought? What the hell did that mean? He'd just lost everything he'd ever wanted.

Leaning his head against the cold stones, Ewen shuddered and tried to blot out the image of Felicity's tears, but her unheard cries rang still louder.

TWENTY-TWO

"We'll take the pair of them off your hands," Dunstan said, kicking escaped embers toward the library grate. "I should never have let Leila convince me to leave them here." Nearly as tall as his host but possessed of a burlier build than Aidan's, Dunstan shot his cousin a glare. "I never should have listened to you when you said you'd look after them. What do you know of women anyway? Especially Malcolms."

Ewen hid his misery by scribbling notes on the back of some useless drawings. He figured Dunstan and Aidan could work out their differences on their own. They didn't want his opinion, wouldn't listen if he offered it.

"There's naught wrong with the little lass," Aidan responded, in an abrupt change of attitude. "She's simply disappointed at not finding her book. It's the other female you should be wary of. If you have ghosts in that bonny place of yours, she'll rout them out and bring down the walls while she's at it."

Dunstan snorted. "If she routs out any ghosts in Wystan, they'll most likely be Malcolm ghosts. She can have good long

311

chats with them," he said dismissively, turning his interest to the view out the windows. "Why did you never tell me you had fields up here? How many sheep can you graze?"

Ewen let their talk go on over his head. The chimney mechanism wouldn't be expensive to make, but the installation would be costly and noisy. He'd have some difficulty selling such a contraption without a sample. And if Larch was really siphoning off income, he couldn't trust the man to make the parts without cheating him. Perhaps he should stay here and look into Larch's shenanigans on his own.

But how could he let Felicity go and never see her again?

Ewen buried his eyes behind his hand. He had nothing to offer her. Nothing. She was far better off in the security of her home, surrounded by those who loved her.

"You staying here, then?" Dunstan slapped Ewen on the back, knocking his quill pen across the table.

Dully, Ewen contemplated the pen's feather, trying not to remember what he'd done with a similar one, trying not to remember Felicity's breathless moan, or the light in her face as he taught her pleasure. She had no ulterior motives to hide, no games to play, no reason to pretend pleasure at his lovemaking. Her honesty had compounded his enjoyment in a manner no experienced female could have done.

"I've work to do," he muttered, snatching the quill back and trying to remember what he'd meant to write.

"We'll be off, then. Leila is eager to return to the babe."

As his brother walked away, Ewen jerked back to attention. "You're leaving now?"

Dunstan halted at the door and lifted a bushy eyebrow. "Isn't that what I just said? I'm taking the girls off your hands."

Aidan's silence rang with condemnation. Ewen could see it in every tense muscle as his host leaned his massive shoulder against the mantel, arms crossed, waiting to see how this scene played out.

Aidan knew Felicity was Ewen's wife. He waited to see if Ewen would admit it.

Ewen stood up and threw down the quill. "I'll go with you. I need to talk with the manager at the mine in Wystan and look at the canal again."

He couldn't let her go just like that. Impervious Dunstan would never understand that Felicity couldn't be left in strange places, that she needed the shelter of the familiar to ground her against unwanted visions. He could see to her comfort, if naught else.

Then he could look about the canal a bit as he had not done before. Perhaps he was missing something. He would be far better at investigating Larch through the materials he'd made than from the books he'd kept.

"I really ought to scold you. Father is calling me a lackwit for not fetching you sooner. He's bellowing so loud I can hear him all the way from London." Taller than either of her younger sisters, with thick black curls she wore unpowdered, Leila took command of the packing, handing a chemise to Dora to stow into Felicity's portmanteau. "But I'm fascinated by this place. I thought Mr. Dougal a homeless adventurer What have you learned about him?"

"That he's a tyrannical bully who doesn't believe in ghosts, like all Ives," Christina grumbled, kneeling to look under the bed.

"He's lonely," Felicity answered. She carefully folded Christina's pink-and-gray gown with its newly attached lace and laid it in the bottom of her sister's valise. One by one, the things that Ewen had admired and touched disappeared into the open bag. She didn't think she could ever wear them again. "I thought you used your perfume on him. You must know more than we do," she added.

"It didn't tell me anything helpful," Leila replied. "Who are Mr. Dougal's parents? Does he own this place? What is his connection to the other Ives?" With blithe disregard of Aidan's maid, Leila swept around the room, searching for misplaced items.

Felicity had no answers. She'd hardly noticed their host's existence. If she concentrated on folding clothing and searching for lost shoes, she might make it through this minute. The hours must take care of themselves.

"Felicity, dear, I really don't think you can take the bedding." Gently, Leila pried the quilt out of her fingers.

Felicity jerked it back and continued folding it. It was her quilt. Ewen hadn't laughed at it. He'd let her wear it. He understood. He was her *husband*. How could he simply let her walk away?

Because he didn't want a wife. Because he didn't want *her*. And foolishly — silly, stupid child that she was — she had thought he did.

Over Felicity's head Leila glanced questioningly at Christina, who shrugged as she emerged from under the bed with a pair of shoes and dust on her nose.

"Dora, thank you, dear. Be a good girl and fetch us some of those wonderful scones Margaret made, will you?" Leila waited for the maid to leave the room before speaking again. "Felicity, would you like to tell me about it? You are giving off such heartbreaking scents that I cannot sort one from the other. Has one of those Ives hurt you?"

"I am fine, Leila," she murmured, folding the quilt ever smaller. "I'd hoped to find a particular book, but it's been sold and no

315

one knows where. I am disappointed, that is all."

"You're a very bad liar, dear." Leila briskly shoved another garment into a bag. "But I'm still not skilled in interpreting what I smell. And even if I know you're feeling hurt and reeking of — I don't know . . . frustration? — I cannot discern the reasons behind those feelings unless you tell me."

"She's in love with Ewen, but he's a bankrupt rake and Father will never let her marry him," Christina said matter-of-factly, rubbing the dirt from her nose. "Besides that, he never stays in one place for more than a week at a time, and would make a perfectly dreadful husband for her."

Felicity didn't have the heart to protest Christina's inconsiderate portrayal of an agony so deep it couldn't be described. She continued forcing the quilt into a neat little square.

Leila's silence echoed ominously. Felicity ignored it. She could only hear Ewen's careless dismissal of their marriage. They'd spent a night and day together that had changed her entire view of the world and her place in it. Did it mean nothing to him? Had he forgotten how he'd kissed her? He'd given her hope and then tossed her aside as carelessly as one would cast aside an outgrown garment.

At that thought, anger swept her with a force so strong she could barely contain it.

She didn't need any man. She'd find out what Mr. Larch and his partners had done and see if it had anything to do with the canal, and then she'd rub the truth in Ewen Ives' face.

And if he still wanted to marry his Harriet, she'd arrange that, too. She was *not* a silly, stupid girl. She refused to sit back and wait for others to make things happen.

Rather than explode with fury, Felicity whirled on her heel and tore open the double-hung mullioned window of their bed-chamber.

She hadn't expected to see anyone below, but she did, and that was all the better. With all the strength in her, she heaved the quilt over the sill at the target of her fury.

"She's your *wife,* much as you refuse to believe it," Aidan insisted, tramping into the slushy snow on Ewen's heels.

"I'll not ruin her life for my mistake." Ewen threw his bags onto Aidan's horse without waiting for permission to take it. He'd rebuilt the man's carriage and fixed his plumbing. The use of his horse seemed a fair exchange.

"You might consider giving Felicity some say in what happens to your marriage," Aidan argued.

"It's not a real marriage," Ewen insisted, bending over to check the saddle girth.

Without warning, a bulky weight hit him on the head, upsetting his balance and dropping him to the icy ground.

"Sure looks like one to me." With laughter in his voice, Aidan walked away, leaving Ewen to wallow in the snow.

Muttering, he yanked the suffocating object off his head and rose in a single movement. Not until he stood dripping and cold beside the unflappable horse did he recognize what he held in his hand: Felicity's quilt.

Gazing upward, he caught Leila looking out a window with a pensive expression on her face. She lowered the sash without saying a word.

Ewen didn't have time to consider how much Leila knew or how she knew or how much she'd heard before the front door opened and a whirlwind of fury exploded through it.

"That's my quilt." Felicity ripped the blanket from Ewen's unresistant hands. "And I *won't* marry anyone. I'll be a hermit or a midwife or anything but a wife. If putting up with stupid, uncaring, blockheaded men is what it means to be a wife, I won't ever marry, and you can't make me."

She swept back inside, trailing the sodden quilt behind her, leaving Ewen stunned and wondering what the hell that had been all about.

"You'll not make it back to Wystan by

nightfall," Aidan warned as Dunstan checked the luggage on the carriage rack.

"The road between here and Berwick is in good shape. There's a reliable inn there," Dunstan replied. "I'll send Ewen ahead since he insists on joining us. You should be relieved to see the last of us."

Ewen mounted Aidan's horse and ignored the niceties of a polite farewell. He was painfully aware that out of the three women inside the carriage, the one who mattered most wasn't speaking to him, and the other two were probably scheming devious tortures to pry every secret out of his head.

He glanced up at the hulking gray stones of Aidan's keep and wished he could have kept Felicity there a little longer. He could have learned more about plumbing, learned to heat the drafty chambers better, and spent more time listening to Felicity as she worked on his notes. Maybe if there had been enough time, he could have figured out the best thing for them to do.

But time was in short supply.

He could follow Felicity to Wystan or wherever the whim took her, try to understand what it was that she wanted, try to make her understand how unsuitable he was, but he would never again enjoy the simple hours of pleasure he'd known within those walls.

He had the canal lock drawings in his saddlebags. When they reached Wystan he'd look them over more thoroughly. He couldn't dismiss what he didn't want to face any longer. Felicity had been right about that. It was up to him to discover what had gone wrong with the canal lock. If it was his fault, at least he would know why he was working to repair the damage. If it was not his fault, then he could bloody well place responsibility on the head of the guilty party.

Either way, he would never be able to pay back the loan. He would never see Felicity again. The few days of her company left ahead would have to last a lifetime.

TWENTY-THREE

"I can sleep in the common room, but we'll need two separate chambers for the party arriving," Ewen told the innkeeper at Berwick. "The chamber for the two young ladies must have the newest mattress in your possession. If you have none new, you will have to send for one. It must be made up with new linen. I'll cover the cost, but believe me, they'll know if the linen is not new."

The innkeeper watched him warily but nodded. Ewen didn't care if the man thought him demented. He couldn't have Felicity suffering from whatever hair-raising events may have occurred in a common inn bed. The night they'd spent together was branded so firmly in his mind that he thought he'd carry the pressure of Felicity's aroused breasts against his chest to his grave, right next to the image of her clinging to him, believing he could keep her safe. That could mean walking around in a state of arousal for the rest of his life.

He'd galloped Aidan's horse hard to arrive here in advance to make arrangements. He had time to spare before the carriage pulled in. Calling for pen and paper, he retired to the tavern. He had to arrange his thoughts before he lost control of them.

Glaring at the hated paper and ink, Ewen sought words that never came easily to him. He could sketch and plan and hammer and tinker, but he couldn't arrange words in the proper order to make himself understood. But he had to start somewhere. He couldn't be in three places at once.

He wrote Drogo a terse note explaining his fear that Larch kept two sets of books. His eldest brother had invested as heavily in the mine and canal as Ewen and had a much better comprehension of pounds and pence. With an earl breathing down his neck, Larch might be forced into honesty.

Nibbling the worn end of the quill, Ewen tried to think of someone in Edinburgh who was competent enough to search for an aging book. Aidan was the only name that came to mind. Instead of arguing with the damned interfering bastard, he should have asked for his help the moment he'd returned to the castle. His life had been turned upside down at the time and asking for help wasn't something that came naturally, so it hadn't occurred to him.

He didn't like asking for help, he realized. Accepting a tankard from the serving maid, ignoring her blatant attempts to attract his attention, Ewen leaned against the high back of his booth and contemplated his sudden insight. He *hated* asking for help. He'd always gone on alone, puttering across the countryside, taking life as it came.

He had two older, reliable brothers who handled family affairs quite efficiently, and they'd freed him from the responsibility to do anything but what he felt like doing — which was why they thought him useless.

Given that much freedom, with his pretty face and the charm he'd learned early on, he'd done what any young man would — enjoyed the ladies and played. No wonder Felicity claimed he lived in the moment. He had no past and no future.

He no longer wanted to be that feckless gallant.

It had taken an earnest young woman with fear in her eyes and the courage to change things to make him recognize that he wanted more of life than his day-to-day existence — that he *wanted* to be the responsible gentleman she thought him.

Shaken by the realization that he didn't want to go on as he had before, Ewen sipped his ale and tried to organize his gyrating thoughts. Did this mean he really wanted to settle down, to have what his brothers had? He'd never considered a wife and children until he'd been told he must marry. He'd not really thought about them even then except as a hindrance to his freedom.

He had to think about them now.

In astonishment, he realized he wouldn't need a second thought if he knew he could have Felicity for a wife.

That he even considered tying himself to one woman shattered all his beliefs about himself, but once he'd grasped what it would mean to have Felicity, excitement mated with logic and their alliance made excellent sense. If this were a perfect world and he could have all that he wanted, Felicity would be his choice. She would make an amiable companion, an enticing bedmate, and a clever partner in his effort to improve the world. In addition, she offered mysteries he could spend a lifetime exploring. He wouldn't need to seek out one woman for her beauty and another for her intellect. Felicity possessed everything he could ask for in a woman.

The matter of children and a home might be terrifying, but Felicity — he wanted her at whatever cost.

Which was his old selfish self raising its ugly head. He was a hair's breadth from bankruptcy, and until his investments started earning money that wouldn't change.

How the devil did one plan for a future when the past weighed so heavily on one's shoulders?

Since he didn't know the answer to that question, Ewen figured he'd best straighten out the coil he was in at present. Then he should plan for several futures. It was rather like considering all theories and experimenting to see which one worked. He could do that.

He'd start with Aidan. The man had books and must know something of what Felicity sought. Let Aidan bluster around and uncover the owner of every tome in Scotland in search of the *Malcolm Journal of Infusions*. It would give his cousin something useful to do besides spy on people and interfere in what was none of his business.

Ewen's pen fairly flew across the paper as he wrote to his Scots relation.

He'd investigate the matter of the faulty canal lock on his own. He could learn to ask others for help if he meant to plan a future, but there were some things he was more qualified to do than anyone else. He could design a canal, but he could not build it alone. Asking for help in personal matters didn't show incompetence any more than did asking for help in building canals, he concluded. It was simply a division of labor.

He still needed someone to produce and sell reflectors if he was to turn a profit on his idea. He'd ask Drogo for recommendations. He would need to develop a network of new investors. He couldn't trust Larch anymore. A broader road to a much larger world beckoned, and Felicity had opened it.

He shook his head and wondered if this

was how his brothers had felt when they'd found themselves making plans on the basis of their wives' odd "visions." The notion ought to be absurd, but it wasn't. He trusted Felicity.

The arrival of Dunstan's carriage prevented further thought on the problem of how he could win Felicity for his own. Since she wasn't speaking to him, the question was moot anyway.

Maybe he could come back in a few years after he'd straightened out his difficulties and made his fortune, and could woo her in the traditional way — if she made good on her vow never to marry. That would be the gentlemanly — responsible — thing to do.

Ewen watched the women descend from the carriage. He saw Felicity's weariness as she leaned on Christina's arm, and noted how she bravely straightened and released her sister once she was on solid ground. He didn't want to risk a wait of years.

She was his wife already. She needed him. Together they were each better people than when they were apart.

Torn in two by that knowledge, Ewen hurried to the yard to greet the new arrivals. He didn't dare risk taking Felicity's arm in front of her family, but he leaned over to whisper, "May I have a word with you?"

With head high, not halting as she picked her way over the muddy yard, Felicity replied,

"Why, have you decided who it is I must marry?"

"Felicity, dammit, I —"

She dropped her fur mantle at his feet. His boots tangled in the heavy mass, and as he tripped and sprawled in the mud, Felicity swept by him without a word.

Christina stepped over him to hurry after her sister. Leaning on her husband's arm, Leila observed her younger sisters' rudeness without comment, waiting with amusement dancing in her eyes as Ewen pushed his face out of the inn yard and sat sprawled where he'd fallen.

By Jupiter, he was an accomplished man comfortable dealing with people on many levels. He should be able to handle this quandary with aplomb.

And yet, one delicate young lady had robbed him of all his mastery.

"Felicity can be singularly uncommunicative when she chooses," Leila said as Ewen pried himself from the muck.

Uncommunicative, by Jove! Did the woman have a brick head? "I thought she made herself rather clear," he muttered.

"If you have quarreled, you will have to wait until she has wrestled with the problem in her own mind."

"And if she reaches the wrong conclusion?" Ewen asked, rising and shaking out the cloak before he dripped mud across the inn threshold.

"Oh, I doubt she will do that. She has an old soul and a clever mind. She simply needs a little more experience and worldliness to make things clearer to her. She is dreadfully emotional and that muddies her thinking."

"Most of the time she is paralyzingly clear," he replied, clenching his teeth, "and it isn't her thinking that is muddied at the moment." Not bothering to brush off the glob of smelly soil sliding down the leg of his breeches, Ewen stomped into the inn.

Leila laughed, and Dunstan sent him a knowing look. Trying to control his panic and temper, Ewen took a deep breath at this sign that they knew and wouldn't interfere. That didn't mean there weren't countless other obstacles in his path, but he could only take them one at a time.

"All is arranged as you asked," the innkeeper assured Ewen as they entered. "My wife will show the young ladies to their room, and if sir and madam would follow me, I will see that all is as expected."

Effectively dismissed, Ewen remained below, directing servants and baggage and the coachman. He could only pray that Felicity's bed was satisfactory and wouldn't terrify her into nightmares. He had no right to go up those stairs, enter her chamber, and ask her directly, even if he didn't fear she'd shove him out a window before he could ask.

It was better this way, placing barriers in

his path to temptation until he'd resolved his predicament. He would take his chances on Felicity working it out in her clever mind and understanding what even he, with all his experience, had difficulty grasping: They were made for each other like nuts and bolts, drive wheels and shafts. One couldn't work without the other.

If he was wrong, then the only person hurt would be himself.

Felicity wrapped her fingers in the quilt covering her lap as the carriage pulled away from Berwick the next morning. She'd caught scarcely a glimpse of Ewen since they'd arrived yesterday, and those glimpses had revealed a proud, handsome man who had done his family duty and gone about his own business. After she'd refused him, he'd not spared a moment to speak with her privately or showed any particular desire to do so again.

Perversely, she had hoped he would insist on speaking with her, that his Ives arrogance would refuse to acknowledge her dismissal of him in the yard. But he hadn't.

Perhaps he had been charming to her in Edinburgh simply because she was available. Perhaps he really did think her a childish nuisance who should marry elsewhere. Perhaps he had only meant to speak to her yesterday to discuss their annulment.

She hadn't thought her heart could break

any more than it already had done, but tears filled her eyes anew. How could she have been so foolish as to believe an accomplished gentleman like Ewen Ives would have any interest in an insignificant creature like her? She didn't even have the backbone to stay angry at him.

Fighting tears, she knitted her fingers together and watched as Ewen rode his mount past the carriage to scout the road ahead. He sat his horse with back straight and head high, his usual winning smile replaced by sternness.

Disguised behind that mask of aloof gentlemanliness lurked a considerate man who had arranged for her bed last night to be free of unpleasant memories. She'd slept as if she were at home. She really didn't think it was a coincidence that she'd been assigned the chamber with new bedding. She'd rather not think how much that had cost him. Even her own sister and brother-in-law had not thought to carry new linens with them for her comfort.

"Did you sleep well last night?" Leila questioned from the seat across from her.

Felicity didn't know how much her older sister sensed with her gift for smelling character and emotions. She'd prefer not to know until she understood her own heart better. "Quite fine, thank you," she replied. And because she couldn't resist a sisterly tweak, she added,

"The inn apparently provided new linens and mattress so I might sleep undisturbed. Father may owe Ewen for the expense."

Dunstan looked up with puzzlement from his perusal of his agricultural journal. "Ewen? Bought new linens? Why?"

Felicity had to smile at her scientifically minded brother-in-law. Dunstan's chiseled visage bore a rough resemblance to Ewen's polished handsomeness, but they were similar in few other ways. Dunstan was a practical man who got things done, but he wasn't necessarily a man who understood women, let alone Malcolms. She was amazed that he and her complex sister managed to communicate in any fashion.

"Because Ewen knows old bedding is sometimes harmful to me," she replied. She didn't know how better to explain it. And she certainly couldn't explain how Ewen knew what her family barely understood.

Smoothly, Leila interrupted before Dunstan could apply his practical mind to that provocative statement "I think we could arrange to reimburse Ewen for all his expenses in looking after the two of you, but he might be offended by the suggestion. We'll offer him the hospitality of our home while he is in Wystan and see if we can compensate him in other ways."

"He was welcome anyway," Dunstan said gruffly. Giving his smiling wife a thoughtful look, he grunted acknowledgment of some mute exchange and returned to reading his journal.

Felicity sighed at the impossibility of ever achieving that kind of communication with a man. How did Leila do it? Her sister was beautiful and high-spirited and charming, but that didn't seem to explain it.

"There is a new color in Ewen's aura," Christina whispered in Felicity's ear. "Or perhaps it is a lessening of gray so that the old colors are clearer and brighter. It has to be a good sign."

"Unless it is the color of riches, it isn't a helpful sign," Felicity murmured in return. She was grateful for Christina's concern, but it wasn't much help.

How would she ever find out if Ewen's investors held some responsibility for his financial burden if she was a hundred miles or more from them?

Would Percy help? Did she dare ask him?

Could she invite Mr. Larch and Lord Edgemont and Mr. Campbell to Wystan Castle? She couldn't. As the wife of an Ives, Leila would have to offer the invitation. Not that there was any reason for the investors to leave the comfort of the city to visit the remote countryside of Wystan — unless they wished to inspect the nearby mine and canal.

Perhaps if they thought Ewen had discovered something about the lock disaster? Would they come then?

And how could she possibly learn what she needed to know from men who were so greedy and evil as to let another man suffer from their misdeeds? If misdeeds they were.

Biting her lip, worrying the quilt between her fingers, Felicity watched Ewen as he urged his horse into an easy trot along the road.

She might be her mother's daughter, but she had a small streak of her father's ironclad determination in her. If she was to spend the rest of her life unmarried, crippled by this gift, she would find a way to make it work for good purposes.

Ewen had given her the courage to try.

TWENTY-FOUR

Hurrying into the breakfast room of the Ives' estate in Wystan the next morning, Felicity halted in disappointment at finding only Dunstan present. "Where is everyone?" she blurted.

"Ewen left early this morning," her brother-in-law informed her without glancing up from his news sheet. "He said something about finding the pieces of the broken canal lock and checking on the rebuilding."

Felicity grimaced at the realization that even obtuse Dunstan had known her only real interest was Ewen.

"Is the canal very far from here?" she asked while holding out her hand to test a chair.

"A few hours' ride." Dunstan shrugged and sipped his coffee. "He should be back by nightfall, if he does not find a reason to dally." Aware that he might have implied something he shouldn't, he glanced up. "Leila said she'd be down presently. Have some of the plum jelly. It's delicious."

Since the taciturn Dunstan seldom said anything so irrelevant, Felicity had to smile. Her new brother-in-law was trying very hard to grasp the frailties and strengths of his wife's odd assortment of relations. She was grateful he did not scowl at her gloves as he once had, and she appreciated his consideration in not offering her a seat she might not find comfortable.

"I hope she brings Verity down with her." Slipping into her chosen chair, Felicity poured a cup of tea. "Your daughter is adorable," she said, congratulating her host on his new offspring.

Dunstan's rough-hewn features and impassive expression broke into the smile of a proud father. "She has learned to follow us about the room with her eyes and smiles when we tickle her. She's a clever thing."

A clatter on the stairs forewarned of the arrival of Griffith, Dunstan's fifteen-year-old son from a long-ago liaison. The boy burst into the breakfast room with a blast of air from the doors he flung wide. "I'm starved. Did Cook make oatcakes? I want to take some with me when I ride into the village later."

"I believe the proper greeting is 'Good morning, Lady Felicity, and how are you?'" Dunstan admonished.

Griffith slid to a halt, blushed, performed a quick bow that revealed his shoulders had once again outgrown his coat, and after stumbling through a proper greeting, grabbed a plate at the sideboard and began filling it up. "Uncle Ewen said I might go with him to the mine if I read up on steam engines and coal, but I think I will learn more if I talk to one of the miners."

With wonder as she nibbled her toast, Felicity watched the boy inhale enough food to feed a village while systematically outlining his energetic plans for the day.

So this is what it's like to live with an Ives, she mused. Drogo seemed to be the only one of them who actually read books. The rest apparently just dived into whatever project they meant to tackle and learned as they went. It was nothing at all like living with her artistic, sophisticated sisters and cousins. She couldn't remember even her far older half-brothers living such rough-and-tumble lives.

She liked listening to Dunstan's attempt to guide his son's more improbable plans down constructive paths. Many men hadn't the patience to deal with childish enthusiasm, but Dunstan didn't blink an eyelash at Griffith's excited explanations.

It was generous of Ewen to offer to take the boy with him. Did he like children? She thought he might be much the same as his brother, accepting children as small adults who needed guidance. That he hadn't yet strangled Christina showed he had a certain degree of patience.

Leila arrived carrying her two-month-old

daughter. Setting aside her teacup, Felicity leapt up to take the flailing infant while Leila filled her plate. "I love that she has dark hair like yours, Leila. And her eyes are nearly as dark as Dunstan's."

"I'm no longer the only black-haired Malcolm," Leila agreed, stopping to kiss her daughter's forehead and elicit a drooling grin.

"Dunstan, you shall have your hands full." Cuddling the blissful infant, Felicity looked up to tease Griffith. "And when you are a grown gentleman, you shall have to escort her about London and teach her to behave. A man can't be improper with a little sister about."

"What if she smells stuff like Leila?" Griffith asked. "Or knows things she shouldn't like Aunt Ninian? I'll never explain it to my friends."

"She's just as likely to bury her nose in books like Drogo or Felicity." Leila took her place beside Felicity so they could share Verity's smiles. "Let's not ruin our enjoyment of today by fretting over tomorrow."

Bouncing her niece, Felicity pondered Leila's wise words. She'd spent her life fretting over things she could not change, hiding in corners to avoid the unexpected. It had not helped or made her any better.

Ewen was right. Instead of trying to change her gift, she must learn to adapt to it.

The infant in her arms gurgled and patted

Felicity's cheek. That seemed sign enough that she had made the right decision.

"I hear you've wed your heiress, lad!" The mine manager pounded Ewen hard on the back, nearly knocking him into the icy canal. "You work quickly."

"How did you hear that?" Irritated at having his thoughts interrupted, appalled that the scandal had traveled so fast, Ewen dug in his boot heels and gazed over the fully operating canal gears, trying to ponder design failure, Larch's fraudulent accounts, and Edgemont's guilt. How did they all fit together?

He could do nothing about investigating the other investors while they were two days' journey away. But while he awaited a reply from Drogo, he might poke around here and find out more of the catastrophe that had brought all this down on him.

"Percy, of course," the mine manager informed him. "He wants to know the date they can expect your investment in the new equipment." Seemingly oblivious of Ewen's ill humor, Mick rocked back and forth, watching in satisfaction as the lock lowered a barge of coal to the next level on its journey out to sea.

"The marriage is supposed to be a secret until we reach London," Ewen improvised hastily. "I can scarcely discuss dowries until we've announced the marriage."

"Of course, of course." Following the path of Ewen's gaze, Mick studied the lock. "You're not thinking that gear will give way as the other did, are you?"

"It seems to be working just as it should." Relieved to be off the more ticklish subject, Ewen returned to his previous thoughts. "It's nearly identical to the earlier design. I cannot fathom how the first one broke. Were there any witnesses I could talk to?"

"Edgemont questioned the barge driver who was in the lock when it collapsed, but the barge is long gone. The man who operated the lock is up on the platform now, if I don't mistake. And there were a few idlers like the ones over there fishing, but I misremember who they were. Plenty of witnesses. The lock filled, the gear snapped, and all hell broke loose. Lost the load of coal, we did."

"I don't suppose there were any remnants of the gear washed ashore?" Ewen asked. The incident had seemed remote to him at the time. He'd been in Bath working on a new design. But faced with the wall of water inside the lock now, he could see the potential for danger. It was a miracle the fishermen had escaped unharmed and only a few chickens and pigs had lost their lives.

"Any old bits would have sunk to the bottom with the coal, I should think." Mick took a contented puff on his pipe. "If there were any parts left, Edgemont has them. Glad he calmed down enough to let you re-design the thing. For a while there he wanted you hanged."

That knowledge didn't ease the churning in Ewen's gut. It merely made him wonder what had changed Edgemont's mind and given him something new to fret about.

"Thanks, Mick. And thanks in advance for having those papers drawn up for me. I'll be out tomorrow to pick them up when I show my nephew around the mine." Ewen watched as the lock closed as it should and the barge continued safely down river. "Before I leave here, I think I'll talk to a few people." He strode off in search of answers.

His interview with the fishermen and the lock operator didn't reveal anything new. The gear had cracked, then bowing beneath the weight of the water, it had fractured completely. The gate across the canal had sagged, the water had roared into the lock, and, ultimately, the whole lock had failed, releasing a pent-up flood.

It had all started with his gear. Why in the name of all that was holy should it have cracked? He'd designed it to bear up under heavy pressure, and the river hadn't been high at that time of year.

Stopping to stare blankly at a new house under construction along the riverbank, real-izing the money he'd borrowed had gone into the rebuilding, Ewen pulled out of his fugue enough to study his surroundings.

"It's a muddy mess, but it will be fine when the work is done," a lanky villager commented, as if following Ewen's thoughts.

Ewen took no offense at the intrusion. "I remember a pretty cottage with flowers here. A bit of grass and a garden, and it will be right again."

"Aye, but the money has to go for pigs and chickens, not flowers. The wife was heart-broken at the loss of her roses, but she likes the new house. Lot less drafty. It's a good thing you're doing, Mr. Ives. Many another wouldn't have owned up to it."

"And I still don't," Ewen admitted. "I can see no reason for the lock to have failed. But a wife cannot go without a home, can she?"

"Well, some might, but not mine. Our children are grown, but she's still nesting. The grandchildren stay the night often, and she wants nice things for them. After all these years she's had to do without to make ends meet, a home is the least I can give her. I'm not usually a hard man, but I'll do what it takes for my woman."

"That's the secret of a happy marriage, isn't it?" Ewen mused aloud. "We do things we might not have done on our own to make our wives happy, and they give what we need in return." He'd already recognized that Felicity offered him opportunities as wide as the horizon. A wife like that wouldn't be a burden but a benefit. Despite his lack of wealth, he possessed a few qualities he could offer her in return. He *balanced* her, as she'd said.

All his jumbled thoughts and fears finally snapped into place like a good design once all the parts were arranged properly.

The older man chuckled. "Aye, and the women know what it takes to make us happy. Men are simple. It's the womenfolk who are difficult to ken."

"Because they insist on talking about things, and we don't listen," Ewen said with a sense of wonder. Perhaps Felicity didn't hate him. Perhaps he'd simply misunderstood her reaction.

Ewen clasped the other man heartily on the shoulder as hope returned in a rush, much as the river poured from the canal lock. "Thank you very much, sir. I'm just learning about marriage, and you've made it simple for me. I'll ask my sister-in-law if she can spare some of her flowers for your wife. Her family believes that plants belong to the world, and they are always willing to share."

"You'll win a friend forever if you can do that, sir. I wish you well of your new bride. If she's half the pleasure mine is to me, you've chosen wisely."

Feeling as if he might explode with something he could not name, something that expanded inside his chest like a hot air balloon, Ewen hurried to find his horse.

He needed to know for certain whether or not Felicity wanted to be his wife. If she did . . . If her coldness toward him simply meant he'd not regarded her feelings as he should have . . .

He had a lot more to learn about women than he'd realized. He knew how to charm them and how to leave them. He'd not learned how to keep one. He could spend a lifetime learning with Felicity, if she'd let him.

This time he identified the emotion swelling within him: the heady excitement of new discovery.

Sitting in the castle's great hall before the roaring fire, waiting for dinner with a book in her hand, Felicity glanced up as the front door burst open. The room was large and shadowed and she was small and tucked into the winged chair, so she didn't expect the new arrival to notice her immediately.

Instead she admired Ewen as he cast off his caped greatcoat, soaked from a sudden spring squall. His black hair glistened with moisture, but he'd apparently taken time to retie the ribbon of his queue before he'd entered the house. He was wearing the dragon vest and a fairly sober green riding coat that emphasized his height and square shoulders. The folds of his jabot were mussed from his ride, his boots were mud caked, and dirt had splashed the frill at his wrist, but all in all he presented a dashing figure.

Ewen reacted with typical Ives energy as his brother materialized from the study to greet him, pounding Dunstan on the back and launching into some involved discussion. The two tall, dark-haired men made a striking picture against the massive tapestries and towering windows of the front hall. They could easily have sported medieval chain mail and carried lances as their ancestors must have, but they fitted equally into this modern world of business and science.

She'd once thought Ives men cold, but knowing them better now, she could see the affection and respect behind their reserve as the brothers approached the fire. They relaxed in each other's company and spoke in short sentences because they understood each other without need for deeper explanation. Despite their fractured upbringing, Felicity understood that all six Ives brothers would stand beside each other, right or wrong, no matter how much they might argue, fuss, and fight behind family walls.

Even Aidan, she realized, was not exempt from family loyalty, cryptic though his relationship to the others might be.

"They stand together in the same way as Malcolms," Leila whispered as she and Christina passed by Felicity's chair to take places on the sofa. "To harm one is to harm them all. It's a good thing they have no foes."

Accustomed to Leila's ability to sense her thoughts, Felicity nodded agreement. "If they have no foes, it is only because others do not see them as we do. Once the world learns of the power they harbor within their minds, enemies will appear."

Leila looked startled at this perception and Christina smirked, but the men had come within hearing and neither commented. Abandoning the garden diagram and chart of flowers she'd picked up, Leila kissed her husband's cheek as he took the seat beside her. "You smell of mud, dear. Are you really thinking of planting the fields here?"

"Someday. They'll take a great deal of marl and a few years of root crops before they'll produce well. Don't worry. I've hired someone to look into it. We'll be traveling south to Drogo's estate as soon as the babe's ready."

Leila cast a glance to Felicity and back to Ewen, who hovered near the fire, warming his hands. "We can all travel together. That will be lovely."

Ewen looked up but didn't respond to the challenge. Felicity admired his fortitude in resisting her sister's manipulations. To argue with Leila would be fruitless.

"What are you reading, dear?" Leila asked, indicating the book in Felicity's hand. "Surely there is nothing interesting in that ancient library."

Felicity glanced at the cover as if just realizing she had the book in her hand. "*A Malcolm Manual on Midwifery.* I think I need something more modern, though. Some of this is little more than superstition."

"Midwifery? Papa would be appalled. That's not proper reading for a young lady." Leila made no attempt to remove the book and returned to jotting notes on her diagram.

Beside the fire Ewen stiffened and reached for the decanter on the mantel. He'd not shaved since morning, and the shadow of his beard darkened his jaw much as the flickering light hid his expression.

Felicity wished she could read his mind. She'd like to know if he understood that she meant it when she said she would stay here and marry no man. It might take years for her to learn to use her gift wisely, and if she couldn't have Ewen by her side to help her, she'd rather do it among family and people she trusted.

She would wait for him, if that's what he wanted. But she'd like to know if she was foolish in believing he had an interest in her and that he might someday return.

Having poured his brandy, Ewen propped one elbow on the mantel and sipped. The piercing look he sent her from beneath his drawn eyebrows shot straight to Felicity's heart.

At least she wasn't an invisible nothing in Ewen's eyes.

TWENTY-FIVE

"Will you trip me in the mud again if I ask to speak with you privately, away from your sisters' prying eyes?" Ewen whispered as he pulled out Felicity's chair from the dinner table. She could feel his lean length and masculine heat against her skin as surely as if they touched.

Since Christina was watching them with amusement from across the table and nothing escaped Leila's observation, Felicity couldn't reply. She merely shivered at the touch of his breath on her nape. The intimacy of his request caressed her jangled nerve endings. She'd never had an assignation with a gentleman, if that's what he was requesting.

Ewen took his seat at Leila's right hand and Felicity's left. Despite the rakish appearance of his mussed jabot and the dark shadow of his beard, he was all that was proper as he assisted Felicity with the dishes the servants offered and carried on a lively conversation that included everyone. Only Felicity could sense his tension.

Had he discovered some means of undoing their marriage? Or uncovered the reason for the lock's failure? Surely he wouldn't discuss the lock privately with her. He would haul Dunstan off to the study and consult with him over the best means of dealing with the problem.

It must be their marriage he wished to discuss.

She could scarcely swallow her food as the evening progressed. Griffith talked excitedly of the morrow's venture to the mine, and Ewen didn't excuse himself from it, so he wasn't planning on leaving immediately. They had time to find a means of talking unheard

But it wasn't just her sisters who stood in their way. After dinner, Dunstan insisted that Ewen retire to the study to discuss some family matter that he didn't think concerned the ladies. Even after the men finished their discussion and rejoined the women at the fire, Ewen had to listen to Griffith regale him with all he'd learned that day.

As Griffith wound down, Leila urged her sisters to go upstairs with her and leave the men to themselves. It all seemed an elaborate plot to keep Felicity from learning what Ewen wished to tell her.

Gnawing at her bottom lip, fretting over how she could possibly see Ewen before breakfast the next day, Felicity scarcely paid heed to Leila and Christina as they played with the wide-awake infant in the nursery. At this rate, Felicity would have to wait until everyone was in bed before she'd be alone.

"Poor Verity will never sleep if you overexcite her," Felicity warned, picking up the book on midwifery she'd carried upstairs with her. "I'm tired and off to bed."

"Wait, and we'll go with you. I've some gowns that no longer fit me that the two of you must look at to see if you'd like them made over for your use." Returning the infant to her nurse, Leila swept them from the third-floor nursery and downstairs to the wing of the castle reserved for visiting ladies.

Leila was doing this on purpose, Felicity decided, resisting the urge to tell her sister to take a flying leap off a broomstick and leave her alone. Leila sensed something, but she couldn't possibly know about her improper marriage. She would have to be patient and wait her out.

By the time Leila and her maid had finished dressing and undressing them in various day and evening gowns, Felicity was on the verge of tears from pent-up frustration. Even Christina had grown impatient and stormed off, carrying an armload of silk and muttering.

"Christina really needs to marry Lord Harry and settle down," Leila said reflectively as the bedchamber door slammed shut behind her sister.

Felicity strained to hear as Christina stopped to speak with someone in the hall. A male voice replied. *Ewen.* He had braved the ladies' wing in search of her. Disappointment welled within her as she heard the sound of his boots retreating. Apparently he'd been warned away.

Satisfied that they wouldn't be interrupted, Leila turned away from the door to examine Felicity untying the bodice of a peacock-blue gown. "A lighter blue kerchief, I think. Give it to Marie, and let her see if I have something suitable. You look as if you're ready to drop from exhaustion. Marie, help Felicity with her corset and put her to bed, would you?"

Before she could find the words to argue, Felicity was enveloped in a night shift and urged between warmed sheets — Leila's way of preventing her from seeking Ewen, no doubt. With the lamps doused and the room quiet, she sank into her familiar mattress — and fretted.

At this rate, she could spend the rest of her life wondering what Ewen might have said to her if they could have stolen a private moment together. If it was bad news, she wanted to know it right now so she could plan for the future. She didn't want to spend the night wishing and hoping for something she couldn't have. If she was to have no use for the book of erotica she'd hidden in her bed table drawer, she may as well burn it.

What she wanted was to spend the night with Ewen. What did it matter if she could never be his wife, since she would never marry anyway? She hated her lonely bed. Throwing off the covers and seeking her slippers, Felicity couldn't lie to herself. It wasn't just escape from loneliness that she sought.

She didn't want to die a virgin.

Not daring to think too hard on what she intended, Felicity pulled her fur-lined mantle over her night shift and cracked open her chamber door. A candle flickered in a niche near the stairs. She heard no voices.

Unlike Aidan's primitive keep, Wystan Castle had been expanded to the inner baileys. The immense structure of solid blocks of stone contained a maze of paneled, tapestried corridors and chambers. Dunstan and Leila shared a suite at the top of the side staircase that led to this family floor. Beyond that was the sweeping main stairs, and past that the wing for housing male guests. She'd found Ewen's chamber in her explorations earlier that day.

Deciding the events of the past week had probably driven her quite insane, Felicity lit a candle from the hot embers of coal in her grate and, carrying the baron's book, slipped into the corridor. If she met someone, she could say she was on her way to the library. No one would believe an insignificant, bespectacled mouse could be embarking on a lovers' tryst.

Of course, it was only a lovers' tryst in *her* mind. Ewen probably meant to tell her he'd discovered they weren't actually married and to apologize for any inconvenience he had caused.

But at least then she'd *know*.

Felicity suspected the corridor must be growing in length as she tiptoed past Leila's room and miles of darkness still lay spread out before her. Surely it hadn't taken her this long to traverse the hall earlier today. Maybe it was a magical castle and the farther one walked, the farther one's destination became.

Finally she reached the door she sought. She took a deep breath and listened for anyone within. Light flickered from beneath the door, but that could be the fire a maid had lit to warm the room. Should she knock? Test the knob?

A bolt slamming below and footsteps echoing against a slate floor startled her into action. Without waiting to see who it was or if they intended to come up the stairs, Felicity hastily turned the knob and almost fell into Ewen's bedchamber.

Sitting up in bed, naked above the blanket drawn to his waist, Ewen looked up, startled from a sketch he was scribbling.

Paralyzed by her first sight of his bare, powerful shoulders, afraid to look too hard at the sculpted planes of his wide chest, Felicity couldn't speak. Couldn't even remember what she had come to say.

Cautiously, Ewen set his pencil beside a

quill and a vase of Leila's famous roses and let the sketch flutter to the floor on the far side of the bed. "Felicity? I had thought Leila would have guards posted up and down the hall by now. How did you get past them?" When she did not speak, he sat up straighter and the sheet slid to his hips. "Is something wrong?"

Yes. No. Who knew? Feeling more than a little foolish, she tried to clear her throat, but she must have swallowed a mouse. And a cat. Like the lady in the nursery rhyme. Words couldn't emerge past the menagerie in her throat.

"I'd get up, but I don't think you're ready for that yet." Amusement began to dance in Ewen's dark eyes as he recognized the reason for her hesitation. "Will you come here? Or at least throw me my shirt?"

Oh, no, she wasn't handing him that shirt. She wanted to see more. Her hands almost shook with the need to touch. His skin glowed bronze and warm in the candlelight, daring her to be bold. Surely touching his chest wouldn't be any more dangerous than touching his hand. Or tasting his tongue.

Drifting toward the bed, enchanted by the play of light and shadow across his hard male muscles, Felicity swallowed the cat and mouse blocking her throat and would have swallowed a bird and a cow, as well, if necessary. "You wanted to talk in private?" she whispered, clutching the book to her chest. She'd say anything, do anything, for the opportunity to get closer to him.

With heart pounding, Ewen watched as Felicity approached. She looked so young with her hair tumbling over her shoulders to her waist. He wished she wasn't wearing the obscuring mantle, but her expression alone could hold him entranced. Her eyes were wide and shining with wonder, and her pink lips had parted so kissably he couldn't look away. Women had regarded him with lust and speculation and slyness and any number of other expressions he could ignore at will, but he was spellbound by Felicity's innocent awe.

"I must talk with you," he replied, "but if you come any closer looking like that, talking is not what I'll do." His voice sounded thick and strange as Felicity's knees bumped against the bed's edge and she hovered within arm's reach.

"What will you do, then?" she asked with innocent seductiveness, eyeing the wide space of the bed between them.

Ewen didn't think that a sensible question, but she didn't seem any more interested in the answer than he was. He held his breath as she bit her lower lip, glanced at him again, then wiggled her bottom onto the bed's edge. The scent of apple blossoms wafted toward him, and he had to bend his knee under the covers to hide what she wasn't yet ready to see.

"I wanted to ask you to consider staying married to me," he blurted out. There, that should shake the intoxicating spell. The words he'd never thought to say certainly shook *him*.

"Oh."

She contemplated him with an owlish expression that Ewen found utterly endearing. He liked it even better that she didn't laugh at the thought of marrying a bankrupt ne'er-do-well. He tried to breathe normally while sitting a hair's breadth from the woman he desired most in the world.

"Does this mean you've been told the marriage is binding and cannot be annulled?" she inquired with a hint of irony.

"No, it means I want to exchange real vows and keep you for my own, but I'm afraid it will be years before I'm able to support you." He hadn't intended to be quite so blunt, but now that she was here, looking like the bride he'd never thought to have, he wanted her answer.

Before he reached for her and put an end to any choice.

"I thought you wished an annulment." She lay the book on the table and settled more firmly upon the covers, her eyes still wide with unanswered questions. "Why did you change your mind?"

"I thought buying your freedom was what a responsible gentleman should do, but it was never what I wanted." Watching the firelight glint off Felicity's golden hair, seeing the trust in her eyes, he knew that offering her happiness was more important than his pride. He had to know what she wanted before he could act.

Rattled when she waited instead of speaking, he ran his fingers through her hair, seeking the assurance that came with physical closeness. She didn't touch him, but she seemed to take pleasure in his stroking.

"It has been brought to my attention that I ought to ask your opinion first," he told her. He would have preferred not baring his soul by asking, but his heart would wither and die if he did not have her answer. "Would you prefer that I obtain an annulment, or could you consider remaining married and trust my ability to pay my debts, even though it may take years?"

She shifted so she could study his face, and Ewen bit back a smile when she had some difficulty disguising her interest in his nakedness. But he wasn't gallant enough not to use every weapon in his arsenal if it meant having her.

"I have no doubt that you will earn your fortune, and I'm not going anywhere that I couldn't wait for years," she answered, a trifle breathlessly. "But I cannot believe you would wish a wife like me. I would be a burden."

When she aired her foolish fear but didn't

refuse him, Ewen leaned against the propped-up pillows and let a tiny ray of hope light the way. "No, you would never be a burden to me. You are my joy." He held out his hand, hoping she would accept it. "But you would be getting a man who can be a blind fool on occasion."

He waited as she studied his hand, then bravely placed hers upon it. He closed his fingers around hers and held tightly while she considered her reply.

"I never thought of you as a blind fool," she murmured, staring down at their joined hands. "You're a man, and you do as men do. But you're the only man who can touch me, in more than just this manner."

With happiness expanding inside him, Ewen tugged, and she slid farther onto the bed, drawing up her legs so that she curled beside him in a puddle of blue velvet. He wrapped his arm around her, and she didn't pull away. If she was reading his lust-filled thoughts, they weren't terrifying her. "I'm not a perfect god of some kind, so if you think it, we are rushing this," he warned in all fairness.

Without her spectacles, she watched him gravely through unfocused eyes, and just that small flaw made his heart go soft and tender. Ewen stroked her delicate jaw with his free hand, and she leaned her head against his shoulder. Thinking that a very good sign,

Ewen didn't deny his urge to press kisses on top of her head.

"I don't think we are rushing anything," she answered slowly, still attempting to be sensible though their blood pulsed hotly. "If we behaved as society required, we would know next to nothing of each other. This way I know you are the husband I'd have, if I could choose."

"You will wait, then?" Heart pounding, he couldn't believe he was asking this of her. Every inch of him froze, waiting for her answer.

"No," she replied.

Ewen gulped and tried to disguise his disappointment, but his heart tore loose from its mooring. The pain was far greater than he'd expected. Tilting his head back to stare at the ceiling, he had difficulty summoning his usual smile and easy words.

Before he could find a suitable response to hide his crashing hopes, she filled the silence.

"I don't wish to wait." She brushed her soft lips against his shoulder. "We're married," she said with soft insistence. "It will only become more complicated if we wait. You might find some easier woman in your travels, and I don't want to miss this opportunity. Does that make me horridly selfish?"

Holding her delightfully rounded form in his arms, Ewen knew he'd never find another like her. He wasn't certain how to convince her, given his past behavior. "You are the least selfish person I know," he said. "I am the one asking too much by asking you to wait. I'm pledging my faithfulness, if that is what worries you."

Lifting her glowing gaze to meet his, Felicity seemed to go all soft around the edges. Ewen's heart beat a little harder in fear and anticipation.

Looking very solemn and young, she clasped his hand with both of hers. "If you wish us to be wed, then I shall vow to love, honor, and take thee in equality for so long as both of us shall live," she promised.

In shock, Ewen recognized the vows of a Malcolm marriage ceremony. He'd attended Malcolm weddings and knew that vow did not come lightly. She'd just pledged to be his wife as if they were standing in a house of God.

Before Ewen could recover his wits, Felicity spread the flat of her hand across his bare chest, and he was lost. Fire licked along his skin and arousal strained his groin. He had done no more than feel the magic of her touch, but he was aflame.

Swallowing the enormous lump in his throat, Ewen repeated her pledge hoarsely. "If you do me the honor of becoming my wife, then I offer what little I have, and that is my vow to love, honor, and take thee in equality for so long as you would have me."

He'd not given thought to a word like

"love." It slid off his tongue without difficulty now. He was more comfortable with desire, and he desired Felicity above all else. Above common sense, it seemed. He was a man who acted in the moment, and this moment was too precious to lose. As soon as the promise left his mouth, Ewen cupped the back of Felicity's fair head and tugged her toward him so that he might seal their vows with a kiss.

The sweetness of her lips seeped all the way into his heart and opened a flood more powerful than the roar of the river. Gathering her in his arms, Ewen drank deeply of her kiss, arranged her slenderness on top of him, and prepared to teach her what she wanted to know.

As much as he would like to fully consummate their wedding vows, he dared not. He couldn't plant her with his child until he'd cleared his debt and his name, and then obtained her father's approval.

But there were many ways in which he could make this night one she could hold warm in her memory until then.

TWENTY-SIX

As she sank into Ewen's kiss, Felicity could do no more than concentrate on the moment.

His brandy-flavored mouth against her lips was all that she remembered and more. Heat and moisture and desire combined with a complexity of tastes and sensations she could spend a lifetime exploring. As she settled against him to investigate the power of his demands, his hand caressed her cheek, cupped her head, and stroked her hair, learning about and claiming her for his own.

His tongue brushed against the seam of her lips, and remembering the pleasure he'd taught her, she opened to him.

Ewen accepted her invitation with a sensual invasion that conquered her mouth and sent tremors of desire to her toes. His urgency caught her by surprise, but the overwhelming sensation of surrendering to his will won out. She couldn't think about anything except his touch, everywhere.

And Ewen's hands did touch her everywhere. At first he stayed outside her cloak, steadying her on top of him with muscular arms and reassuring caresses along her back. Then the pressure of his masculine heat through the layers of bedclothes sensitized her to the shape of him beneath her, and as if knowing that, he grew bolder.

While his mouth and tongue plied their wicked spells, his hands slid beneath the cloak. Felicity gasped as his skillful fingers stroked her bottom through the thin cloth of her night shift. She could feel the imprint of each finger, and if she let herself think, she would have a goodly idea of how that felt to him.

She didn't dare think. Couldn't. She simply responded to sensation, and that sensation included the hard masculine ridge swelling against her belly. For the first time she understood the excitement of traveling new roads, and she loved the freedom to explore that he offered.

Ewen's mouth whispered kisses along her jaw as he shifted position. "I want to lay you back against the bed, but you haven't tested it," he warned, letting her know they'd reached a new guidepost along this particular path. "Will the mantle protect you?"

Nothing else could have warmed her more thoroughly than his thoughtfulness, even in passion. Nodding because she couldn't speak through tears of wonder, Felicity let Ewen lay her in the center of her fur-lined mantle. Through the flickering candlelight she examined the handsome planes of his face. The intensity of all his being focused solely on her thrilled her nearly as much as what they were doing together.

"We are given only one wedding night," he murmured as he leaned close and brushed a curl from her cheek. "I want to teach you that you have nothing to fear from me or what we do together. If I should do anything that causes you pain or alarms you in any way, you are to stop me. Will you do that? If I have your promise on that, I'll not worry so much about shocking you."

"I promise," she whispered, "although if it's very shocking, I cannot always help my reaction."

She loved his smile. It was so confident and tender and . . . appreciative, as if what she had said was wonderful instead of annoying.

He pressed a kiss on her cheek. "Perhaps I should start with familiar sensations first," he murmured. "Ones that can't shock."

Before she could question, he rolled over and grabbed the quill from the bed stand. It had a huge, fluffy feather on it, not the usual goose quill.

A wicked gleam lit his eye as he leaned over her again. "We were interrupted in our experimentation last time. Let's review, shall we?"

Ewen hovered over her in all his masculine glory, square shoulders and bare chest masking any view of the room. Daringly, she stroked the bronzed, taut skin over the muscular hills of her husband's chest.

Love and desire and admiration and a blur of other emotions she could not properly define seeped from his mind to hers as he let her explore. Love? She wasn't certain. Ewen didn't think in such terms. But he radiated warmth and protectiveness and . . . It was impossible to call it love. But it felt just as good.

The feather stroked her cheek. "My turn to touch," he whispered.

She couldn't let him go, not now that she had dared caress him. She let him tease her with the feather, felt its sensual tickle down her neck, anticipated the tingle in her breasts as he traced closer to them. But she kept moving her fingers over his chest, absorbing the sensations of soft dark hair, the flexibility of muscular planes, the response of hard male nipples.

Ewen untied her chemise ribbons to the waist. The heat of his hand so near her breasts jolted her more thoroughly into awareness. Her fingers froze where they were as he peeled aside a corner of her opened bodice, and the feather trailed over the upper curve of her breast.

"I want to see more of you, Felicity," he murmured, pressing kisses to her ear. "Will you let me undress you?"

The mere question shot hot spears of pleasure to her lower parts. She couldn't reply, although she thought she nodded. He seemed to take her silence for the answer he sought.

Slowly, irrevocably, he peeled both sides of her shift away, exposing her breasts to the room's chill. Not that she felt the cold while Ewen's gaze warmed her. His eyes had gone nearly black as he slid the frill of linen off her shoulders, trapping her upper arms against her sides. Her nipples tightened into aching points, and she almost melted beneath the image in Ewen's mind.

He wanted to lick her there!

"You are made so beautifully, my love. You were designed to overflow a man's hands."

His words enhanced her desire. She wanted more than just his hands on her. She wanted what she saw in his head, but she didn't know how to ask for it.

"I'm all out of proportion." She whispered the first thing that came to her mind, an old complaint.

Oh, my, Ewen's smile was like the rising heat of dawn. Laughter and pride emanated from that smile, and Felicity nearly lost his reply in her admiration of the contrast between white teeth and bronzed skin.

"Your breasts are larger than the rest of you only because you are young. In time you will fill out and be lovely and round like your mother. You will fit into my big hands everywhere I touch. For now I will satisfy myself with the promise of your perfect breasts."

Amazed at Ewen's plain speaking, Felicity grew hotter under his warm observation, losing her shyness over her near nudity. He traced the feather around her aroused nipple, and her thighs parted in reaction, which elicited another heart-melting smile of admiration from her tormentor.

"You are so sensitive, I will find it hard to go slowly. I want to bring you to the peaks over and over until you are so lost in pleasure that you will not notice when I devour you."

She did not completely comprehend his meaning, but his tone washed over her in ripples of delight. She cried out in protest when Ewen rolled away again, but he returned holding one of Leila's precious roses. The rich fragrance wrapped around them as thoroughly as the sensual spell he cast.

In the back of Felicity's mind, she knew Leila was perfectly capable of choosing a dangerous scent that would wreak havoc with their senses, just as her mother's candles filled entire ballrooms with smells of peace or happiness. But if Leila had tinted the rose with one of her fragrances, it wouldn't be a harmful one. At best, it would only enhance what was already happening between them. It would be just like her sister to encourage sensuality once Felicity was brave enough to act on her own. An act of approval for her newfound maturity.

She gasped as a petal fell on the hollow of her throat. Looking up, she read the satisfaction in Ewen's face while he tugged another petal loose and let it flutter to her breast.

"There is nothing harmful in the petals, is there?" he asked, watching her closely as he dropped another.

"No, they feel . . . like silk. And smell like heaven. But . . ." She gulped and sought the courage to speak her desire. "I want to touch you," she whispered.

"Anything for my lady." With a tug, he freed one arm from her imprisoning shift, then the other.

Fur caressed her back and shoulders when the top half of her gown fell away, leaving her exposed to the waist. She didn't have time to feel shy. Ewen dropped another petal on her belly, and something lower quickened.

She understood the basics of where this led, but she would rather experience it than think about it. She raised her hand to trace the muscled length of Ewen's arm while he continued dropping petals on her. She was clothed in roses and didn't mind her nakedness. He was still wrapped in blankets, so she couldn't feel any more than the half leaning over her.

"Now you'll only be kissed by roses," he explained, pressing his lips to the petal at her throat.

Sheer delight shivered through her as Ewen

kissed the rose petals not only at her throat, but on the curve of her breast and in the hollow between and —

His mouth closed over the tip of her breast, and his tongue licked her aroused nipple.

Lightning struck and electricity sizzled straight to the place still concealed by the folds of her shift. He didn't release her at her cry but nuzzled further, suckling and kissing until her hips lifted and petals floated everywhere.

When she dug her fingers into his arm and whimpered for something she couldn't name, Ewen filled his hand with her other breast. He teased the nipple with his thumb, and she saw — oh!

Felicity closed her eyes but the image didn't go away. She saw what he wanted to do next. Saw what he kept hidden beneath the covers. Understood how it would feel to him to ease the pressure where moisture flowed between her legs. He craved it, needed it —

Ewen suckled deeply of one breast while his hand squeezed the other encouragingly, causing the ache between her legs to grow and spread.

The image of Ewen covering her with his body, filling her with his heat, elicited wild and uncontrollable urges. Felicity cried out in alarm as the sensation built, but Ewen didn't hesitate. He took both of her breasts in his hands, massaged them until she quivered, and covered her cries with his mouth. His tongue filled and invaded. Her hips writhed, her womb spasmed, and pleasure spiraled upward and spread to her fingers and toes and spun her head until she nearly fainted from pleasure.

Barely conscious, she collapsed against the fur. As the feverish heat of her skin cooled, languor followed, and Felicity wanted no more than to curl up in Ewen's welcoming warmth and sleep.

His chuckle warmed her ear. "I didn't think it possible to experience anything new in an act as old as the ages, but you, my wife, have gifted me with a rarity."

Sleepily, she raised her eyelids to study him, but he was smiling fondly, so she needn't fret. Basking in the title of "wife," she closed her eyes again. "How?"

"Most women do not reach the peaks from the simple acts of kissing and fondling. I cannot wait to see how you respond when I claim you fully."

Heat flushed her cheeks as comprehension came to her.

He hadn't even touched her in the place where men and women joined. And the male part of him that matched the womanly part of her was aroused and in need of release. He craved the pleasure he had given her, but she sensed that the act he desired wouldn't be so gentle a pleasure as hers had been.

"Will you claim me now so I might know what it is like?" she asked, still dazed by all the impressions she was absorbing.

Ewen kissed her forehead and cupped her breast in his palm. "Not tonight. I've given you enough to keep you entertaining warm thoughts of me until we can be man and wife in the eyes of the world. I'll not damage you by giving you a child we cannot yet support."

That hurt, but she could not tell if it was because she objected to the incompletion or because it physically hurt him to deny her — and himself. But he liked her touches. That much she knew. Perhaps if she touched and fondled as he had . . .

He'd spread her mantle on top of the blankets. He hid his nakedness beneath the covers so she couldn't even feel his toes. That could be corrected.

Fully awake again, fascinated by the fleeting impressions she received when she touched him, awed by the power of what he had just done to her, Felicity rolled from the bed Calmly, she let her shift fall to the floor.

Captivated, Ewen watched her beauty unfold from the chrysalis that had protected her. Her high, full breasts narrowed to a tiny waist and rounded hips in a perfect hour-glass. Silver-blond hair tumbled to her waist, a lighter shade than the curls between her thighs. Pert pink nipples pouted as temptingly as her full lips. She was every man's dream. He didn't know why she thought herself insignificant. She was magnificent.

Felicity wrapped her mantle around her shoulders, threw back the bedcovers, and slid between the sheets.

The fire in her fingers stroked him.

Ewen almost choked on his gasp when her hand lingered where he most needed her. He'd tried to protect her from his lust, but she knew what to do as if born to it.

"You like that!" she murmured in awed pleasure at his reaction. "I can do for you what you did for me."

"Felicity —" He ground his teeth to keep from groaning when she boldly circled him with her fingers and stroked him exactly as he liked.

"Show me more," she whispered excitedly. "Tell me what to do. I've never touched anything so fascinating. You're so *big*, and hot, and hard . . ."

He would be rolling on the floor laughing at her pornographic description if her perceptive fingers hadn't manacled him to the bed. Between choking laughter and moans, he couldn't speak. But that didn't seem to matter. She knew when to increase her speed, how to intensify the pressure, and knew instantly the moment he needed a squeeze at —

He spilled his seed all over her fair hand,

and reached to grab her shoulders before she shied away in surprise or terror.

"Felicity, you are a gift from heaven." He pulled her down so he could spread kisses across her cheek. "I have found the only woman in the world who knows exactly what I need, and if I have to hire myself out as a slave to keep you, I will."

She stared at what must be his crazed expression before she slowly relaxed and teased him a little more with her fingers.

"I did the right thing?" she asked hesitantly.

"You did the right thing perfectly. I think your gift has just found its purpose." Ignoring her shocked expression, Ewen tugged her down. "Snuggle closer and let me kiss you before I send you back to your room. This night will have to keep us warm for a long time to come, so let's do it properly."

"I don't see why we can't just tell everyone we're married," she argued sleepily.

Put like that, he didn't either. He'd forgotten every reason he'd imagined to keep away from her. As her silken thigh brushed his rough one, Ewen surrendered the fight with a groan of pure pleasure. "I'll go to London and tell your father everything. I just wish I had found something at the canal to prove my design wasn't at fault, but I suppose there is no changing my debts at this point. So your father will simply have to bellow and try to take off my head."

"And we must hope he does not find a solicitor to nullify our vows. I'd hate to have to run away to Scotland all over again."

So would he. Tucking Felicity into the curve of his arm, Ewen began to dream of a future he'd never thought to have.

TWENTY-SEVEN

Waking alone and in her own chamber the next morning, Felicity wondered briefly if she'd dreamed the events of last night, but the burn of Ewen's whiskers lingered on her cheek and breasts. Blushing, she pulled the covers around her and contemplated never leaving her bed again.

She was married to Ewen Ives. It seemed much too incredible to believe in the bright light of day. It didn't help that the vows hadn't been said before family or consummated, or that she still woke alone.

Vaguely uneasy at the thought of being a wife only in private, she flung back the covers. It was just a matter of time until Ewen spoke to her father. She could pretend she wasn't Mrs. Ewen Ives in public a little longer.

Casting off her uneasiness as she washed, Felicity refused to think of complications. It might take years, but Ewen would eventually settle down and provide a home for her. He could invent and she could take notes, and they wouldn't have to pay a secretary. Anything was possible.

By the time she arrived downstairs, Ewen

and Griffith had left for the mine. She hid her disappointment that he hadn't waited, but it would have been difficult to pretend nothing had happened between them if he had.

She spent the morning persuading Leila that they must leave for London soon. She wanted to be with Ewen when he approached her father. The Marquess of Hampton was a terrifying man, but he could also be reasonable. Eventually.

While Leila tended to the baby, Felicity sat before the fire in the great hall with a newer book on midwifery that must be from her cousin Ninian's collection. She jumped in surprise as the door knocker rattled. Ewen couldn't have returned already, and he wouldn't knock.

An aging servant emerged from a side room to open the door just as Leila descended from the upper floor. Relieved that she didn't have to act as hostess, Felicity watched with curiosity as the servant ushered in the new arrivals.

"Sir Percy Larch and Mr. Robert Larch," the old man intoned, accepting the gentlemen's cloaks and hats.

A quiver of anxiety rattled Felicity's nerves, but she remained where she was while Leila swept across the huge hall to greet their guests. Would the visitors mention her and Ewen's "marriage"? How would she explain to Leila? Could she ask them to keep it quiet if she got them alone?

"Good morning, gentlemen. What brings you here on such a fine day? James, fetch us some coffee and tea, would you?" With the charm she'd used to conquer society, Leila led the men toward the fire.

"We're looking for Ewen," Sir Percy said easily. Then catching sight of Felicity, he smiled and bowed. "Good morning, my lady. This is a pleasure."

Still uneasy, Felicity gestured toward a seat nearby. "It's good to see you again, sir. Ewen is at the mines with his nephew. Stay and have a bite to eat before you hare off looking for him."

She didn't like the way Robert Larch remained standing, pacing back and forth before the fire. She knew that these men hoped to obtain further financing from Ewen, but surely they hadn't come here to collect their funds. Had there been some new disaster to visit on his head? Perhaps it hadn't been Robert's avarice in the books and someone else had stolen from them?

While Percy and Leila exchanged pleasantries, Felicity watched the large man at the fire. Robert was older than Percy, possibly in his forties, but still a strong, active man. Today he had condescended to wear a modest bagwig, but he appeared uncomfortable in it. She suspected he was more at ease in his foundry wearing the crude dress of his workers.

She admired Ewen for his impartiality, but after what she had seen in Robert's office, she didn't trust this friend of his. If she touched Robert Larch, would she see the guilt he harbored? Did she dare?

"I'll fetch Verity and show her off," Leila said gaily. "I have no idea where Christina has got to. Felicity, be a dear and entertain our guests, will you?"

Setting aside her book and removing her spectacles while Leila dashed upstairs, Felicity wondered what she was supposed to say that would be entertaining.

"I pray you will not mention to Leila anything we have told you in confidence," she said, unable to introduce small talk when more weighty matters occupied her mind. "We are waiting for her to recover her health before returning to London so Ewen might speak with my father."

Percy looked shocked and Robert frowned.

"You did not have the marquess's permission?" Percy asked. "He has control of your dowry, does he not?"

"It's a mere formality," she said, trying to sound confident. "My father will do as I ask. But he would not be happy to be the last to know."

Percy attempted to disguise his concern, but Robert stood with his back to the fire, looking at her as if she were an insect to be crushed.

"Time is running out," he grumbled. "We have located the equipment the mine needs and must have Ewen's investment or find another. He promised us that he would obtain the funds soon."

"He owes the bank because none of you would pay for what your lock has done," she said in a spurt of anger. "I think you owe him rather than the other way around."

"Now, Felicity," Percy tried to placate her, "the lock was Ewen's design. If it failed, then he must be the one to pay."

"It is the same design being used now, isn't it?" she demanded. "And has that failed?"

"Don't waste time arguing with a woman," Robert said wearily. "They have no comprehension of business. We should travel on to the mine while the weather is good."

Felicity wished she could smell guilt as Leila could. The thought of touching the burly man at the mantel repelled her. She wasn't likely to see anything of use even if she did touch him, but she had to try — for Ewen's sake. A man who cheated was capable of other crimes.

"How does the mine pay for the equipment?" she asked with feigned interest, returning her spectacles to her nose so that she looked harmless. "Does the owner deliver it and the mine give a bank note?"

"Robert found a mine in Cornwall with just what we need," Percy answered. "He is to take the funds to the owner and have the equipment shipped to the port here, where it will travel directly up the canal to our mine."

"And I suppose you simply accept any price Mr. Larch names and hand him the money without question, do you not?" Felicity continued studying Robert's expression without looking at Percy. "Did it not occur to you that he might be pocketing a substantial profit for his trouble?"

Stunned by her perception of business affairs as much as by her accusation, Percy didn't immediately reply. Robert, however, looked as if he might turn purple.

"Do you say I cheat?" he roared.

"I say it is very likely that you have in the past, so you might in the future," she said simply, before turning to Percy. "You know my gift. Do you wish me to touch him and tell you what I see?"

Percy looked thoroughly shocked.

Robert pulled back his long coat and propped his fists on his hips. "They hang witches where I come from," he said.

Felicity summoned all her courage. For Ewen's sake, she must do this. Steeling herself, she rose from her chair. She faced Robert with the same pugnaciousness that he showed her, although she shook inside at her daring. "They hang thieves where I come from," she retorted.

As she'd known he would do, Robert grabbed her as if to shake some sense into her.

Felicity swayed at the blast of images and perceptions accompanying his grip, but she remained standing, concentrating on the memory embedded in Robert's hand and not on her reaction to it.

Guilt. His fingers clenched around the broken lock gear that Edgemont had thrown on his desk. The alloy he'd used to make it hadn't held. He shouldn't have used the cheaper material. But Ives always insisted on the most expensive ore, as if they were all as rich as earls. Aristocrats like that didn't know the meaning of money. Let him pay for the destruction.

"You!" Felicity shouted, dizzy with the vision she clung to. "It's your fault the lock failed, not Ewen's!"

"That's a lie! You cannot know that." Robert flung her arm away as if burned.

Still faint from the strength of the vision, sick to her stomach at what she'd seen, Felicity stumbled beneath the ferocity of his gesture.

"Felicity!" Percy jumped forward to steady her.

"Let us be away from here," Robert growled. Heedless of Felicity's distress, he clapped his hat on and prepared to walk away.

"Wait!" she cried. Hoping to hold him

until help came, she pulled away from Percy and reached instinctively for Robert's coat.

This time, when Larch brushed her off, the pain of his animosity struck with such force that she crumpled before Percy could catch her.

Felicity's head connected with the stones of the hearth. Percy's terrified cry followed her into the encompassing blackness.

"If steam can pump water *out* of the mine, can't it pump water *into* a house?" Griffith asked excitedly, following on Ewen's heels as they entered the hall.

"It would require a huge boiler, wouldn't it? We could heat the water —"

Slamming the door closed behind them, still wind-tossed from the elements, Ewen and Griffith stopped in their tracks at the sight of servants milling at the foot of the staircase. A grim-faced Dunstan ran down the stairs, and seeing the new arrivals, hastened in their direction.

Felicity. Ewen had no idea why fear stabbed his heart. He just knew that for the first time in his life, he had someone to care for, someone who was wholly his to shelter, and the responsibility weighed on him. Even knowing his wife's fragility, he'd neglected her to play in the mines as if he were a free man.

Clenching his teeth against terror, Ewen

watched his grim-lipped brother cross the hall.

"There's a physician in Berwick," Dunstan said as he approached. "If you ride fast, you can be there before dark. Take a fresh horse."

"What happened?" Ignoring Dunstan's orders, Ewen scanned the hall for Felicity. She wasn't by the fire with a book in her hand, looking up with a welcoming smile.

"Leila says it isn't just a faint this time. She's hit her head, and we can't revive her. I was off to Berwick, but Leila's hysterical —"

Ewen shoved past Dunstan and flew across the floor to the stairs. His heart had stopped beating the instant his brother had said "faint." *Felicity.* It had to be Felicity. He wasn't going anywhere until he'd seen her.

"What the devil happened?" he shouted as Dunstan chased after him.

"One of the Larches apparently touched her. Just fetch the physician. There isn't anything you can do." Dunstan grabbed Ewen's arm.

Ewen jerked away and kept running. "She's my *wife,* dammit. *You* fetch the physician." Without another word of explanation, Ewen slammed past the maid carrying a bowl of water from Felicity's room — the room he'd taken her to in the early hours after a night more magical than any he'd ever known. He couldn't have lost her already.

Leila glanced up in surprise, but Ewen saw nothing except Felicity's white face against the pillow. Blood seeped through a bandage near her temple, and she lay so still that she didn't seem to breathe. Horror nearly flattened him. They'd physically *hurt* her! How much of her condition was weakness from her vision and how much from physical damage he could not hope to fix?

Falling to his knees beside the bed, he grabbed her hand where it lay unmoving upon the covers — the hand that revealed the world's mysteries, the hand that caressed with gentleness and wonder. Surely her magical fingers could feel him now. "I'm here, Felicity. Wake up and tell me what happened. I'll take care of it. I'll make it go away."

She didn't respond. Terror choked his throat. He couldn't hear her breathing. Ignoring Leila's and Dunstan's shocked stares, Ewen cradled Felicity's face in his palm until he could feel movement. Her pulse beat. Barely.

"Felicity," he whispered, alarm taking root when she didn't seem to feel his presence. She *had* to feel him. She knew his innermost thoughts, understood him far better than he understood himself. She had to wake. He had to find out who had done this to her. He had to fix it somehow —

"Griffith is old enough to ride for Berwick," he shouted at Dunstan over his shoulder. "Send him. I can't leave her."

Feeling Dunstan's hesitation and subsequent departure, Ewen tried to breathe evenly, as if that would force life into Felicity's lungs. He caressed the soft skin over her cheekbone, pushed a curl off her forehead, wrapped her hand in his and held it against his rough jaw.

"What happened?" he demanded hoarsely, not tearing his gaze from Felicity's eyelids. Was that a flutter? Did she feel him yet? Surely the strength of his panic ought to be reaching her. It was clawing through his skin and would become a physical manifestation if she did not wake shortly.

Leila answered softly. "The Larches were here. I went to fetch Verity while Felicity entertained them. Sir Percy started shouting, and I ran back down to find him cradling Felicity on the floor and Robert calling us meddling witches. I didn't see what happened."

Larch! "Where are they now?" Ewen asked murderously. "Where are the lying, scheming bastards?"

"Sir Percy was quite confused. I don't think he harmed her," Leila warned. "He said she had one of her weak spells, that Robert grabbed her, and she started shouting at him. She said something about Robert being guilty, not you. Then Robert brushed her away, and she fell. Percy is quite beside himself. His cousin refused to stay, and I could not hold him."

Bowing his head to the mattress, Ewen fought back tears. He'd told Felicity to use her gift, not abandon it. And she had, for him. He'd been given the grave responsibility of taking care of this fragile creature, and he'd failed her. Failed her utterly. She'd warned him that Larch might not be what he seemed. *He* should have confronted Larch.

"I will do anything if you will wake, my love," he whispered so only she could hear. "I will spend the rest of my life hunting for your book so you may be rid of this terrible gift. I've been selfish in encouraging you to use it. If I can prevent it, I will never have you suffer this pain again. Please, love, hear me."

His tortured plea fell on deaf ears.

"Get up off the floor and take a chair," Leila murmured, touching his shoulder. "We can only wait and see what happens."

He didn't know how to wait. He'd always taken matters into his own hands, made them work, made them whole. He couldn't sit here and watch Felicity's life slip away and do *nothing*. He detested helplessness more than anything.

Frantically, Ewen rose, and ignoring the offered chair took the bed beside his wife. His *wife*. And he'd broken her already. Leaning over Felicity on one elbow, he ran his hand everywhere, touching, caressing, trying to find the place where she had gone.

No response.

He had no idea of time as he tried everything that came to mind, bathing her poor, abused forehead, talking for her ears alone, lifting her arms and caressing her breasts, ignoring the shocked, silent stares of everyone coming and going. She'd been so responsive last night, so eager to learn. How could she lie here so cold now? There had to be something he could do, some touch, some word, some action . . .

Doors opened and closed. Voices swirled around him. Ewen didn't listen. If he could focus hard enough, maybe he would reach her. Maybe she could read his mind again. Feel his heart. Feel his love.

He loved her. He knew what love was now. It was tears and devastation and wonder and pleasure and all the emotions he'd been afraid to experience until he'd held Felicity in his arms. He couldn't lose her like this. He'd die with her, if he must.

A door below slammed so loudly that the old walls shook. A roar of rage reverberated throughout the maze of corridors.

Ewen didn't need to know the voice. He recognized the anguish. Not raising his murmurs over the bellows below, he continued talking soothingly to Felicity and didn't look up when Felicity's father, the powerful Marquess of Hampton, blasted into the room like cannon fire.

"What the devil have you done to my

daughter!" he shouted in a voice that rattled the rafters.

"I married her," Ewen declared without deviating from his concentrated effort to will Felicity awake.

Did he imagine it, or had Felicity's eyelashes fluttered?

"You've killed her!" the marquess shouted in rage.

"No, I've loved her," Ewen whispered, heart in throat as he wondered if they were not the same thing. He hadn't known how badly love could hurt.

Yet it could also heal. His love had to heal Felicity, as hers had restored his life to something worth living.

Her hand twitched in his.

"I'll have you hanged," the marquess roared.

"Not if you love her as I do." With broken-hearted satisfaction, Ewen watched Felicity's eyelids lift to reveal the crystal clarity he so adored. She stared right at him and her fingers clutched his, before her lashes fluttered closed again.

He loved her, and because of his irresponsibility he'd almost lost her. For her own safety, he would have to leave her with those who could stay with her as he could not.

But if he never did another thing in his life, he would find that damned book of hers so she would never suffer for him, or anyone else, again.

TWENTY-EIGHT

Ewen loved her.

Felicity could feel it in his fingers where they clung to hers. She'd not doubted his love. That he admitted it aloud filled her with wonder, especially with her father roaring like a lion with a sore paw.

But there was something else there, something she couldn't quite interpret. She tried to hold on to Ewen's hand as he drew it away, needing to know what was behind the sorrow she felt in him.

Her head ached. Her father's shouts pounded like the ocean against the cliffs. She couldn't make heads or tails of what he said.

Ewen sounded curt and clipped. Leila's voice sang like musical notes between the shouts of the men. Christina said something sharp, but the voices turned against her.

If only her head didn't hurt so. She wanted Ewen's soothing caress back. There was something she must tell him . . .

Larch. It had to do with Larch.

She tried to speak, but no one seemed to be listening. A gentle hand laid a cold compress against her forehead, soothing some of the pain. The scent of roses wrapped around her. She tried to lift her hand to grab her sister's attention, but both Leila and Christina were speaking in low, angry tones, driving the men away.

She listened for Ewen, recognized his whisky-warm baritone under and between the others. For a moment he bent over her, but she couldn't keep her eyes open. She wanted to tell him not to worry, that she was fine, but the words seemed to come out as a murmur. He stroked her cheek with the back of his hand, and her mouth relaxed in a smile.

He loved her.

He was leaving her.

Panic. She struggled to wake, to shove aside the covers, to run after him. Leila held her back, her words a calming string of notes to which Felicity paid no heed.

She could hear them moving away. Dunstan had arrived. They were going away. She couldn't let them go.

"It's all right, Felicity. They'll just argue and storm about." Leila spoke into the quiet left by the closing door. "You must rest. You can tell them everything later, when you're feeling better. Let me give you this tisane. Ninian always recommends it for aching heads."

Felicity winced as Leila lifted her head, but she drank from the glass held to her lips. She needed to feel better immediately. She needed to see Ewen.

The throbbing behind her eyes didn't ease. She held them closed, waiting for the pain to go away. Clouds of sleep rolled in, and she fought them.

"Not yet, little one. Sleep now. It will be all right." Leila's soothing singsong voice relaxed her.

And she slept, consumed by storm-tossed dreams.

"I thought I told you to stay away from her!"

The angry command and the thud of a door opening jarred Felicity from a drug-induced sleep.

"She's my wife. I have every right to be here."

Ewen. She closed her eyes and drew in the bliss of knowing he claimed her fully and proudly, despite her father's irate protests. Not many men could stand up to her father. Pride eased her fretfulness.

"She's not your wife in England. And she won't be your wife in Scotland for long. I've already written to the Earl of Middlesea. He'll silence the witnesses and untangle the legalities. You bungled it all. If she tells me you tried to consummate this charade of a marriage, I'll see you hanged."

"She's in pain," Ewen exclaimed. "Keep your voice down."

Footsteps moved away from the bed, and their voices lessened as if they had stepped into the hall. But they were too angry to be quiet.

"You're a madman if you think your blustering will stop me or Felicity," she heard Ewen growl. "I didn't want things to happen this way," he continued. "We were on our way to London to obtain your blessing. But if you would throw your daughter away by denying her what she wants, then I'll be happy to take her from you."

Her head ached too much to be certain if this was a good or bad argument with her stubborn father. She simply let the power of Ewen's convictions seep into her and heal her fears. Ewen loved her. He would make everything all right. Ewen always fixed things.

"I've arranged it so you'll go straight to debtors' prison should you ever set foot near her again," the marquess shouted. "I've bought your overdue note from the bank. It will take only my command to see you locked up and the key thrown away."

Felicity recognized the cold tone in her father's voice, and she froze, waiting for what she knew would follow.

"No one in his right mind will loan you enough to repay me." Satisfaction colored the marquess's next words. "I promise not to call in the loan, as long as you stay away from Felicity."

She wanted to leap from the bed and race to the hall, screaming protests, but she could scarcely lift her head from the pillow. Her father was the very devil himself. Ewen must choose between prison and giving her up. If he went to prison, he'd be giving her up anyway. Unfair!

Fighting the covers with hands that shook and legs that wouldn't obey, she listened in horror for Ewen's reply.

His tone was as cold and angry as her father's.

"You are a fool if you think Felicity will pay heed to anything you say after this, my lord," Ewen said in a voice that could have halted stampeding elephants.

No one ever called her father a fool. The marquess advised *kings*. She marveled at Ewen's temerity at the same time that she held her breath, waiting for him to continue.

"You are a fool to suffocate and imprison your daughter behind closed doors." Ewen lowered his voice to one of reason. "What you should be doing is looking for the book she ran away to find, the book that will allow her to stand on her own."

Felicity breathed a sigh of relief. He wasn't taking her father's bribe. He understood what she needed. She had feared his sense of responsibility and honor would drive him away.

But her father would have Ewen thrown in prison if he did not leave! Horror returned as

Ewen continued speaking in a low voice that didn't disguise his rising fury.

"I had these papers drawn up and meant to offer them to you in exchange for Felicity's hand." Paper rustled. "Instead I'll trade my entire investment in the mine and canal for the note you hold and for my freedom, so that I might find what she needs."

Stricken by the immensity of his sacrifice, knowing he had worked years and put his heart and soul into building a future with those investments, Felicity gathered the strength to pull back the covers. The voices were moving away. She couldn't hear her father's response. Ewen mustn't give up everything in exchange for a debt he shouldn't even owe. The canal failure wasn't his!

In her haste to follow, her foot caught in the heavy comforter, and she nearly fell out of bed. She knocked a book from the bedside table when she grabbed at it, but the sound was muffled and no one came running. She couldn't hear their voices. They were leaving. She had to stop Ewen.

He was leaving her. She might never see him again. Her father could hide her away forever. She couldn't bear to live without Ewen at her side.

She cried out, but the sound was feeble. She attempted to untangle her foot, but her knees were even weaker than her voice. In frustration she smacked the unlit oil lamp off the table, causing a loud thump of metal against bare wood.

The low murmur of voices returned. Footsteps scurried. Finally disentangling her limbs from the covers, Felicity stood shakily beside the bed, holding on to the bedpost to keep from falling. "Ewen," she tried to call, but the sound wouldn't reach past the door. "Father —"

The door thumped open. In relief, Felicity waited for Ewen to rush in and catch her in his arms and tell her everything was fine now.

Instead Leila swept across the threshold bearing a tea tray. "Back in bed right this minute, young lady!"

"I must talk with Ewen." The words were little more than a frantic whisper. "Please, Leila."

Her sister looked sympathetic but did no more than set the tray on the table and bend over to retrieve the fallen lamp. "The physician said you must rest in bed. I'll not have anything else happening to you. *Maman* would have my head, and rightly so."

"I must tell him something — now." She tried to convey her urgency, but swaying in a nightgown and speaking in whispers didn't lend the proper effect.

Catching her shoulders, Leila gently pushed her back onto the mattress. "It's too late to tell him. He is gone."

"He can't be." Stunned, frantic, Felicity struggled to rise again. She'd just heard them outside the door. She could run after them —

"He had words with Father and stormed out the front door some minutes ago. Now lie down. We need to build your strength back up."

Ewen couldn't be gone. He wouldn't leave without her, would he?

Of course he would. All the fears and insecurities she'd thought to overcome washed over her now. He'd surrendered his only hope of income. He had nothing left with which to build their future. He would be too honorable to return until he had something to offer.

Felicity slid back between the covers and buried her face in the pillow.

In the morning when she was stronger, she would tell her father exactly what he had done. She would never return home again. She would wait until Ewen came back for her.

He *would* come back. Or she'd perish of a broken heart.

Icy rain dripped off Ewen's hat brim as he climbed down from the steed he'd appropriated from Dunstan's stable. In his hand he held the reins of the stallion he'd taken from Scotland earlier. Aidan's forbidding gray castle loomed through the damp mist. He didn't even know if his damned rambling relation had stayed home for a change, but he had to take the chance.

He housed both horses in the leaky stable, covering them with moth-eaten blankets and feeding them oats he'd brought with him, then trudged through the rain and mud to the front door.

The door swung open without his resorting to the clangor of bells.

"Lost her already, did ye?" Aidan asked, waiting for Ewen to drip across the threshold before slamming the door against the howling wind.

"Almost. And I can't risk it happening again. I have to find that book she was seeking. It's too dangerous for her to go about prying into men's secrets."

Aidan snorted and stalked toward the library, where a fire burned in the grate. "She's a Malcolm. There's no stopping her."

"Larch nearly *killed* her. Even Felicity agrees her gift is dangerous."

Ewen hated to see her marvelous gift destroyed, but the danger to her life wasn't a fair price to pay.

"And what do ye mean to do about it?" Aidan asked with suspicion, feeding more coals to the fire, illuminating books stacked haphazardly across the floor.

"Find the *Malcolm Journal of Infusions* I told you about in my letter. She says it contains a formula for ridding herself of unwanted

Malcolm gifts. Nesbitt sold it. I must find out to whom."

Aidan looked at him oddly, but Aidan was odd anyway. The man had a castle and land and did nothing with them. He wandered about the countryside, interfering where he shouldn't, instead of making something of what he had. Ewen didn't care what his bastard-born cousin thought; he simply needed his help. "I need to know the names of booksellers and collectors in the area who might buy antique journals of herbs and such."

His host raised heavy black eyebrows and regarded Ewen with eyes more ebony than his own. "The city is littered with foolishness like that. I've enough right here to keep an army occupied for a year. I have been searching through them since I received your letter." Aidan gestured broadly, indicating the dusty, cobwebbed shelves holding books with lettering long since faded. "Surely a man of intelligence doesn't believe such nonsense holds anything of value?"

Ewen hadn't, not before Felicity, but he would accept her faith in books. "I must try," he said stubbornly. "Felicity believes it. And I believe in Felicity."

As if Ewen had passed some test, Aidan nodded curtly and lit the lamp on the giant oak beam that served as mantel. "May as well look here, then. It's too wet a night to be goin' into the city."

"The book was in Nesbitt's library," Ewen protested. "Unless you bought it from him, it won't be here."

Aidan shoved the oil lamp at him. "Nesbitt sold that lot decades ago. If I know aught of my mother at all, it will more likely be here than elsewhere. I think you are dinged in the noggin to encourage this foolishness."

Ewen couldn't keep from staring. He supposed all men had mothers, but why would Aidan's collect ancient books on Malcolms?

Aidan took no notice of his astonishment. Turning his back on the room, he studied the wall of untouched books in front of him. The threads holding his sleeve to his faded velvet vest had worn thin with age, and a small tug would separate the seam. The vest itself was cut wide and long in the fashion of an earlier decade, with a linen back and sleeves and torn lace at the wrists. Like all Ives, Aidan wore his black hair in a queue, but he used a leather thong and not a ribbon to tie it back. Dressed as he was he could never pass for a gentleman, but in his casual arrogance he could never pass for less.

Shaking his head to be rid of irrelevant observations, Ewen lit another lamp and turned to study a different wall, daunted by the task to which he'd been set. They would have to remove each book from its place to find its title. Not one of them appeared to be less than a century old. The bindings had frayed and the titles faded to illegibility.

He hated this task. He needed to confront Larch and Edgemont. He needed to sell his chimney reflectors and start a new company. But for Felicity's sake, the book must come first. Resolutely, Ewen reached for the first tome on the bottom shelf. His head ached just thinking of the labor ahead. But he owed her this.

Had he not distracted her, Felicity might have found the volume on her own, and Larch would never have had reason to harm her.

He'd wring Larch's neck for that — as soon as he had Felicity's book safely delivered.

TWENTY-NINE

"Here's another that mentions infusions." Aidan flung the dusty book on the library table, adding to the stacks already accumulated there. "She may have misremembered the title."

As he kneaded his forehead, attempting to ease the thumping ache behind his eyes, Ewen lifted his gaze from the ancient hand-lettering of the book in front of him to ponder the stack growing at his elbow. Groaning, he scanned the shelves they had yet to work through. They had been at it for days. And nights. The clock had chimed midnight hours ago, and they were only halfway through the room. He didn't think he'd had more than an hour's sleep, and that only because his head had collapsed on the table from exhaustion.

"Surely these all can't be Malcolm tomes," Ewen protested for the millionth time. "Did the blamed women do nothing but scribble all day?"

"Can't always tell which ones are Malcolm and which ones aren't," Aiden replied. "They weren't much on autographing their texts. Some of these journals stretch back centuries. It's a wonder they have any blunt left after buying all this paper and ink." Aidan flipped open a page, disturbing a cloud of dust.

Ewen sneezed, massaged his head again, and reached for the ale they'd dredged from the kitchen along with a hunk of cheese and bread. "You belong in Bedlam for harboring this rubbish," he muttered.

Aidan ignored the insult and returned to perusing his obviously unread collection. Why the devil did he keep the blamed books if not to read them? Ewen sighed and returned to scanning brittle pages of spidery handwriting. The author of this particular tome had raised herbs. His sister-in-law, Ninian, would enjoy it. He was half tempted to mix one of the recipes to see if it would cure his headache. But then he'd need another to ease his strained eyes.

Setting the book aside, he reached for the next book in the stack, *A Journal of Infusions and Poultices.* Damned women needed to read each other's books so they would quit repeating themselves.

The title page read *A Malcolm Journal.* Well, at least he knew this one was written by a Malcolm. He hadn't been certain with some of the others.

This one had promise.

Once he'd found the right journal, he would allow Felicity some time to put it to use, and let her be the one to tell him farewell. By then she would recognize that he wasn't the white knight she needed to keep her safe from harm.

To rid the persone of afflikshuns of the flesh and minde . . .

Ewen blinked, and the lettering seemed to grow alternately large and small. He could scarcely make sense of the archaic spelling. *Of partiklr intrst to wymn of deliket constitushun . . .*

Ewen groaned and held up his spinning head with one hand as he strained to read the faded ink.

A broad hand clapped his shoulder, and another removed the book from beneath his nose. Aidan's voice rang inside his head like pounding church bells.

An infusion for the removal of unwanted and dangerous Malcolm gifts. Take one leaf of fox-glove, mix generously with —

Ewen slumped in his chair until his head bounced off his folded arms. He'd found it.

"I don't know how I'll repay you, Dougal, but I will." Exhausted, but feeling alive for the first time in days, Ewen mounted Dunstan's horse. With the book safely inside the bag he'd thrown over the saddle, he was torn between joy and regret.

He wanted Felicity to be safe and happy, and the book would provide her only chance at that.

It would also mean she would no longer need him to shield her from the effects of her gift.

The wretched book would end any hope he had of keeping her.

But Felicity's safety and happiness came first. He could fix this one wrong and ride off, secure in the knowledge that never again would she be harmed by her gift — or by him.

"The heat from your fireplace reflector is payment enough," Aidan assured him. "Although it might have been more useful to repair the roof," he added with a hint of dryness.

"You don't need me for that." Ewen took up the reins, eager to be on his way.

With a wave of farewell, he kicked his horse into a canter. The sun was shining. Perhaps it was a sign that all would be well.

He prayed Felicity had recovered but hadn't left for London yet. He didn't know how he would get past her devil of a father, but he must. He had to let her know he hadn't forgotten their vows, that he hadn't used her for his own pleasure and then abandoned her. He would let her be the one to realize she had a future again, though not with him.

And then he had a small matter to settle with Robert Larch.

While staring out the open window at the branches swaying in the moonlight, Felicity wrapped her arms around her ribs. It was unusually warm for so early in spring. To-morrow Dunstan and Leila would depart for the Ives estate in Surrey, taking Christina with them and leaving Felicity behind, despite her father's strong objection. She had told him she would only run away again, and keep running away, if he attempted to return her to London.

Her father had ridden off in a rage to Edinburgh, determined to erase all trace of her marriage, thinking that would stop Ewen. He might well succeed, but he didn't understand that Ewen was her future, no matter what.

She supposed it would be lonely in this great drafty castle on her own, but it would be infinitely preferable to returning to the social whirl of London. Perhaps she could make friends of some of the village people. And she'd have her books to occupy her.

Once everyone had departed, would Ewen return? Or had he gone off on another of his expeditions? Had he already forgotten she existed? She had no difficulty understanding that he could both love her and forget her. His mind was so far above such domestic concerns as home and wife that he could forget to eat if not reminded.

Or he could think the honorable thing to do was to stay away until he earned enough to provide for her. Since he hated pen and ink, she couldn't expect to receive any letter of explanation.

Smiling fondly, if wryly, at this observation,

Felicity watched the sliver of road visible through the trees guarding the castle. Leila had insisted that Felicity stay in bed all week, but her head was better now. The mending gash looked ugly, but she could think again. It was foolish to believe Ewen would arrive simply because she was up and about now.

She was more likely to see her father tearing down the moonlit road. The others waited for his return before taking the yacht to London. She wondered if he'd succeeded in having her marriage declared null and void. Her father simply couldn't accept that earthly laws could not nullify the spiritual vows she'd exchanged with Ewen.

Felicity pulled the draperies to shut out the silver light and turned back to her empty bed. Once her head had stopped hurting she'd written to Drogo, Earl of Ives, trusting him with all she'd learned of Robert Larch, hoping he'd pass the information to Ewen. She couldn't prove Larch's guilt or Ewen's innocence in the lock failure. She couldn't force the other investors to repay Ewen for their share of rebuilding the village. But if Ewen could uncover Larch's perfidy or if Drogo could demand his books, they and the others could refuse to do business with a man of malice and greed.

She settled into bed with another book on midwifery. She'd learned that Ninian had trained some of the village women in physicking. Since the villagers couldn't read, perhaps one day she could act as their repository of knowledge.

She'd rather be Ewen's repository of knowledge.

It wouldn't do to fall prey to loneliness so soon. She'd made her decision and wouldn't back down. She would wait here until Ewen returned for her, no matter when that might be.

She must have eventually dozed off, because when she woke again the lamp had burned out. She tried to remember the sound that had woken her. The clock chiming on the landing?

A music box tinkling.

Startled completely awake, Felicity sat up. A tiny ballerina in a box on the bed stand danced around and around, her dainty foot lifting and bending as she pirouetted to the strains of Bach. Even more elaborate and beautiful than the precious enameled bouquet Ewen had given Felicity at her come-out, the dancer seemed to be alive, awash in moonlight.

Moonlight. But she'd closed the draperies.

Carefully lifting the musical figurine, heart beating in time with the music, Felicity turned toward the open window.

Ewen stood in silhouette there, one broad shoulder propped against the frame, arms crossed, wind-tossed queue tumbling over his shoulder.

Terrified and elated, uncertain what he expected, Felicity met his shadowed gaze. "Thank you," she whispered. "She is even more beautiful than the flowers." Fear clamored in her chest as she realized that the last time he'd given her a toy, he'd left London and not returned. "Does this mean you are leaving again?"

Ewen stepped away from the window. He'd thrown his hat and greatcoat over a chair. He carried with him the scent of fresh night air and the masculine fragrance of sandalwood shaving soap. He'd shaved recently. For her?

"That's up to you." With the economy of movement of a man comfortable in his body, he crossed the room and lifted the delicate figurine from her hands. "I think this is Austrian. Someone abandoned her because she didn't dance anymore. She only needed a little care to bring music into the world again. People are in too much haste to throw away that which they once valued."

Felicity's fear subsided. She didn't need to touch him to understand what he was telling her. He'd never abandon her, no matter how difficult it might be to accept her frailties. "I still have the doll I was given one Christmas. She is tattered and torn and more precious to me than diamonds and gold."

Ewen set the ballerina on the dresser as the figurine wound down. Cautiously, he lowered his heavy weight to the bed's edge. Had she not known his gentleness, his masculine presence would have overwhelmed her

"How is your head?" he asked gruffly, brushing a finger over the small bandage she still wore on her forehead.

She couldn't see his expression but she sensed his uncertainty, as well as his relief that she'd understood him. He was so clear to her. The bond between them was forged of something stronger than mere words. "On the mend. I really am quite strong, you know."

"I should have been here to protect you. After what you told me, I should have given orders for Larch to be denied the house. I wish I knew how to take care of you as you deserve."

Before she could protest his foolishness, he produced a small leather-bound volume from his pocket and presented it with a flourish. "I found the book."

Startled, she nearly jerked her hand away from the unexpected object. She had almost come to terms with living with her gift forever. Now he was confronting her with a challenge she no longer felt prepared to take.

She took a deep breath and calmed down. She had to learn to master her volatile reactions. With awe she accepted his gift. "Where? How?" She stroked the volume and sensed no evil in it. It had been many years since someone had touched it. She could feel only Ewen's great exhaustion on it.

Fear curled in her stomach. Now that she had the means to be rid of her hated gift, she would have to make an irrevocable decision. Would her mother weep if she did this? Would her Malcolm relations scorn her? When the book had been a distant impossibility, those questions hadn't been real. Now they hit her with their immediacy.

"Where and how isn't what's important right now," Ewen said, interrupting her fretting. "I don't know how much time we have before your father throws me out the window. I no longer have a future to offer you. The book gives you a means of freeing yourself to marry elsewhere once your father nullifies our marriage. I want you to know that I will not hold you to any vows we made in the heat of the moment. You are free to do as you think best."

"And you?" she asked, because she needed to hear the words. She hugged the book against her chest "Do you wish to be free of me?"

"No," he said harshly. "But I speak from a wealth of experience and know what I want. You are young and have years ahead of you to regret any hastily made decision. I would give you time to learn what you want."

Ewen gave her the book to free her, even though it meant destroying the gift that might save his future. She ought to feel guilty that concern for her had diverted him from his own concerns. Did he truly think she could ever find a man who loved her more deeply? She shook her head at his absurdity, forgetting that he could not read her as she did him.

He started to stand up.

Clasping his coat, Felicity tugged him back down again. "I may not have the experience that you do, but I know to value a man for his honesty and his abilities rather than for his wealth. I know when a man loves me instead of my title or dowry. I know when a man sees beyond my weaknesses to the person I can be if I'm allowed to grow and learn. If you believe in me, then believe in my love and know there will never be another."

Ewen sat still for a moment, measuring her words, absorbing them. He closed his eyes and a shudder rippled through him. Blindly yet unerringly, he cupped his hands around her face, stroking her while he steadied himself. Opening his eyes again, he leaned over and wrapped her in his arms.

"Love can't feed you," he warned, his voice raw with emotion.

"Food for the stomach is easy. Nourishment for the heart is rare," she whispered into his coat collar. "I'd thought never to feel your embrace again."

"I was afraid you'd already be on your way back to London. You realize the difficulty ahead of us, don't you?"

She nodded. Her father could apply pressure to Drogo to have her thrown from the castle. Ewen could provide her no home. She could be forced to return to her father's house, where she would cause dissension in her family if she chose to be rid of her gift.

A thought occurred, and she kissed the hard line of his jaw. "I can always stay in Aidan's keep. I wager even my father couldn't find a means of threatening someone who has nothing."

Ewen chuckled. "Aidan would be pleased to have you, knowing I would fix the crumbling disaster just to keep you warm. And if we cannot marry in England without your father's permission, Scotland would be the place for us. Could you accept being so far from your family?"

"You are my family now. And if the book works, I can follow where the need takes you without harm."

"I have nothing," he warned, setting her away from him. "I have an idea of how to use the chimney vents, but it may take months before I see any profit."

"Let me go with you," she pleaded.

He kissed her nose and hairline and shook his head. "You need to consult with Ninian and your sisters before recklessly using that book. We have a lifetime ahead of us. Let me make it a happy one. Can you wait for me?"

She shook her head. "You have spent your life roaming the earth, fixing broken things that don't belong to you." Concentrating hard on what she'd learned from touching him, she did her best to interpret the emotions and thoughts rioting through him. "I am asking you, for once, to think of yourself, to take me for your own, and make me into the home you've never had."

As she clung to his hand, Felicity could feel his confusion and knew he struggled between his need to claim her and his fear of harming her. She waited, praying he would accept that she would not break in his care.

"I can't bear to hurt you," he whispered, cupping her jaw in his hand.

Felicity kissed the palm of his hand. "You will not break me, and if you leave, I will follow. You may as well surrender." She touched his jaw and turned his head so she might find his lips with hers.

Ewen hesitated, but hearing her certainty, he let her greater understanding fill his heart. He didn't know how he would make this right, but he would accept her word that it would be, because he needed Felicity to give his life hope and meaning.

Succumbing to her request, he drove his hand into her tumbled hair and tilted her head to better access her mouth. His tongue took instant possession, telling her of his desire in the only manner he knew. Responding with the craving he had taught her, Felicity twined her tongue with his, wrapped her arms around his shoulders, and offered all she had for his taking.

Ewen caressed her breast through her nightclothes, felt her arousal, and tried not to panic at the consequences if he went too far. Coming up for air, he studied his wife's up-turned face in the moonlight. Silver bathed her features in purity, and trust shone from her eyes. Her halo of ringlets wreathed soft shoulders as porcelain as those of the balle-rina he had given her. She was a precious gift he must cherish for the rest of their lives. He was terrified of failing her, but if she trusted him, he would not run away from the responsibility.

He wanted to begin by doing the right thing, but desire inflamed him and he could not think clearly. All he could see was the haunting woman who truly loved and desired him just as he was.

"I want to make love to you properly this time," he warned her, so that she understood fully. "I have come with protection that might shield you from children, but there are no guarantees."

She nodded. "I know. A woman never goes into marriage expecting them. I can care for your children."

The idea of Felicity bearing his child alarmed and excited him. He kissed her in gratitude for her understanding, but there was one more thing he would make clear.

"I want to do this now, before you lose your gift. I want you to know how I feel when I claim you, how important you are to me, so that in the future if I should ever give you reason to doubt, you will remember this night."

Her eyes widened in surprise before her lips curved in understanding. He could almost feel the pull of her amusement.

"I am fully prepared for days of neglect, sir. I am capable of entertaining myself. But at night, I mean to have your full attention."

And so she would. Without further argument or warning, Ewen lowered his head and claimed her mouth again. He risked all — for both of them — to take her like this, but this time he would not stop until he had set aside all notion of her belonging to anyone else but him.

Right or wrong, they would be bound for life.

THIRTY

Drowning in the sensations pouring through her fingertips and all the places Ewen touched her, Felicity was the one to pull back this time.

"My turn," she whispered.

Ewen looked startled, then amused. He brushed a stray curl from her cheek and traced his finger down her fair skin. "Your wish is my command. What would you have me do?"

"Undress." She'd never said such a bold thing in all her life. But with Ewen she could say anything. Freedom blossomed and took root somewhere behind the place he now caressed. She shivered as his knowing fingers rubbed her aroused nipple.

Delight and amusement lit his eyes, but he obediently released her to shrug out of his coat. "How far?" he asked, daring her to speak up.

"Completely," she answered, already admiring the manner in which his shoulders moved as he removed his vest. He wasn't as big as his older brothers, but he was far larger than she, and proportioned in such a way as to make a woman weep in gratitude.

"To be fair, you'll have to remove your shift," he noted, wrestling with the knot of his cravat.

She loved the way Ewen's eyes danced with joy and life and desire. They could live in hedgerows and be poor as church mice, and it would make no difference to her as long as he looked at her like that. Teasingly, she lifted her hair on top of her head so that her throat was bare and her shift slid off one shoulder, allowing him a glimpse of what he most hungered for. "Eventually," she agreed.

His gaze became very focused after that. She could feel it burn straight through the linen of her bodice to all the parts below. He wrenched off his neck cloth and untied his shirt strings. Before she could absorb the full impact of rippling muscles draped in linen, he stripped off his shirt and flung it over a chair to join his coat and vest.

"Oh, my." She couldn't stop the exclamation. Moonlight bathed his broad shoulders and powerful arms. A shadow of hair delineated the hard curves of his chest before descending and narrowing toward the waist of his breeches.

Where his hand rested.

Gulping, Felicity watched in fascination as Ewen unfastened the buttons. She could see the male part of him straining against the tight cloth, and skittish, she dropped her gaze. "Boots!" she whispered. "You haven't removed your boots."

He chuckled, and she was glad he couldn't see her blush.

Obediently, he sat on the side of the bed and tugged at his loose riding boots. "Lower that little frill over your shoulder, madam," he whispered, leaning toward her. "Give me incentive to do this properly."

With heat flushing her skin at the thought of being so brazen, Felicity slipped the loose neckline of her gown off her shoulders, where it barely clung to the curve of her breasts. Ewen's abrupt intake of breath aroused her as surely as if he'd touched her.

His second boot crashed to the floor, and he cursed under his breath. They both waited to see if anyone came running, but the house remained silent.

"Father isn't here," she whispered. "Christina is closest, and she sleeps like the dead."

Ewen pressed a kiss to her bare shoulder, then rose to finish unfastening his breeches.

This time she didn't avert her gaze.

Moonlight illuminated the full male beauty of him as he peeled off his breeches and stepped out of them. She had seen the etchings in the book, but they could not compare to the reality. Stunned, Felicity had no sense of fear, only awe. When he waited patiently, making no move to force his attentions on her, giving her time to study and conquer her missishness, she borrowed from his composure and let her gown slip off her arms and down to her waist.

Ewen was beside her instantly, pushing aside the blankets, helping her discard her nightclothes, skimming his hands over her nudity as if to worship her.

"I have no rose petals tonight," he murmured. "Nothing to come between us. How does this feel?"

"Wonderful." She sighed in pleasure as his hands drifted to a halt at her breasts. "You cannot hurt me, Ewen. I feel the love in your touch, and it's like . . . I can't describe it. It's like nothing I've ever known."

"Good." In satisfaction, he bent to kiss her thoroughly, sprawling his heavy frame along her slighter one.

So many sensations overwhelmed her at once that she couldn't separate one from the other. His mouth and tongue fed the desire bubbling in her veins. His hands roved and caressed and aroused until she arched her back, her breasts pressing into his palms in an abandoned plea for more. Felicity returned his kiss, urged deeper exploration, took his straining arms into her hands and stroked until he moved over her.

The flick of Ewen's tongue against her achingly aroused nipple brought a gasp to her lips. His hair fell forward, brushing her sensitized skin as he suckled, and she nearly wept with the pleasure of it. She removed the ribbon of his queue and wrapped her fingers in his hair, not wanting to let go, but he knew what she wanted better than she did. Ignoring her grasping fingers, he carried his kisses from one breast to the other. The hard heat of his arousal rubbing below her belly opened rivers of need.

Rolling to one side, he took advantage of her surrender to part her thighs with his hand. Felicity wept as Ewen finally — at long last — touched her where she most needed him. Too lost in the sensations swirling through her, she merely obeyed the command of his tormenting fingers until she opened and arched and accepted the strangeness of his intrusion.

She bit his shoulder to keep from crying out as his fingers gently explored, teaching her the mysteries she'd longed to unravel. He plundered deeper, keeping time to her writhing cries, until she could no longer tell what was him and what was her and a bubble of joy grew inside her womb.

When she thought she surely must come apart from the power building within her, Ewen applied both thumb and finger, and the bubble burst and shook her with quakes of desire and surrender. She whimpered as the explosion slowed and curled up against him, needing his strength to hold her together.

Clasping her tightly, Ewen murmured loving suggestions into her ear and began his sweet torture all over again.

"Did you ever read the whole book Nesbitt gave us?" he whispered, as his hand cupped her breast and teased the crest and his kiss seared along her jaw.

"I . . . I tried." She could barely speak as the hot, heavy male part of him rubbed against her belly and thighs, awakening her need all over again. "Some of it did not seem quite . . . feasible."

His laugh was warm against her ear. "Oh, it all is. I shall show you in the nights to come. But we will start with the basics this night. The first time may hurt, and I want to be in a position to soothe the sting."

He rolled over and reached for his clothing, removing a prophylactic from a pocket, and Felicity watched in fascination as he donned it.

She could not imagine how they would fit together. She could see for herself that Ewen was much larger than she could be. What if she couldn't satisfy him? But the craving was so strong she would accept any explanation, anything at all to ease her hunger. "Then please teach me," she whispered back. "I want to be your wife in all the ways I can be."

"Just touch me in any way that pleases you, and I'll do the rest." Propping himself on his elbows over her, Ewen bent to spread his kisses along her jaw.

Fully aware of the cold air against her skin and between her thighs, sensing his heat within reach, Felicity slid her hands up his arms and accepted his tongue into her mouth. Her hips arched, brushing against him. Sensing that he wanted her to touch, she ran her hands over his shoulders and down his chest, teasing his male nipples until they hardened into tight points just as hers did. She couldn't reach far enough to touch the part of him that ached to be grasped, but he solved that problem on his own.

Felicity sucked in her breath as Ewen parted her legs and pressed his maleness into the opening he'd made liquid with his fingers. A riot of sensations swept through her from all the places they touched — not just hers, but his as well. She knew the joy he experienced, the fear of hurting her, his pride in claiming her. His emotions multiplied her own until she nearly wept with the wonder of their joining.

As he inched deeper, she felt him absorbing her, becoming part of her. By the time he pierced the barrier of her innocence, they had become so completely one that she wasn't sure if the cry she heard was his or hers.

"Quickly this time, my love. I cannot hold back much longer. Hold on to my arms and follow me," he murmured against her ear.

She couldn't translate the meaning of his

words with her mind, but her body under-stood his desires, as if touching him accessed his deepest yearning. As if in these moments she shared her gift with him, and he was filled with the knowledge of it.

His thickness stretched her, but not painfully. Responding to his need, Felicity wrapped her legs around Ewen's hips, lifting herself into him. The action took him deeper, until he groaned and began to move within her. Felic-ity's hips rose and fell with the gentle rhythm he set, pushing higher, harder, reaching for a rainbow just beyond her grasp —

Ewen caressed the right spot and the rainbow shattered, coloring her world in infi-nite beauty. Sensing that Ewen's urge was yet to be satisfied, Felicity reached for the last bit of untouched sky, arching to take him deeper still.

Ewen accepted her invitation and entered her so completely she thought she might burst with the fullness. He took his pleasure with great, driving thrusts, until his body quaked and spilled inside her with such grati-fication that she understood that no shield could prevent him from filling her with his child, should the fates choose to grant them one.

Accepting that prospect with the languor induced by their mating, Felicity held him tightly and smiled.

He stilled above her and inside her and

rested his forehead against hers. "My word," he whispered, "is that what you see and feel?"

"Not until tonight," she murmured, as shaken as he by the experience, by the gift that until now she had viewed as a curse.

Ewen released a sigh and slowly removed his weight to the mattress, taking her with him to lie at his side. Content, she curled up in the curve of his arm, resting her knee over his muscled thigh.

"Will we do this again tomorrow?" she whispered.

"Umm." He tickled her ear with his tongue, shooting a sensual shiver up her spine. "If you're very, very good, we'll do it again tonight."

Felicity was always very, very good.

Ewen insisted on slipping from her bed in the early hours of the morning. Until he had arranged the legalities of their marriage and secured a place for them to live, he could not risk involving the rest of their family in his battle with the marquess.

Felicity watched him go with regret and yearning. She wasn't the kind of person who enjoyed sneaking behind the backs of others.

But she would do anything necessary to continue sharing Ewen's bed, and that included following him to Scotland and Aidan's castle if she must.

Before he left, Ewen laid another present

upon her table: a book of bound blank pages and a pencil. Only the first page held writing, and she recognized Ewen's scrawl in the words *"An Ives Journal of Contraptions."* Laughing, she stroked the empty pages with pride, knowing that this gift more than anything proved he was ready to share his future with her.

Returning the notebook to the table, she stretched in the gray of early morning. She could feel the ache where he'd claimed her, torturing her into physical awareness, and she stared at the ceiling while her heart pounded in anticipation.

Ewen Ives loved her. Her, Felicity, the undistinguished, hysterical Malcolm. He'd scarcely given Christina's beauty a second look, barely knew sensual Leila existed. She would have to make Ewen as proud of her as Dunstan and Drogo were of their Malcolm wives.

She wasn't entirely certain how she would go about that if she rid herself of her gift, but she didn't know how she could roam the world with him otherwise.

She picked up the Malcolm journal Ewen had left for her and read the page he had marked. She wasn't an herbalist like her cousin Ninian, but the ingredients for the infusion didn't sound too difficult to obtain.

Ninian was in London with Drogo. How could she ask her for help without returning to the city with her family?

Felicity climbed out of bed and washed in the cold water in her basin rather than waiting for the maid's arrival. Ridding herself of her gift was something she couldn't discuss with Ewen. She needed the combined wisdom of her family — without her mother's knowledge of her intentions. Not an easy task.

Fretting over the decision, she hurried downstairs to the breakfast room and halted abruptly at the scene within. Her hesitation didn't prevent the two men at the table from politely rising at her appearance.

Drogo, Earl of Ives, had arrived. This was his castle. He could forbid her from staying here after the others left. Gulping back her fear, Felicity studied her brother-in-law.

Standing beside Dunstan, Drogo appeared taller and leaner, with introspective eyes that revealed nothing. Imposing in his fashionably embroidered vest and elegant frock coat, disdaining wig and powder as his brothers did, Drogo looked the part of aristocratic earl far more than did Dunstan, who favored rural broadcloth and boots.

"You are up early, Lady Felicity," the earl said with the same gravity he might use in a Parliamentary speech.

She wasn't good at making small talk, and the Earl of Ives possessed a formidable presence that unnerved her. Still, this was Ewen's brother and Ninian's husband. She should not judge on appearance.

"The day promises to be fine," she murmured. "Please take your seats. I only meant to grab a piece of toast. Did Ninian come with you, my lord?"

"She did. She has decided to take up residence here until she hatches our daughter. She assures me this time she will have a girl."

Oh, yes, Ninian was having a baby. She'd forgotten. Felicity's hopes rose. Ninian wouldn't let the earl drive her away. And now she wouldn't have to go to London for Ninian's help in understanding the infusion recipe. Perhaps she would be cured and could go with Ewen when he left for Edinburgh!

If her father did not return immediately and throw all her plans into disarray. . . .

"I did not mean to intrude on your discussion." Felicity helped herself to a piece of cold toast and backed away.

"Did Ewen come in last night?" Dunstan asked. "I thought I heard him on the stairs. We need to talk with him when he wakes."

With cheeks flushing furiously, Felicity bit her lip, straightened her shoulders, and accepted that the whole world knew Ewen had chosen her. If only her parents would accept that! "He's back but exhausted and still sleeping. I could send a maid to him if you wish."

"We can wait." Despite his formidable

presence, the earl spoke mildly, and his expression evoked understanding. Not a hint of smirk or sneer touched his features as he gave Felicity his full attention. "I trust you are feeling better this morning? Ninian was exceedingly worried."

Ewen's brothers might be large and prepossessing and often curt, but they were considerate gentlemen. The earl had obviously given into Ninian's pleas to leave early for Wystan so that she might see to Felicity's care. Felicity curtsied in acknowledgment of that fact. "I am well, thank you. You really did not need to rush here on my account."

For a moment she wished her mother had accompanied Ninian. But her mother had made her disapproval of Felicity's wishes clear. The marchioness would never agree to using the book Ewen had found until all other alternatives had been exhausted.

"We could do no less, especially after I received both your and Ewen's missives. It seems there may be a rat in Scotland to be uncovered."

He believed her! The Earl of Ives believed what she'd told him about Larch. And Ewen had actually applied pen to paper to write him. That had probably convinced Drogo most of all. Pride surged through her that her gift had stirred an earl from his mighty tower.

A commotion in the great hall ended further

discussion. Felicity attempted to steel herself against the onslaught of furious vibrations she recognized so well; her father had returned from Edinburgh. May the goddess rain curses!

"Where is he?" the marquess roared, sweeping into the dining chamber still wearing his greatcoat and swinging his ebony-headed walking stick. "I've brought the magistrate with me. So help me, I'll have the boy bound and shipped to the colonies if he so much as —"

"He's not a boy, he's my husband." Hands on hips, Felicity stepped in front of her father before he could start threatening her brothers-in-law. "You may bellow all you like, but you will not change my mind."

"I don't need to change your mind." The marquess turned to shout at someone in the hall. "Upstairs and to the left, Walker! Drag him from bed if you must."

Thank goodness Ewen had gone to his own room and not stayed in hers! If she could get past her father and outside, she could take the servants' entrance and perhaps warn Ewen before anyone found him.

"If you hurt him, I'll disown you," she declared rashly. "I shall never go home again." Lifting her skirts, she raced past her father and into the great hall. His footmen blocked the stairway, but she wasn't so foolish as to lead them directly to Ewen.

With her father's protests ringing in her ears, she ran for the front doors.

No one halted her. Her father still thought her a foolish child who would run away when crossed. But she was a woman now, a wife, and she would do whatever it took to defend her future with Ewen.

Racing across the immense lawn in the direction of the rear kitchen, Felicity hesitated when the hedge rustled a few yards ahead of her. Fearing it might be another of her father's servants, she sought a safer route.

Instead of a servant, Robert Larch pushed through the bushes. "I've been waiting to talk with you, miss."

Why in the name of the goddess was he here? Had he returned from Scotland with her father? He did not sound as if he meant to exchange pleasantries, and he blocked her path to Ewen. Caught between Larch and her father, Felicity kept her distance, uncertain which way to flee. "Then I think you had best call at the house in a proper manner," she answered.

"I'm not a wealthy man," he continued, as if she had said nothing. "I don't live in a grand palace like that one." He nodded at Drogo's home. "I don't have earls and marquesses on my family tree."

She couldn't argue with that. She saw no reason to mention that having stubborn, powerful earls and marquesses on the family tree tended to be more of a nuisance than a convenience. Perhaps she could ease around Larch as he talked . . .

Robert apparently didn't expect a response. "I don't know what you and your witchy sisters believe, but I'm a respectable man with a family to support. I'll do what I must to protect them."

Remembering this was Percy's cousin and Ewen's friend, Felicity attempted to determine where his topic led. "As we all must," she agreed. He seemed reasonable, but if she had interpreted her vision correctly, he may have cost Ewen a fortune.

"Just so you understand," Robert said, as if she had agreed with whatever was in his head. "If you tell people I'm guilty of things only you can see, I'll have to report your witchcraft to the Earl of Middlesea. He detests witches and thinks they should all hang."

Eyes wide as she grasped his threat, Felicity lifted her skirts and prepared to run. But Robert grabbed her arm.

THIRTY-ONE

Already half dressed when he heard the explosion of Hampton's arrival, Ewen hastily shrugged on his coat and glanced out the window to be certain an army of foot soldiers didn't accompany the marquess.

From this angle he could see only the coach rattling around the corner after dropping off its wealthy owner in the front. He could climb out the window, down that outcropping of stone to the porte cochere, and escape with no one the wiser. He didn't think the marquess a man prone to hearing reason when it came to his daughter. If he was to have anything to offer Felicity, he couldn't do it from prison.

Felicity! He couldn't go without saying farewell. He'd thought he'd have time this morning to say all the words women needed to hear. He'd hoped to have time to talk with Dunstan about seeing to Felicity's welfare before he left to repair his fortunes. His discussion with the marquess earlier had been fruitless. Nothing less than cash in hand would convince the man he could take care of Felicity.

Hearing loud voices echoing up the stairs,

431

Ewen knew his time was running out.

Opening the window, he found a foothold in the old stone and began working his way down to the flat roof below. If anyone in the stable yard saw him he'd be in a trouble, but under the circumstances this seemed the most expedient means of reaching Felicity.

At the porte cochere Ewen halted to survey his surroundings. Something seemed to be off kilter, but with the marquess bellowing inside and his henchmen crawling around outside, he couldn't tell what else might be wrong.

He dug his boots into the tangled vines and stones of the column leading to the ground and landed safely on the gravel drive.

Felicity's scream broke the quiet morning air.

Without hesitation, Ewen ran toward the sound. Rounding the corner of the castle in such haste that he slid and threw gravel from the drive, he arrived in time to see the bright yellow of her gown fall to the ground near the hedge. Fury and terror displaced all other considerations. Someone had touched Felicity and made her faint. That someone would die.

As the man straightened, Ewen recognized the bastard. *"Larch!"*

Looking up in panic, Robert turned and fled. At any other time in his life Ewen would have chased the foundry owner, brought him crashing to the ground, and beat his face into a pulp for daring to accost Felicity. He would have received great pleasure in doing so.

But not with his wife lying broken and still on the ground. Reaching Felicity, dropping to his knees, Ewen lifted her fair head from the drive, terror freezing all his working parts as he pushed her hair back from her already bandaged brow.

"I'm fine. Go after him," she whispered furiously, eyes flashing in her pale face. "Make him tell my father and Drogo what he's done. Stop him!"

Relief flooded him, but still he hesitated, unwilling to leave her — until she struggled to sit up as if she would run after Larch herself.

"Don't move," he ordered, then leapt to his feet and covered the uneven ground in long strides.

Robert had a head start but no expertise in running. Ewen was nearly on him when Larch stumbled over a root. His pace slowed, and Ewen grabbed him by the flared tails of his old-fashioned coat. Larch lurched forward, caught himself, and turned around, swinging.

With all the force of his indignation, Ewen plowed his fist into the man's jaw. He was a lover, not a brawler, but the crunch of bone against bone felt thoroughly satisfying. Larch crumpled.

But the larger man grabbed Ewen's ankle and jerked. A moment later he was on the ground with Larch, his head spinning from the abruptness of his fall. Before he could catch his breath, Robert pounced, grabbing him by the throat and squeezing.

Felicity's irate screams echoed from a distance. Fighting back, Ewen dug his fingers into Larch's bulky arms and attempted to tear him away. Abandoning the effort to break Larch's hold before he expired from lack of breath, Ewen emulated his opponent's tactic and wrapped his hands around Larch's throat. Using the leverage of his long legs, he whipped Larch back to the hard ground.

Robert squeezed harder. Ewen gasped for air and attempted to beat Larch's head into the ground. Larch loosened his grip in his effort to knee Ewen in his softer parts, but he wasn't in a position to achieve a good blow. Ewen returned the favor with more accuracy and Larch blanched, but his fingers still clung desperately to Ewen's throat.

"Let him loose, you monster!" Felicity cried from nearby.

Ewen hadn't the breath in him to tell her to run. For all he knew, Larch had more men in the bushes waiting to carry her off. Unable to beat Robert into insensibility, Ewen released his grip on his opponent's neck and poked him in both eyes. Larch howled.

A large stick wielded by gloved hands crashed against Larch's arms, encouraging him to release Ewen. Free at last, Ewen leapt to his feet.

As he stood over his nemesis, fists at the ready, Ewen heard his brothers' feet pounding down the gravel drive. "Stand back, Felicity," he said. "I'll not have him grabbing you again."

Ewen didn't have to look to know she was there, stout oak branch in hand, waiting for Larch to rise. Pride and joy filled him at her courage.

As if the Fates conspired to rain all the heavens down on him at once, the Marquess of Hampton reached him first, followed closely by Dunstan and Drogo.

Larch struggled to sit up, rubbing his eyes and cursing. Seeing not just Ewen but two more Ives glowering over him, he appeared to think better of rising.

Felicity slipped her hand into Ewen's, and he inhaled so quickly in relief that he nearly reeled. He might never be certain she was safe unless she touched him.

Ewen bent to place a hasty kiss to Felicity's head and studied her to see if she'd been injured in any way.

"I did it," she said triumphantly, her shining eyes looking to him for approval.

"You didn't faint," he said with understanding. At her beaming smile, he added, "You didn't react emotionally but captured the moment."

She nodded vigorously, although she clung to his hand for support. "I did. I used my gift and it didn't hurt." She sent him a worshipful gaze. "I'm not helpless. In time, I can go wherever you go. Perhaps I can even use my gift for good purpose, as I did with you and Percy."

Warmth and love flooded him, but Ewen only had time to wrap his arm around her waist and hug her, murmuring so others couldn't hear. "You have never been helpless, my love. You are the most courageous person I know. You will give me failure of the heart if you touch the Larches of the world, but I must admit, last night was a revelation I wouldn't mind sharing again."

Felicity all but purred at the reminder.

"Will someone please explain what is happening here?" the marquess shouted. "Felicity, let go of that demon!"

On the ground, Larch rubbed his aching eyes and attempted to wiggle his way out of trouble. "She's a lying witch," he protested. "If she ever sets foot in Scotland again, I'll have her hanged for her trickery."

Felicity tensed, but Ewen massaged her shoulders as the marquess abruptly swung his attention to the villain in the road. "Who the devil is this ninnyhammer?"

Robert blanched.

"I thought perhaps he was a friend of yours," Drogo said sourly, nudging Larch with his toe to see if that would stir him into rising.

"Can't say that I recognize him," the marquess responded, "but if you don't remove your rake of a brother from my daughter's presence, I'll have him thrown in the deepest dungeon in all England."

"Then you'll have to throw me in the dungeon with him," Felicity asserted, returning her father's hostile glare.

Ewen noted Dunstan and Drogo stepping away from the fray, not in cowardice but in appreciation of an equal fight. This time he allowed an open grin as his amazing wife cocked her pretty elbows and placed her hands on her hips in a defiant stance any fishwife could appreciate.

Before the marquess could quit sputtering, Felicity pointed at Larch. "That man stole from Ewen and Percy and the other men who trusted him. Then he used inferior materials to build the lock, causing the canal to fail and a flood to destroy homes and farms. I saw it when he grabbed me. And now he's threatening me to be quiet about it."

Ewen heard no hint of fear in her voice, just righteous anger. Despite her father's scowl, he hugged her reassuringly. "Larch is full of bluster, love. He thought he'd scare a timid mouse and didn't know he'd threatened a lioness."

Felicity crossed her arms and nodded in

approval. "I think I could learn to like being a witch."

Ewen could see Dunstan and Drogo hiding their smiles as the marquess roared at this nonsense. Ewen had teased his brothers often enough about marrying witches. It wouldn't hurt if they evened the score.

In the meantime, he had the little matter of a marriage to protect. "I can't prove what Felicity is telling us, my lord," Ewen said, cutting into Hampton's blustering, "so I'm still bankrupt. Even should Drogo go over the books and recover any funds, I doubt there would be enough to keep Felicity as she should be."

Although if Felicity's vision was right and Larch was hoarding the cash he'd stolen, Drogo might recover enough to buy the needed mine equipment. Since the marquess now owned Ewen's portion of the mine, Ewen wasn't inclined to share that possibility with him.

"If you are patient," he continued, amazed that the marquess was still listening, "there are dozens of ways in which I can support her. For Felicity's sake, I'd ask your approval. She does not like being a disobedient daughter. I think you should trust her judgment and wish her well."

Hampton glared through stormy eyes that resembled Felicity's when she was angry. "She's not old enough to know her own mind. I suggest you wait until you've made your fortune and give her time to learn the ways of the world."

"I suggested that, my lord," Ewen admitted, "but she refused."

In disdain, Dunstan shoved Larch back to the ground with his boot. "Why don't we remove our guest from this little discussion? Perhaps we could ride him on a rail back to Edinburgh while you settle it."

"You can ride your damned brother on the rail with him!" Hampton roared.

Ewen didn't bat an eyelash at her father's curses, Felicity observed with pride. Her husband merely stood up to her powerful father as if the marquess were no more than any other man. "Then you must ride me on a rail, too," she reminded him with just a small dose of Christina's sauciness.

"He has no means to care for you," her father insisted. "His reputation precedes him. I will not give you to a philandering —"

"Felicity has chosen me, sir. Do you truly believe she would choose wrongly?"

Felicity noted with satisfaction that Ewen had succeeded in tumbling her father off his high horse. The marquess looked momentarily flummoxed.

"You do not deserve her!" her father repeated for good measure. "Prove that you can care for her as her family does."

While Dunstan and Drogo grabbed Larch's

arms and hauled him toward the stable, Ewen and Felicity's father adopted the postures of men about to settle down to a furious argument. Her father had the advantage of position and flaunted it in his lace jabot, fine coat, and neatly clubbed wig. Ewen had obviously been caught by surprise. His hair fell over his brow and down his nape, his jabot remained loose over his untied shirt laces, and his coat looked as if he'd slept in it. He certainly didn't appear like any suitor she'd ever had, but she had confidence in him.

Deciding Ewen would be better off fighting with her father while she wasn't around, Felicity hurried toward the women gathering on the lawn.

She was a wife and a woman. Now she had to decide if she wished to be a witch.

Ninian rushed to encompass her in an embrace, examining her bandages and checking for bruises. "I shall beat Ewen to within an inch of his life if he is responsible for bringing that brute here," she declared.

Hugging her cousin, Felicity continued toward the house. "Ewen is my husband. If anyone beats him, they will answer to me."

"You really, honestly married Ewen Ives?" Christina cried, racing after her. "It is not a hoax to force Father to let you stay here?"

"We exchanged vows," Felicity replied. "They may not be legal in England, but they're enough for me."

Leila rushed to stand in front of her before she could escape into the house. Gently, she touched Felicity's cheek, so Felicity understood she meant no harm. "There is great disparity between the two of you. You are a bookworm and a homebody, and Ewen is a ladies' man who has no use for books or settling down. How can you be certain his goal is not your dowry?"

"He married me knowing Father would never approve and grant him my dowry." Felicity gathered her skirts and pushed past her older sister. "I'll show you how I know our marriage is right."

Her older sisters and cousin followed obediently as Felicity ran through the great hall and up the stairs to her chamber. She picked up the ballerina Ewen had given her and thrust it into Leila's hands.

"That is how I know. This is the only gift a man has ever given me that vibrates with sincerity, with thoughts of me and none other. I can feel the hours Ewen spent repairing the mechanism and turning it back into a thing of beauty and pleasure. I can feel the love he poured into it. I can feel his joy in thinking it would please me. There is not one thought or memory that reverberates with greed or lust or dishonesty of any sort. No other suitor could have given me this."

While Leila turned the key to play the music, Felicity snatched up the battered journal and shoved it into Ninian's hands. "And here. Ewen spent this past week looking for this, just for me, no doubt incurring a crashing headache when he might have been investigating Larch and saving himself."

Christina looked over Ninian's shoulder as she flipped the pages. "*A Journal of Infusions and Poultices?*" she asked in surprise.

"The title is not quite right, so he must have read hundreds of old books to find this one." Felicity found the marked page and pointed to the recipe. "There. That's why he sought it: to ease my pain, to give me freedom from this disability that causes me as much harm as good."

Ninian read the recipe with surprise. "You would be rid of your gift? It has become so harmful that you would dare try this?"

With care Felicity took the ballerina back from Leila, feeling the love pouring through her fingertips. Last night her gift had showed her how to give her husband pleasure. Today it had revealed the villain who would have robbed Ewen of his future. Tomorrow what else might it do? Allow her to help a child of her own? Her gift might cause her suffering, but it could also produce great good, especially with Ewen to balance out her fears and teach her courage. Taking a deep breath, she made her decision.

A cheery, singsong "Hello, is anybody home?" carried down the hallway before Felicity

442

could speak. All four Malcolms swung, wide-eyed, toward the doorway.

"Mama?" Felicity whispered. It couldn't be. How would she . . . ? Lifting her skirts, she raced out of her bedchamber to greet her mother.

"There you are, my darling girl," Hermione sang, reaching out to hug her wayward daughter. "Here we all are," she cried, glancing over Felicity's shoulder at her other runaway daughter and their co-conspirators. "My, how sweet all of you look!"

They all looked guilty as sin, Felicity concluded with a hidden smile as her mother released her from her embrace and went to hug the others. She caught her mother's cloak as it tumbled off her shoulders, and Christina rescued a scarf that threatened to fly from Hermione's throat.

"Now, tell me what this is all about." Hermione swept into the room, observed the old journal in Ninian's arms, and glanced out the window to the drive below. "The road is full of Ives, and blessed if your father isn't out there with them. I expect thunderclouds to roll in any minute."

Felicity and Christina launched into hasty, apologetic explanations, but Hermione waved her hand impatiently. "Yes, yes, of course. You are naughty, but I never expected less. It's a family trait." She held out her hand to Ninian. "May I see the journal?"

Handing over the book, Ninian studied Felicity with the empathy that was her Malcolm heritage. "I fear testing so dangerous a recipe."

Felicity clasped her hands as her mother scanned the formula. "I have decided not to try it," she admitted. "Not while I have Ewen. I could not bear losing the ability to feel the love in his touch."

Hermione beamed approval and slapped the book closed, raising a cloud of dust. "Of course, dear. I knew once you developed the courage to go out on your own, you'd find your own happily ever after." She returned the book to Ninian so she might embrace Felicity once more. "Sometimes we simply need to grow into our gifts."

Thoroughly relieved that her rebellion was forgiven, Felicity returned her mother's hug and, for almost a whole moment, forgot the sound of angry male voices drifting upward through the window. She flinched at a particularly loud shout.

Releasing Felicity, Hermione tilted her head. "I think right now, though, we should arrange for a proper wedding."

Unhappily aware of the unlikelihood of that, Felicity gazed out the window overlooking the drive where the men were still arguing. Her father's coach now waited in the drive while Drogo appeared to be giving the driver instructions and Dunstan tied Larch's hands behind his back. Her father and Ewen were so busy posturing and arguing that they didn't notice. "I don't think Father will agree to any such thing. Ewen and I will have to live in Scotland until I come of age, I suppose."

Hermione peered over Felicity's shoulder and laughed. "Nonsense. Ninian, can you make a rowan ring? Leila, ask the housekeeper for her best white linen. Christina, fetch your sewing kit. We can make capes from a sheet."

Puzzled, Felicity studied the scene outside the window and instead of the makings of a Malcolm wedding, she saw nothing but trouble. Ewen was gesturing furiously. Her father, his arms crossed over his chest, was shaking his head. "They are more likely to kill each other than agree to a marriage," she said. "I don't believe Ewen will leave me, as Father is no doubt insisting he do."

Coming up behind her to look as well, Leila laughed and squeezed Felicity's shoulders. "You must learn to study the way men hold themselves when they are talking about money. They are negotiating your dowry, dearest."

Hermione beamed in approval at her oldest daughter. With a shooing motion, she gestured at the rest of them. "Come along now, we have a wedding to plan."

In amazement, Felicity remained at the window to watch a while longer. Ewen wasn't angry. He was arguing. And boasting. She could see it in the way he held his shoulders and gestured as if he were explaining something to a man of little understanding.

"Your other suitors were mere boys," Leila murmured, steering Felicity from the window. "You have found yourself not only a man, but one as strong as Father. Your gift has served you well."

Her gift had brought her Ewen. Sweeping out of the room behind the rest of her family, Felicity allowed joy to carry her.

THIRTY-TWO

Ewen listened only long enough to hear Dunstan order Larch remanded into the care of the magistrate. Then he swung on his heel and hurried back to the house. Now that he had hammered out the broad terms of the marriage contract with Felicity's father, he could let Drogo handle the niggling financial details that he and the marquess so loved to negotiate. Ewen had only one goal of his own in mind — seeing that Felicity was safe and well.

To his surprise, as he approached the castle, the women poured through the open doorway and down the stairs dressed in their best apparel. He spotted Felicity instantly, garbed in a shimmering silk so fine he could not tell if it was rose or silver or some color in between. Real roses adorned the decorous coronet of hair upon her head, and he slowed his stride to admire the welcoming smile on her face.

To his pride and pleasure, he realized she'd left off her heavy gloves. In her bare hands she held a bouquet of flowers from the conservatory.

Behind the women walked a man Ewen

couldn't identify. Frowning, he increased his pace as Ninian halted to whisper in the man's ear. He knew a Malcolm conspiracy when he saw one.

Confirming his fears, Dunstan fell into step beside Ewen. "Ninian is about to cause trouble," he said. "I've seen that look on her face before. And Leila is smirking like a cat in cream. You're in for it now."

Ignoring Dunstan's warning, Ewen hurried to take Felicity's hand and press a kiss to the healing head wound she'd hidden with curls. The scent of roses enveloped him, and he thought he'd remember this day, from now on, every time he smelled a rose. "It's done, my love. Your father has agreed to our marriage." He wanted to bellow his triumph like a stag choosing his mate, but he thought his wife might prefer a more civilized approach.

"We thought as much." She looked up at him with shining eyes. "You seemed most forceful in your insistence. I do love a man who knows his own mind."

"And I do love a woman who lets me speak it," he replied. He was grinning like a fool, no doubt, but he couldn't help it. She was so adorable he wanted to carry her straight up the stairs and to her room beneath the eyes of both their families. He was well and truly snared, but then so was she. He could see it in her glowing eyes when she looked at him. He thought that a fair exchange for the pounding excitement in his chest.

"I have agreed to form a new consortium that includes your father in any future ventures. And, best of all, he's agreed to provide your dowry so we might live anywhere we choose."

"I wish to live wherever you are." Standing on her toes, Felicity kissed his jaw. "But I think we ought to call Edinburgh our home for now. It is not so very far from your projects here, and there are more people in the city to whom you can sell your heat deflectors. Besides, there are many fine booksellers, and I could tend Aidan's library. Do you think he might let us stay in the castle if we fixed it up?"

"I have the suspicion that the more we fix up that heap of stones, the farther from it he will wander," Ewen warned.

"He wants a wife," Felicity confirmed. "He will find one if he is not tied down."

Feeling the hair rise on the back of his neck, as if just speaking of his cousin would produce him, Ewen scanned the thick woods ahead. "Mayhap the man *needs* to be tied down," he said, his suspicion confirmed. He hugged Felicity and pointed her in the direction of a still figure leaning against a tree trunk, watching the spectacle on the lawn.

"You must ask Aidan to join us," Felicity murmured. "He is one of the family now, and our friend." She curtsied as the broad-shouldered figure in the shadows greeted her with a tip of his hand to an invisible hat.

"Hurry along, now," Leila called gaily, shooing them toward the forest of oaks and rowans that separated the lawns from the road. "Reverend McIlvey cannot stay long."

"Reverend McIlvey?" Tearing his gaze from his nuisance of a cousin, Ewen glanced around.

Looking resigned, Dunstan was trudging across the lawn toward the stranger Ewen had noted earlier. What he hadn't noted was that the stranger wore a clerical collar. With a frisson of alarm lingering from his bachelor days, Ewen sought out Drogo and the marquess. Both men were arguing amicably and following Dunstan toward the woods at the edge of the lawn. Without prompting, Aidan peeled away from the tree trunk to join them.

Ewen tugged Felicity's arm through his as a means of steadying his rising nervousness. He studied his sisters-in-law. They were carrying white linen and woody circlets and hurrying to meet the men in the clearing among the trees.

Taking a deep breath, he glanced down at Felicity's serene features. "This isn't legal in England anymore, you know. I must have a license."

"Reverend McIlvey is related to the archbishop. He says he will help us obtain the special license and will perform the church ceremonies later. But for now he does not mind performing the traditional Malcolm ceremony while our families are here." Steadily, she continued across the lawn to join her family.

"Your father will accept that?" Ewen asked in amazement, glancing toward the marquess. The older man looked back with what appeared to be wicked triumph. Or maybe that was just his imagination.

"Of course. Malcolms have married this way for centuries. It is only for the sake of society that we ever use a church," Felicity said.

As they arrived in the clearing, Ninian tugged Ewen to a position on the clergyman's left. "Stand here. Christina, give me a cape."

Too stunned to argue, Ewen allowed Felicity to be torn from his grip while her sisters wrapped them in impromptu capes and fastened them with the gold pins required by Malcolm ritual.

Leaning forward so Ninian could place a circlet of twigs on his head, Ewen heard Dunstan whisper to Drogo behind him, "Ten pounds says she'll have a son after the first of the year."

Straightening, attempting to keep the ridiculous crown in place, Ewen glanced anxiously at Felicity. Standing in front of the minister between him and her father, she seemed unaware of the whispered conversation.

"Ten says the boy will arrive next summer," Drogo countered. "Ewen is too much a gentleman to burden her so soon, and too fond of roaming to settle down easily."

Uncertain whether that was a compliment or an insult, Ewen tugged at the cape strangling his throat. A child? He'd barely accepted his need for a wife. His gaze drifted to the clergyman who was preparing to publicly seal his fate.

As if that were the signal to begin, McIlvey nodded and began droning the words of the marriage ceremony.

"Twenty says it will be a fair-haired boy in exactly nine months," Ninian murmured behind Ewen in the serene voice of certainty.

His brothers' appalled gasps almost distracted Ewen from the service. Gulping and glancing down at Felicity, he recognized the mischief in her eyes. Relieved that she heard and didn't mind, he let her amusement soothe his rattled nerves. He wouldn't think too hard about children while pursuing the business of taking a wife. Living in the moment had its advantages.

"Ives men don't have yellow curls!" Dunstan protested in a loud whisper. "It's like cattle. Black bulls only produce black calves, even if the heifer is white."

Attempting to say her vows with a solemn

face, Felicity giggled at Dunstan's argument. Ewen couldn't prevent a smile from curving his lips. For once his adorable wife wasn't fretting about a thing.

"What if the black bull who mates with a white cow was born of a white cow?" Leila asked with feigned innocence. "It seems to me that your mother's hair is quite fair."

Even the minister was beginning to look a little confused as Felicity laughed outright and Ewen grinned instead of observing the solemnity of the occasion. After all, they'd already made their promises once. This time was just for family.

Only the request for the ring brought the assembly back to the moment in a whispered rush of panic.

"A ring!" Ninian murmured in dismay. "I did not think of rings."

"Give them ours," Drogo muttered. "This ceremony is improper enough as it is."

"You can't take off your rings!" Christina cried. "How unromantic."

Warmed by the golden sun, happy within and without, Felicity ignored the rising confusion and watched expectantly as Ewen fumbled about in his pockets and produced a bundle of thick wires that glittered in the sunlight. Their audience grew sufficiently silent to hear a robin caroling in the bushes while Ewen twisted the wires into two braids and worked them into circles.

"I thought silver might make a good conductor," he murmured after handing the impromptu rings to the bemused minister to bless. "But it doesn't."

"Then perhaps it will serve us better as reminders of our vows," Felicity said. With love in her heart, she held out her hand so Ewen might slide the wire ring over her finger.

As Ewen repeated the clergyman's phrases, "With this ring, I thee wed . . ." a cloud of doves exploded from the rowan bush, spiraling high into the sky over their heads.

"Oh, my," Ninian whispered in awe. "I think the goddess has just given her blessing."

With joy rising where there had once been emptiness, Ewen ignored the rumbling argument that ensued. Bending over, he pressed his mouth to Felicity's and fed off the wonder of love. The only goddess he heeded was the one in his arms, the one whose magic touch had healed the broken places in his heart and taught him the power of love.

ABOUT THE AUTHOR

The author of more than thirty romances, PATRICIA RICE was born in Newburgh, New York, and attended the University of Kentucky. She has two grown children and lives with her husband of many years in Charlotte, North Carolina. To learn more about Patricia Rice's books, visit her Web site at www.patriciarice.com.

The employees of Thorndike Press hope you have enjoyed this Large Print book. All our Thorndike and Wheeler Large Print titles are designed for easy reading, and all our books are made to last. Other Thorndike Press Large Print books are available at your library, through selected bookstores, or directly from us.

For information about titles, please call:

(800) 223-1244

or visit our Web site at:

www.gale.com/thorndike
www.gale.com/wheeler

To share your comments, please write:

Publisher
Thorndike Press
295 Kennedy Memorial Drive
Waterville, ME   04901